Praise for
The Gauntlet Runner Series...

"Bailey is an incredible writer and his long hours of research are evident."
Anne B. for Readers Favorite

"Bailey's commitment to both sound research and strong character development make this series a 'must read' for anyone interested in British North America. Whether enthusiast or newcomer, Bailey brings the 18th Century to life in vivid detail."
Brady J. Crytzer,
Author of *Guyasuta and the Fall of Indian America*

"Mr. Bailey does a remarkable job with his descriptive depth of historical detail along the Eastern Frontier. This novel is definitely a page turner!"
Tim L. Jarvis, Author of *Shadows In The Forest,*
Woodland Warriors of the Mississippi Valley

"Once I started reading The Gauntlet Runner, I had to keep going to find out what happened. This story goes way beyond the typical names and dates of usual histories, and takes us right into the center of events as they unfolded."
Alan McGillivray, Author and Historian

"S. Thomas Bailey makes the battles vivid and real."
Trudi LoPreto for Readers Favorite

"Author S. Thomas Bailey did a wonderfully fantastic job in describing and recreating what the frontier life must have been like for the families and for the men fighting…"
Sylvia H. for Readers Favorite

Produced by:

FriesenPress
Suite 300 – 852 Fort Street
Victoria, BC, Canada V8W 1H8

www.friesenpress.com

Distributed to the trade by The Ingram Book Company

Shades of
Death

The Gauntlet Runner Series

S. Thomas Bailey

Dedication

To Maria, Madison, and Kennedy, who have enjoyed and endured our new journey, meeting great friends and visiting amazing places.

Also, to George Lower and the wonderful folks at Lord Nelson's Gallery in Gettysburg, PA who gave a little known author an opportunity to succeed. I will forever be in their debt. Thank you!

Author's **Notes**

My first award winning novel in the series, The Gauntlet Runner, was an adventure. I realized it would be a lesson in learning not just about writing but in a medium that would explain, entertain and educate the reader. At the same time, I was conscious of the fact that I didn't want to bog down the story with too many facts just to prove that I knew the time period. Opinions vary, critics are everywhere but my bottom line was I did this out of my passion for this amazing time period and out of respect for the actual settlers who forged a path for me to do this.

My fascination and appreciation for the French and Indian War period has grown even more since spending time with many fellow authors, re-enactors, living historians and artisans through a great year promoting my first novel.

Book II, Shades of Death was a personal highlight for me. I spent my youth in the Grand River area and especially around Lake Erie. It was wonderful to reminisce about spending long summer hours canoeing, swimming or just being around the lake. I experienced the varied weather that could spew up without notice and the incredible pull of the undertow. The winter was spent skating or walking miles onto the frozen ice until we couldn't see the shoreline.

This is the second book in the continuing series surrounding the Murray family. Enjoy Jacob and Maggie's struggles and hardships as they fight to reunite and survive. Continue to watch for future novels in The Gauntlet Runner Series and most of all, explore, visit and read more about this great time in history.

A special thanks to Todd Price for providing the amazing cover art, "Extra Coat". I liked the piece so much I purchased the original art work and it is displayed proudly in my home office. Thank you to Kim McDougall of Blazing Trailer for the great cover design. Thanks once again to John Allen of Induna Art & Design for the maps of the Ohio Valley Region.

A final special word of thanks to several people who helped and supported me through this journey including, Catriona Todd, who did an incredible job with editing my manuscript and dealing with me over several months...not an easy task! Frank and Lally House, Donna and Jack Vargo of Beaver River Trading Company, and the great staff at the CLA.

"Savages may indeed be a formidable enemy to your raw American militia; but upon the King's regular and disciplined troops, Sir, it is impossible they should make any impression."

~Major General Edward Braddock, during conversation with Benjamin Franklin, as reported by Franklin in his autobiography, first published in English in 1793.

"Who would have thought it? We shall better know how to deal with them another time."

~Braddock's last words to his officers before he passed, July 13, 1755

"When a white army battles Indians and wins, it is called a great victory, but if they lose it is called a massacre."

~Chiksika, Shawnee

Chapter | **One**

"Get back!" Jacob Murray hissed, pulling on Joshua's arm.

He had searched far too long and risked more than most men to get his family back. After getting this far, he could not risk getting himself captured and most likely killed in some godforsaken French outpost in the middle of nowhere.

He could see the dampness seeping from the heavy oak palisades that encased the soldiers inside Fort Machault. Jacob could practically smell Maggie's sweet strawberry perfume waffling around his head. The maddening thought that she was so close yet unreachable agonizingly gripped his insides.

This was no time to panic or do something foolish that might endanger him or the two young men that faithfully stuck by his side.

They could do nothing now. Hiding within the thick underbrush, just beyond the forest line, he was lucky none of the fort's sentries spotted his attempted advance.

"Damn it lads, looks like we missed our chance," Jacob whispered.

Before he could finish his thought, the forest echoed as three French regulars struggled to swing open the main gate. Jacob could hear them groan under the weight of the massive door.

Powerless to do anything more, Jacob watched as a large carriage, drawn by six massive work horses, rumbled out of the fort. The only things he could see past the resulting dust storm were two armed guards stationed at the rear and the driver positioned on the top slanted seat, lashing at the horses to pick up their pace.

Struggling to identify the occupants of the carriage as it passed directly by his position, Jacob was tempted to jump out and stop it. The ten French regulars and four Huron scouts that accompanied the carriage changed his mind. Following behind them were two full supply wagons packed with merchandise and drawn by two teams of horses.

The ground vibrated with the pounding of the heavy wheels and the trampling hooves of the horses digging into the dirt path. Jacob was close enough to see the sweat already pouring off the horses as they galloped by.

Frustrated at this sudden turn of events, and left watching as the carriage followed the only passable trail towards Fort Duquesne, Jacob called to One Ear.

"Did you not say that during your visit inside the fort, an officer mentioned the French merchant who purchased Maggie needed to first visit Fort Duquesne?"

"Yes, Mr. Jacob, I did," One Ear politely replied.

Jacob felt helpless; he was still not certain Maggie was even in the carriage.

"Damn the bloody French, I need to see who is inside. That massive carriage will never make the entire trek, unless they dismantle it and haul it over the mountains. Most of the passes barely fit two men abreast, and what of the swamps or endless river crossings?"

The two young men remained silent, content to stare at the fort in hopes they might spot Maggie.

Jacob sat for a moment in deep thought. He was contemplating his next move and wanted to calm his emotions before he acted in a way that might jeopardize his chances of ever reuniting with Maggie.

"I have no choice but to find out who is in that bloody carriage," Jacob muttered to himself as he turned to the young man next to him. "One-Ear, if you would be so kind, I need you to stay here to watch for any sign of Maggie. If by chance she is still in there, I can't risk the chance of losing her again."

"I will do that for you, sir. I will follow if Miss Maggie is taken away from here."

Jacob nodded at him, "Good lad."

"Now for us, Joshua, you will come with me and we must hurry to cut off the carriage before they reach the first portage route. We do have the luxury of time since the trail is much easier on foot and we can catch up pretty quickly.

The two young men hesitated for a moment; they had never been away from each other for well over a year. Ever since One-Ear was brought to the Huron village that had adopted Joshua, they had been side by side. Even their fellow villagers recognized their bond and always permitted them to hunt and fish together. One-Ear's adopted Huron parents were relatives of Joshua's, and they spent many occasions together. Despite Joshua's white heritage and One-Ear's Cayuga blood, they were very close and their families called them brothers.

Jacob noticed their initial hesitation, "I will make sure we join back soon. If Maggie is with this merchant fellow, then we will take her and head back to you, One-Ear. You will do the same if she is still within the fort's walls."

"Right, sir, but what about weapons?" Joshua inquired. "We will need something to fight off the regulars and their Huron escorts."

"Ah, yes, Joshua, weapons. I honestly don't think much of a French-made musket but for now it will have to do."

Jacob took a moment to survey the fort and surrounding fields.

"They must retrieve their water from the river. A regular work detail should be out fetching water, so they would make for some easy pickings. What do you two think?"

"I don't feel safe being anywhere near this fort; the sooner we get some muskets and move out the better," Joshua said, keeping his gaze upon the fort. "The guards watching from the walls make this more difficult than it might appear."

"Not to worry, if we are careful they will not even know we are here. Now, One-Ear, watch for any movement or signs of Maggie. If they attempt to move her, please make sure you follow her, understand?"

One-Ear nodded and the two others crawled their way through the brush as far as they could. They stayed low to the ground and watched the high palisade walls for any signs of French guards.

Jacob counted only two men scanning the fields, moving in opposite directions atop the walls, covering the entire fort's perimeter.

He was careful to time them and knew there was only a brief moment in their routine when the two guards were not watching over the front gates. Jacob was thankful the main gates remained closed, mostly because of the inflated numbers of Indians staying in the area. Even with their apparently strong alliance with the local tribes, the French understood that rum and Indians did not mix well together.

Jacob and Joshua could see that the guards were not the most dedicated watchmen, taking several breaks to talk and exchange food.

They knew one of these small moments of inattention would be their chance. The small, cleared area just in front of the fort's main gates was open, but the concern was for the numerous tree stumps that pocked the clearing. A runner would have to dodge the massive stumps and Jacob could not see an easy path through.

While the two guards once again exchanged pleasantries, Jacob and Joshua made their move.

"Stay close and run as fast as you can to the far western wall," Jacob whispered as he stood up and ran full speed through the stumps. He knew at any moment the Frenchmen could turn around and sound the alarm. In seconds, the field would be inundated with French regulars, and he and Joshua would probably be shot.

As Jacob sprinted, he felt Joshua pass by him and dodge his way to the relative safety of the western wall.

He arrived a few moments after Joshua, and the two pressed tightly against the outer wall and waited to catch their breath. "Good job, lad. We made it this far, it would be a shame not to find us some muskets now," Jacob spoke softly as he made his way towards the north side of the fort.

Joshua didn't reply, concentrating more on his footsteps and what was ahead of them.

Reaching the northwest corner, they were greeted by another open field that led down to the river. This field was much larger and completely exposed to the guards still patrolling above them. Jacob took time to think what to do next.

"Damn, we would have to be invisible to make it across this field," Jacob said.

Joshua simply nodded and knelt down to see what faced them on the north side of the fort.

"We are wasting time just standing here, and the longer we linger the greater our chances of getting shot grows. I am going to scout around the side and see if there is another way to get down to the river. Stay put and I will be back shortly."

Jacob moved along the wall and made it to the large blockhouse that held the first of four cannon positions. He stood directly under the structure and could hear the voices of the two guards.

Ready to keep moving, he was startled by a loud snap and a faint, mumbling voice.

His immediate thought was of Joshua, and he instinctively returned to where he left him. His fears were met as he found no trace of the teenager where he had left him.

A lone Indian lurking about the outer walls of the fort, ally or not, would not be greeted with open arms. Most likely a knife or bayonet would be his only greeting.

Before he could look for any clues of what happened, Joshua reappeared behind a small line of bushes that framed the open field. Jacob noticed that he held a musket in his hand and a big smile on his face.

Waving him to come near, Jacob said, "Thank God you are alright, lad."

"More than alright, sir," Joshua proudly replied as he pulled another French musket from behind his back.

"Where, boy?" was all Jacob could say.

"I followed two French soldiers that went off into the woods and I figured they had to relieve themselves. Not the smartest pair since you usually have one stand guard while the other does his business. They also left their muskets several paces from them. I just grabbed them and to make sure they wouldn't alarm the fort, I smashed their heads with a small rock." Joshua smiled at his bold accomplishment.

"Did you kill them?"

"No, but they will have sore heads for a bit. I also grabbed a few more things from our generous Frenchmen."

Joshua proceeded to place two powder horns, a cartridge box and a small sack of lead balls on the ground. He also pulled an axe from behind his back. Jacob just stood and looked at the nice cache of items Joshua confiscated.

"Damn good work, lad, much better than I could have imagined. Now, we had better be off before the soldiers wake up or are reported missing to the sentries. There is no need for more Frenchies out in these woods."

Jacob pushed ahead and moved quickly back towards the main trail.

"Damn fine job, Joshua," he said again, squeezing Joshua's shoulder proudly.

They immediately went to find One-Ear where they had left him, but were surprised to find him nowhere in sight.

"This is not like One-Ear to just leave, maybe he saw Maggie," Joshua said, as Jacob searched around the general vicinity.

"We have no time to wait or look for him. If we don't leave now, we will lose the carriage in the dark. One-Ear is a smart lad; we can meet up with him after we catch the merchant," Jacob offered, dashing onto the trail before Joshua could object.

The trail was easy to follow, the carriage and size of the escort party left a traceable path that even the youngest of trackers could follow. The pair used an older, much rougher cut Seneca trail that ran parallel to the main French-used trail.

It wasn't long before they caught up to the first line of stragglers, visibly tired from the march. The difficulty was that the carriage was not intended for such uneven, rocky trails, and the men were forced to pry the heavy wagon out of several holes along the way.

Jacob noticed two soldiers beginning to lag farther behind the main unit. Even as the Huron scouts attempted to push them forward, they were obviously tired of the march.

The noise from the sheer weight of the carriage rocking across the uneven terrain, not to mention the two wagons stacked with supplies, could be heard for miles. The dust they kicked up left the escorts' once nice white uniforms covered in dirt and most of their faces caked with dust.

Most of the men looked miserable and moved as quickly as they could to end their painful ordeal.

The constant jarring and wrenching of the carriage, Jacob imagined, must be difficult for the passengers inside. He even saw the two drivers almost fall off their perch on a number of occasions as the massive wheels rolled over the endless stumps that littered the trail.

Moving much more easily than the French, Jacob and Joshua raced farther ahead and took up positions behind two massive birch trees. There was a steep cliff in the trail, and the French would be forced to carry the carriage and wagons down in pieces.

The first of the group to arrive were the two Huron advanced scouts. They stood above the drop-off and Jacob could hear them talk about something.

"Joshua, can you make out what they are speaking about?"

"They are concerned about the cliff and what the French are thinking of doing with the heavy carriage. One feels it would be better to take the longer route around and avoid this place."

Jacob paused briefly, "I wish we could get closer and understand what direction they are considering."

"Let me go talk with them," Joshua quietly suggested. "As a Huron, they would welcome me and have no concern how I got myself here."

"Are you crazy, lad? Would they not be suspicious of a young warrior just walking into their camp?"

"On any long scouting trip, the Huron usually come and go as they please," Joshua explained. "I know it upsets the French because they never know how many Huron scouts they have with them at one time. It is actually easy just to join the group, and they would not think anything of it."

Moments later, the main column of soldiers arrived along with the carriage. The officer in charge of the escort met up with the scouts and listened to their suggestion. Jacob could clearly see that the officer would have nothing to do with the idea of the longer route, and left the two Huron warriors shaking their heads.

The soldiers quickly unhitched the horses and led them over to a small patch of grass. Jacob knew that the animals must be suffering and that the meager grass would not come close to filling their empty bellies. His experience with the Virginia militia throughout these parts had taught him that not many horses could make such a trek because of the lack of good grass and water.

The carriage sat unhitched while the two drivers remained on their high perch, scanning the area for any signs of trouble.

Jacob finally heard the carriage door screech open, unfortunately the occupants used the opposite side door and no one was visible yet.

"Damn. Joshua, you stay put while I work my way around to get a better look."

"Take care, sir, and watch for the Huron scouts," Joshua whispered. "I'll keep you covered from here."

Jacob crawled on all fours and whispered back, "Keep your head down and if I get into trouble, get the hell out of here…understand?"

Joshua gave a quick nod and remained watching the trail.

Moving slowly, Jacob worked his way farther down and across the open trail despite the presence of two French sentries. They had their sights on a couple of porcupines making their way up one of the many oak trees.

Jacob made his move and with two swift leaps, he reached the relative safety of a huge tree. Stopping a moment to catch his breath, he moved into the thickets and could almost see the other side of the carriage.

After a few agonizing minutes, he made his way nearer, but could only see one figure, standing with his arms folded. Jacob was now close enough to the French that he could hear their constant murmurs, but was unable to make out what they were saying.

Pushing even closer, he caught the end of an argument between an officer and a civilian. He had no idea what they were talking about, but the officer departed, visibly upset.

Waiting for the right moment, Jacob could hear the grunts and shouts of the soldiers removing the massive wooden wheels from the carriage and rolling them towards the cliff face. Others were starting to dismantle the main body of the carriage, while most were struggling to lower the first wheel down the cliff. Large pulleys, normally used on ships to tow the heavy sails, jerked wildly as the wheel was slowly lowered down.

The men had not yet even started to work on the two wagons stacked full of merchandise headed for Fort Duquesne.

Jacob moved even closer to the lone man, guessing this was the French merchant from the fort, and could now smell the musty odor of cologne emanating from him.

Finally getting a clear view of the merchant, Jacob could see he was an over-weight, unimpressive stock of a man. He was noticeably uncomfortable within these woods and was entirely out of his element. The much more civilized streets of Quebec were more to his liking and Jacob imagined he had never worked a hard day in his life.

The man's dark blue silk outer coat and matching breeches gave him a colorful appearance, sharply contrasting with the greens and browns of the forest. Adding to his appearance was a poorly-fitting powdered wig and a smallish felt tricorn hat that barely covered his over-sized head. He constantly dabbed his nose with a white perfumed silk cloth that he kept stuffed in his left sleeve.

Jacob fought hard not to burst into a fit of laughter at this French dandy, yet he harbored an immediate hatred for this man whom he suspected had purchased Maggie.

Realizing the deadly consequences for what he was about to do, Jacob decided he had no choice but to act.

After a quick glance towards Joshua, Jacob sat his musket against the tree and unhooked the bayonet from the barrel. It was not the most effective weapon on its own, but he had no other choice.

Cautiously standing up, he was now presented with a much better view of the entire situation. With the soldiers and scouts busy working on the carriage and wagons, the merchant stood completely unguarded. Noticeably out of place, the merchant impatiently paced while the others struggled with the task at hand.

With one quick lunge, Jacob had his large right hand over the startled merchant's clammy mouth. At the same moment, he had the bayonet pressed up against the neck of the terrified Frenchman.

"Don't fight, merchant, I mean you no harm," Jacob whispered in the man's ear.

Instinctively, the man attempted to resist, but, although he outweighed Jacob, his strength was no match for the experienced woodsman.

Moving quickly to get out of the sight of the hard-working soldiers, Jacob jerked the merchant violently towards a large hemlock tree that more than shielded them both.

Carefully pulling back his hand, while keeping the bayonet pressed firmly against the man's neck, Jacob again whispered, "I just need to know about the English woman you met back at the fort."

Defiantly glaring at him, the merchant spat, "Monsieur…"

Pushing the bayonet deeper into his fat jowls, Jacob retorted, "In English, you fat bastard."

"A woman, all this for a woman?" The merchant scowled.

Losing his patience, Jacob drove his fist hard into the man's ribs and covered his mouth once again to ensure he didn't yell out.

The force of the blow pushed the merchant forward with all his weight and Jacob was knocked back, barely catching his balance on a thick, low-hanging branch. In the confusion, Jacob pulled back on the bayonet and drove it into the man's shoulder. He could see some blood seeping through the man's white neck cloth, and as he stumbled to get to his feet, his grip on the merchant's mouth loosened enough to allow the man to scream.

The merchant's horrid shriek resonated through the forest and within seconds, several soldiers and the four scouts were scattered into the woods. Jacob realized he was caught and impulsively threw a sharp right hook into the mouth of the merchant.

Jacob simply put his hands up as the man slumped to the forest floor. The soldiers had him surrounded and all he could do now was offer them a smile.

From behind, an officer pushed his way around the men and demanded, "What is the meaning of this? Monsieur LaMont, are you injured?" He motioned for one of the privates to offer the merchant some assistance.

The officer then turned his attention towards Jacob, who had taken several punches from his captors and had his hands bound behind his back, "You are a thief, monsieur? No, you would have killed him by now. What problem do you have with this merchant?"

Jacob remained silent and stared at the now recovered LaMont.

"Sir, I have no time for this. I care little for you, but if you refuse to explain your actions, maybe I will permit our Huron friends have some fun with you."

"I am not a thief…" Jacob replied but was cut off by the merchant.

LaMont shouted, "All he wanted was to know of some poor English woman I purchased back at the fort."

Touching his bloodstained shoulder and noticing the large blotch on his new French silk neck cloth, he added, "And who will pay for my clothes, they are worth more than six months of your officer's wages?"

The disgusted officer looked at LaMont and mockingly replied, "I will send my entire crew to search this ungodly place for silkworms to weave you another. Just be happy you are alive and can continue on."

Motioning two soldiers to remove LaMont from his sight, the officer returned his attention to Jacob.

"I truly wished you had killed that man and saved us all many problems. Sadly, monsieur, I must know what your intentions were with our wonderful merchant?"

As LaMont was being escorted back towards the makeshift encampment, he screamed at Jacob, "That English woman is mine. She is my property and will be shipped to Quebec with the rest of my goods."

Jacob vainly attempted to kick at the man but was restrained by the two soldiers. He could only shout back, "You are a dead man and I promise you will never make it back…"

He was cut short as the two soldiers drove their fists into his back, forcing him to fall to one knee. Before he could recover, LaMont was gone.

Jacob once again remained silent.

"Fair enough, you two scouts make sure his arms are bound tightly and then secure him to one of the carriage wheels. My patience is running thin with this thief, so drive a hatchet into his skull if he acts up."

The officer, with much more pressing concerns on his mind, turned his back on Jacob and headed back towards the work crew.

Knowing he was probably not going to survive much longer, Jacob's last hope was that Joshua might have managed to escape and was making his way back to One-Ear.

All he could think about was Maggie. If the merchant was telling the truth, she was now headed in the opposite direction. Jacob cursed under his breath that he had been so close to her but his own impatience had convinced him to the follow the merchant! Now she was hundreds of miles away and he could only pray that One-Ear was close to her. His only solace was the fact that he now knew where she was headed, but that would be a moot point if he didn't improve his situation.

Deep in thought, Jacob was jerked back into the moment as two Huron warriors pulled him through the brush and pushed him down onto a large wooden carriage wheel. A torturous pain shot through his shoulders as he was unable to stabilize himself and landed awkwardly on the heavy wheel.

Before he could manage to regain his balance, the two wrapped his hands and arms around the thick spindles with wet pieces of deer-hide rope. They pulled tightly on the rope and Jacob could barely wiggle his fingers as the rope dug into his wrists.

As he was unable to move for himself, they dragged him to a tree and pushed him up against its massive trunk. He was able to prop his feet against a nearby tree stump and, making sure the wheel stayed relatively stable, press himself backwards, thereby keeping most of the pain in his shoulders to a minimum.

His new position presented him with a good view of the work party and the surrounding forest. Surveying the forest line, Jacob was shocked to see Joshua still remaining exactly where he had left him.

Attempting to shake his head to signal him to leave and get back to One-Ear, Jacob could only watch as Joshua slowly worked his way around to the area where he was being held.

Jacob continuously monitored the work crew and the growing number of Indians that were all around the small camp. He certainly did not want Joshua to suffer the same fate that lay before him; moreover, Joshua was now his last hope of finding Maggie.

Distracted by Joshua's movements, Jacob failed to notice the French officer and several militiamen approaching his position. He could not make out their muffled voices through all the noise from the work crews, but he could see them speaking and pointing in his direction.

After some brief discussions, the officer stepped forward saying, "Monsieur, you are in luck today. A company of French regulars, Canadians and our Indian allies have arrived to assist us. They have just left from Fort Duquesne and are on their way towards Quebec."

Jacob knew these same men were part of the French contingent that had defeated Washington at the dreadful Fort Necessity only a few months earlier. He thought they might have even participated in the murdering and torching of the wounded at the abandoned fort.

Ignoring the officer and simply staring down at the ground, Jacob listened as the Frenchman continued.

"Gentlemen, this one is strong and tried to kill my only passenger, Monsieur LaMont." Jacob could hear several of them laugh as the officer continued, "Englishman, these men and some of their Huron scouts will be returning to Fort Duquesne to escort you to the stockade there. The fort's commander will be left to decide your fate, but I must warn you, he is supposedly good friends with LaMont and has nowhere near my patience. God be with you."

Jacob understood that his situation had just become worse. He expected to be beaten along the way and then what was left of him would be thrown into the stockade. He would be left to rot or, if he was lucky, sentenced to hang. Despite all this, his lone thought was that it meant added miles between him and Maggie.

"If you have nothing to add, you will leave shortly. Good bye and good luck." Jacob looked up as the officer mockingly bowed his head and left.

It wasn't long before his escorts, six French regulars and four Huron warriors, gathered in front of him.

Two of the warriors pulled him up and cut him free from the wheel. Before he could rub his tired wrists, they slipped a trump line around his neck and secured his hands behind his back.

Jacob struggled to walk as he was shoved ahead by his indifferent escorts. His legs had been in such an uncomfortable position that they were numb. He fell before he managed to regain his strength.

Standing upright, he finally got a good look at the Huron warriors assigned to him. They still had their faces painted and their bodies showed the signs of the battle. One in particular had blood stains on his chest that appeared to be from someone struggling to fight him off. Three still carried several dried out scalps that decorated their thin breech cloth belts. One proudly wore a coat once the property of a soldier from the Carolinian Independent Company.

The only warrior that appeared out of place was a young man that had a much cleaner appearance. He was shirtless and his face was almost completely blackened with soot. A simple deer-skin breech cloth and a dark blue pair of leggings covered the rest of his body. He seemed much less threatening than the others.

One of his fellow warriors handed him the trump line as they left to run ahead of the French regulars. As they left, the young warrior pulled gently on the line and stopped to adjust the line around Jacob's neck.

"Mr. Jacob, it is me Joshua. I will keep you safe and you will live to make it to the fort."

"Thank you, lad, but you should have run when you had the chance," Jacob whispered. "It is no use if we are both dead."

Nonetheless, Jacob was relieved to have Joshua by his side.

Still fiddling with the line, the two failed to notice the merchant LaMont quickly approach them.

Before they could react, he awkwardly punched Jacob in the face. His extra weight made up for his lack of co-ordination and the impact splattered blood on both of them.

Jacob's nose was a bloodied mess as LaMont pulled his face close. Joshua attempted to intercede but was shoved aside by the much bigger man.

"Don't you worry, I will take good care of your woman…I promise you that."

The merchant then pulled Jacob's hair and forced his head back. He was about to strike him again, but Joshua managed to step in between them.

"My prisoner."

LaMont stopped; the threat from even such a small Huron was enough to make him withdraw.

He stepped back and adjusted his shirt, saying, "I will see you hang. I will take pleasure watching your body twitch as your neck stretches and your last thought will be of me and your woman."

Controlling his own reaction, Jacob stared directly at the merchant and replied, "It will be my pleasure to kill you and watch the wild animals feast on your fat, spoiled carcass."

The commotion caused several soldiers to rush over, but LaMont brushed them all aside and returned to the relative safety of the work crews.

"You alright, sir? Sorry I couldn't stop him…"

"No bother, lad, I've been in much worse pain," Jacob replied, managing a smile.

Joshua then pulled on the line and they picked up their pace to catch up with the others.

Chapter | **Two**

Maggie was tired and upset that she would be leaving the peaceful confines of this small fort. For a very short moment, her life seemed calm, and the thought of trudging through the endless forest towards the fort at Niagara made her recall everything she had experienced over the last several months.

Her French was not as strong as her husband's, but she had overheard that she was to be moved to the French fort by the falls. The merchant who had purchased her wanted to meet up with her there and prepare for their journey to Quebec City in the early spring.

"Madame, you will be leaving shortly," the compassionate commander of the fort awakened her from her thoughts. "Is there anything I can do to make your trip somewhat bearable?"

"No, sir, you have been kind enough, and I will always remember your thoughtfulness," was all Maggie could manage to say.

"I am truly sorry, madame, but if I may, my youngest son Fredrick will be accompanying you to Niagara. I have personally requested that he ensure your safety. He is respected by our Huron allies and they will listen to him if the situation warrants. Please stay by his side, if you will. Sadly, I must return to my duties. Your beauty will be missed, madame. God be with you." The commander tipped his hat and left Maggie standing alone in the small courtyard.

Moments later, a handsome young French soldier approached her and introduced himself.

"Madame, I am Fredrick Duval. Did my father have a chance to speak with you?"

Initially, Maggie was taken aback by the Frenchman's grasp of English. He was older than she had first imagined, but he still had the softness of a teenager. He was much shorter than she and although he carried himself with confidence, he didn't come across as a spoiled son of a French officer. Fredrick looked at home in the wilderness, and he dressed more like a trader than a soldier. His leggings, breeches and short vested waist coat were all made from tanned deerskin, and his Indian-made moccasins were well worn. Only his clean tricorn hat trimmed with yellow lace indicated he was French.

He reminded her of Jacob, if a bit more refined, and Maggie felt that her trip might be somewhat more tolerable.

"Thank you, Fredrick. Your father was kind enough to inform me that you would be my escort." Maggie found herself genuinely smiling for the first time in months.

"Father always had a weakness for a beautiful lady, if I may be so bold."

Beautiful was something Maggie had not been called for what felt like a lifetime. Hearing it made her blush, and it reminded her of how Jacob made her feel when he was with her.

"Merci, sir," was all she could say.

"Regrettably, duty calls, and we must be leaving shortly. We must reach Fort Le Boeuf in two to three days. It is a rough march, through terribly cut trails and miles of swamp. I have requested a horse to make it some degree more comfortable for you. Do you ride, madame?"

"Please call me Maggie, and do not go out of your way, Fredrick. I do ride but I am used to the difficulty of the trail and have travelled through much worse."

Fredrick politely excused himself and left Maggie alone once more.

She took a seat on an old stump the soldiers used for a chair and watched as the fort came alive with frantic activity. The small escort party readied its equipment and packed supplies on two small wagons. Several Huron scouts filled their waist sacks with a variety of dried meats and freshly baked corn bread loaves.

Maggie certainly did not want to make this trip, not only because of the long, inhospitable trail, but because it only increased the distance between her and Jacob. She had slowly begun to understand that once she crossed into Canada, any hope of reuniting with her husband would be lost.

Her prospects were grim at best.

"Madame, it is time for us to depart," Fredrick said politely, interrupting her thoughts. "Please gather what you may, we are ready to leave."

Maggie nodded but said nothing. She simply stood up and waited for the main party to leave. A Huron scout gave her a tightly packed sack that had a few pieces of corn bread and dried deer meat. She smiled her gratitude and placed it over her shoulder. Except for a new pair of moccasins the fort's commander had given her, the only possessions she had were the clothes she was wearing, and they were pocked with holes and snags. A few months earlier, she would have been embarrassed to be seen in such tattered attire, but now they represented her struggles to survive and she wore them proudly.

Watching the escort party ready themselves for the long trek, Maggie counted ten French regulars, four wagon drivers and more than a dozen Huron scouts. Added to their caravan were a few traders and four pack-horses laden down with a number of supplies.

Maggie understood that the Huron scouts were unpredictable and their numbers tended to swell or decrease as they saw fit. Staying close to Fredrick was imperative, as was keeping up with the main body of soldiers.

Just as they were organizing, Maggie noticed several of the scouts leave the fort and head up the trail. She assumed they were sent out ahead of the others to ensure the trail was safe and cleared of any dangers. The Huron were feared in these parts by the local Delaware and Seneca people, so any trouble with other Indians was unlikely. The threat of running into any British troops, since most were still recovering from their recent defeat and had withdrawn to the fort at Will's Creek, was also improbable.

Maggie was thankful the early morning was sunny and clear. The first leg of the journey would hopefully be made easier by the fair weather, and she was told the trail ahead was relatively flat since most of the high mountain ranges now tended to spread towards the New York region. She was relieved that they wouldn't have to navigate similar ridges to those she had been forced to travel back near Fort Duquesne.

It wasn't long until the entire company was deep into the dark reaches of the forest where the high canopy shrouded the ground from all but a few remnants of sunlight.

"Sorry, madame, but I could not find a suitable horse for you to ride. Most of the animals in these parts are either old or better used as pack-mules."

Maggie looked behind her, as Fredrick startled her with his sudden apology.

"No need for your apologies, Fredrick," Maggie replied as he moved to her side. "The walk will do me good."

A brief, uncomfortable silence overtook the two until Fredrick said, "Just keep by me and you will be safe. With all these savages around, I really never know what they might be thinking. They come and go as they please and you can lose count of them at any given time. Not the best situation out in these godforsaken woods, but the Huron make good scouts and I would trust most of them with my life."

Maggie did feel much safer with this group and felt less of a captive. Free to walk unabated and not hindered by having her hands tethered together, Maggie did have more moments to enjoy the landscape. Fredrick's company also added to her comfort and she appreciated the safe feeling he gave her.

"Merci, Fredrick, your friendship is very comforting."

"My pleasure, madame. Please excuse me, but I must check ahead and get a report from the advanced scouts." Fredrick tipped his hat and she watched him move towards the front of the caravan.

As he moved up, Fredrick glanced back and offered, "My men have orders to keep you safe, but please keep up. The savages do enjoy watching for stragglers."

Maggie smiled and watched him rush forward.

Her thoughts immediately returned to Jacob and the confusion she felt not really knowing if he was dead or alive. She could never betray their love, but if he was dead and the children most likely adopted into their captors' tribes, where was her life heading? Fredrick's kindness more than just made her feel safe, and it was certainly nice to have another white person to converse with. Yet the chance that Jacob might still be alive kept any thoughts of her feelings buried deep inside her. Maggie knew that she would have to do just about anything to survive and, for now, Fredrick made her feel protected and less vulnerable.

"No need to worry, I will keep you safe, Miss Maggie," a familiar voice whispered.

The voice made her stop.

Turning towards the whisper, Maggie, managing to hide her excitement and careful not to draw any unwanted attention towards them, replied, "One-Ear, you are alive!" Her first thoughts were to grab him and hug him like he was one of her own.

Not wanting his fellow Huron warriors to suspect he knew this English woman, One-Ear maintained his distance, but gave her a quick smile as he said, "I have always been alive; I just was waiting for you to leave the fort."

"It is so good to see you," Maggie gushed. "Where is Joshua? I hope he is with us."

"Please keep your voice down; remember, I am Huron and fit in with these dogs," One-Ear smiled proudly. "I will stay close to you and make sure they keep their distance. Joshua is well, but I have news about your Jacob. We must keep things quiet and not draw any unwanted attention to ourselves."

Just as he attempted to explain, Fredrick abruptly returned.

"Move away you savage, leave this fine lady alone and get back with the other scouts." Fredrick raised his hand to strike One-Ear just as Maggie stepped between them.

"This young one is no threat. He was just keeping me company and walking with me."

One-Ear remained in front of Fredrick and simply stared at the angry Frenchman.

"Get with the others," Fredrick ordered and pointed One-Ear to move away from Maggie.

Saying nothing, One-Ear departed and left the Frenchman with Maggie.

Having no other recourse, she could only watch as One-Ear slowly moved ahead of the main unit. What of Jacob? Could he be alive, or had One-Ear heard of his fate from another Indian? Wanting desperately to know, she clung to the knowledge that the trail was long and One-Ear was a loyal friend who would be back as soon as he could.

"My apologies once again, madame," Frederick said, his eyes following One-Ear's movement toward the other forward scouts, "the savages have no sense of manners. I swear to you he will not bother you again, be sure of that."

"Please, monsieur, there was no need to keep him away, he is just a boy," Maggie said, hoping Fredrick would not stop One-Ear from speaking with her again. His mention of Jacob excited her and she desperately wanted to finish their shortened conversation.

"It is your choice, madame. Just be careful, these Huron can be devils, no matter how young."

Changing the topic, Maggie asked, "How does the trail look ahead?"

"Clear, thank God. With the English languishing back at Will's Creek, we have little to worry about, just as long as the savages stay loyal. One can never trust them or this wilderness.

"The sooner we make it to the fort at Niagara, the better. The big lake makes the weather unpredictable in these parts. One of these wilderness outposts would not be a good place for a lady to have to overwinter if we are delayed."

As Fredrick spoke, he assisted Maggie over a large fallen tree.

"When do you expect to reach Fort Le Boeuf?" Maggie asked as she held Fredrick's outstretched hand.

The dead tree was partially sunken into the trail floor but it still reached up to Maggie's hip. One of the Huron held his arm out to steady her and she offered him a friendly nod. He didn't return her smile, but simply glared and returned to the front of the small column.

"We must arrive by later today or early tomorrow," Fredrick replied, "because if we lose more time, our Huron friends will leave us and we will have no chance of reaching Niagara before the first snow fall. The Huron want to return home and ready their villages for the winter months. They know they can move much faster without us, so I must keep them happy."

A young private approached and interrupted their conversation, "Monsieur, the Huron scouts say we are only a few leagues away from Fort Le Boeuf. They want to get there before nightfall."

"Go inform them we will keep up if they continue to lead the way." Fredrick directed the private.

"The sooner we get there and leave, the better off we will be," Fredrick said, returning his attention to Maggie.

The feeling of not being a captive made her enjoy the long trek. The trail system between the forts was so much better developed than she had experienced earlier. Fredrick had told her that this was a main trade route from Quebec and was well travelled by traders, soldiers and savages.

Maggie had seen no sign of One-Ear since they had spoken earlier, and she hoped that they might have a brief moment at Fort Le Boeuf to continue their conversation. Her mind was full of thoughts of Jacob, and she just wanted to find out what One-Ear knew.

She had dared once to ask Fredrick about One-Ear, but he immediately dismissed her question.

"What is this savage to you?" he asked suspiciously.

"He is nothing but a boy and I have a mother's instincts," was all she offered.

"No need to worry, he is only a Huron and they always seem to manage," he replied brusquely.

This exchange was followed by a long stretch of the trip where Maggie was left to herself. She strangely appreciated the freedom and enjoyed that she finally had a moment to see the vastness of the countryside. She was worried, however that their last conversation about One-Ear had somehow bothered Fredrick. He had not checked on her or asked her if she needed anything for several miles and she hoped he was not insulted by her concern for the young Huron boy.

Finally, after noticing Fredrick checking on the wagons and the pack-horses, she was relieved that he worked his way back to her.

"My apologies for not being a better escort, but the scouts were pushing hard to make it to the fort. I am happy to say that the fort is just on the other side of the small meadow directly ahead. We have a small crossing at a place you English call the French Creek."

Maggie could now clearly see smoke billowing above the northern skyline and assumed it was from the nearby fort. She was hoping they were preparing for the column's arrival, and the thought of a hot meal made her pick up her pace. The last hot meal she had enjoyed was back at a peaceful riverside camp with a couple of Huron warriors, her now dead Dutch friends and the two young adopted Huron boys.

"This fort is small, honestly not much more than a supply depot, but I know the commander well," Fredrick offered as he kept the stretched out column moving ahead. "He will make sure we are well fed and have comfortable lodging, far from the luxuries of Quebec but good all the same."

"My idea of luxury is far from anything you are used to in Quebec. All I desire is a good fire, a pot of stew and good company," Maggie replied.

Chapter | **Three**

The French regulars and their Huron guides maintained a frantic advance through the dense forest. Jacob had his fill of trekking along this trail, and even the thought of what awaited him at Fort Duquesne didn't slow his pace. All he wanted was to rest his sore feet.

He was so thankful that Joshua was guiding him, even though part of him wished the young man had escaped back to find One-Ear. The two were left to themselves for most of the trip, except for the odd Huron who gave Jacob a shove to remind him who was the boss.

Jacob knew that once they reached the fort, he would most likely be thrown into a musty old stockade, where he might be lucky enough to avoid the lash, but would surely be hanged. He could feel that an early fall was already in the air, and during the wilderness winter, one less mouth to feed in a small garrisoned fort would be better for everyone.

Jacob knew all too well the harshness of the long winter months in these parts. His father always told him that you live and work in the spring and summer months, prepare in the fall and try to survive the winter months to start the cycle all over again. He guessed winter could be here as soon as a month, two at the most. The birds were already flying to warmer regions and the vermin were busily gathering what they could for their winter storage. Another tell-tale sign was the leaf-bearing trees, which had become a colorful blend of reds, oranges and yellows. The trail was becoming bogged down with a fresh floor of leaves each morning, and at times the sky was a blizzard of falling foliage that made the footing quite treacherous.

Soon enough, the trails would be impassable and he thought of Maggie being trapped inside some French fort with a tiny garrison of unfortunate souls. Jacob fell into a reverie as he thought of the winters he had passed at his cabin. The snow always came fast and thick. Most times he would just finish clearing a narrow pathway when another storm would pass, forcing him to clear it again. He shuddered at the thought of having to relieve himself in the middle of a freezing, dark night. Even the wildlife found a warm cave or old hollow tree to stay warm and sleep through the worst of the winter months.

He didn't want to even think of the deep freeze of December and January. It could get cold enough that some men would never awaken in the morning, frozen right in their beds. Jacob had heard stories of how a man could have his breath taken away by the bitter cold and would soon starve to death rather than face the harsh freezing winds.

"Sir, we must keep moving," Joshua said as he kept a watchful eye on the scouts just ahead of them. "I have some stale corn bread and a few berries. I fear we will not be stopping until we reach the fort."

In an attempt to keep pace, Joshua accidently pulled hard on Jacob's neck rope, but apologized for his efforts.

The two stayed a few paces behind the main body of regulars and far enough out of earshot from the two Huron escorts that they could safely converse without being noticed.

"Why didn't you run, lad?" Jacob asked. "I would have hardly held it against you."

"Nowhere to run, sir, One-Ear is the only friend I have, and he is with Miss Maggie. I have no attachments to these heathens, so I guess sticking with you was my best option." Joshua smiled.

Before they could continue, they heard the French just ahead talking. As they rounded a sharp curve in the path, they noticed the regulars taking cover in the woods. The two Huron in the rear pushed past Joshua and rushed towards their fellow warriors.

Joshua pulled Jacob off the trail and took up a spot within some shoulder-high brush. They both intently watched as a few of the French soldiers spoke with the two advanced Huron scouts. They had run back to the main body just moments earlier, causing all this commotion.

Too far to hear anything, Joshua just sat and watched the rather animated conversation between a French officer and his two Huron scouts.

"What do you suppose they are all bothered about?" Joshua asked, keeping his eye on the conversation.

"They either ran into some lost English hunting party or something is happening at the fort, who knows?" Jacob guessed, knowing there would be no Englishmen alive this far north of the fort.

Soon it was clear to both of them the reason why the Huron scouts were so excited.

A small group of captive British soldiers were being marched by several Delaware and Seneca warriors towards their winter villages. They must have been imprisoned at Fort Duquesne after the defeat at the Great Meadows.

The soldiers, ten in number, had been repeatedly beaten and not well taken care of. Most were an encrusted, bloody mess and their skin had a sickening translucence to it. It was clear the French soldiers were attempting to control their Huron scouts from attacking the much larger Delaware party.

The Huron warriors were feared by most of the Woodland tribes in these parts. The only tribe that challenged them was the more northwestern Ottawa, who were respected by all tribes for their fearless fighting skills. When possible, even the Huron avoided contact with the Ottawa. They were a favorite of the French in battle, who used them as 'shock troops' because of their bold nature.

Despite the pleas from the French, the threat of a stand-off was increased when the Huron blocked the trail as the Delaware approached. The French regulars were clearly not interested or willing to sacrifice themselves for some tribal dispute and took up position behind the Huron. It appeared they wanted to, at the very least, discourage the Delaware from attacking.

"What the hell are they doing?" Jacob asked.

"The Huron are a proud people and they expect the Delaware to pay them for passing them on the trail," Joshua explained. "It is much like a parent asking a child to share in their good tidings."

"What child wants to share?" Jacob asked drily.

"Nothing good will come from this," Joshua quickly added, "You must stay here, I need to show them I am with them and not afraid." He quickly tied Jacob's tether line around a large oak tree and ran up the trail.

The standoff lasted for only a few moments as the Huron listened to two Delaware plead their case. Without the threat of a shot or battle, the Huron simply stepped aside and let the Delaware party pass.

As the battered prisoners passed, a Delaware brave passed a rope line to one of the awaiting Huron. Four English prisoners were pulled away from the others, leaving the remainder to continue on with their Delaware captors.

The Huron scouts stood proudly as the party passed; not one Delaware warrior dared to look at them, but remained stoically glowering at the trail without acknowledging their presence. They were soon well up the path and around the sharp turn, heading towards their nearby village.

Now with four new prisoners added to their party, Joshua was passed their ropes to watch over them along with Jacob. The four new men appeared to be walking ghosts. None uttered a word or glanced around the area. None raised his head to see their new captors.

Jacob kept himself away from them; their smell made him wince, they were no better than upright corpses. They made no noise, they simply let Joshua lead them.

The column quickly got back on the trail and increased its pace, determined to make up for the time lost during the delay. Joshua kept a steady march but was aware of the brittle nature of the men, so he eased up when they appeared winded.

As they moved along, Jacob watched the men as they struggled to walk even a few paces without stumbling. He tried on a few occasions to identify what regiment the men were from, but without any visible markings or coats it was impossible to know. One man appeared particularly familiar, but without hearing his voice or seeing any distinguishable part of his uniform, Jacob was left to wonder and observe.

After several hours, the column stopped by a fast moving stream to refresh their canteens and catch their breath.

Joshua pulled the five prisoners over to a shaded area and loosened up the ropes on their wrists.

"Please do not run we have warriors ahead and behind us. You will be dead either way."

"We are dead now," one of the men said weakly, "the only choice we have is a quick death or long torturous one." The man looked up, but remained in place with the others.

"There is not much left of them, I think they have already died on the inside," Joshua said as he loosened Jacob's wrist ropes.

"Poor bastards; try to find out from the talker where they are from," Jacob said after he settled on an old stump that sat beside the stream.

Silent once again, the small group of prisoners remained together with their heads down. They didn't even attempt to speak amongst themselves. It was like they were all in their own horrible world, afraid to talk about it.

Joshua approached them, "Do you have names? Where are you from and how did you get yourselves captured?"

He waited a few moments and was ready to leave them until the same man spoke again, "We are all from South Carolina. We were captured while we were on a patrol to search for deserters. We ran into a band of Delaware and Seneca warriors by mistake and they overwhelmed our much smaller group."

"How long have you been prisoners to the Delaware?" Joshua asked the lone speaker, while the others remained with their heads down.

"A few weeks...why do you care about us, savage?" he replied.

"No reason, Englishman; do you have names?" Joshua pressed the prisoner, while Jacob listened from the stump.

"Still not sure why you care, savage, but I'm called Duncan, they are Stuart, Collins and Peck. What are your plans for us, Huron?"

"Not my plan, we head to Fort Duquesne," Joshua offered.

He left the four to their pains and sat with Jacob.

"They said they are South Carolinians, captured on some patrol for deserters. They call themselves Duncan, Collins, Peck and I think Stuart."

Jacob sat up and interrupted him, "Did you say Stuart, Stuart from South Carolina?"

"I'm sure that is what he told me, why?" Joshua asked.

"Damn, just my bloody luck."

Before Jacob could explain, the French and Huron were back on the move. Jacob knew there were only a few more hours before they reached

Fort Duquesne and then his life would be in the hands of the French garrisoned there. His hope for leniency was dwindling as he got closer to the fort.

Added to his problems was the same Private Stuart whom he had knocked unconscious, left without a weapon and whose boots he discarded in the deepest part of the vast wilderness. Jacob had saved his life from a band of Huron warriors, but he expected little thanks for that. Also, the fact he was a deserter was something no soldier would soon forget.

Stuart was nowhere near the same man Jacob knew a few months earlier, but he was still a threat. Worried enough about what he would be facing soon, Jacob certainly did not want Stuart to have enough of his wits about him to finger him as a deserter. Regular enlisted soldiers, French or English, had no love for men who deserted them, even though many had thought of doing so themselves.

A couple of hours into the march, the forest finally opened into a large, freshly cut field. The field was speckled with rows of tree stumps and Jacob noticed the remnants of a make-shift village.

At the point of the open field sat the impressive Fort Duquesne. He had last seen the fort from well above the western ridge, but the closer he approached, the more impressed he became.

Fort Duquesne was strategically placed on a relatively flat piece of land that jutted out into the Ohio, Allegheny and Monongahela Rivers. The English called it 'The Forks' and had originally attempted to build a small fort on this site. The small force was removed by the French who claimed the place as their own. This act was the prelude to the eventual battle at the Great Meadows.

Jacob could see that where the fort sat, anyone attempting to paddle past would be spotted miles away. The deep forest on either side made it next to impossible for a large army to attack by land. It appeared the only weakness was in the form of high ridges that were set on either side. Jacob thought well-placed cannon or mortars could do some damage if placed on the high bluffs.

Upon their approach, the Huron forced the prisoners to carry several heavy bags of flour and sugar before they entered the fort. The Carolinians could barely hold themselves up but they each held a bag.

Since the last time he had observed the fort, Jacob could see many more French regulars laboring to build up the deep earthen works that surrounded the wooded side of the fort.

There was also a number of Canadian militia mingling about, not doing much of anything. The only Indians were the Huron scouts that had been his escort.

"Stay close to me, sir, I will need to find out what to do with you," Joshua whispered. "Don't worry, I will not leave you alone for long. I will find a way to overwinter at the fort."

"Don't get yourself into any trouble, lad," Jacob replied, watching the large wooden doors swing open to let them pass. "God only knows how long I might be in here. It could be months or days, depending on whether they hang me or decide to waste food on me over the winter."

Slowly making their way into the fort, Joshua still held the neck ropes of the prisoners and watched as one of the fort's officers greeted the column. A couple of the French escorts and one of the Huron spoke with the officer, and Jacob could see they were looking towards the English prisoners.

A fellow Huron called to Joshua to take the four Englishmen to the stockade near the back of the fort. Joshua pointed to Jacob but was told to only move the others.

Joshua told Jacob that he needed to stay behind and immediately took the others to the stockade.

Jacob stood alone with several Frenchmen and the Huron scouts standing about. After a brief moment, Jacob had his hands released and another officer pointed towards one of the packed supply wagons that had been part of the column.

"Empty this wagon, Englishman, and put the sacks into the supply hut."

Without any help, Jacob emptied the entire contents of the wagon while several French regulars and the Huron scouts stood by and watched.

He counted twenty sacks of flour, three large kegs of salted pork and dried cod, two barrels of brandy and wine and an endless amount of sugar and salt. He lost count of the muskets, powder horns and wooden powder kegs he unloaded, and must have taken four trips to take crates of bread into the hut. By the time he was finished, the hut was jammed to the ceiling and that didn't include the muskets and powder that were piled just outside the door. His back and arms throbbed, but he gave his captors no satisfaction in knowing he was tired.

When he finished, they offered him no water or food, but two soldiers simply pushed him across the courtyard and into the stockade.

With one small, barred window, the stockade was dark and rank. The smell of death was in the air and Jacob could only see two small cells, no more than six feet across. There were no beds, only a meager floor of rotting straw. There was no place for privacy, and if one had to relieve himself, Jacob guessed there were very few options.

Jacob was greeted by a sickly old French soldier who was obviously too ill to perform his duties so he was stuck in here to guard the prisoners. He simply grunted and mumbled something inaudible under his breath to the two soldiers who had pushed Jacob through the courtyard.

He could see that the four men who arrived with him had been thrown into the first cage, and he assumed he would be put with them. There were two other shadows sitting in the next cell but it was impossible to see them clearly with the poor lighting. The cells were only separated with old wood piled up to make an unstable wall, but were anchored by heavy bars that framed the entire room. A heavy wooden door kept the men inside and made them think twice about escaping.

Jacob was surprised when the guard stopped him from entering the first cell. The old man grabbed him by the arm and shoved him into the other occupied cage. Before he could regain his balance, he stumbled over the outstretched legs of one of the men in the cell. Jacob managed to stay on his feet, but only by bumping into the far wall.

The guard laughed and pushed the heavy door shut, locking it and spitting at the men before he turned his attention towards the other four prisoners. He spat at them also, before shutting the large outer door of the stockade and perching himself on a rickety stool nearby. He was soon fast asleep with his red woolen garrison cap pulled over his eyes.

"Bloody good way to treat prisoners, aye lad?" one of his cellmates asked. "Not that we would treat them any better."

His voice sounded so familiar that it made Jacob think back to his short-lived military service at the Great Meadows.

Before he could remember the familiar voice, the man introduced himself, "I am Robert Stobo and this one is van Braam. We were officers not long ago."

Jacob saw it was the same officer who had befriended him. He appeared relatively healthy, maybe somewhat thinner but his spirits were noticeably high considering his circumstance.

"No need for introductions, sir, I know you both all too well," Jacob nervously replied.

"How so, lad?" Stobo asked as he managed to get to his feet.

"Do you remember a Jacob Murray from the Virginia militia?"

"Aye, lad, I do. He was a good man, only who is he to you?" Stobo became more curious about the large, bearded prisoner standing in the poor light.

"I am the same man, sir, just a bit more unkempt and ragged," Jacob smiled and offered his hand.

"Damn, Murray, I thought you would be dead by now. How is that brother of yours, Israel as I remember?" Stobo accepted Jacob's hand and appeared happy to see him again.

"Sadly, Israel was murdered by the Huron and French militia after we surrendered the fort. Not sure if you heard, but I deserted not long after-wards. It was only a matter of time before the French, English or savages were to capture me."

"Sit, lad; I am deeply sorry about Israel. He was a good man for sure. As for your desertion, bad thing yet there must be more to the story." Stobo released his grip on Jacob's hand and offered him a seat beside him.

Sitting beside his former captain, Jacob started to explain how he got himself in all this trouble.

"Not much to explain, sir. After the one-sided battle, I witnessed how the savages, with the encouragement of the French, treated the injured and sick men left at the fort, I felt I needed to find Israel after being forced to leave him behind. I was frustrated and upset about dragging myself back with our defeated army, and I know it was the wrong thing to do…" Jacob stopped himself.

"No need to re-live the past, lad. How did you manage to get yourself in this place?"

"Well, after returning to the burnt out fort, I returned to my home in Pennsylvania. The rumors of the Huron raiding the frontier proved to be true, and I found my cabin a smoldering ruin. I found no signs of my wife or kids, so my only recourse was to go after them. At the moment, I most likely will be hanged for attempting to kill some fat French merchant who has purchased my Maggie and is set to take her to Quebec."

"You sure got yourself into some trouble, son," Stobo said wryly before trying to reassure the younger man. "Honestly, faced with what you have told me, I would have done the same. Let me see what I can found out about what the French have planned for you. I have a good relationship with some of the French officers and, despite my accommodations, they treat me relatively well."

Jacob remained seated and watched his captain call for the guard, "Hey private, let me out and take me to see your commander." He turned back to Jacob, saying, "They usually permit me time to walk the courtyard and I have even been escorted outside the main fort for a longer stroll. I gave my word to the commander that I would not attempt an escape, in exchange for some certain privileges."

The guard stumbled from his deep sleep and, once he gathered his wits, he rushed obediently over to the door and nervously attempted to jam his keys into the lock.

"Oui, monsieur," he mumbled.

"I will return soon, lad, so get yourself some rest and I will do my best to find out what they have planned for you," Stobo said and dusted himself off as he walked with the guard into the courtyard.

"Murray, get up, lad," Stobo said, shaking Jacob's shoulder.

"Yes sir, sorry sir." Jacob quickly got himself up off the floor.

"You will be fine for now, lad. Lucky for you, most of the regulars here dislike the merchant you threatened. We just need to keep you out of trouble and show them you are a good lad."

Clearing his eyes, Jacob replied, "I will do my best, sir, I have no desire to be part of a hangman's rope."

"One more thing, what do you know of the young Huron hanging around the fort?" Stobo whispered.

"He might prove to be my only way out of this mess," Jacob explained. "He is actually an English boy who was captured a few years back by the Huron. The boy has been a godsend to me, and I would be dead if not for him. He also knows of my wife and helped her as well."

"He certainly might prove to be helpful," Stobo agreed, as he stared silently into the darkness. "Now get some more sleep."

"One last thing, sir, is Captain van Braam in bad shape? He has not made a sound the whole time I've been here, except for a few groans." Jacob looked at the crumpled form propped in the corner next to him.

"He has proven to be useless. All the Dutchman wants to do is die. He knows he let Washington down back at the Great Meadows, and his own incompetence cost his friend some standing within the Virginia community."

Chapter | **Four**

Maggie's pace increased as the Huron scouts up ahead veered to the left and continued on a much smaller-cut trail that presented a nice view of a river. She could now see the fort and was shocked by its size. Fredrick had mentioned earlier that the fort was no more than a supply depot, but Maggie could see that if it was ever attacked, the soldiers inside would have difficulty defending it against even a small company of men.

It was crude and as basic as any fort she had seen in the frontier wilderness. In Scotland, such a structure would not even be used to house livestock. The thoughts of overwintering in it made her shiver. It consisted of four house-like structures that doubled as the outer walls, and four bastions that had only two cannon mounted in each. She knew these provisions wouldn't be much of a deterrent to an attacking enemy.

Maggie assumed the fort's only saving grace was its location. It was too far, for the moment, to be attacked by the English, and the native tribes who inhabited the area were allies with the French and posed no threat.

Getting a better look as she moved closer, Maggie noticed that since the fort was so small, the garrisoned soldiers not on duty were forced to make their living quarters outside the main structure.

Maggie saw this fort as Fredrick described it, a storage depot, and nothing more. Even as the small party approached, they were informally greeted by two guards resting on two empty oak barrels.

With only a slight nod, Fredrick and his men walked past them and followed the dirt path towards the fort's front gates. Maggie had drawn particular attention from the two men, as well as a few onlookers posted on the upper bastions. She guessed that most of these men had not seen a white-skinned woman for several months and the sight of one reminded them of much better times.

"Stay close, Maggie," Fredrick said, seconding her thoughts as he fell back from the front of the column. "I feel these poor bastards haven't set their eyes on many women out in this wilderness for a while. You have certainly piqued their curiosity."

Maggie saw the Huron scouts stop by the front gate and remain outside the walls; it appeared they had no wish to enter the fort. She quickly glanced around to find One-Ear, but he was not with the others. She could only pray he was safe.

"Monsieur Duval, I am surprised yet glad to see you here at my fort; how is your father keeping?" the fort's commander asked, quickly donning his coat and hat to make himself appear somewhat presentable.

Maggie had to keep herself from nearly laughing out loud when she first got a glimpse of the commander. He stood no more than five feet tall, and was just as wide. He waddled more than walked and his fat red cheeks and welcoming smile reminded her more of a favorite uncle than a French officer. She thought he was probably the right size for such a small fort.

"Commander Savard, it is good to see you again," Fredrick said. "May I introduce Madame Murray?"

The commander attempted to bow, but his oversized belly prevented him from doing so. Maggie smiled politely as he unceremoniously grasped her hand and lightly kissed it.

"Madame, you certainly make this dreary fort a much more attractive place," Savard said, tipping his hat.

"You are too kind, sir," she replied as she pulled her hand back and hoped there was a place inside to wash his filthy stench from it.

Savard again took her hand and escorted her into the fort. Her larger stride made the much shorter officer struggle to keep up with her. She could see Fredrick smiling at the sight of the two of them.

"Come, Fredrick, a glass of wine is awaiting us in my quarters," Savard suggested.

"Before we indulge ourselves in your wine, may we splash some water on our faces and have my men taken care of?"

Savard's smile left his face as he motioned to two of his men to come over, "Please take care of these men and draw some water for their horses."

Fredrick excused himself as well, addressing Savard, "I will be with you shortly; I need to ensure our scouts are in good order."

"Now, madame, please take a moment to freshen up and come back with Fredrick to enjoy a drink with us," Savard said, turning his attention back to Maggie.

"Thank you, sir," Maggie politely replied and followed Fredrick to find where she might be resting for the night.

Looking about the fort, Maggie noticed it was even smaller than it appeared from the outer walls. There was a small chapel, an open-air guard house and what looked like a doctor's quarters. Along with Savard's house, the four structures were what made up the main walls of the cramped fort.

She was also struck by the lack of signs of any Indians either inside or outside of the fort. Maggie could only think that it had to do more with the time of year and that they were busy preparing their villages for the long winter months.

Fredrick stopped to speak with a kindly-looking older gentleman for a few minutes. "Madame," Fredrick said to Maggie, "the good doctor has offered his home for your comfort. He said he is leaving for Fort Presque 'Isle immediately and would be honored if you slept there tonight."

"Please make sure you thank him for his kindness," she said and smiled at the older man as he moved to depart the fort.

Maggie made her way to the doctor's home and knocked, just to make sure that no one was still within. She slowly opened the unlocked door and stepped into the darkness of the front office room. The smell engulfed her immediately; it was an odd combination of stale blood, medicinal supplies and several dried herbs that hung from the ceiling. Once she adjusted to the strong odors, she was impressed by the spaciousness of the office. She walked past the doctor's equipment and furniture to the back of the room where she saw a door that she assumed led to the sleeping quarters.

Again, she knocked on the slightly opened door before walking through. Though the room was dim, she could make out a large wooden-framed poster bed and a cozy fireplace in the far corner. Maggie was looking forward to finally having a comfortable night's sleep as a bed was something she hadn't enjoyed for months. The thought of not sleeping on the cold ground or a hard wagon bed made her wish she had declined Savard's offer of a glass of wine.

She found a pitcher of cool water and quickly washed her hands and face. The doctor had a small looking glass, and Maggie peered at her reflection. For the first time, she felt uncomfortable with her appearance, having been battered by months on the trail and the lack of good washing. Her normally lengthy, well-combed hair was matted and braided back, almost reaching her belt line. Her clothes were caked with dirt and hadn't been washed for months. Even with the onset of winter, she dreamed of a hot bath and a freshly dried dress.

Feeling briefly refreshed, Maggie slowly made her way towards the commander's home and could feel the air getting noticeably chillier as the sun set. The nights had become much colder and the leaves on the trees were rapidly changing color and raining down on the vast countryside. It was hard to gauge the weather or the time of year while actively trekking through the thickness of the wilderness, but once the trail opened to a clearing, the cold fall winds hit pretty hard. Her only hope was that they would move swiftly enough to reach Niagara before the snow was too deep to pass.

Maggie scanned her surroundings as she walked, and only counted maybe fifteen, possibly twenty regulars that manned the fort. Once winter struck, these men would endure the bitter cold and thick snow from October through to April, and possibly into late May. She honestly felt sorry for these poor souls, and even though her life was destined to be in the hands of some rich Quebec merchant, she wouldn't change spots with any of them.

Except in dreams of being posted within the walls of Quebec City, these men would not see any outsiders for several months. Even then, it would be only the odd trader or Indian. It was a lonely, mundane existence that she wouldn't wish on any man.

She reached Savard's door and lightly tapped on it, hoping they might not hear it, thus giving her the excuse to return to her warm bed. She heard the door being unlatched and opened slowly in an effort to keep the cold air outside.

Fredrick greeted her with a pleasant smile as the rusted hinges of the door creaked and echoed throughout the fort. She stepped in and immediately felt the warmth of the roaring fire heating the entire front office of Savard's home. Maggie was impressed by the fine furnishings in the officer's quarters and saw Savard standing over the fire moving some of the wood around to keep it burning.

"Madame, I am so honored you could make it tonight," Savard greeted her kindly. "God knows, this fort is not used to such beauty, no offense Fredrick. I hope you found your sleeping quarters acceptable, madame. I should apologize for the rather strong medicinal odor, although I suspect a tent full of men would not smell much better."

Without asking, Fredrick placed her arm in his and walked her over to the fire and a chair placed just off to the side. Savard noticed Fredrick's directness and smiled.

Maggie's first instinct was to pull her hand back but it would make for an uncomfortable trip towards Niagara. She certainly did not want Fredrick to get the wrong idea, but his protection was something she needed for the time being.

"The room is perfect, and having a bed is certainly a luxury I did not expect this deep into the wilderness; merci, monsieur," Maggie responded.

"We are not heathens, madame. We might be a lifetime away from Quebec, but we do our best to remain civilized despite our predicament," Savard stated.

Maggie politely nodded at her host and decided to leave such conversations alone.

"I asked Fredrick how a beautiful English woman like you got herself involved in all this mess," Savard commented, changing the tone of the conversation.

"Well, I am Scottish and my involvement was not of my choosing, "Maggie boldly snapped back. "The French and Huron decided this all on their own. They took my children, burnt our home and murdered my friends. My husband is off fighting them and we hope to send all of you back to Quebec as soon as we can."

"Please accept my apologies for my fellow countrymen; the savages I can't make excuses for, so let us share a glass of wine before we all continue on with our misfortunes," Fredrick interjected, attempting to end the conversation.

At first, Maggie ignored Fredrick's offer of wine, but she reluctantly accepted. Savard, still wishing to provoke his guest, raised his glass and offered a toast, "To France and to war."

Maggie simply stared at the fire and did not return the toast; she placed her full glass on the small side table beside her chair. Savard noticed that he had upset his guest, yet he still decided to continue with his conversation.

"If I offended you, madame, my deepest apologies," Savard smirked. "I should be much more prudent in the company of the fairer sex." Savard smirked.

Maggie had thoughts of reaching over and smacking the impish little man but decided that imagining it served her just as well.

"Sir," Fredrick began, "please bear in mind that Madame Murray is our guest and should be afforded respect as such. Remember, we are French gentlemen not the English." He was half-hearted in his defense of Maggie, being careful not to overstep his authority and place.

"You are right, so permit me to rephrase my ill-humored toast – to peace and happiness," Savard said, looking directly at Maggie.

Maggie ignored the toast and left her glass resting on the side table.

Fredrick quickly redirected the conversation with Savard, "What is the news of the English in these parts?"

"All I have heard is that we routed them near Fort Duquesne and sent them home in tatters," Savard replied. "There is a rumor that they have called on a newly appointed general from England. I recall his name is Braddock, but I know little about his experience. I see him as little threat to us or Quebec, especially if he has never fought in this horrendous wilderness before. If he thinks this is like the open fields of Europe, we will soon be toasting another French victory."

Before they could continue their one-sided exchange, Maggie interrupted, "Gentlemen, I should return to my room and let you both talk about your war stories. I have no interest in two countries fighting over acres of wilderness that God knows no sane person would want to inhabit."

Fredrick attempted to speak but Maggie said good night to them both and stepped outside into the chilly night air.

Upset with the commander's arrogance, Maggie knew her temper would get her into trouble and it was best for her to return to her quarters. She had made it across the dimly lit courtyard and was about to open the door to the doctor's house when she heard Fredrick call out to her.

"Madame, I am sorry for the idiot's manners. I trust you now understand why he is stationed out in this unimpressive fort versus back in Quebec?"

"No apology is necessary, I truly am tired and it is late," Maggie replied. "I need a good night's rest so I am ready for our long journey in the morning."

"Nonetheless, I am truly sorry he was so rude. We must leave by the first light; it is a short walk to Fort Presque 'Isle and then we can canoe the rest by way of the lake. Please rest and I will send one of the men to wake you by sunrise. Good night, madame." Fredrick politely bowed and walked back towards the commander's quarters.

Strangely, Maggie was excited about the prospects of travelling by canoe. She thought it would be a pleasant change from all the trudging she had done on foot over the last several months. She had done a little canoeing on a few of the small lakes near her home, but had never experienced or seen the large lake they would be journeying on.

She was also beginning to grow quite fond of Fredrick and appreciated the way he made her feel safe.

Morning came too soon for her liking, but she did get a good night's rest. The bed was an extra special treat and if it hadn't been for the light knock on her door, she would have slept most of the day. It only took her a few moments to put her clothes back on, re-braid her tangled hair and then start a small fire in the doctor's wall-sized fireplace in the far corner of his front office.

She went to the door to see what the morning would bring weather-wise and immediately noticed a packed haversack resting on the door's frame. She picked it up before stepping back into the room and closing the door behind her.

Carefully opening the pack, she was pleasantly surprised to find a new pair of men's breeches, along with a clean woolen over shirt. A pair of socks was tucked inside the shirt's sleeve and a light brown overcoat finished off the thoughtful gift. A small card fell to the floor as she tried on the breeches. She picked it up and read:

> *"Madame, please accept this small gift to ensure your comfort on the last leg of our travels. Although it may be more fitting for a man, I am certain you will be the envy of us all."*

> *Warmest Regards, Fredrick*

The thoughtfulness made her smile and Maggie happily put on her new, clean clothes after briefly warming them by the fire. She actually had worn an old pair of Jacob's breeches before while she worked the farm, and they were much more practical than a dress.

Once she had put on the breeches and the large, comfortable shirt, she found a small vest and a red woolen cap that she stuffed back into the haversack.

Along with a good night's rest and her fresh attire, Maggie stepped out into the sunny courtyard and was politely greeted by the busy soldiers. She noticed Fredrick ordering some of his men to prepare the horses and wagons, while the Huron remained waiting outside the opened gates of the fort.

Fredrick spotted her and immediately approached, "Good morning, madame, was your night favorable?"

"Very much so, monsieur, and I must thank you for your kind gift. It was a very pleasant surprise this brisk morning."

"I see you found everything and you look much more comfortable. I thought a fine women sitting in a canoe with a dress on would be rather distracting to the others." Fredrick smiled.

"Thank you again for your thoughtfulness, Fredrick."

"If you are all in order, then we must be leaving immediately. The weather appears favorable and the trek to the lake is only a short, easy nine miles. I sent a few of the Huron ahead to ready the canoes and wait for our arrival. I must speak with Savard before we depart and I will pass on your thanks to him."

Maggie watched Fredrick walk away. She was almost happy to be with him and her thoughts of her family were so far out of reach that she decided to live in the moment. It was not because she didn't want to think about Jacob and her children, it was really the only way she could cope; it was the only part of her life that she could control at the moment. She had experienced and witnessed so much over the past several months that she had forgotten what Jacob smelled like after he had returned from a long hunting trip or how it felt when they touched each other. Her life now was filled with the intensity of just surviving and Fredrick by no means made her feel the same way Jacob once made her feel, but he provided some security and that gave her hope, and hope was far better than the thought she might never see her family again.

Chapter | **Five**

"Jacob, I am going for a little walk," Captain Stobo said, "would you be so kind as to pass me pen and paper so I can take some notes? Soon enough you will be able to accompany me, but let us gain their trust first."

Jacob watched as Stobo simply walked out of the cage, pleasantly greeted the lone guard and stepped unescorted into the courtyard.

Alone again with the silent, brooding van Braam, who remained slouched over in the far corner, Jacob wondered why the Dutchman did not receive the same privileges bestowed on Captain Stobo.

There were constant moans and murmurs coming from the other cell that housed the North Carolinians. Jacob decided to work his way closer to hear what he could from the men. He stood in the open doorway but was immediately warned by the guard to sit back down.

After only a few minutes, Stobo rushed back into the small cell. Warning Jacob to keep his voice down and sit in the far corner with him, Stobo whispered, "What kind of trouble did you get yourself into lad? I briefly spoke with the fort's commander and he mentioned that the merchant you attacked is very high-powered in Quebec City."

"That fat pig bought my Maggie; all I did was scared him a little—and I recall I might have threatened to kill him," Jacob said with a smirk.

"Damn it, lad, you certainly made a pretty important enemy," Stobo explained, taking care not to let his tone alarm the guard. "I heard the commander shares your general dislike for the merchant, but pressures from Quebec might force his hand in how he treats you.

"You might have forced my hand as well. We might need to get you out of this place sooner rather than later. My fear is that once this merchant arrives, our options will be limited."

"Is there word when he might be arriving?" Jacob asked.

"From what I can gather, he is expected any day now. I will need some time to think about our problem and hopefully we can get you out of here. Do you know if that Indian boy is still around?" Stobo asked, as he pondered all the options.

"I have not seen or heard from him since I was placed in here, but I know he is around. The lad is a good one, and he had his opportunity to leave me earlier but decided to stay by my side."

Ironically, as the two continued to talk, they heard a commotion at the entrance to the stockade.

"Leave, you savage, or I will shoot you dead," the guard warned an Indian outside the view of the two captives.

"I see my white prisoner now, you let me go and I will be quick," the Indian said calmly.

Jacob immediately recognized the voice of Joshua and told his captain, "That is the lad…"

Before Jacob could continue, Stobo was out in the hall, attempting to calm down the guard, "He is a fine soldier, please let the savage pass; the lad is a friend."

The guard looked towards Stobo; although he was an English prisoner, he was still an officer. Any insubordination by him would not be looked upon well by the French officers in the fort. Also, Stobo had been granted certain privileges, and the guard obviously did not want to land himself in trouble because of some wild savage.

Having few options, he decided the best course was to relent, "Go, Huron, but not for too long."

"Merci, sir," Stobo said politely, nodding to the guard who ignored the gesture and returned to his stool.

"Come, boy, Jacob is in here with me," Stobo said as he waved Joshua forward.

Seeing him through the dim light, Joshua moved quickly to get out of earshot of the guard, replying in perfect English, "Thank you, sir, I am sorry for the problem."

With all the noise, Jacob had risen to his feet just in case his captain needed any help, and he greeted Joshua as soon as he saw him, "Joshua! Good to see you well. This is Captain Stobo. So what news do you have for us?"

"Pleasure to meet you, sir," Joshua said, shaking Stobo's hand, "and good to see you so alive, Mister Jacob. My news is not good, I fear. The merchant fellow has just arrived and is not overly happy you are still alive. He had hoped your dead body would be hanging from a tree to greet him outside the fort's walls."

Stobo was clearly upset and paced around the small cage. He kicked at van Braam's outstretched feet, saying, "Get yourself on your feet, you lazy Dutchman, and go find me some information on this French merchant. I want to know why he is here and what he wants." Grumbling under his breath, van Braam pushed himself up and did as Stobo ordered. It was the first time since Jacob had been at the fort that he saw van Braam actually move, albeit rather slowly and methodically.

Jacob waited until van Braam had walked out of the stockade before asking, "Honestly, what use will he be to us, sir?"

"None whatsoever, I just didn't want him to be a part of this," Stobo explained. "We will need to get you out of here tonight or tomorrow. Joshua, do you know where the merchant is now?"

"He is in the main courtyard, ordering the soldiers around," Joshua replied. "The commanding officer is not very happy with him, and I think that Mr. Jacob might be used to get the merchant on his way."

"I see, and that makes some sense. Murray, you really know how to get yourself into trouble with anyone of authority. I know that the commander of this fort would just as soon sacrifice you in order to get some peace back into his life. The garrison needs to get ready for the winter and all this merchant is doing is slowing his men down." Stobo continued pacing the floor as he spoke.

With all of their thoughts distracted by plans for Jacob, they had failed to notice that some of the Carolinians were listening to their conversation. Jacob had paid little notice to them, and it hadn't occurred to him that Private Stuart was actually getting some life back into his beaten body.

"What about us, Captain?" a voice barked from the adjoining cell.

Jacob and Stobo both turned and saw Stuart, finally standing, leaning against the thick cell wall.

They now realized that the private had been eavesdropping on the entire conversation and knew enough that he wanted to be part of this.

"It is you, Stuart, I feared it was you the first time I laid my eyes on you, but I hoped you were already dead," Jacob snapped.

"No such luck, deserter," Stuart shot back. "I knew I would track you down some day."

"This is no time for past feuds, you fools," Stobo admonished the men. "If you both want to live then keep your tongues in your head, or I will let the hangman do his work on the both of you."

"I don't answer to prisoners, my duty is to take this man back and see him hang under a British flag," spat Stuart.

"Watch yourself, lad, I am still an officer in his Majesty's Army, and any further insubordination will result in your hanging, understood?"

"No disrespect, sir, I am just doing my duty," Stuart said as he stared towards Jacob.

"Murray, you are determined to have yourself hanged by either side, be it French or English. For now we must look at what is at hand, getting you both out of here. Then you are free to continue your petty issues outside, agreed Stuart?"

"Yes, sir."

"Are you in agreement, Murray?"

"Yes, sir."

Just as they tried to continue, van Braam strolled in, totally unaware of what was taking place.

"Captain, this merchant LaMont is a powerful fellow," the Dutchman began, "I am told he has the ear of the King of France and is not afraid to use such influences. He appears to wield his authority freely and often. As for you, Murray, he wants you hanged before he is set to leave in two days."When he had finished speaking, he simply returned to his corner and tucked his head into his knees.

He said nothing else, and Stobo requested no further information from him.

"Joshua, I need you to leave and find out what you can from your Huron brothers; go now and be safe, lad," Stobo said and patted him on the shoulder as he left.

"Let's take a moment to consider our options," Stobo continued. "Jacob, I have been making notes and details of this entire fort and have sketched almost every square inch of this place. Washington would be very interested in this information, and I need you to take it to him."

"Washington? With all due respect, sir, he has no use for me and, might I remind you, he was the officer who placed a bounty on my head. I fear hanging might be a better option for me." Jacob was puzzled at the mere suggestion of the plan.

"That's the best idea I heard since you arrived," Private Stuart interrupted from the other cell.

"So true, Murray, and keep your comments to yourself, private, or you will find more trouble than you could ever imagine," Stobo snapped. "My thought was to write a personal letter to Washington to explain your situation and how you bravely helped me out. The information I will give you regarding the inner workings of this fort should be more than enough to sway him."

"Fine, but what of Stuart and the other men?" Jacob countered. "Certainly they are in no shape to make such a journey?"

"Private Stuart will accompany you to Washington's camp at Will's Creek. He will vouch for your bravery and honor, correct, private?" Stobo leaned over towards Stuart's cell as he spoke.

Jacob was uncomfortable with the idea of Stuart's word, but he also knew that he had no choice. Stobo still had good standing within the officers' ranks, despite being stuck in Fort Duquesne's stockade.

"I still feel Stuart is in no shape to travel the distance to Will's Creek." Jacob mildly protested.

"What about the others?" Stuart added. "I cannot be expected to just leave them here to rot."

"Two can move more swiftly and you can't have men slowing you down," Stobo said firmly. "As for you, Murray, you will have to make sure he makes it. In the same letter I will mention the private's role in this. You must put your petty differences aside if you both want to live. Do I have your word?"

The two nodded to Stobo but did not look towards each other.

Jacob was excited about the prospects of his freedom, even with his uneasiness about Stuart. The thought of travelling with him did not sit well, nor did he trust Stuart's word, but he was obligated to his captain. The idea that there was a chance to be pardoned for his desertion also gave him some renewed energy.

The two men rested for several hours until they were both awakened by a large crash that reverberated throughout their cells. The door of the stockade smashed open and knocked the unsuspecting guard off his stool.

"Where is my prisoner?" a loud voice bellowed. "Let me see the worthless bastard."

Jacob had only a moment to clear his head before two French regulars pulled him by his arms and forced him to his feet.

Captain Stobo immediately got to his feet and vehemently protested, "What is the meaning of this?"

Jacob could now see it was the merchant, LaMont. He had finally bullied his way around the fort and was seeking his revenge.

Spitting as he talked, LaMont replied to Stobo, "This is my prisoner and he will be hanged."

Jacob attempted to struggle free at first, but was met with a swift punch to the face. He could hear Stobo's commanding voice once more, shouting, "I will not stand for this, where is the commander?"

"He is occupied at the moment and will not be available until nightfall; this is no concern of his or yours, Englishman," LaMont replied arrogantly. He nodded to one of the soldiers, who quickly struck Stobo in the stomach with the butt end of his musket.

As Stobo crumpled to the floor of his cell, clutching his abdomen in pain, LaMont smirked and said, "He is mine, and you would be smart to stay out of this, sir. An Englishman has no rights in this fort, so tread lightly."

The two soldiers firmly held Jacob's arms behind his back and pulled him into the stockade's cramped passageway. Jacob made a conscious effort to stop struggling and conserve his energy, so he said nothing as the soldiers secured his arms with a line of rope and shoved him into the open courtyard. He fell to his knees and strained to regain his balance while they tugged harder on the rope.

LaMont caught up to the men as they stopped. He gripped Jacob's hair and pulled the man's face even with his own, growling out, "The tables have turned once again. I assure you, this will be quick since I must return to your wife as soon as possible. I will be sure to treat her well in your absence." He paused and pulled sharply on Jacob's hair before whispering near his ear, "I will enjoy this as much as I will enjoy your wife."

Jacob was filled with rage, but gave LaMont no satisfaction. His calmness seemed to provoke the merchant even further.

A swift knee to the ribs brought Jacob to his knees, yet he defiantly gathered his breath and stood back up.

LaMont raised his fist to strike the defenseless Jacob but was blocked by an unsuspecting hand.

"What is the meaning of this? Have you lost your mind and forgotten your place here, Monsieur?"

Jacob saw that the commanding officer had returned to find the fort in chaos. He watched with pleasure as the merchant struggled to explain himself in front of the angry officer.

"Stand down, men," the officer shouted. "You have crossed the line, Monsieur LaMont. We may be in the wilderness, but I am the officer in charge of this fort and I will not tolerate such insubordination by some civilian. This prisoner is in my stockade and is under my protection until the due course of law dictates otherwise. I know your influences reach as far as France, but I assure you my duties reach just as far." He was clearly enjoying his opportunity to lecture the arrogant merchant.

Jacob had been released and stood back to enjoy the scene, rubbing his wrists, worn raw by the exuberant soldiers' ropes. He looked around and finally spotted Joshua. He was leaning proudly against the large beamed entry gate, with a broad smile across his face.

Jacob knew it was Joshua who had run to find the officer and tell him of the happenings back at the fort. Jacob returned the smile at the brave young man, understanding that Joshua had saved his life once again.

"Return this man to his cell," the commander ordered his men. "As for you, merchant, count yourself lucky I do not free the prisoner to make this a fair fight. This conversation will continue in a more private setting and any mention of the King or your friends back in Quebec will only serve to add to your troubles."

Jacob could see that the merchant was barely able to hide his displeasure at being so humiliated in front of the entire fort. It was rather pleasurable to watch as the merchant fell in step behind the officer as they headed towards his quarters.

"You must be part wildcat, lad," Stobo laughed as Jacob walked back into the cell, relatively unscathed.

Jacob smiled and took a seat on the damp, straw-covered floor. He was exhausted and still inwardly shuddered to think about hanging from a tree while the fat merchant laughed at his broken, limp body.

"No time to rest, Murray, we must get you out of here as soon as darkness hits us," Stobo pressed. "I am sure that the commander will grow weary of the persistence of the merchant and give into his demands. Your neck is not worth all the trouble that will result from the merchant's possible connections."

"What about you, Captain, why don't you come with me instead of the useless Stuart?" Jacob asked, hoping that Stobo had considered the possibility. He wasn't entirely sure what was holding his captain back, but knew better than to push him.

"Honestly, I don't trust Private Stuart either," Stobo said quietly, "but you will need some help to make this trip. You will have to keep an eye on him for sure. I wasn't going to tell you this, but after I was struck with the rifle and you were taken out to the courtyard by the guards, I saw the merchant talk to Stuart. I couldn't hear anything, since I was lying on the floor, and it did appear to be a one-sided conversation, but I still found it odd that the merchant would waste his time on a lowly private. We can't let anything interfere with our plan, and once you are on the trail, if you feel it makes more sense that Stuart should meet an untimely death, so be it."

Before they could continue, the door of the stockade opened once again. Jacob saw that it was Joshua and as he moved to greet him, Joshua yelled, "Sir, the Huron are ready to leave and our coming to retrieve their captives. They are looking to take you with them back to Canada!"

Joshua barely got out his last words as four Huron braves boldly walked into the stockade, ignoring the guard's warning to stop.

"Get down, Murray, I'll try to negotiate with the savages," Stobo said as he stepped into the now crowded hall.

The Huron burst into the first cell, which housed the Carolinians, and quickly put ropes around three of the men's necks. They appeared to leave Stuart alone then turned their attention towards Jacob's cell. Stobo blocked their way and that slowed them down enough to give Joshua time to protect his property.

"That one is mine, he is property of the French and I have traded for him to be my prize." Joshua stood his ground and, to his surprise, they left Jacob and pulled the three struggling Carolinians out into the courtyard.

Jacob remained sitting and looked towards Stobo and Joshua as he asked, "Why did they leave Stuart? He is in better shape than any of the others."

"Not sure, maybe they worked out a deal with the French," Joshua guessed. "I fear the others will not make it far on the trail towards Canada, and most likely will be put to the knife and scalped. The Huron want to get back home and the three white captives will only slow them down."

"The boy is probably right," Stobo said. "They would have gotten something much more useful in Stuart, but the others will soon be a war prize, destined for a scalping pole.

"Young man, please see what is happening with our old friend the merchant. We are considering making a move tonight, if all falls into place. I need a set of eyes out in the courtyard to make sure nothing surprises us."

After everyone had cleared out and they were alone once again, Stobo answered Jacob's earlier question, "God knows, I would love to leave. I really should, but I can't leave van Braam behind here alone. I also gave my word to the French that I would not attempt to flee. I gave no such word not to help a fellow prisoner escape though."

One of the reasons Jacob trusted this man was he really cared for his men. He proved that back at the Great Meadows and once again within the walls of this stockade.

"I understand, sir, so what needs to be done?"

"It is pretty simple and should work as long as we can keep the merchant out of our way. We will just walk right out the front gate. The French have no reason to think I will escape, and will think nothing of us walking the grounds. I guess the sentries will assume we need to relieve ourselves and will be more concerned in keeping themselves warm during the cool night. Your role is to make it look like the two of you attacked me and ran off."

"I must tell you again that the thought of taking Stuart with me is a concern," Jacob said. "I don't trust him to keep his word, and did you notice how the savages came in and took his friends? They didn't even look at him; didn't that seem odd? What about the conversation with the merchant?"

"Don't concern yourself; the letter addressed to Washington explains everything, and Stuart will have no way to betray you or me," Stobo replied, obviously tired of Jacob's objections.

"That is, if we even make it to Will's Creek," Jacob added as Stobo handed him a sealed letter, making sure that Stuart could clearly see the exchange.

The captain then motioned for Jacob to sit and search the straw by his feet, where he found another thicker package, which he hid in his left moccasin. Stobo watched Jacob and explained, "There is some detailed information in there that Washington will be particularly interested in, so protect it with your life. That goes for you as well private." He shot a glance directly at Stuart.

"If you are recaptured by the French," Stobo continued, "the information will be easily traced back to me and it will mean a death sentence for us all."

Jacob finally understood that his escape was not just about his own freedom. His captain trusted him with his own life as well. Whatever the package held, it was critical to Washington and to Stobo, and Jacob couldn't fail to reach Will's Creek.

Finally, Stobo handed him a small, deer-skin package, which Jacob unfolded. It was a small patch knife with maybe a six inch well-made blade and a sturdy handle made from an old deer antler. Jacob smiled his thanks for the gift.

Leaning over so Stuart could not hear him, Stobo explained, "Just in case things get out of hand; it's not much, but it's better than an empty hand. And I expect it back when we meet again."

Quickly wrapping the knife back up and tucking it into his shirt, Jacob called out to Stuart, "Get up, private. You need to get yourself ready for our journey."

Stuart only looked up at him from his corner and said nothing.

"Are you deaf, man? Get yourself up now," Stobo bluntly ordered the indifferent private.

Jacob impatiently watched as Stuart finally got himself up and slowly brushed himself off. He still made no eye contact with either man as he meticulously cleared himself of all the straw that stuck to his clothing.

"I know you know the trail up on the ridge, Jacob," Captain Stobo said. It is important that the western ridge is cleared well before sunrise. The patrols are sporadic at best and the only threat you might run into is a hunting crew. The other factor will be the darkness. Most of this wilderness is treacherous even in daylight, so watch your step and keep moving. We are lucky since most of the Huron are well to the north of us and the Delaware and Seneca are too busy setting up their winter camps to be worried about two white men wandering the trails."

"All I need is for Stuart to keep pace with me and we will be safe," Jacob said.

"Worry about your own scalp, deserter, and we should both be fine," Stuart replied.

"Damn you two, enough with the bickering! Maybe I should just escape instead and leave one of you behind to rot in the straw," Stobo angrily suggested.

"No need, sir," Stuart meekly replied.

Jacob said nothing, although he knew the sun would be setting in less than an hour, and that left little time for him to prepare for the escape. Stobo had also mentioned that he got word out to Joshua to meet them outside the fort at dusk.

Stuart sat by himself in the first cell while Stobo continued to whisper to Jacob, "Take these moth-eaten wool blankets, and I have been borrowing some leather straps to secure them. They should keep you warm during the cold nights. You have seen this fort from above so you know that the earthen works that surround the outer defenses are lower as you move towards the river. I suggest taking that route rather than heading towards the main trail that cuts up the eastern side of the ridge. Godspeed, son, and keep moving no matter what you hear or see behind you."

"Before we leave, I need to know what Stuart was talking about with the merchant. How do we know he isn't planning to double cross us?" Jacob earnestly suggested.

"If it puts your mind at ease then I will ask him."

Stobo got up and called out to Stuart, "Private, come closer, we need to speak about our plan."

Jacob remained behind Stobo, waiting to see how Stuart would react to their questioning.

"What do we need to go over, sir?" Stuart innocently asked.

"To be perfectly direct, Stuart, I just want to be reassured that you are loyal to our plan."

Before he could reply, Jacob stepped forward and said, "Forget all this talk, Stuart, you were seen speaking with the merchant and we want to know what you were talking about."

Stuart laughed at the implication and replied simply, "He asked about the Ohio Company's trading post at Will's Creek."

"That's all you talked about?" Stobo asked quickly, before Jacob could step in again.

"Not much else to it, sir, I told him I knew nothing about it and he left it at that," Stuart explained and returned to the solace of his own cell.

Stobo decided not to push the point and left Stuart to his own thoughts. He offered only one word to Jacob, "Satisfied?"

Jacob was far from satisfied but realized that Stobo wanted him to concentrate on the escape plan and not be distracted by anything else.

He decided not to offer an answer.

The rest of the time they all sat quietly. Jacob's only thought was on getting out of this place and reaching Washington as soon as possible.

The smell of cooked stew and baked bread filled the air and streamed through the stockade. Soon the soldiers would be sitting down for their nightly meal, and that would give the prisoners a brief moment to launch their escape. Hungry soldiers would hopefully care little for three Englishmen wandering around the courtyard.

Jacob knew that the French would not suspect that anyone would be foolish enough to escape into the woods at night. The deep forest was next to impossible for even the most seasoned trapper to navigate during the night, so the French knew that anyone venturing out would either get himself lost or make a good dinner for the vast array of wildlife that inhabited the woods.

Even if there were savages to worry about, Jacob felt comfortable enough that he would never be followed at night. Most Indians feared the night and believed the spirits came out then and did not welcome anyone who might venture out. He knew that they would normally wait until dawn to track anyone foolhardy enough to enter the forest.

With most of the soldiers eating their nightly meal and only a few unlucky sentries manning the upper walls, Stobo waited until the lone cell guard left momentarily to grab his rations. They now had their opportunity to leave relatively undetected.

"It's time, gentlemen, gather what you need and let's move out." Stobo kept his eye on the stockade door.

Jacob was up and ready to move, the excitement and anticipation made his heart pound with the thought of being free.

"Keep close," Stobo whispered, "and stay tight to the walls. The men will be too busy with their food and drink to notice us, but let's be safe. Any noise tends to carry for miles around here, so be quiet."

Jacob watched as Stobo headed out into the dark night, but took the lead when the captain signaled him ahead. Stobo then took up the rear to ensure the two men kept moving, without running into problems. Stuart remained close to Jacob and carefully watched every one of his steps.

They made their way quickly to the main gate and were extra cautious as they passed under the torch-lit bastion. It was manned by a single guard who appeared to be waiting out his time before he could get his fill of the stew. Realistically, it was next to impossible to see anyone approaching or leaving the fort unless they were right in front of the torch.

Jacob easily slipped the lock off the small soldier's entrance door that was used for easier access for patrols, instead of the much heavier main gate.

He was careful not to let the old hinges give up their plan and only opened the door just enough to fit through sideways.

Even though the countryside was blackened by the night, the openness of the earthen works made Jacob feel the exhilaration of his imminent freedom. His excitement was quickly dashed as he noticed a dark figure standing on the small bridge that linked the fort to the main trail. He put his arm out to stop Stuart and Stobo from giving up their position.

"For God's sake, who could that be?" Stobo leaned forward to whisper to Jacob.

The three men stayed still and watched the lone figure; he was easier to see since he was obviously smoking a pipe. Jacob could see the smoke surrounding his head and the glowing embers every time he puffed.

"Who would be foolish enough to be out this far from the fort's walls at this hour?" Jacob asked the others.

As they hesitated, a voice from above on the ramparts called out, "Messieurs…"

They had been spotted.

Trying not to panic, Jacob moved quickly for some cover while Stuart did the same. Stobo was much less fortunate.

The still unidentified individual standing on the bridge had been alerted by the guard and ran back towards the fort.

The guard yelled out once again, this time much louder, "Messieurs."

Jacob could now only watch as Stobo was approached by the smoking stranger. It was LaMont, the merchant.

A single shot rang out and echoed through the cold night air. Jacob heard the bullet sail by him and hit a large tree stump. The prisoners had little time to act; the merchant had grabbed Stobo by the arm and he had put up little resistance.

Before Jacob could fully react, Stuart stood up and called out in a poor mixture of English and French, "Monsieur LaMont, the Englishman is here."

Jacob was confused with everything that was happening around him, but he instinctively pulled out the small patch knife Stobo had given him and charged towards LaMont. He knew he had precious little time to reach the merchant before the field would be teeming with heavily-armed French regulars.

With all his strength, Jacob drove his shoulder into LaMont's back, just as the Frenchman was turning around to look for him. The force drove the man face-first onto the hard ground, pulling Stobo along with him. Jacob's forward momentum brought his full weight onto the dazed merchant's ribs.

Grunting with the effort of rolling the heavy Frenchman over onto his back, Jacob quickly plunged the small knife deep into the man's stomach. He could see the utter fear in LaMont's eyes, and just before his last breath left his body, Jacob pulled out the bloody knife and drove it between the merchant's ribs. He twisted the knife as he knelt near the man's ear. "This is for my Maggie," he whispered hoarsely as the merchant expired.

In all the confusion, neither Jacob nor Stobo noticed Stuart running towards them with a large rock above his head.

Jacob could do nothing but kick at Stuart as Stobo attempted to block his assault. Just as Stuart was about to bring the rock down on Jacob's exposed head, a shot whistled past Stobo's left shoulder. It hit Stuart directly in the forehead, throwing his body backward as the rock fell feebly to the ground. Stuart was dead; Jacob and Stobo stood stock still, awaiting a similar fate.

"Mr. Murray, get over here before the French are upon you."

It was Joshua once again.

Jacob, with a helping hand from Stobo, was up and running as fast as his trembling legs could carry him. They followed Joshua's calls to a small clump of cedars just a hundred paces to the west of the bridge.

He spotted Joshua through a small break in the trees, smiling proudly and rapidly re-loading his musket. Stobo was right behind him as the sound of several French regulars forming a line echoed through the earthen works.

"Thank God you can shoot, son," Jacob said as he ducked down and patted Joshua on the shoulder.

"I must second that, lad, one hell of a shot in this darkness," Stobo added as he knelt down to catch his breath.

Joshua said nothing, keeping his eyes peeled for any visible movement in their immediate area.

"What the hell was that all about?" Jacob asked, careful to keep his voice low. "I knew that damn Stuart couldn't be trusted; he was planning this the entire time we were planning our escape."

"I knew something was happening when the merchant man was out alone in the bushes," Joshua replied. "Nothing good ever comes from a man like him deciding to take a walk in the dark."

"It appears that Stuart scoundrel wanted to get the best of us," Stobo said as he shook Joshua's hand. "Thank God you were here, boy, to watch our backs. I will be forever grateful to you."

It appeared the French were not advancing, and only a small detachment was searching around the bridge. They seemed more interested in returning to their dinner than looking for anyone out in this darkness.

"Now what, sir?" Joshua whispered to the captain. "Surely, you can't go back?"

"I have no choice, lad, but the two of you need to get yourselves out of here now. Don't worry about me; I'll wait a few moments while the French fuss about the bodies and then make my way back into the fort. If I time it right, I should be able to just walk back into the stockade with no one being the wiser. If I get caught, I'll just explain that Stuart and Murray escaped and I was out trying to find them to bring them back. Now go, lads, before we are all recaptured and my story is wasted."

"Thank you, sir, thank you for everything," Jacob said as he and Joshua moved out along the tree line.

"Godspeed, lads," Stobo replied as they both disappeared into the darkness.

Not turning around, Jacob sprinted until he reached the trail opening to the upper ridge. He could feel Joshua on his heels, and they both stopped just inside the trail. Jacob took one last look at the fort and prayed his captain was safe by now.

He could see the fort's outer earthen works were full of torches, and the glow gave him a good view of the small detail moving the two dead bodies back towards the fort. He could not see any sign of Stobo and assumed he had worked his way back inside. The soldiers' voices carried through the cold night air and, as his captain had suggested, they were not as concerned about the two dead men as they were about their food getting cold.

Before they started to head up the side of the steep ridge, Joshua presented Jacob with a musket and powder horn, and smiled, saying, "I know you have a preference for English-made muskets, but this French piece should serve us well. We must keep moving; if we reach the top trail before light, we will be well ahead of any patrols the French might send out. Please, sir, let's go."

"Yes, Joshua, lead the way, Jacob replied as he tossed the musket over his shoulder with a small pack of supplies, relieved to be away from certain death.

Chapter | **Six**

After an unusually pleasant trek, Maggie was happy to finally reach the next outpost in the French chain of forts.

The last few miles of the trip presented Maggie with her first views of the grand lake they called Erie. She had seen an ocean before, but she was captivated by the wondrous, endless rich blue color of the lake water. Part of the coast was bordered by high, windswept bluffs, and she could tell that this peaceful lake could quickly change into a threatening, churning body of water.

"Don't be fooled by its beauty, the Indians will tell you that without warning, the waves can stir up and swallow several canoes with one quick thrash," Fredrick interrupted her thoughts.

"That's hard to imagine when you look out at the calm waters now," Maggie replied.

"If you look right past that grouping of chestnut trees," Fredrick said, pointing, "just to the west, you can see the fort. She sits on the southern shore, and it certainly has to be the most peaceful setting of all the forts we have seen."

Maggie could now easily see the fort the French named Presque 'Isle. It appeared very different from the other French fortifications she had seen over the past several months. It had the same general shape with four bastions but from this distance it appeared that the outer log works were shaved down and stacked one on top of each other. LeBoeuf and Machault had a more traditional upright stockade that had the heavy wooden logs driven into the ground.

Fredrick explained that this was the first in the southern chain of forts, which were used to protect the French trade route to Louisiana. Presque Isle's primary functions were as a supply depot and staging area for traders. A well-built stone structure behind its outer walls held most of the supply of powder for the fort network.

Less than a mile from the fort, Maggie noticed a crew of soldiers out cutting down trees and splitting them up for firewood. Once the crew had noticed the small column, they happily greeted them and offered some water. As they moved closer, a scouting patrol met up with them and escorted the column the rest of the way to the fort.

"They seem to be happy to see us," Maggie said, as she and Fredrick walked side-by-side to the fort's front gate.

"The nice weather would make any garrison cheerful," Fredrick said. "They need to take advantage of days like this to cut wood for their fires and hunt for game to supply them with food through the winter. Winter hits them particularly hard around here, and the harder they work now, the easier winter will be for them. Once the snow falls, they will have no chance to cut wood or trap game."

The field in front of the fort was dotted with tree stumps and endless piles of cut wood for winter fires. Although the soldiers were all busy working in the fields, they all took time to greet the new arrivals.

Maggie saw another trail cut into the side of the high bluffs that led down to the water's edge. There was a landing area with a crudely built dock that jutted several feet into the shallow water. She could see seven large canoes and a dozen or so Huron scouts mingling around the canoes, readying them for the next leg of their journey. The canoes were crammed tightly with supplies and covered with large blankets to keep them from moving about through the water and shifting the load. Maggie could not see One-Ear among the Huron and hoped he was somewhere nearby preparing for the trip. She had not had an opportunity to continue their conversation and her thoughts of Jacob and what One-Ear knew of him exhausted her. She just needed a moment to talk with him and finally know what had become of her husband.

Even as the daylight gradually started to give way to the impending darkness, the soldiers continued working hard cutting massive piles of hard wood to build up their supply for the winter. Maggie knew that winter could last far into May in this rugged wilderness, and you always had to prepare for the worst. She noticed several other soldiers coming from the fort with lit torches to provide light for the cutters to continue late into the night.

The gates of the fort were wide open as Maggie and Fredrick stepped under the massive log frame and entered the inner fort. She immediately saw the massive stone magazine that Fredrick had told her protected the valuable powder supply. Four other buildings framed the walls and must have been the officers' quarters and the regular soldiers' housing. With the bitter winter, the men would not be expected to live in tents like they did throughout the spring and summer. Maggie imagined they preferred these cramped conditions to somewhat roomier tents that were left vulnerable to the harsh elements.

"We will have a short night, madame," Fredrick addressed Maggie. "The canoes will leave just before sunrise. The Huron know these waters better than most, and they like to be safely off-shore as soon as possible. I must excuse myself now to speak with the officer in charge to find us reasonable accommodations for the night."

Maggie was left alone and decided to walk around the fort. With the garrison so alive with activity outside the fort, the small column had not been afforded a formal welcome. In fact, Maggie had not seen an officer since they had arrived, and knew that the lack of housing would probably mean an uncomfortable night's sleep.

Fredrick returned only a few minutes later and Maggie could see he was not impressed by the housing arrangements offered by the officer. Fredrick shook his head, saying "I am so sorry, but all they have for us is some old tents and a few empty horse stalls. Not as nice as our previous night, but thankfully we will not be here long."

Maggie was tired and she would have gladly slept outside. At least the stall was private, and the soldiers had cleaned it out and laid down fresh straw that provided a nice coating of insulation from the cold air. They were also kind enough to give her a nice woolen Indian blanket and, despite the odor of horses, she was more than comfortable.

The early morning wake-up call was very unwelcome and the light frost that covered the ground was certainly an unexpected and unpleasant way to be greeted.

"Madame, we must get ourselves down to the canoes before the Huron leave without us," Fredrick called from outside her stall. "They are worried about the ominous northern sky, and the threat of an early winter storm does not sit well with them. They tend to worry about the silliest of things."

Maggie arose and quickly made her way down the sloped bluffs to the landing area. The French garrison had cut a narrow path down the side and planked a few spots with some cut wood to keep the loose sand in place. Maggie paused to look out at the lake that was now considerably darker and more windswept than the peaceful waters of yesterday. The violent, cascading white-capped waves kicked up and pushed the light canoes dangerously close to the shore. She couldn't imagine how they would be able to stay upright considering how the waves were already smashing the fragile-looking canoes. More canoes had been added to the flotilla and as she got closer, she was surprised at how long they actually were. Most were packed in the middle with supplies and had enough room for two, maybe three paddlers.

The northern sky did look awfully dark and the thought of being caught in the middle of the lake in a storm made Maggie think twice about getting into any of the canoes. Her spirits were raised when she saw One-Ear already sitting in one of them, providing some much needed weight to help the canoes maintain their balance against the waves.

"Hurry, madame," Fredrick urged, "we must leave immediately or risk being in the middle of a storm. Please get in the canoe nearest you." He now appeared concerned about this part of the voyage.

Hearing Fredrick call to her, One-Ear finally looked up and offered Maggie a reassuring smile. Each canoe was manned by a soldier and a Huron paddler. Maggie took her place in Fredrick's canoe and was accompanied by one of the older Huron paddlers. The weight of three adults and the supplies made the canoe sink close to the water-line. Once they began to paddle every stroke jerked the canoe back and forth, splashing ice-cold water all over them.

Maggie was impressed by Fredrick's skill with a paddle. He managed to keep up his stroke with the much more experienced Huron paddler who sat in the back so he could steer them out into the open waters of the lake. By the time they had worked their way out of the landing area, Maggie was soaked and the addition of a stiff north wind made her shiver uncontrollably.

She watched ahead as the other lead canoes headed directly towards the fast-approaching storm. They maintained a swift pace, and she was impressed by the speed of the heavily-laden canoes as they skimmed over the lake. The lake did her best to pull them back towards the shore, but years of experience navigating such waters gave the Huron paddlers a distinct advantage. The canoes were nearly two miles out into the open waters before the lead paddlers turned to the east and ran parallel to the jagged shoreline.

There was very little conversation and Maggie felt rather useless as all she could do was watch their progress and keep her movements to a minimum. The paddlers were all struggling in the rough waters, but they remained determined, and the fort at Presque 'Isle was soon only visible far off in the distance.

The lake was particularly unforgiving and once the group was deeper into the open waters, Maggie could barely make out the outline of the shore. The dark blue water became almost mesmerizing.

A few hours passed by quickly, and the paddlers began slowing their pace considerably. The combination of the powerful waves and the distance they had already travelled had fatigued most of the men. Maggie could hear Fredrick screaming back at his Huron paddler, but the noise of the winds and waves increased as they advanced and she could barely make out what he was saying.

It appeared to her that the Huron paddlers wanted to locate a safe place to beach the canoes and wait out the fast-moving storm. Fredrick was clearly attempting to encourage them to keep paddling and try to ride out the storm on the water.

The lake decided for them.

Maggie was spellbound as a blinding, black curtain of rain swept across the sky. The rain was hard, a mixture of ice-pellets and pounding showers that stopped the canoes like they had hit a wall. The combination of being almost stationary in the water and the swirling winds resulted in the lead vessel being thrown off course and violently capsized. The two paddlers frantically struggled to stay above the water as they grasped at anything that would help them stay afloat, but the heavily-laden canoes sank immediately. The others did their best to reach the men, but the storm came on so hard that they were forced to fight their own battle with the lake.

Maggie watched in horror as the two men were thrown around by the surging waters; they would be pulled under the churning water, just to pop back up a few seconds later. Only a minute passed before they slipped below the water and never re-surfaced.

Shouts and panic filled the air as two more canoes flipped over into the cold water. The howling wind, torrential rain and heavy supplies combined to make it impossible to keep the canoes from overturning. The harder the paddlers fought, the harder the waves ravished the sides of the defenseless men.

Maggie held the sides of her canoe with a firm grip and after only a few minutes, all but two canoes had succumbed to the lake. She could see One-Ear and his fellow paddler power their way across and over several massive waves in a vain attempt to reach the shore.

Fredrick and the Huron paddler saw what the other remaining canoe was trying to accomplish and they managed to maneuver their own canoe directly behind them. Luckily, the wind had shifted to the south and aided their struggle towards the shore. The pounding waves now hurled them directly towards the safety of the sandy shoreline.

It appeared that the two canoes had paddled through the worst of the storm until one last massive wave smashed them from behind. One-Ear's canoe was pulled up almost out of the water then driven nose first back into the frigid lake. His canoe split almost cleanly in half, and pieces of it floated on the surface.

The same wave hit Maggie's canoe with such force that it threw Fredrick and the Huron paddler over the side. She managed to keep the canoe upright, but with no one to guide it, she could only hold onto the sides with all her strength and let the lake take her where it wanted.

As Maggie scanned the water around her, she could see One-Ear struggling to keep his head above the choppy water. She called out, hoping that he could hear her, "One-Ear, swim to me!"

Somehow, One-Ear found the strength to reach the front of Maggie's canoe and held on, waiting for a break in the pounding waves. He did keep the canoe relatively stable with his added weight, and that meant that it kept Maggie from falling into the cold water.

She could not see any sign of Fredrick and despite her frantic shouts, he never returned her calls. She feared the worst.

Amazingly, as precipitately as the storm hit, the lake calmed down long enough for One-Ear to pull himself up with a helpful hand from Maggie.

"Thank God you made it, I was sure the lake was going to take you!" Maggie cried as tears of relief flowed down her cheeks.

"No fear, the Cayuga people paddle this lake all the time," One-Ear said, smiling through uncontrollable shivers. "We never let the lake beat us, despite her best efforts."

Left without paddles, the two could only pray that much smaller waves would guide them into land. Their mutual silence was broken by a loud shout from behind them.

"Madame, over here! Can you reach me?"

Maggie and One-Ear could only just make out the dim figure of Fredrick bobbing up and down with the waves. He was too far to reach with an extended arm, and without a paddle, they were forced to merely watch him and hope he would be pushed toward them.

Maggie could now see he had managed to attach himself to a small barrel that must have been emptied of its contents. It provided him with and the buoyancy he needed to keep his head above the water.

One-Ear searched under the tied-down supplies and managed to pull a long piece of heavy rope from within the pile. It took him several difficult tosses to come close to Fredrick before the rope finally landed directly on the barrel.

At that same moment, the waves picked up again and pushed them towards a tiny cove, formed by centuries of pounding waves eroding the sandy shore. The beach was punctuated by large boulders and rocks, and Maggie prayed that they would be able to control the canoe enough to land on one of the open spaces.

Fredrick was barely able to keep a firm grasp on the slippery, water-logged rope as the canoe continued to struggle against capsizing. The canoe was taking on water, and both Maggie and One-Ear frantically pushed water back overboard with their freezing bare hands. Their efforts were futile and the water began pulling the canoe under.

Anticipating a plunge into the icy water, Maggie desperately reached out to grasp One-Ear's hand. Just as their fingers touched, the canoe jerked forward sharply, and then halted suddenly like it had hit an invisible wall.

They were still several hundred yards from the safety of the shore, yet the canoe had simply stopped in its tracks. Maggie had no idea what was happening as she sat and watched One-Ear leap out of the canoe and appear to be standing on the water.

Noticeably excited, he shouted, "It is sand! We have landed on a large track of sand! I have seen this before, many years ago when I was younger. My father took me west of here to a place he called Long Point; we walked almost to the middle of the lake and only got our moccasins wet. He told me there were many sand islands in the middle of this lake and, since it was shallow in some places, it was a bad place for canoes." One-Ear laughed as he pointed to the distant shore, adding, "Bad for canoes, but good for us!"

Maggie happily jumped out of the canoe and joined him, "When I was a small girl, my father used to take me out into the ocean after the tides dropped. We would collect tiny clams and shrimp, but he warned me that the water comes back fast and unforgiving to swallow back up the land. I remember a story of a neighbor who had drowned when he was caught out as the tides returned, they never found his body."

They both took a moment to check out the sandy shoreline and celebrate their luck.

One-Ear returned to the canoe and noticed that the sandbar had ripped apart the underbelly, rendering it useless in these waters. He immediately pulled off the deerskin that was used to protect the supplies and rummaged to see what would be useful to them.

He looked to Maggie to give him some help and saw her holding the rope they had tossed out to Fredrick. She gazed out into the deep water, saying nothing.

One-Ear rushed to her side as she hysterically started to pull the rope back towards them. The water had soaked it and it was now almost too heavy for both of them to manage.

Grasping her hands to stop her, One-Ear said, "There is no one on the other end; the poor Frenchman could not have held on any longer. The water is cold and the added weight of the rope meant he could not have survived. The lake is cruel at times."

Maggie was obviously distraught and One-Ear could see she was saddened by Fredrick's death. "Miss Maggie," he said, "the lake takes what she wants, and so we can only thank her for sparing our lives. I am sorry that the Frenchman had to die, but we must keep moving or we might meet the same fate."

With still several hundred yards of lake separating them from the safety of the shore, One-Ear grabbed the same rope they had used to help Fredrick to secure it to the front of the damaged canoe.

"Let us see if we can pull this along the sand, we will need the supplies if we reach the beach safely," One-Ear said frankly.

Maggie recognized that their ordeal was far from over and she assisted One-Ear with the rope and together they pulled the cracked underbelly of the canoe out from the sandbar.

"How long is this sand island?" Maggie asked as she continued to pull with all her strength.

"It is difficult to say," One-Ear said, keeping his eyes on the sand and water in front of him, "we can only keep moving forward and wait. The sand might drop off without warning, so we must be careful. I have seen some go from solid sand to a sudden ten foot drop back into the water. Just move with me and follow my steps."

A lone paddle from one of the overturned canoes drifted right into their path, and One-Ear used it to test the sand's depth as he continued forward.

Maggie just followed his lead. One-Ear was careful not to walk in a simple straight line and, after struggling to pull the damaged canoe along the sand, they decided to conserve their energy and leave it beached on the sand bar.

"Can you swim?" One-Ear asked Maggie, not raising his head as he continued to jab at the sand ahead with every step he took.

"I am comfortable, but honestly I have not swum for a few years," Maggie replied, carefully keeping her eyes on One-Ear's feet as he moved. "Please don't be concerned for me, I'll be sure to keep up with you."

One-Ear paused to scope out the water ahead, fully expecting the sand island to fall into the water at any moment. He warned Maggie over his shoulder, "You need to watch out for the lake pull. This water is bad for catching a swimmer or fisherman by the leg and dragging him under. I lost a good friend to this lake's pull and we never saw him again."

The distance to the shore shrank as they weaved their way along the massive sand island. The water was now up to their knees and Maggie could feel the tug of the water on her legs. Thankfully, the water level appeared to be fairly constant and they had not found an open section of the lake. The only issue they had was the wind, which began howling and pushed their soaked clothing against their already chilled bodies. Maggie thought that in some ways, it might have been better in the water than being so exposed to the open air.

Not far from the shore, Maggie could see that the small cove would provide them ample protection from the cold, and once they had built a nice fire, they could forget about the freezing lake. She watched One-Ear continue to push down on the paddle until he jabbed at a place in the water where the paddle didn't stop. Maggie was watching and grabbed him before he followed the paddle into the deep water.

She remained still as One-Ear jabbed the paddle to his left, right and then a few paces ahead, but it continued to hit nothing. Their choice was now made for them.

"It drops right in front," One-Ear said, "so it would be best if we swim for the shore. We might get lucky and land on another sand island, so I will go first. Wait for me to call you forward; we should be on shore soon enough."

Maggie watched him slowly step off the sand bar and splash into the deep lake water. He swam maybe twenty feet and stopped again.

"Come, Miss Maggie, it's not too deep and I can feel the sandy bottom again," he called back to her.

Without hesitation, she stepped into the water and swam as fast as she could directly to the spot where he stood. The waves were picking up once again, but thankfully they actually helped her move towards shore.

One-Ear reached out for her hand and pulled her up onto the under-water ledge. The wind hit her hard as she was now soaked to the bone. The thoughts of a roaring fire and the short distance remaining to walk helped her ignore the cold.

"We are good now, we only have a short walk the rest of the way," One-Ear reassured her as he pointed to a small point on the beach.

They both made it fairly easily to shore, considering the struggle they had just experienced. The clean sand felt extra good on her feet as she stopped to look behind her into the far off horizon. She could still see their canoe sitting alone, surrounded by miles of water.

Wet, freezing and tired, Maggie just sat for a moment on one of the many boulders that protected the small cove from the wind. She looked out at the now peaceful lake for any sign of survivors but couldn't even spot a canoe or any trace of their recent ordeal. It appeared that the lake had swallowed up the canoes and taken them away. She thought for a moment about Fredrick and felt a sting of pain in her heart, though she had only spent a little time with him. Having One-Ear by her side made her feel safe, and she knew that they would be able to make it through this together.

"No time to sleep," One-Ear said, interrupting her thoughts, "we need to gather some dry wood to start a fire or we will both die, wasting all our hard work to get here. I have to go back for the canoe, so please find us some wood and we will have a much better night."

Before she could protest his return to the water, he was gone. She realized the supplies on the canoe would make things that much easier but she wished he had given her a little more time to recover from the tragedy.

Understanding the importance of organizing as much as they could before nightfall, Maggie started to gather what she could. Most of the wood in and around the small beach area was wet and useless, so she decided to venture a little farther inland. She climbed over several of the boulders to see what was around and saw only beach and sand dunes to the west. Walking towards the east, she found the massive boulders quite challenging to maneuver around. After clearing most of them, she noticed a smaller beach that was littered with debris.

Curious, and not having much luck finding an adequate supply of fire wood, she worked her way inland before finding an isolated trail that took her towards the other beach.

Entering the opening to the beach, she was greeted with several bodies of the same soldiers who were part of her group. Two of their bodies were pushed up against the jagged edges of some rocks, while another lay face down in the sand with the tide rolling over him. She ran down to see if any had miraculously survived, but found all three dead. Searching a little longer, she located the bodies of two of the Huron just at the mouth of a small interior creek.

Not wanting to get herself lost, and seeing enough death, Maggie decided to head back towards the other cove.

She discovered a small path that appeared to head west and decided to take it in hopes it would return her back to where she started. With her gaze fixed farther up the trail, Maggie tripped on something nestled in a small grouping of waist-high rocks. She looked down and saw that it was an arm. Frightened at first, she knelt down to see if it was attached to anything.

Before she could check it, she heard an incoherent groan coming from the rocks. Maggie reluctantly felt the arm and found it was warm. She checked for a pulse and, although faint, there was one. She gently pulled on the arm and heard another groan.

She attempted to pull the man free, but he was wedged pretty tightly within the rocks. Maggie started to climb the rocks to see if she could get a better view of the man. The rocks were pushed against a large sand dune and when the tides were higher, the water-line reached right to the sandy cliff. Once she made her way to the top, she could see the prone body had been pushed between two larger boulders. The sand had been driven against the rocks and covered most of his body.

Maggie slowly lowered herself down into the middle of the rock formation and marveled that the tide could be powerful enough to drive a man's body into such a place. She could still barely reach the man, but did manage to pull him closer and turn him on his side.

It was Fredrick.

She immediately screamed for One-Ear, not sure if he had returned from the canoe.

Struggling within the confined space, she used all her strength to pull the unconscious Fredrick upright. As soon as he sat up, he violently spit up a stomach full of lake water and gasped for air. Maggie pushed him forward and forced his head down. That worked, Fredrick caught his breath and some color started to return to his face. His breathing became much steadier, but he was unable to speak. He did recognize Maggie and offered a weak smile.

"Miss Maggie, where are you?" the distant voice of One-Ear called out.

"I'm down near the creek within the boulders; I found Fredrick," she returned his call.

She pulled herself back up to the top of one of the larger boulders and saw One-Ear making his way down the dune pathway. He spotted her and waved to acknowledge he had seen her.

One-Ear swiftly worked his way down between the rocks and he saw Maggie holding Fredrick in her arms; he appeared dead. He placed his hand under the Frenchman's nose to check his breathing.

"He is alive—not much, but alive," One-Ear assessed.

"When I got to him, he did open his eyes for a moment but fell back to sleep," Maggie said, barely able to hold back her tears. "He is very weak and we need to get him out of here."

Moving him gently, they managed to pull Fredrick up and One-Ear placed him on his own back. With Maggie bracing him and helping him to balance, One-Ear got him out of the rocks and safely onto the small beach.

"Maggie, I found another canoe that drifted into some weeds; if we get the Frenchman into it, we can float him back to where we came ashore," One-Ear suggested.

"Why would we take a chance on move him again, can't we just keep him on this beach until he recovers?" Maggie asked, keeping her hand on Fredrick's arm.

"Too much death here, it's not safe for us or him," he replied, pointing at the bloated bodies of the dead soldiers that littered the area. "I must bury them soon or the wolves and coyotes will be upon us. I'll get the canoe and you can get the Frenchman to the other side of the dunes."

One-Ear reentered the water and waded back towards their beach. Maggie sat by Fredrick's side, trying to make him as comfortable as she could. She watched his chest struggle to exhale and she prayed he wouldn't die. The same feeling of helplessness that she experienced when her children were taken away from her by Huron raiders engulfed her; she didn't want to lose another person she cared for.

Maggie felt she had suffered enough loss over the last few months—more than anyone deserved.

Chapter | **Seven**

With every few steps, Jacob turned to check on the activity back at the fort. The night exposed the soldiers' torches as they searched the outer fields for any sign of those who had just murdered the merchant and the English prisoner.

His thoughts were filled with worries for Captain Stobo. He prayed that his friend had made it back safely to the stockade and would not be implicated in the killings. Jacob felt some remorse for the death of Private Stuart, but was glad death meant he couldn't identify the captain as the ringleader of tonight's escape. By contrast, Jacob felt no remorse for the dead merchant, as his death gave Jacob some brief solace that Maggie would be free of the man's slimy grasp.

It would be challenging enough for him and Joshua to make their way up the roughly cut trail during the day, but it was no more than three feet across and the darkness complicated each step they took. An illuminating full moon would have been nice, versus the dull cloud cover that made it even darker than usual.

They were careful not to make too much unnecessary noise, but the trail was full of prickly bushes and unrelenting over-grown tree branches that smacked them with every misstep. The unevenness of the trail certainly added to their struggle, numerous fallen trees, stumps and large roots littered their path and were visible only after they had stumbled over them. Joshua did an admirable job guiding them through the maze of obstacles and was careful to give Jacob fair warning of anything in their way.

The two stopped a few times to rest and listen for any patrols that might have been sent out to search the upper trails. Unlikely as it might have been, they both had to be vigilant in case the French decided not wait until sunrise to hunt for their escaped prisoner.

Jacob knew that by first light, these woods would be swarming with French regulars and their Indian allies. The more distance, no matter how difficult, they put between themselves and the fort, the easier their trek to Will's Creek would be.

"Once we reach the summit," Jacob said quietly, "we can use a side trail that I have used a few times. It is well tracked and we will be able to put a good distance between us and anyone sent out to search for us. If we reach it before dawn, we might even be able to use a torch to give us some light if we see fit." He kept his voice low, ever mindful that voices could travel for miles through these ridges.

Jacob had difficulty catching his breath as they ascended the steepest part of the ridge. Keeping his musket at the ready as he climbed complicated his effort, but is weapon meant the difference between life and death. A weaponless man mixed with this vast wilderness could prove fatal. In addition to threats from human enemies, there was an ever-present risk of becoming prey for cougars, bears or wolves that prowled the woods, especially at night.

"If we keep moving we should be good," Joshua murmured. "My only fear about using the side trails is that the Delaware and Seneca use them as well, so we must be extra careful."

They reached the top of the upper ridge together and quickly took in the majestic sight below them. The midnight sky was beginning to give way to the slowly rising sun. The fort appeared so far away that even the once numerous torches appeared to be a waning threat.

"I must thank you, lad, for saving me again," Jacob said, grasping Joshua's hand. "My life is certainly in your hands. God knows if you hadn't shown up back there, I would be dead."

The two shook hands for a moment and Joshua offered a brief smile as he said, "We must go, we can't lose any more time to this darkness."

They pressed on.

The pair maintained a frenzied pace for several miles before the stress of the previous night's events and the intensity of their travels caught up with them. They were fatigued and their pace gradually began to dwindle, Jacob's more so than the younger Joshua's.

"We should really think about stopping and giving our legs some rest," Jacob suggested. "If we don't stop soon, come daybreak we will be too tired to move and we might find ourselves making critical mistakes. I know a place we can rest a mile up the trail, it should provide some shelter and an opportunity for us to sleep and eat."

They covered the distance in short order and along the way, they crossed the grounds of a small plantation. Jacob immediately realized that the French had set fire to most of the buildings and cleared the outer fields of any useable crops. Most of the outer structures had burned to the ground and their charred outlines were all that remained. The main building was partially collapsed and left to rot. Jacob and Joshua could not chance it falling on them as they slept, so their only option was the open-air stable that faced the west woods. There was nothing left of value and any food stores had been taken by the French or Huron raiders.

"I knew the owner of this land and I can only hope he escaped before the French arrived," Jacob said as he looked around. He saw the look on Joshua's face and knew that the young man had hoped for a more secure place to rest. He tried to bolster the young man, saying, "It is certainly not what I expected, but we should be able to rest and hunt us some food. A couple hours are all we will need and then we can be on our way."

Jacob put his pack in the stable and checked out the edge of the woods adjacent to the large field. He easily picked up some tracks and knew there would be something to eat if he worked quickly. The area was pocked with deer tracks and numerous smaller vermin. It was a good place to hunt and the almost leafless trees provided some great views of the deep forest.

Joshua stayed busy gathering up some wood for a much needed fire. He had been taught early by the Huron to always keep a good fire starter on him, and many times it had come in handy during one of his long winter hunts. It was only a matter of moments before he had a good fire roaring. The warmth was most welcome considering, the pre-dawn air was particularly cold and the signs of an early winter were all around.

A piercing crack shook the walls of the stable as several mourning doves flew out from its rafters. Joshua instinctively jumped to his feet and grabbed his musket. He raced towards the woods where he had last seen Jacob, but there were no signs of him. Trying not to panic, he ran into a small opening in the forest line to search.

Shortly after Joshua ran down the rough cut of the path, he saw Jacob huddled over a small buck. He was carving it up, pulling large chunks of meat off the hind quarters and removing most of the skin. Bloodied from his work, Jacob stood up and noticed Joshua grinning at the scene.

"Hungry lad? It was certainly a meaty creature," Jacob said.

Before they returned to the plantation, Joshua sprinkled some dry tobacco over the deer carcass as thanks for providing them a meal. "The Huron taught me to always give thanks to our fellow creatures for providing us food," he explained.

They left the remains of the buck behind to be eaten by the woodland animals that inhabited the area. Joshua made sure to drag it several yards into the woods to keep any animals away from their makeshift camp.

The meat cooked up well and a small nearby stream provided them some fresh water. They enjoyed a hardy meal and, with their bellies full, it was time to get some much needed rest. Their plan was to rest until sunrise and get back on the trail. Joshua was not comfortable with resting here and preferred to keep moving towards Will's Creek.

It wasn't long before the two packed up their gear and wrapped up the remaining small pieces of deer meat for the journey. Their pace was steadier, the short rest having given them both a renewed sense of energy. Soon Jacob began to see familiar landmarks that gave him a much safer feeling.

It was difficult to pass through this area without thinking of his brother, Israel. This was where Jacob's life had changed forever. He was hit particularly hard as they followed the trail into the large opening of the Great Meadows. The area looked sadly peaceful covered in the morning frost.

He could still see the French and the Huron refusing to step into the openness of the field, remaining hidden in the woods before fanning out and surrounding the ill-equipped men outside the fort. From the distance, he could still make out the burnt ruins of Fort Necessity. The stench of death still lingered, even after several months had passed and several heavy rains had fallen.

Jacob slowly continued through the meadow and avoided looking towards the remains of the poorly built fort. He wiped his eyes as he thought of Israel and wished he had found his brother's body to at least have some sense of closure.

"I'm sure we just need to get past this bend and work our way along the bottom ridge, my cache of supplies should be nearby," Jacob broke the silence. Joshua remained silent, giving Jacob the space he needed to face his demons and pay respect to the men who died here.

Jacob understood that Joshua knew little of what had taken place in this relatively peaceful meadow only a few months earlier. In time, he would tell him the story of the one-sided battle and of his brother, but now was not the time.

The two worked their way along the trail, which was much easier than the uneven trails they had experienced earlier. The English axe men had clear-cut the trail and, with assistance from men like Jacob, uprooted the tree stumps and cleared any debris. The heavy wagons and cannon had also pounded the dirt down, thus providing for a much more solid footing. It was relatively level, considering its location so far into the wilderness.

Not expecting to run into any French patrols this far south or English, who were back at Will's Creek licking their wounds, they were less cautious and stayed to the main trail. They were not very far along the trail when they heard faint voices coming from beyond a sharp elbow on the pathway.

"Stop, can you hear that?" Jacob asked quietly, grabbing Joshua by the arm and pulling him hard into the dense brush. "I can't make out what they are saying, but we need to move. I'm not even sure if they are English, French or savage."

They tumbled into the waist high underbrush. Jacob pushed Joshua even deeper into the forest then straightened himself up and peered over the highest brush.

Four Delaware warriors were running at top speed, quickly covering the ground where Jacob and Joshua had just walked. A number of woodsmen were giving chase and a couple at the front of the group stopped to fire shots at the Indians, but both missed their intended targets. A few of the men looked familiar to Jacob, but at this distance it was difficult to make them out.

Several of the other woodsmen moved forward and shot wildly, striking trees and splitting branches. A number of them slowed to re-load while Jacob and Joshua remained hidden, waiting for them to pass.

Jacob had no plans to give up his freedom this easily, even with the letter and map that he still kept tucked into his moccasins. These men wouldn't even give him a chance to explain before they opened fire on him. He certainly wasn't ready to chance it, not this soon.

He and Joshua waited a few extra minutes to make sure all the men had passed them and once they agreed it was safe, Jacob stood up and ran across the trail to the other side. Joshua tripped slightly but was right behind Jacob and they didn't stop until they had both reached the lesser travelled path to the north.

"Sorry for my carelessness," Jacob said. "We should have been on this path all along. I have always preferred this old Indian trail and have never seen any signs of the Delaware or Seneca using it. They likely feel it adds too much time to their travels and they really have nothing to fear by taking the main trail. After the English widened and cleared it even more, they could move much swifter over it then most trails in the area."

"No reason to apologize," Joshua replied, "I thought we had safely passed any serious threat."

"I'm not sure if the English even know this trail exists," Jacob pondered aloud, "the only white people who use it now are trappers and the odd hunter. It runs through a number of steep crags and high, rocky ridges. It is slower, but any time we lose will be made up by having a much safer trip. One of my cache spots is just off a side trail, only a mile or so from here.

The two sprinted along the relatively even trail until they reached a sharp rise in the path. As they neared Will's Creek, Jacob decided they should take a moment to locate the place he had stored some of the supplies he had taken from the dead retreating soldiers he found when he deserted.

Jacob realized that as they were only a few miles east of the fort at Will' Creek, he was also only a few miles away from George Washington and his former militia mates whom he had deserted. The letter from Captain Stobo was still tucked into his moccasin; it was possibly his only chance to clear his name but he was hesitant, not sure if Washington would pardon him despite his captain's recommendation. Jacob was fully aware that Washington held Stobo in high regard, in addition to the fact Stobo volunteered himself to be held in a French stockade until a prisoner exchange was arranged.

Jacob felt he had not only run from the militia but from his fellow volunteers. He honestly didn't know how they would react. If Washington actually pardoned him, would they accept that and still want him to fight by their sides? Even with his captain's blessing and the map that might save some of their lives, he feared they would care little and force Washington's hand to punish him.

Another reason he hesitated was that if he went back, he would be expected to fulfill the remainder of his service term. That meant he would not be able to go after Maggie until well after next spring, assuming Washington wouldn't decide to extend Jacob's time commitment to the militia in exchange for his pardon. He was not ready to face so many unknown possibilities, not to mention, what would become of Joshua?

The young man had done so much for him and he couldn't imagine leaving him now in order to fight with the militia. First he had helped Jacob find Maggie then remained with him throughout being re-captured. Mostly though, he truly felt he owed the young man for his life. Both the French merchant and the turncoat Stuart had wanted him dead and if it had not been for Joshua's quick thinking, they would have succeeded.

Putting all that behind him, Jacob and Joshua kept moving.

"Joshua, keep your head up, I think we are in the area where I left my supplies," Jacob called back to Joshua just as another loud crack made them both stop.

Jacob instinctively veered left and off the trail; he reached out for Joshua who had rushed forward. He pulled him forcefully towards the cover of the woods.

"What was that, boy?" Jacob whispered as they both ducked down and waited.

"Not certain, but it sounded like musket fire again," Joshua replied.

Jacob looked between the thick cover where they hid, watching for any signs of who might have fired and who the shot was intended for.

The vastness of the wilderness tended to project noises for miles, so when he didn't hear any return fire, he assumed it might have been an echo from a greater distance. Jacob slowly stepped from the security of the woods.

"Sit here and watch my back," he said. "I think it might have been a far off hunter and we just caught the recoil of his musket."

No sooner did he step onto the open trail than he felt a musket ball brush by his left ear. It clipped his ear lobe, causing it to leak blood down into his shirt and inside his ear. He vainly tried to clear his ringing head from the load blast when he saw the shooter just down the trail.

From twenty or so paces down the path, charged three of the four crazed and screaming Delaware warriors from earlier, now aiming their vengeance against him. Their faces and upper torsos were covered in tattoos, but they did not have their bodies painted. That meant they were not a war party but were most likely just out hunting when they were attacked by a patrol, probably from Will's Creek.

Jacob noticed that two of them had discarded their muskets after firing them at him and were instead hurling themselves towards him with war clubs raised. The third Delaware still carried his musket but was not in a position to fire it.

Regaining his wits and calming himself down, Jacob called to Joshua for help, but the young man was already aiming his musket at one of the savages. He fired and snapped back the head of the lead runner. The savage tumbled backward and now laid face down as the other two hurdled over his body.

"Reload, lad, and I'll cover you," Jacob yelled as he shot at the other war club-wielding Delaware, striking him just below his ribs. The force of the shot knocked the wounded warrior back, directly into the path of the last savage. This Delaware managed to dodge his now dead mate, but that gave Jacob the moment he needed to re-load and aim. Joshua stood nearby with his musket raised and ready to fire in the event Jacob's musket misfired, as they tended to do at the worst possible times.

Jacob stood tall and waited until the savage was almost on top of him before he pressed the trigger. The blast hit the Indian in the neck and he stopped like he had hit a wall. It felt like forever as the savage remained upright but frozen. Joshua was ready to discharge his musket until he noticed the savage's eyes roll back as he finally fell straight backwards.

The forest fell silent – no more war cries, no more musket fire just peaceful stillness. The smoke from their own muskets dissipated and presented Jacob and Joshua a clear view of their handiwork.

Less than ten paces away, a lone Delaware was face down encircled in a pool of blood from a large wound in his neck. The other two were only a few more paces behind him, stiffened by death and already covered in the mass of flies that seemed always close by.

"Be careful, we need to make sure their all dead; great shot by the way, Joshua," Jacob warned.

Jacob kicked at the first savage to see if he would get a reaction from him. Satisfied that the warrior was dead, he continued cautiously towards the other two. He looked back at Joshua in time to see the young man out a small knife he had concealed in the pouch around his neck and pull back on the first savage's hair. The boy was just about to press the knife against the dead Delaware's forehead when Jacob ran over and grabbed the knife out of his hand, screaming, "Stop! What the hell are you doing, boy?"

Stunned, Joshua looked up and said, "I would expect the same from him."

"We are not them, and we have no time for this," Jacob said. "Take what you want from them but leave their scalps intact, the wolves will have their way with them soon enough."

Once Joshua released his grasp on the man's hair and stood up, Jacob returned his knife, saying, "The noise we just made could be enough to alert scouts from the garrison at Will's Creek, not to mention the men we already saw chasing these Delaware we just dispatched. Let's gather their muskets, clubs and hawks and get moving so we don't get ourselves into more trouble."

Joshua took the powder horn and ball pouch from the dead savage he had been ready to scalp. Jacob decided to scavenge a decorative neck sheath and accompanying bone-handled knife that was around the last Delaware's neck. The raw hide neck sheath was intricately beaded and woven with flattened porcupine quills. It measured the length of Jacob's hand, from the tips of his finger to his wrist. The knife had been well taken care of and sharpened to produce a clean cut when needed.

Joshua noticed the knife sheath now hanging from Jacob's neck but said nothing.

After scavenging what they could, Jacob sprinted up the trail with Joshua keeping up right behind him. Watching what was ahead of them, the two said nothing but kept a steady pace.

Once they felt they had put enough distance between them and where they had left the Delaware warriors, Jacob slowed down to survey the area. Joshua broke their tense, self-imposed silence, saying, "Sorry about back there, I lived a long time with the Huron and they instilled some things in me that are very foreign to white people who don't understand their ways."

Jacob remained watching the upper trail then replied, "Joshua, your steadiness during our battle was something to be proud of. We both know and have seen that most men would have run under the same circumstances. You were brave to stay by my side once again and not opt to run. Honestly, you have had a number of opportunities to leave me behind and you have always stayed by my side. The aftermath was from your Huron influences and I will never think less of you for reacting that way. As you know, I have two boys who I pray are still alive, and might be living the same life you were forced to."

Joshua smiled and replied, "My life with the Huron people did teach me many good lessons. My respect for nature, my ability to survive in the wilderness and my fighting skills are all thanks to their training."

"I do understand," Jacob said, not wanting Joshua to feel like he did anything wrong, "but I have seen the remains of my friends mutilated by the Huron and I would not wish that image on anyone, white or Indian. You did nothing that any other man might not have done after a victorious battle, and I know the English can be just as disrespectful to the dead."

Without saying much after that, the two made their way quickly to the lower ridge and off the trail. They began the short accent to where Jacob remembered spending his first night alone after his desertion. He wasn't totally certain this was the way since the hordes of fallen leaves had obscured some of the trail and this far into fall everything appeared very different.

"It should be here, between these high cliffs," Jacob called back down to Joshua as they climbed the rock face. Their extra loads did make the climb somewhat harder, but they watched each the other's step.

Jacob made it to the top and pulled Joshua up over a small crevice. The two entered the concealed and rocky fortress, which had not been disturbed since Jacob's last visit several months back.

"Looks like no person or thing have found this place since I used it," Jacob said.

"How could anyone find this place unless you got yourself lost and stumbled upon it by accident?" Joshua said as he scanned the perfectly formed high rocks that presented such an ideal place to stay. "I'm still trying to figure out how you happened to find this spot in the first place."

Jacob laughed at Joshua's comment and went straight to the place he had buried his cache. It was not buried too deep in the moss covered ground, and he pulled out several canvas bags, shaking them clean of dirt. He tossed one over towards Joshua who untied it and emptied out its contents.

At the moment, they had more than enough weapons, powder and supplies taken from the Delaware, but what the bags carried could be used to supplement other necessities for their travels.

While they both searched the bags, Joshua asked, "What is our plan from here? Winter is coming on fast and our options will be seriously limited if we wait too long."

"God, I hope we have a couple weeks before the heavy snow hits us," Jacob said, sitting down and leaning against the flat stone wall. "My thought was to head towards my old homestead, although the only problem is there is not much remaining of the cabin. That means we are a good day or two walk from it and we will need to build us a winter cabin. You will see it is a great spot with plenty of game, a reliable water source that we can draw from through the winter, and I know the area better than most men."

"Why can't we just stay here?" Joshua replied. "The forest should have plenty of game and the rocks would shield us from most of the heavy snow. What happened to going to speak with Washington at Will's Creek?"

"I thought of this place too, but the patrols from the fort would be too close and it's evident after today's fight that the Delaware are nearby as well. Any person with the slightest of tracking skills would be able to just follow our path up here, no matter how careful we were. I think our best bet is the homestead, and then we can visit Will's Creek in the early spring and speak with Washington. All we need to bring along is a couple of axes, and between the two of us we can have a nice cabin built to wait out the winter."

"I will go with you wherever you feel is best," was Joshua's simple reply.

Tired from the day's walk and the encounter with the Delaware, the two gathered up some leaves and moss to make two comfortable beds. They were relatively safe from attack as the only way up to their shelter was by a narrow path, and any such movement would be heard by either one of them well in advance.

Daylight hours were shortening and taking advantage of a natural over-hanging cleft; they even had the luxury of a small fire and ate a hardy meal of squirrel, raccoon and a large rattlesnake that they had accidently disturbed while gathering up leaves. The remaining cooked deer from the previous night was sliced into thin pieces then hung over the fire to make some nice jerk for the next leg of their trip.

As the morning dawned, the first rays of sunshine stretched through the mass of trees and forced down small narrow beams of light that looked like they were sent from heaven. Jacob always loved this time of day, and in the wilderness, fall mornings were especially beautiful. The massive maple trees had almost lost most of their lower leaves and the colorful pattern of oranges, reds and browns brightened up the woods and were a nice change from the normal sea of green. The coolness of the early morning air combined with the light frost that covered most of the exposed ground looked peaceful and out of place in world of death and war cries.

Jacob knew all too well that they must make it through the mountains before the first of the heavy snows. It was unusual not to have some snow on the ground by this time and he wasn't sure what they might find once they hit the higher ridges to the south. They could find a foot of snow or worse, impassable mountain gaps and no way to reach his homestead until spring. They certainly did not need anything slowing them down, especially considering they had a good week of long, hard work days awaiting them.

Shelter was one thing, but Jacob hoped he would have time before the cold weather hit to set enough trap lines around the usual reliable haunts. Some nicely salted meat and warm furs would be most helpful during the cold winter nights.

"Sorry to get you up so early, Joshua," Jacob said, but we need to get moving if we want to reach the mountains by tonight. If we push through the night, my land is not far from the bottom ridge line and we should be there by this time tomorrow." As Jacob explained, he packed up his bag and was ready to move out.

Joshua had barely enough time to rub his limbs to get some circulation back in them and his response was tinged with sarcasm, "Sounds wonderful, let me get my gear and I'll be with you in a second." Jacob pushed hard and Joshua matched his every step. As they reached the small gap in the mountains and took in the beautiful countryside, Jacob felt more relaxed and was filled with memories of his family and home. He began to enjoy this last part of their journey through these familiar parts, and once they arrived on the outskirts of the large valley that housed his homestead, he increased his pace even further.

He stopped for a moment to let Joshua catch up and when the young man moved to his side, Jacob said with a grin, "Sorry about how hard I am pushing. I can't believe we've covered so much distance already, but it is sure great to travel through a place that is so familiar to me."

It was already well past midnight, but they decided to keep pressing on towards Jacob's homestead. After a short time had passed, Jacob paused, saying, "If we keep moving, we'll be there before dawn. I have travelled these trails in the dark so many times I think I could close my eyes and still make it safely. How are you doing?"

"Tired but excited to reach your land, I can rest once we get there," Joshua replied as he waited for Jacob to lead the way.

They slowed their pace a bit, being careful in the dark and cautious of the many nocturnal hunting creatures around. Just before the sun started to rise, they reached the trail that would take them directly to Jacob's plot of land.

Jacob could see the charred remains of his cabin as they walked into the clearing and he was blindsided by all his old memories. The countless times he would return from checking his trap lines and be joyfully greeted by his kids who would jump all over him like he had been gone for years. The familiar sight of Maggie standing in the field collecting corn or working the outer field – even with her apron dirty and her hair mussed from the activity, she was beautiful. Jacob hesitated as these images washed over him.

"You alright, sir?" Joshua asked, as he stepped in front of him to take a look at the nice-sized plot of land.

Jacob did his best to suppress his emotions, but the sight of his burnt-out cabin hit him hard. He could still smell Maggie's fresh bread baking over an open fire and the noise the kids always made. It was a noise he had always complained about but, by God, he would trade anything to hear their screams again and feel Maggie's loving embrace for just one brief moment.

He stood, almost frozen in his tracks, as Joshua slowly stepped through the trampled and withered remains of Jacob's last corn crop and headed directly towards the blackened, charred pieces of logs that lay heaped where once a happy home stood. Respectfully, he stopped before he got to the torn down fence that surrounded the cabin and knelt on one knee.

The land had not changed much since the last time he had been here, and discovered what had happened. The field was starting to overgrow from lack of plowing, but it was nothing a little of hard work couldn't clear once they built a place to overwinter in.

When he looked back at Joshua, the young man was now on both knees with his head down, he appeared to be crying. Jacob had felt a fleeting moment of hesitation before rushing to the boy's side. As he got closer, he could hear his deep, uncontrolled sobs.

"Joshua, are you alright son?" Jacob asked as he tried to hold back his own tears.

"Sorry, sir, it reminds me so much of my parent's farm," Joshua explained through his tears. "I never got to see it after they were killed and all I remember is seeing my mother's body lying by the front door and the cabin catching fire. The Huron just took me and beat me because I cried."

Jacob clutched the boy and cried with him.

The two lone figures held each other in the ruins of the burnt out cabin, releasing emotions that had been bottled up for far too long. It was the first time Jacob had honestly understood what truly linked them together. It was so much more than just Maggie.

They both had their happiness and security ripped from them and they both knew their lives could never be what they once were. Jacob held

Joshua like he was his own son, knowing their bond would give them hope and the feeling of family they had thought was gone forever.

Joshua said nothing and cleared his eyes, but Jacob said, "Thanks for making me feel like a father again."

With the rejuvenation of spirit brought on by what they had shared upon arriving at the remains of the cabin, Jacob and Joshua were able to focus all of their energy and emotions on the task at hand, building a place to protect them from the approaching winter.

During the next few days, the two of them cut, scrapped and gathered logs to build their new structure. Jacob couldn't bring himself to build over the old cabin, so they laid an outline nearby that was roughly a twelve-by-twelve foot square. The finished product wouldn't be anything fancy, but it would be enough to keep them warm and keep a decent fire for cooking and warmth.

Jacob was impressed by Joshua's eagerness to work hard, even past autumn's early nightfall. They always kept a good-sized campfire going to give them adequate light so they could work long after dark.

In addition to their building project, the pair worked to build up a means to feed themselves throughout the winter. Jacob appreciated Joshua's company while setting trap lines and before long, they had fresh meat every day. Joshua smoked some of the better cuts the traditional Huron way. He had put up a small smoke house and hung pieces of deer, bear and raccoon over a small fire. It did a great job drying out the meat and would prove to be handy on snowy days when the trap lines would be impossible to get to.

After a week of hard work and fighting through a couple days of wet snow, they stood back to admire their still roofless new home.

"It looks God-awful and I do pray the first strong wind whipping down from the mountains doesn't knock it down," Jacob laughed as he patted Joshua on the back.

"I think it is a fine place and I am proud to call it home," Joshua responded earnestly. "It is much better than the inside of a French stockade or a cold, drafty Huron winter hut."

"You are quite right and I second that," Jacob replied.

The main structure was complete and sturdy. They had been limited by time and proper tools, so they rough-cut notches in the logs, and pressed dirt, leaves and bark into the gaps to provide some insulation from the increasingly colder nights. The floor was basically packed dirt with leaves and moss mixed in to keep the morning ground frost from leaching into their beds.

They had collected enough rocks to build a suitable fireplace and used a combination of dirt and clay to bond them together. They also decided not to build in any windows in an effort to lessen the amount of cold air that could seep in.

They did however cut in a couple angled musket ports on each wall that they could close tightly with a wooden latch, much like Jacob had done in the old cabin. In case of an attack, they would prove to be helpful fending off a surprise raid from either a roving Indian hunting party or a British patrol still searching for deserters.

The roof proved to be the most challenging part of constructing the small cabin. They already had the frame built and now spent almost two whole days cutting massive trees into planks that would be attached to the frame. Jacob was careful to angle the roof so the snow would not accumulate and add extra weight. Neither man wanted to wake up to a collapsed roof in the middle of the winter. They strung the planks together tightly and added mud to the gaps before piling fir branches over the planks and mud.

The interior was simple. In addition to the small stone fireplace, there were two rough-hewn beds made from the leftover roof planks. They were merely meant to keep them off the cold floor, not really for comfort. Both beds were covered with various furs taken from the animals they had trapped over the past week or so. Jacob and Joshua stuffed leaves and branches under their beds to give them some added insulation from the cold.

It was certainly far from elaborate, and nowhere near as nice as his previous cabin, but it provided a secure roof over their heads and a good, warm break from the increasingly colder nights. The fireplace was a godsend. In addition to the good amount of heat it put out, it turned out to be a perfect place to cook all the meat they were lucky enough to trap.

Snow was in the air every day now and once the sun went down, the nights were freezing. It was so cold that the small creek had nearly frozen over in spots and it was solid enough they could stand out almost to the middle without fear of falling through. Thankfully, it was a fast-moving creek and rarely, if ever, did it completely freeze over. As it was the only source of water for miles, the pair made it part of their routine to check on the creek and clear any ice build-up. Jacob also knew it was a great place to trap beavers and since their arrival, they had taken three large males and one old female.

The next several weeks kept Jacob and Joshua routinely busy checking trap lines, hauling fresh water from the creek and keeping up with their constant need for firewood. These tasks were made easier after Joshua made two pairs of Huron-style snowshoes that helped them glide across the deepening snow.

They were also very vigilant in checking the area for tracks and signs of traders or trappers who might have wondered off the main trail. Their muskets were always with them and the spare pair was kept by the fireplace, loaded and ready for a quick fight.

The trap lines provided them with a nice supply of winter wildcats, some deer and small vermin. Snow rabbits were in great numbers in the area, and they sustained the men once the deer moved farther south to avoid the heavy snow. Jacob also caught a lynx and several coyotes that were made into thick fur clothing that was especially useful when they went out before the sun rose.

The first heavy snow hit them almost three weeks after they arrived and it trapped them in the small cabin for over a week.

"Sure hope this isn't a sign of the kind of winter we are in for," Jacob said after they had been stuck in the cabin for four straight days. They could barely open the door to retrieve the firewood they had piled just beside the entrance. "I really hate having our trap lines left unchecked for this long."

"I can remember the first winter my family experienced in New York," Joshua reminisced. "Our cabin was near the mountains and thankfully my father had us prepare for the oncoming snow. We had one storm that piled the snow over our cabin and once it stopped it took us over three days to dig out. My mother wanted to move back to Scotland but my father explained to her that with this much snow, we wouldn't be able move until

June, at the earliest." Joshua laughed as he remembered his short time with his family.

Jacob was impressed with the skills Joshua had learned from the Huron and how invaluable they were to both of them. He fashioned a couple of pelts into warm hunting gloves and made two long winter wraps from the many coyote furs they had accumulated. He also was good at sewing with dried deer tendons and made the warmest winter hats that Jacob had ever worn. When the two ventured outdoors to hunt or check trap lines, they looked like beasts walking upright.

"The Huron taught you well, Joshua," Jacob said one day as they came in from their chores. "The winter gear you have made for us keeps me so warm that by the time we return to the cabin I am honestly sweating."

Even with the winter hitting the area particularly hard, the pair was more than prepared to deal with anything the season decided to throw their way. With all they had been through, Jacob and Joshua felt a certain bond and enjoyed their solitary time together. When they were not working they spent time talking and enjoying each other's company.

Chapter | **Eight**

One-Ear did his best to bury the swollen bodies of the soldiers and Huron that had washed ashore. The sand was easy to dig into and he tried to bury them as deeply as he could. He wasn't sure how well the sand would mask the smell and fully expected to find the beach dug up by the wild dogs and coyotes that inhabited the area. At the very least, he wanted to make it difficult for them and try to keep them off the other beach where he and Maggie and the Frenchman had taken up residence.

With Fredrick moved to the other side of the cove and well taken care of under Maggie's watchful eye, One-Ear searched the area for any signs of a white settlement or Indian village.

"Miss Maggie," One-Ear said, "we are miles from the fort and nowhere near the great falls. We must find ourselves a place to stay through the winter or we will all die."

Even in Maggie's caring and capable hands, Fredrick was showing few signs of improvement. She and One-Ear both understood that and an injured man would only slow them down once they needed to move.

"He took too much water," she said, fighting back tears. "I don't know what more we can do for him."

"Miss Maggie, boil some water on the fire and I will mix a soup made with wormwood, marjoram leaves and a sprig of tansy that my people sometimes use to help when one of the villagers suffers from stomach and breathing pains."

Maggie watched him take a small pouch from his belt and start to grind up a mixture of leaves on a flat rock with a stone. She had the water boiling in minutes and waited as One-Ear brought over a handful of crushed leaves and dropped them into the water.

"Mix the water until most of the leaves are gone and the soup is a dark brown color," he said as he sat back and watched her.

Maggie did as he instructed and within a few moments, the leaves appeared to be dissolved. The water did turn a dark brown, but the smell made her turn her head away from the boiling pot several times.

"What is this?" Maggie asked. "The smell is dreadful!"

"We have to get some of it in his stomach, and then we wait," was One-Ear's only reply.

Maggie spooned some of the putrid liquid into a small cup and walked it over to Fredrick. She slowly dripped some over his lips and he winced from the taste. After getting as much as she could into his throat, Maggie struggled to keep the barely conscious Fredrick upright so he could swallow.

Satisfied that she had given him enough, Maggie looked up from her patient and noticed that One-Ear was busy fashioning a bed from the remains of one of the two salvaged canoes. He stuffed it with some leaves and moss to pad the bottom and make it somewhat comfortable. At the very least, it would keep a person off the damp ground and give some relief from the elements.

One-Ear slowly moved Fredrick into the canoe and covered him up with an old wool blanket to keep him as comfortable as they could. The canoe's sides did provide some shelter from the winds that had been increasing with intensity as the days passed.

Fredrick showed little improvement from One-Ear's mixture and Maggie continued to monitor his breathing and do what she could to keep him comfortable. She could sense that One-Ear wanted to talk with her about their situation and what they might do with the sickly Frenchman. When she had determined that Fredrick was sleeping soundly, she walked up the small trail that led to the upper cliff and found One-Ear checking the traps he had set around the camp.

"One-Ear something is bothering you, have I insulted you in some way?" Maggie asked when One-Ear noticed her approach.

She watched him as he re-set the traps and moved a few into better positions. He took a moment to reply to Maggie's question.

"I think the Frenchman is dying and he is slowing us down," One-Ear said frankly. "Miss Maggie, if we don't find a place to spend the winter we will also die. Even if he feels better from the drink, he will not be able to travel far and the longer we stay on the beach, the harder it will be for us to prepare for the winter."

Maggie feared this was what he was worried about, so she asked him flat out, "What should we do with Fredrick, just leave him to the wolves?"

"That might be for the best," One-Ear said without emotion. "I have found an old cabin that is maybe two miles from here, but the Frenchman in his current condition could never make such a journey. We must decide where he dies, on the beach or on the trail. If he was a Huron, we would leave him so he didn't slow down the rest of us."

Maggie was taken aback by his blunt, unfeeling response. She could never leave Fredrick behind and decided he had to be taken with them, regardless of the outcome.

"I will carry him myself, he will be my responsibility," she replied, visibly upset with the conversation. "I have seen too much death to just leave him behind."

There was nothing else to say and the two slowly walked back towards the cove. One-Ear stopped just short of the small, roughly-cut trail that lead down to the beach and said, "I do not understand what you want from this Frenchman. You have been on this beach for almost a week and you have never asked once about your husband. Have you forgotten him for this man?"

One-Ear did not wait for her response, but left Maggie standing at the trail head. She knew he was right and was overcome with guilt, not for forgetting about Jacob, she could never do that, but she had let her immense loneliness cloud her memories.

She sat down and wept. Not for herself, but for Jacob, Mary, James, Becky and Henry. After months of simply trying to survive, her emotions exceeded her strength and she collapsed into wrenching sobs.

After a few moments of letting go all her pent-up emotions, she composed herself and slowly made the short walk back towards the beach. As she moved around the rocks she immediately noticed One-Ear standing over Fredrick's canoe. Fearing the worst, she screamed, "Stop! For God's sake, stop!"

One-Ear turned and looked at her curiously as she ran at him as fast as she could.

"What is all the shouting about, madame?" a voice came from the edge of the water to her right.

Maggie stopped in her tracks. She had been so focused on what One-Ear might be doing, that she had failed to notice the man bent over the edge of the shore, splashing his face in the water. Fredrick stood up and looked at Maggie.

She tried not to show too much emotion, yet she made it obvious that she was happy and relieved to see him alive and upright. "My God! How long have you been up?" she cried out.

Maggie watched as he slowly walked towards her, taking his time to carefully plant each step gently in the soft sand. She could see he was still extremely weak and he had lost weight from his ordeal.

His breathing was still labored and his voice was weak, but he offered a smile, saying, "When I awoke, I was alone and I worked myself out of the canoe. I had to get some water, my mouth tasted like I ate some rotted grass."

"Well, it is certainly wonderful to see you up," Maggie replied.

"I was initially worried I had drifted here and was all alone, until I saw the savage."

Maggie turned her attention towards One-Ear and saw that he was watching their conversation. He was still standing over the canoe. "Sorry I yelled at you," she said. "I wasn't certain what you were doing."

"Not what you thought, Miss Maggie," he replied and turned back to work on the canoe.

Fredrick had managed to work his way over to her and Maggie spoke to him with an edge in her voice, "The one you call 'the savage' was the one who saved your life. If it wasn't for him pulling you from the water then making an herbal soup that kept you alive, you would be dead."

Her directness took Fredrick by surprise and made him stop, saying, "I must apologize to him and offer my gratitude for apparently saving my life."

She noticed One-Ear was looking towards the two of them again, this time with disgust. He called out, "We need to move from this beach, the sky is showing signs of a bad storm moving in from the north. The color of these clouds usually means snow."

One-Ear ignored Fredrick's attempt at an apology and started to pack up some of the supplies into the canoe that was once the Frenchman's bed.

"Fredrick is still in no shape to travel," Maggie immediately protested.

"The savage is right, the sky does look menacing and that leaves us little choice but to move from the open area." Fredrick interrupted.

Maggie considered continuing with her protests but noticed that One-Ear had fashioned a walking stick for Fredrick to assist him on the trail.

"The 'savage' has a name, Fredrick," Maggie said, continuing her verbal attack on Fredrick's disrespect towards her friend. "He is called One-Ear and he is not a Huron but a Cayuga warrior. Look what he has made for you; his skills in fire making and scouting the area saved us both and we should be indebted to him."

Fredrick offered no reply.

Maggie watched as One-Ear brought the sturdy walking stick to Fredrick and offered it to him. He demonstrated how it fit under the armpit or could be used as a staff. It appeared to be solid enough to bear the weight of a much heavier man. Fredrick tried it and immediately began to move much easier than he could without it.

"Merci, One-Ear, I feel much better with this," Fredrick offered.

One-Ear remained silent and simply returned to tying down the packed canoes, readying them to pull along the trail. He reinforced the rope they had used to pull the canoe to shore by weaving it together with some reed stalks he had gathered from around the cove. He attached a length of this rope to each canoe then secured one of the canoes to a rock on the beach, planning to return for it after he got Maggie and Fredrick to their destination.

One-Ear dragged the other canoe to the start of the cliff trail then waited for the others to go ahead of him. Maggie let Fredrick go in front of her so she could guide him as he stepped up to the pathway.

As the path leveled to a more manageable trail, Maggie looked back at One-Ear, who effortlessly pulled the packed canoe behind him, and asked, "How far is the cabin you talked about?"

"Maybe a mile or two, we will make it there well before nightfall," One-Ear replied. "I have prepared it for us and it should be a warm, safe place for us to wait out the winter."

"You can't seriously be thinking that we can survive the winter in this wilderness?" Fredrick interjected.

"Honestly, what are our choices?" said Maggie. "Once the snow hits, most of the trails and small hunting paths will be virtually impassable. You should already know this, Fredrick; the snow stops everything, even the Huron and Delaware."

"The garrison at Niagara will be wondering why we haven't arrived and they will certainly send out search parties to find us," Fredrick said in a last-ditch effort to keep the party moving towards the fort, despite the pending weather.

"Snow and cold will make their search impossible," One-Ear said. "Even the Huron would refuse to travel these woods and make such a long trip. If your search parties did come, they would be looking along the shoreline for you and not in the forest. We must make the best of what we have and make the trip to the fort once the winter ends." He pulled the canoe past the others, not waiting for them to decide what they wanted to do.

Maggie caught up to One-Ear and tried to lift the other end of the canoe to at least take some of the weight off of the young man's shoulders. She did her best but found the canoe heavy and awkward. He appreciated her effort, though, saying, "Thank you, Miss Maggie, but I am used to pulling this weight. When the Huron first took me from my family, they forced me to carry much more than this."

They were not long on the main trail when One-Ear took a left turn and pulled the canoe onto a much narrower path. This trail was a bit more of a struggle for the hikers, especially since it was nearly smothered by low trees and overgrown bushes. Thankfully this part of the trek was brief and they soon walked into an open meadow where the cabin sat in the far eastern corner.

Maggie was both relieved and happy at the sight of the cabin. It appeared to be a solid structure and she could see that One-Ear had done some work clearing the long grasses that had surrounded it. He had even repaired a small hole in the roof.

For a simple trapper's cabin, it was much larger than she had expected. There was still some work to do. The one and only window was in need of repair and the wall-sized fireplace needed to be cleaned out and checked to see that there was nothing living inside of it.

"Do you know who lived here?" Maggie asked as she walked around the cabin.

"He looked like an English trader," One-Ear replied.

"Did you know him?" Fredrick asked. As he also checked around the simple cabin, he appeared far less impressed than Maggie and One-Ear.

"I found him dead just behind the back of the cabin," One-Ear said, "I would guess he met up with the Shawnee or Seneca.

"What did you do with his body?" asked Maggie.

"He had been there for a few weeks, but I put him in the ground deep enough to keep the wolves away."

The cabin was fairly clean, considering the circumstances. It had a separate room with a bed and the main living area had a nice wooden table for meals. There were a few cups and plates, as well as a good supply of deer, wolf and bear skins for bedding and warmth. It appeared to be a sturdy structure and the roof was solid enough to hold the extra weight the snow would put on it.

"I wonder why the Indians killed him but didn't bother to take his supplies," Maggie said as she found an old straw broom and began to sweep up the floor.

"They must have been moving quickly through the area and just found him outside," One-Ear offered as he began to unload the supplies from the canoe.

Fredrick did very little to help and simply sat on one of the two chairs at the table.

One-Ear left Maggie to bring the rest of the supplies into the cabin while he returned to the beach to pull the other canoe back up the trail.

When he returned, Maggie helped him cover their tracks to the cabin by dragging pine branches along the leafy path from the main trail to the meadow. Maggie felt oddly at home. She kept busy dusting and clearing the cobwebs from the corners. She even fashioned an old deerskin drape for the window and was impressed at how quickly the place shaped up. No sooner did One-Ear have the fireplace cleared out and cleaned of leaves and twigs, than Maggie had a roaring fire going and it instantly warmed the entire cabin.

The smell and atmosphere brought back wonderful memories of her home back in Pennsylvania. It was difficult to hide her sadness–even if she could have returned home right then, there was nothing left of it but some burned-out rubble. Besides, she had no family to return to and the thought of their whereabouts just added to her misery.

As they days passed, Fredrick got noticeably stronger, but he did very little to contribute around the cabin. One-Ear, however, diligently set trap lines around the area and brought back a constant supply of river perch and sunfish from a small brook he had found just north of the cabin.

"He is French, they tend to be a lazy and expect everyone else to do their dirty work," One-Ear commented to Maggie one day when he brought several good-sized river trout back to the cabin.

"Did your people always fish during the winter months?" Maggie asked as she set them to boil in the large iron pot over the fire. She would make a nice stew with some herbs and roots.

"Not the Huron, they like salted fish but it is too dry for me. I think it was because they travelled great distances and keeping their food salted kept it edible for much longer. My own people have always fished through the winter. We would just cut a hole in the ice, although that was very difficult when the ice was really thick. When the lake didn't freeze completely over, we would walk for hours to find the open waters and catch many perch and trout."

"Did you ever worry about falling through the ice and into the icy water?" Maggie asked as she continued to work.

"My father would not let me go out on certain days and taught me how to check the cracks for safety. He would tell me stories about how a few of our people every season would get caught out on the ice piles or go too far out onto the lake when the weather was warm and fall through a cracks."

Once the winter hit, it was merciless. Maggie realized how much colder it was than Pennsylvania and she could not believe how much snow fell each day. The winds howled all night from the north and each morning they were greeted by a fresh blanket of snow.

No matter how much snow fell, One-Ear was up at dawn. He would strap on his hand-made snow shoes and go out to check on the traps he maintained around the perimeter of the property. Maggie saw how hard he worked and it made her work that much harder, and it definitely affected Fredrick. He had regained his full strength and now obsessively cut wood, patched any drafts in the cabin walls and a few times a week he would catch up with One-Ear to help with the trap lines.

As time passed and they fell into more of a routine, Maggie noticed that One-Ear and Fredrick had learned to like each other. One-Ear saw how hard the Frenchman worked and Fredrick began to greatly respect the younger man's skills in hunting and trapping.

Maggie quickly learned how to preserve any meat One-Ear was able to bring back, by cutting it into thin slices and curing it over the fire. This provided them with easy, quick meals and was especially helpful on the days when even One-Ear could not venture out into the snow.

Noticing the night sky was starting to descend later and the mid-day sun was much brighter, Maggie hoped the worst of the snow was now behind them. She also started to see and hear hordes of migrating birds pass over the cabin. At times, their numbers would darken the sunny skies and the noise was deafening. The nicest part of the burgeoning season was the welcoming change in colors that surrounded the small cabin. The trees sprouted new and healthy leaves, the deer herds were out early grazing in the open fields and the cool nights were more sporadic.

March was a time of transition and she could see that One-Ear was eager to be on the move. He would regularly make his way down to the small cove where they had arrived months earlier, to see if the French and Huron were moving past yet.

Fredrick was also excited that winter was ending. He was noticeably happier and he began his days by taking long walks to the beach or hiking up the northern trail. He hadn't stopped talking all winter about moving on to Niagara when the weather improved.

One-Ear and Fredrick continually spoke with one another of plans for heading towards the fort, but Maggie did her best to ignore these conversations and went about her daily routines.

She was in a quandary. Moving onward to the fort at Niagara placed her farther away from any chance she of seeing her family again, and it doomed her to be a servant to the French merchant's family. At least in the cabin she was no man's slave and free to come and go as she pleased. She thought rather harshly of Fredrick as well. Could he just abandon her at the fort after all they had been through? Her life at the cabin was simple and she did not want to leave.

She purposely slowed her daily pace down as the men obviously worked harder in preparation for their departure. She spent more time out in the blossoming meadow than inside the cabin. Even though its single window allowed a nice stream of light and fresh air to circulate, she could not stay inside with chores she would need to complete in order to leave her safe haven.

Maggie had dreaded the inevitable conversation about when they would leave, but it came much sooner than she had anticipated. Just as March cleared out leaving the fresh air of April to consume the countryside, Fredrick and One-Ear walked into the cabin and found Maggie cleaning up after baking some cornbread.

"Madame, we must talk," Fredrick started, without his normal friendliness.

Maggie bristled and kept her back to the men. She did not want to hear this.

"Miss Maggie," One-Ear said softly, knowing that Maggie would be ready to fight all suggestions about traveling to Niagara, "the trails are clear and winter has left only a few memories behind. We need to prepare to leave for the fort at Niagara before the forests are full of French and Huron."

"What is at Niagara that makes both of you want to give this up?" Maggie countered. "I lost this once and I don't want to leave it all behind again."

"This, madame?" Fredrick asked, surprised at Maggie's reaction. "This was only a stop for us. We…I need to get to the fort; they are expecting me to arrive. We all know they will send out patrols for me."

"You need to go to the fort," she said, looking him straight in the eyes. "After all we have been through, you just expect me to give up my freedom and become some merchant's servant girl?"

"Miss Maggie, we can't stay here," One-Ear tried to reason. "I have seen signs that the Huron are on the move again. They are moving south so we must head north."

"I have nothing to the north, One-Ear, you should know that better than anyone," she shot back, watching as the two men put their heads down to avoid looking at her.

The conversation ended, but they all knew that they would need to leave sooner rather than later.

Maggie watched as the men packed for the trip but she refused to help. Little had been said since the last futile exchange and she did nothing to show the others that her mind had changed.

"As of now, we are far enough away from the main trail between Fort Niagara and Fort Presqu'Isle that the Huron have no idea we are here," Fredrick tried again to reason with Maggie. "Yet I must agree with One-Ear that it is certain the French and Huron are on the move south. Down by the lake, we have seen a number of large canoes and a French bateau carrying marines. It will not be long until someone stumbles upon this place. Do you think it is safe now to have a fire that might attract the Huron to us?"

He and One-Ear continued to pack supplies, clean their weapons and dry out as many pelts as they could for trading along the way. They needed to pack light to move faster, so they had to be selective with what they took. They didn't want to weigh themselves down and become easily tracked.

Maggie had fought as long as possible, but she had seen for herself the French and Huron on the lake and had even heard voices carrying from the main trail. She realized it would be much better to be a French servant than to be re-captured by the Huron.

She knew they had to move on.

"Fredrick," Maggie began as she put together some food for their journey, "how can you just let me be taken by the merchant and what of One-Ear? Are you that willing to just abandon us?"

"I don't know, madame, but it is my duty to deliver you to Fort Niagara. Word must get back to my father that I am alive, a dispatch has most likely reached him by now that I never arrived."

Maggie understood she had no options. She could consider escaping with One-Ear, except the lake and trails were now teeming with the enemy. That option would only serve to put them both in danger; a fast-moving army would have little use for two prisoners and would probably kill them if they were captured.

Staying with Fredrick would provide some security that should enable them to pass through the French territory towards Niagara without fear of being attacked by the Huron or the Canadian militia. Maggie understood that her realistic options were few, so she decided to follow him and pray that he might find a way to release her from her obligations to the merchant.

Any travel by the lake, although it would cut several days off their trek, would be foolish since there was a noticeable increase in traffic on the lake every time they checked from the cliffs.

"We must be cautious where and when we travel," Fredrick said. "Despite the fact I am a French officer and the son of a respected senior officer, the Huron and even the Canadians are unpredictable and their loyalties tend to lie where it best benefits their own cause."

One-Ear knew that this deep into the wilderness, a lone Frenchman in the company of an Englishwomen and a young Huron scout would not afford Fredrick much authority with the Huron. They would easily kill them all, take their supplies and leave them for the wild cats to feast on.

Maggie and Fredrick waited for One-Ear at the cabin while he made one last check on the beach to cover up any signs they had been there. He had also stripped the small cabin of anything that might alert the Huron that they had stayed there. He buried most of the items that they could not carry and hid the ashes that had accumulated in the fireplace in the tall grasses in the fields.

Fredrick was noticeably anxious to leave and stood pacing by the pathway that they planned to take towards the fort. Maggie was getting nervous since One-Ear had been gone for over a half-hour and should have been back by now.

"Should we go and check on him?" she asked Fredrick, who had now moved into the center of the field. "It is certainly not like him to be so long."

Before he had a chance to reply, they heard One-Ear shouting and racing down the trail from the small cove.

"Miss Maggie, run! The Huron and a number of Canadians have landed at the cove and are searching around the area!" One-Ear ran past Fredrick who had his musket raised to cover him if he had been followed.

Maggie instinctively raised her musket as well, and they grabbed what they could and ran deep into the forest cover of maple, oak and chestnut trees. They couldn't run too far since they would have made enough noise to attract the Huron and would have been easily overtaken.

They stopped only a few paces into the woods and took cover behind a massive oak tree that provided them great cover and a clear view of the small cabin. A few moments later, Maggie noticed a small band of Huron carefully entering the outer field and spreading out to search for any signs of the cabin's inhabitants.

They remained quiet and well-hidden as they watched the Indians scour the field. The Huron were being cautious, leaving three warriors at the mouth of the trail to provide cover for the others.

Two Huron worked their way to the front of the cabin as more warriors entered the field, swelling their numbers to well over twenty. Maggie watched the two circle the cabin, trying to see through any cracks in the log work. They pushed on the window to see if it might open up but it had been latched from the inside and didn't budge.

"Why are they wasting their time here? This place is no real threat to them." Maggie whispered to One-Ear, as he intently watched the Huron flood into the field.

"They must have found the remains of some of the French soldiers I buried on the other beach," One-Ear whispered, keeping his eyes on the cabin. "With the winter melt, along with the increased water level of the lake, the waves hitting the beach must have pulled off some of the sand and exposed their remains. I guess they are checking to see if there are any survivors."

"Shouldn't we move before they decide to search the woods?" Maggie nervously replied.

Maggie saw that Fredrick was making sure nobody came up from behind, as One-Ear continued to observe more Huron surrounding the cabin.

"If we move, we take the chance they will see or hear us," Fredrick finally whispered, not taking his eyes from the small pathway they would use to escape. "With all these packs, they would be all over us in seconds."

"Then we should just leave the packs, they are useless if we are all dead." Maggie continued.

After a few minutes spent checking around the exterior of the cabin, the Huron finally pushed open the front door. They carefully walked into the cabin and checked inside. It didn't take long for them to realize no one was inside and were satisfied that it was just an old, abandoned cabin. They quickly departed back towards the cove trail.

Maggie and the others waited for almost a half hour before they decided it was safe enough to move.

"They appear to be gone," One-Ear said as he stood to get a better view of the field. "I should really check down by the lake, but we have wasted enough time and need to get moving."

Fredrick helped Maggie to her feet as they gathered up their supplies. "How far is the fort at Niagara from here?" she asked One-Ear, to get him to focus on moving away quickly.

"It is not a place I have ever done on foot, the lake is much faster and much easier," said he replied before pulling on his pack and gathering up his musket.

"I would venture a guess it is a good week's walk from here," Fredrick added, sounding somewhat discouraged. "I don't really know the shape of the trails, especially since we need to avoid the main trail."

Once they had all their gear, they decided to take a trail that roughly followed the high, wind-swept cliffs of the lake. This way they could observe the movement on the lake and avoid any chances of running into the Huron and Canadians who are travelling overland on the heavily-used trader routes.

Maggie was nervous during the entire first leg of the trek. Every sharp corner or slight elbow in the trail was a potential place for an ambush. The trail was extremely narrow in most places and they were forced to walk single file. One-Ear kept well ahead, searching the upper trail to make sure it was clear. Maggie let Fredrick take up the rear position, several yards behind her.

The overhanging branches and the thick, unruly underbrush that suffocated the forest floor were constantly catching on her clothes or snagging on her pack. Maggie kept her musket at the ready and vigilantly kept her eyes and ears focused ahead to listen for any problems One-Ear might run into.

The hardest part was that they all had to remain silent and only use hand signals. One-Ear had warned them that voices carried and they certainly did not want to alert anyone of their approach.

After several hours of non-stop, intense walking, Maggie was happy to hear One-Ear double back and suggest they might want to rest at a secure spot he had noticed up the trail a ways.

They were all fatigued, especially Maggie, who carried the added burden of what awaited her at Niagara. She was slowing noticeably as she watched One-Ear run ahead of them to make completely sure the site he had seen was safe enough to stop and rest.

By the time Maggie and Fredrick found One-Ear, he was waiting near an isolated landing area that overlooked the lake. It was several yards off the trail and concealed by dense wild strawberry patches that provided great coverage from any passerby that happened to be using the trail.

Maggie thought it was a great place, the ground was sandy and the lookout was nestled with large rocks that they could safely watch for any passing canoes on the lake. The ground was soft enough to sleep on and the few small trees provided more than enough cover from the wind.

The only nuisance was the sand flies that inhabited the area and added to the hordes of mosquitoes and other biting flies that were everywhere; plaguing them without mercy.

Maggie had learned enough from her earlier travels that any exposed skin would be bloodied by the ever-present insects. She kept a piece of cloth tied around her neck to keep them off her back and, even though she was hot from the long sleeve shirt, breeches and long socks, it was far better than being bitten and itchy. A good fire always was a good way to keep some of the flies away, but that was impractical now since it would only serve to give their secluded spot away. Much like voices carried, smoke could be seen for miles and they didn't want to make it easy for the Huron to locate them.

Maggie noticed that One-Ear had picked several spring berries and she laid out some corn-bread and dried fish on a small blanket for them to enjoy.

It felt great to be off her feet and she took a seat on one of the rocks that presented her a beautiful panoramic view of the entire eastern end of the lake. The sun was pretty high in the mid-day sky and the fresh air blowing softly in off the lake provided some much needed comfort from the last several hours of walking.

One-Ear took a seat right beside her and offered her some berries that were barely ripe yet. She tried some and immediately reacted to their tart taste. Taking a quick drink from the water canteen she kept over her shoulder, she asked, "What land is that just below the horizon?"

The distinct, cloudless sky provided a clear view of a large coastline that sat almost directly across from where they ate.

"That is where some of my people live," One-Ear said wistfully as he gazed towards the distant land. "Most of the Cayuga settled in the lower area near the great falls, but some of my own family moved across the water to find better hunting grounds. It is where many Huron lived, but most of their large villages are farther up the large river there. My family lived there for several summers on the lower banks of the river, right where it flows into the lake. The land was full of game and the river gave us fish to eat whenever we needed it."

"It sounds wonderful; we must go there one day," Maggie said cheerfully, sensing that he was eager to speak of those happier days. "Why did your family ever leave?"

"My father was an important elder in our clan and he felt that back in our other home decisions were being made without his counsel. I know he never wanted to leave; he left my older brother behind to lead the people that wanted to stay there. I think his plan was to return, but the Huron raiding party changed all that. It is sad because when we lived in that new home of ours near the river, our Huron neighbors were farmers and traded their corn for our fish. They never bothered us as long as we stayed off their land."

Maggie noticed he was fighting off his emotions, so she left him to his thoughts and took a bite out of a piece of corn bread.

He remained looking off into the horizon and continued, "We would catch large fish that sat on the bottom of the river, and they had long, stringy whiskers that could give you a painful sting if you were not careful. My father called it a mudfish and some of us called it a catfish because of its whiskers. It tasted really nice mixed in a big pot of corn, roots and vegetables."

Once again they both sat and watched over the lake. Maggie remembered a much simpler time and wished they both could return to their much happier lives.

Maggie took a moment to check on Fredrick and noticed him stretched out on one of the wool blankets, fast asleep. She thought this might be the only chance she could have a free moment to talk with One-Ear about what they might want to do about heading towards Niagara.

"I hope you understand that I have no intentions of going to the fort," she said quietly. "We both know that my life would be basically over. I will be forced to become a servant-maid in Quebec, or worse, France. If that happened, you would be unable to help me and we would never see each other again." Maggie watched Fredrick as she spoke, to see if he was really sleeping or listening to their conversation.

"Miss Maggie," One-Ear said, "I do know that once we get to the fort, any opportunity to escape will be gone. I think Fredrick will have little to say if the merchant still wants to take you. I promised to keep you safe and I will do so."

Maggie smiled at him; she had hoped that his compliance with Fredrick's eager travel plans was just to keep Fredrick happy until they could escape the Frenchman.

"We have little choice but to escape before we get too close to the fort," she said as she watched the rhythmic waves plowing against the sandy shore below. "It will be next to impossible to make it to the fort without being captured by either a French patrol or the oncoming Huron. I know that Fredrick will have no choice but to give me up and my fear is that if you help me escape, he will have you hunted down."

"I promised Jacob that I would keep you alive and safe, so that is what I must do. I fear little action from the French since I am a Huron and they do not want to upset them their ally. Without the native people, they have no chance to defeat the English."

"I am so sorry that I never spoke to you about Jacob, but I fear he has given up his search for me," she said as her eyes filled with tears. "There has been so much time and so many miles between us that only a miracle could ever help us find each other again."

"Your husband is out with Joshua searching for you. He was with us outside of Fort Machault. They left me behind and followed the merchant towards the fort at the Forks. I'm not sure where they may be, but I know that with the new season, they will be both out looking for us."

Maggie cleared her eyes and pressed One-Ear for more information, "What did he say, word for word? How do you know that it was my Jacob?"

"We told him that you were with us and got yourself captured by the French. That is why I went into the fort to get you, but the merchant had purchased you by then. So when he found out that you might be going with the merchant, he took Joshua with him and left me to watch for you if you were left behind. His plan was to stop the merchant to check if you were with him."

"How do you know it was really Jacob? He was with the militia in the Ohio Valley, how did he get to the fort?" She needed more details. The thought that it might really be Jacob and that he was out there searching for her gave her some shred of hope they might see each other again.

"He told me who he was; he could have easily killed both of us, but he chose not to. He had the same kindness in his eyes as you have."

They both sat for a moment as Fredrick rolled over onto his side. He remained fast asleep, so they continued to plan their escape.

Maggie was full of a renewed hope that she had lost several months back. She would absolutely not allow herself to be escorted to Niagara by Fredrick. If she and One-Ear could have escaped right that moment while he slept, they would, but common sense dictated that they would have to be careful of what they should do next.

"If we want to escape, we need to do it soon," One-Ear cautioned. "The closer we move towards the fort, the deeper we get into French territory and the threat of patrols and hunting parties."

"What do you suggest?" Maggie asked simply. She knew that she had to trust One-Ear and that he would get her to safety.

Just as the young man was about to answer, Maggie pulled on his hand and slid down the rock. She pointed over the rock as One-Ear signaled her to remain quiet. She watched him slowly poke his head up over the rock to see why she had so abruptly ended their conversation.

Together they could now clearly see five large, flat-bottom boats. The crews rowed feverishly despite the fact that each boat had its bright white sail unfurled. The vessels were manned by over a dozen, white-coated French regulars and guided by a dozen or so birch bark canoes, each packed with five Huron and several Delaware warriors.

"Don't talk, we can't have them know we are here; besides, Fredrick might want to speak with them and we would lose our chance to escape," One-Ear whispered, intently watching the flotilla's fast approach.

"Why would Fredrick want to speak with them?" Maggie quietly asked.

"They are a detachment from the fort, most likely sent out to locate any signs of me, Madame," Fredrick's voice resonated unexpectedly behind them, catching them off-guard. They had no idea how long he might have been standing there.

"I can assure you, they mean us no harm and I will speak with them," he continued. "It will certainly make the long trip much easier if we have a safe escort by water all the way to the fort."

Maggie moved aside as Fredrick stepped forward to see over the large rocks. Just as he did so, One-Ear viciously swung a large piece of a fallen oak branch and struck Fredrick directly in the face.

Taken completely by surprise by One-Ear's attack, Maggie screamed without thinking. The force of the blow knocked Fredrick backwards and he slumped against a nearby chestnut tree.

He was dazed and bleeding heavily from his eyes and nose. He struggled to get on his feet but fell face-first back to the ground. One-Ear approached him as he now lay motionless.

One-Ear tossed the piece of branch down and ran to the top of the rocks. He knew that Maggie's scream would have been heard for miles and the boats below would have easily been alerted. Peering down he saw that the French soldiers, along with their Huron and Delaware allies, had already beached their vessels and were securing them to some trees. A couple of officers were pointing directly at the spot One-Ear was careful not to reveal their location. A few had already begun to scale the steep, sandy cliff.

"Keep back, Miss Maggie, the French heard your scream and they are working their way up the cliff," One-Ear said as he watched her stand over Fredrick's lifeless body.

One-Ear fearlessly stood atop of the rocks to get a better view. A few careless musket shots struck well below his feet. He could clearly see that the soldiers were struggling with the unstable sand and the lack of hand holds on the cliff face. The Huron were all out of their canoes and stood on the congested beach, contemplating which route to take.

The French regulars continued to pelt One-Ear and Maggie with musket fire, but were too far out of range and only struck rocks and trees well below them. They knew they had to get out of there before the men figured out how to reach the top.

"We have to move, the French will be here soon," One-Ear directed Maggie. "Grab what you can carry and just run; head north and don't look back until you are well clear of these cliffs."

Maggie stood, momentarily frozen, but a stray musket ball bounced off the top rock, hitting the hemlock tree where they stood and sent shards of branches down upon their heads.

She took one last look at Fredrick's bloodied body, oddly praying he might still be alive.

"Don't bother with him, grab a musket and run," One-Ear shouted, trying to get her to move.

She was stunned, and watched as he smashed two of the muskets against the rocks and tossed them over the cliff. He also pushed some old, dried out logs over as well. Maggie assumed he wanted to at least slow the French down.

He turned and scooped up two haversacks, throwing them over his shoulders, and pulled her onto the trail. "Now run!" he cried. "And don't look back! I will hold them off as long as possible. Now, run!"

The excitement in One-Ear's voice made her snap to attention. She could hear the voices of the French soldiers as they struggled to work their way up the cliff. Their shouts filled the woods and made her feel surrounded, and she began to run.

Without turning back, she heard the echoes of two shots and could now only pray that One-Ear would soon be right behind her. She ran for what felt like an hour. When she finally felt like the French threat had dwindled, she slowed her pace to see if there was any sign of One-Ear behind her. She didn't see or hear anything.

Frightened and alone, the shock of how quickly everything had happened kept her moving. With no sign of One-Ear, and having no sense of where she was, Maggie slowed her pace to regain her composure. Her arms and face were scratched and rubbed raw by the endless bushes and trees that choked the small trail, and she was very thirsty from all the running.

As she cautiously approached a sharp elbow in the trail, she decided to climb up a small embankment that provided her with a view of the trail in either direction. From this spot, no one could see her, and no one could pass without detection.

Struggling to catch her breath from all the running and the surprise attack, Maggie laid out on her stomach and watched the path from her high vantage point. She ate a few small pieces of corn bread and took several drinks from the wooden canteen she had over her shoulder.

Thankfully, after about a half-hour of watching and praying, Maggie spotted One-Ear running awkwardly down the path. He stopped several times to re-adjust the bags he had grabbed, and the two heavy muskets that constantly struck his legs as he ran.

Standing up to check into the distance, Maggie could see no signs of the French or Huron. Just before he was near her position she called down to him and waved her arms, so he would see where she was.

One-Ear turned and made his way up to her. Before he could say any-thing, Maggie greeted him with a hug and kissed his forehead.

He smiled and said, "They stopped chasing me after only a few miles. I think they were more concerned with their injured officer than some Huron boy. They did shoot at me a few times, but I think they were only trying to scare me. I don't even think the Huron scouts bothered to scale the cliff; they just watched over the canoes instead."

Catching his breath and eating a piece of dried meat that Maggie had offered him, One-Ear took off all the gear he had struggled with and sat on a piece of soft moss.

They were clearly both exhausted but knew they had to keep moving.

All Maggie could think to say was, "Now what do we do?"

Chapter | **Nine**

The isolation of the valley created almost its own climate. The mountains provided some protection and at times insulated Jacob's small plot of land from the bitter cold that normally engulfed the rest of the lower region.

They certainly had their share of snow, but that was far better than the freezing temperatures that would soon arrive. When it snowed, they could still trek out to traps and find them full, but when the bitter cold set in, even the animals did not venture out of their dens.

In addition to hunting and trapping when weather permitted, Jacob and Joshua made regular trips to the nearby creek to maintain their water supply. They also kept themselves busy by chopping wood and clearing the snow off the roof and repairing the numerous drafts created by the constant winds.

The long winter provided them with some quality time together and they grew very close. Jacob missed his children desperately and although Joshua was not their substitute, he brought out Jacob's fatherly instincts and their bond grew stronger. They spoke about many things; Jacob spoke of his wife and children and Joshua spoke of his parents and the Huron and One-Ear.

"How long were you with the Huron?" Jacob asked one early morning while the two shared a nice hot meal of river trout stew and grounded chestnut coffee.

"My family had just moved to a nice ten-acre plot at the foot of the Adirondack Mountains. We had just finished a three year indenture term for our sponsored voyage from Cork and my father was so excited to finally own his own property. My older brother, Jeremy, and I helped him work the land and build a nice four room cabin. My two sisters, Mary and Tess, helped my mother make curtains and weave some nice wool blankets."

Jacob could see that rehashing the past was causing Joshua to get emotional, so he said, "We can speak later, lad; I didn't mean to get you upset."

"It is hard to think about, but it's no more than what you have been through," he said, taking a deep breath. "I think we had just been at our new home a little over two months when we got word from a couple neighbors that the Huron were raiding some of the nearby farms. I will never forget that morning and the noise the warriors made. There was a fog-like mist that covered most of the lower region and my father and brother were out clearing some rocks from the front field. They had no chance. I was on the front porch, cleaning some pelts when I heard the deafening shrills from the attackers and saw my father run back towards the cabin. He had left his musket near the fence that surrounded the field, but he was run down before he could get to it. Jeremy was taken down by a large Huron who smashed his skull with a war club. My mother ran outside to see what was happening and was greeted by a musket ball that struck her just below her chest. I had managed to grab a loaded musket from inside and got one shot off, but it was too late."

"It sounds like you did everything you could," Jacob offered, patting him on the back as he refilled the young man's cup with coffee. "The Huron are known for their early morning raids and they strike fast with brutal efficiency. You should not feel any shame, lad."

Joshua smiled and continued, "The Huron easily overran me and my sisters, tied us up and made us walk for miles. We were then forced to watch them raid several other farms and murder all the settlers. To this day, I am not sure why they let me live. Mary and Tess didn't last long; they cried most of the way and couldn't keep up with the pace the Huron were keeping. During one of our stops, two of the Huron took them both into the woods and when they returned without them, I knew they had been killed. Thankfully, they left them unmolested and, like my parents, didn't scalp them. Once I was among them, I learned they didn't always scalp their victims since they didn't prize white scalps as much as other Indians'. The scalp represents the warrior's soul, and when you scalp your victim you take their soul. I think they saw no value in the white man's soul at all until the French started paying for them."

The two men exchanged many stories and memories, some of which they had never shared with anyone else.

By God's grace, the winter broke early and the longer days of spring gave them both a renewed sense of energy.

"When do you think we can make the trip to Will's Creek?" Joshua asked one day while he took a brief break from chopping wood.

Jacob had noticed that Joshua must have grown three or four inches during the winter and he stood almost as tall as himself. In fact, Joshua was wearing some of Jacob's old clothes and without his Huron gear, on he reminded Jacob of himself at his age.

Jacob knew he would have to decide what to do with the information entrusted to him by Captain Stobo, but he had little stomach at the moment to face Washington and his old mates.

"Let me think about that while I go out and check the trap lines," Jacob said.

"Do you need a hand?" Joshua asked.

"No thank you, son; I need a bit of time alone to think," Jacob replied as he grabbed his musket and walked up the trail to check his lines.

"I'll be back before nightfall; take care of yourself," Jacob called back just before he entered the woods.

Jacob had let his hair grow over the winter, and if he didn't tie it back he looked like a wild man. Joshua would laugh every morning when he saw Jacob get up. The long hair and unruly beard he sported presented a rather untidy picture. He shuddered to think what Maggie would think if she saw him; the kids probably wouldn't even recognize him. Returning to

Will's Creek the way he looked now might be the only way to avoid being arrested for desertion.

Jacob reached the first trap, which was set up almost a half-hour from his homestead. This deep into the wilderness, any sound tended to carry and he could hear the voices of two men making their way down the trail. He imagined they were inexperienced woodsmen, since they continued to make all kinds of racket, appearing to care little about their chances of being ambushed.

Jacob knew better than to make so much noise in these parts; there was always a roaming band of Delaware or Shawnee hunting or fishing near this particular spot. He knelt down to let the men pass within a few feet of where he was waiting. He could see they were two older men, dressed in faded buckskin and fully armed, carrying several cleaned pelts. Jacob's curiosity got the best of him as he casually stepped out from behind his concealed position.

"Gentlemen, could you make more noise?" he said as they almost walked directly into him.

Startled and confused, the men immediately dropped their pelts and raised their muskets.

"I mean you no harm; I'm just out checking my trap lines and heard you coming," Jacob explained. "We don't get many folks this far south."

His attempts to diffuse their fears failed as they both stood their ground and kept their muskets cocked. "Are you looking for some trouble, mister?" one of them finally barked.

"No trouble, men, just a word of advice," Jacob said. "I could hear you coming from a mile back and you are both damn lucky I wasn't a Delaware hunting party ready to ambush your sorry backsides."

"Sorry, mister, but the savages don't scare us much," the same man replied, keeping his musket pointed at Jacob's chest. "It's the thieves and low lives that might kill a man for his furs that we worry about."

"Now, it is pretty plain that if I wanted both of you dead I would have never given up my hiding place," Jacob said testily. He was now clearly offended at their insinuation that he was a thief. "I would have shot you both from the trees before you could have gotten a shot off."

"I'll give you that, but what do you want?" the man replied without moving his gun an inch. "We are on our way to Fort Cumberland and want to reach it by nightfall."

"Fort Cumberland? I have lived here most of my life and I have never heard of such a fort," Jacob snapped, wishing he had his musket in a better position.

"It's at Will's Creek; some new British Major General re-named the place. His quartermaster is buying all kinds of supplies and paying top dollar for it. We just wanted to get there and get some of his money for ourselves." The man's tone was a bit friendlier and he had finally lowered his musket.

Jacob moved completely onto the trail, interested in this news of Will's Creek. He politely offered his hand and shook both of the men's hands. He passed them each a piece of tobacco for their pipes and they happily accepted.

"I'm Murray from the valley; can you tell me a little more about this fort and this new British General?" Jacob asked, trying to fish out some more information.

"I'm Wells and this is my brother-in-law, Kenton; we are from near the Susquehanna just east of here," the talker said.

"I know the river and area well, beautiful country if I remember correctly," Jacob replied.

"There are rumors the British are thinking of attacking the Fort at the Forks," Wells explained as he lit his clay pipe, "but we don't know what to think of that. We heard he brought a few thousand soldiers with him as well."

"Are Washington and his Virginians still at Will's Creek?" Jacob asked eagerly.

"Last time we were there he was, but can't say for sure now," he replied, pausing to take a long draw on his pipe. "That British Major General, I think his name is Braddock, has recruited most of the able-bodied men around and called on New York and Maryland territories to send men. We met up with a man a ways back who said there were now several hundred militia men there now and he wasn't sure about the regulars."

"Braddock must be serious if they are going to march through the wilderness to try to take Fort Duquesne," Jacob said thoughtfully.

"Not much of our concern to be honest. The French never gave us much trouble and we like what they are paying for furs and such."

"You best be heading on," Jacob said. "Just make sure you keep the noise down. I would hate to find you both dead and scalped somewhere along the trail." He exchanged polite nods with the men and watched them disappear up the trail.

Jacob now knew what he had to do. Captain Stobo was relying on him to deliver his notes to Washington. He owed the man a lot and it was the least he could do for him.

The only complicated issue was the pardon note. Jacob didn't trust Washington or the army's law to protect him from any possible repercussions. He decided he would deliver the map and save the note for a better time. His only hope was that no one would recognize him and he could go about his business without fear of arrest.

Not wanting to wait much longer, Jacob left his lines and rushed back to Joshua. He ran most of the way, slowing to a walk when he reached the trail that led him to his homestead. Joshua was still working hard splitting wood and stacking piles of wood for the fireplace.

Careful not to startle him, Jacob called out, "Joshua, that's enough wood for now."

Joshua stopped and rested his weary arms on the axe handle. He pulled off a small rag that was around his neck and wiped the beads of sweat that had drenched his face and arms.

"Back so soon?" he called back. "I assume we had a bad day on the lines?"

"Let's get some food in our bellies," Jacob said with a smile, patting Joshua on the back as he passed him. "I have just heard some news of Will's Creek, and we need to talk about what to do with the maps."

Joshua nodded and scooped some water from the rain trough and poured it over his head. Jacob grabbed some wood and walked into the cabin where he laid out some meat and bread on the table while he waited for Joshua.

When Joshua had made himself comfortable, Jacob told him what he had just learned on the trail. "First, Will's Creek is now called Fort Cumberland. There is a Major General Braddock running the army and he is recruiting militia from the Maryland territory all the way to New York.

I ran into two old trappers and they were on their way to the fort to sell their furs and they told me of the news and that the army was preparing for an attack on Fort Duquesne." Jacob explained.

"Does this Braddock fellow understand the terrain between the forts?" Joshua asked, shaking his head and letting out a low chuckle. "How is he going to get his army through the mountains, swamps and trails that are meant for two or three men standing shoulder-to-shoulder?"

"He sounds like the typical British officer who thinks his army is invincible," Jacob said dryly as he tore off a piece of bread and tossed it into his mouth. "Most of his men have never seen a forest this thick, not to mention the Huron and Delaware that they will run into. The trappers were not certain, but it should be safe to assume that Washington and his Virginians were still at the fort, so we need to pass on Stobo's map as soon as we can. They also mentioned that the army's quartermaster was buying up all kinds of supplies. Horses, wagons, furs and all sorts of materials are being brought in from all over and they are paying top dollar for it all."

"Are you not still concerned about the desertion charges on your head and that Washington might recognize you?" Joshua asked.

"The map Captain Stobo gave me should be enough to save my neck. The trappers also said the army is recruiting every healthy man available, so we might consider joining up." Jacob suggested.

Jacob felt comfortable enough that the way he looked now covered up any signs of his previous appearance. Washington would have no way to know him, and his former mates hopefully would not recognize him. He should be able to just blend in with the rest of the recruits.

"Why would you even consider joining up with the militia again?" Joshua asked curiously. "What about Miss Maggie and One-Ear? Are we just going to forget about them and go on with our lives?"

"I thought about this, lad. If the rumors hold true, the trails from here to Fort Duquesne will be packed with soldiers. Even well to the north, the French will get word of the English intentions and every path, trail and waterway will be swarming with French regulars, Canadian militia and Huron. Where are we to go? It will be impossible to go anywhere without the threat of getting ourselves caught up in the middle. My thoughts were to join up so we might have an easier and safer route north."

"You do make some sense, but do we really want to be in the British army?" Joshua said quietly as he cleared the table and sat by the fire.

"Trust me, lad, if we watch each other's back we will be fine. Now let's get some sleep and we'll head out at first light."

Both men awoke well before dawn and decided to head out early. It was still dark, but Jacob knew these trails and felt comfortable walking it in the predawn darkness.

Joshua wore a new pair of buckskin pants and a freshly-sewn hunting shirt tied with a red sash. An old tricorn hat he had trimmed down for himself completed his ensemble, and now all vestiges of his past Indian life appeared to be gone.

"You certainly make a good white man, lad," Jacob laughed when he saw Joshua in his new woodsman attire.

The trail remained quiet most of the way; they only saw a couple patrols and a small work details. Jacob assumed that they were sent out just to keep them busy and active. He knew that the army didn't like its men to be too idle because that just lead to a lack of discipline. Discipline was the backbone of the British army.

They reached the outskirts of the Will's Creek area just after the morning sun cleared the ridges. The traffic on the trail had increased noticeably and they had run into several men from the Ohio Company who had storage facilities on the western river side of the new encampment.

The fort sat on a small rise at the base of the mountains. Jacob and Joshua stopped before they entered the freshly cut outer field where a small contingent of British regulars were monitoring the traffic arriving from the eastern wilderness.

"Before we go much further and have no time to talk," Jacob said, "I want you to call me John Sims instead of Jacob Murray, just in case anyone might think they recognize me. In due time, I might show my face, but for now I prefer to be just another settler interested in joining up and looking for some adventure."

"Makes sense, so who am I?" Joshua grinned.

"You will be my eldest son, Joshua. We are two Pennsylvanians who came to pass on some information to Washington."

They didn't want to stand around too long, just in case they attracted unwanted attention from the English guards. They slowly made their way over Will's Creek and were immediately impressed by the number of soldiers and civilians that covered the several acres of the fort's open fields.

There was an entire field of bleached white canvas tents that were in perfect rows and appeared to go on forever. The far field was being used for the various militia companies and new recruits. Their limited organization and lack of discipline made a stark contrast in the layout of their camp.

The noise produced by all the men and civilians resonated throughout the open field. Some of the men were being drilled endlessly and the barking orders of their sergeants echoed loudly. Others were busy cleaning their weapons while many more were moving cannon and mortars across the parade grounds in several large wooden wagons.

Another part of the field contained large pens that housed not only the army's horses, but enough cattle and pigs to feed the army two times over. The noises of the animals added to the general din.

Some of the British regulars stood around mocking the raw American volunteers as they attempted to perform their drills. The colonial militia's recruits were far less disciplined than their English counterparts, yet in the deep wilderness, their skills should be well used and appreciated.

Unfortunately, Jacob had experienced firsthand how the British felt about the colonials. If Braddock was anything like the other English officers, the American militiamen would not be used as they should be, but would be consolidated into the regular force, made to utilize British tactics while wasting their own skills.

The men's dress was as varied as their backgrounds and skill levels. The British soldiers, of course, wore their signature red coats, white breeches, and blackened linen thigh high leggings while many volunteers wore buckskin clothing or their own civilian garb. Jacob recognized a unit of grenadiers by their high-peaked, mitre-style headgear. He had heard of this elite group of fighters before, but had never seen them up close. They were more than impressive and he thought they looked rather regal, but out of place in the wilderness.

Jacob could see that Joshua was intently watching over the mass of men and equipment. He took a seat on a small embankment overlooking the entire encampment and motioned Joshua to do the same, asking, "What do you think about all of this?"

"Colorful, to say the least," Joshua finally replied. "Their bright red uniforms can be seen for miles, though; they will make nice targets for the French, not to mention the Huron."

They continued to scan the grounds before venturing down into all the chaos.

"Look at those men over by the main entrance," Jacob pointed out. "They certainly appear to understand that blending into the environment is the best way to survive in the wilderness."

"I think they are part of a ranging company," Joshua said. "There were a few of them in New York and New Hampshire and they always tended to dress in greens and browns. The Huron encountered them a few times and they were very skilled fighters, well-adapted to wilderness fighting."

"That sounds like some good fun!" Jacob said with a grin.

As they pondered what their next move should be, Jacob noticed an older gentleman dressed in a smart red jacket and riding a large black stallion. He was presiding over the parading troops and speaking with another officer whose back was facing them.

Jacob recognized this other officer, it was Washington. The man's unusual height made him stand out and from this distance, Jacob was certain it was his former commander.

"Let's get down into the action and see what we can find out," Jacob suggested as he stood up and brushed off his pants.

"Are we ready for this?" Joshua asked nervously. He received no response from Jacob, who had already managed to work his way down the small hill.

Joshua caught up to him at the bottom and found that the ground-level view of the encampment was even more impressive. It seemed larger and busier than it had from above.

Jacob confidently walked right past the two British regulars who were guarding the advanced pickets. The two soldiers looked at them but said nothing. As they made their way along the rows of tents, they got some friendly nods from some of the militia who waited around for their next set of orders.

Jacob could hear some strong Scottish accents calling out instructions and that made him feel somewhat at home. He checked back to make sure Joshua was keeping pace and saw that the young man was just as interested in all the sights as he was.

They worked their way through the hectic mass of men to the main parade ground. Here some of the inexperienced militia men were being drilled by an impatient sergeant who barked out his orders.

As he got closer to the tall officer he had seen earlier, Jacob confirmed that the man was indeed Washington. He approached his old commander slowly. Washington was not in conversation with the older officer and several woodsmen. Jacob and Joshua stood back and listened.

Jacob assumed that the older man in the red coat was the Braddock gentleman he had heard about. He was struck by the age of the Major General, who had to be over sixty years old.

Catching the end of the conversation, Jacob heard one of the local woodsmen trying to explain to the officer how the French and Indians in the wilderness fight.

"With all due respect, sir," one of the woodsmen said in an exasperated tone as he vainly attempted to educate the British officer, "the savages will not move from behind the trees. The French are no different. Their regulars have adapted well to wilderness fighting and will fight the same as their allies."

"Damn the savages," the officer replied arrogantly, dismissing all suggestions from the woodsman. "If they decide to cower behind the trees then so be it. As for the French, if they choose to do the same it will be more than their honor they will lose."

Jacob watched as Washington stepped in and said, "Sir, these men have fought the savages in these parts for decades and we must, at the very least, consider their ideas. Wilderness fighting is vastly different from the open-field battle tactics that are used in Europe. I can speak from firsthand experience that no matter how much you prod them, the French will not leave the cover of the trees."

"We must...we must?" the older gentleman said with a scowl. "If the bloody French decide to fight like savages then we will charge into the woods and let them taste our bayonets."

"Sir, we just thought your men should be aware of what they will be facing," the woodsman countered politely. "Formations and drills won't help them once the fighting starts."

"I am sure these savages have never faced the discipline of the British a soldier before; my guess is that they will merely run at the sight of us," the officer snapped back.

"So be it," the woodsman said, clearly frustrated. "I have one last item though, sir. The terrain you're about to face is unforgiving. Mountains, swamps and cliffs are what you are up against. Your equipment and cannons will be next to impossible to move over most of this wilderness."

"We have a detachment from the royal navy that will assist us in moving what needs to be taken over any of the mountains or cliffs," Washington said in another attempt to calm the heated situation.

Having stood back long enough, Jacob stepped forward and brashly added his thoughts of the impending situation. "Dragging cannons, wagons and horses," he said, "will only cause your entire army to slow down. I have made the trip from here to Fort Duquesne dozens of times and it proves to be most difficult even as a lone traveler on foot."

Washington gave Jacob a look of contempt, barking out, "Who are you to interrupt this private conversation?"

Respectfully tipping his hat, Jacob introduced himself, "I am John Sims and this is my eldest son Joshua. We are here to offer our assistance and by the looks of things, you certainly need it."

Braddock scoffed at the very idea that an insolent backwoodsman could be superior to his army, but Washington simply asked, "Have we met before Sims? I am Lieutenant-Colonel George Washington and this gentleman is Major General Edward Braddock, appointed by the King to rid our country of the French."

Jacob respectfully bowed his head, but fought back laughter at the notion that this old man was to be the savior of the wilderness. "I have never had the pleasure, but your reputation does precede you, Lieutenant-Colonel," he said.

"Enough of this idle chatter," Braddock growled, obviously losing his patience with Jacob's overconfidence. "Let's get on with things and find these men a unit to attach themselves to."

"Before you go, Major General, I have a message to pass on to you from a Captain Stobo; it is addressed to the Lieutenant–Colonel," Jacob said quickly as he pulled out the sealed document from his coat pocket.

"And how do know of Captain Stobo?" Washington asked suspiciously.

"I honestly don't know him well," Jacob said slowly. "I was passed this note by the Captain at Fort Duquesne. I didn't ask too many questions, but I do know there is a map enclosed, and it should provide you with some information about the fort." Jacob smiled coyly and carefully handed the information over to Washington. He and Joshua stood back and watched as the two officers read the notes and looked over the detailed map.

"Who is Captain Stobo?" Braddock asked.

"He was one of the officers transferred to the French to appease them while we sent back their prisoners we had detained here," Washington explained. "He is a good officer and one of my most trusted advisors."

Braddock appeared satisfied before turning his attention once more towards Jacob, saying, "Explain how you came to acquire such valuable information."

"As I said earlier, it was passed on to me directly from Stobo's own hands," he replied, becoming uncomfortable with the tone of the conversation.

Braddock and Washington returned to examining the information. Jacob had had enough and politely tipped his hat to excuse himself.

Before he had a chance to leave, Braddock abruptly stopped him by saying, "You mentioned something of an attack; how would a woodsman in this wilderness know of such an attack? Should I assume you are loyal to the King and not the French? How do we know you are not acting on their orders and trying to mislead us?"

Jacob was visibly insulted by the tone of Braddock's questions. The insinuation that he was not a loyal subject clearly was meant to push him into saying something he might regret, but he refused to take the bait.

"Sir," he said evenly, "you obviously have not been in this territory long and I will forgive your question of my loyalty to my King. As for the French, if I was working with them I would have simply put a musket ball in your head and end all this foolishness. Your mind appears to be made up already and I pray to God your fine British regulars don't get our militia boys killed."

He could see that this proper English officer resented the very thought of a common colonial doubting his military strategy, let alone his right to question any man's loyalty. Jacob took particular joy in watching Braddock's face redden with anger over his insubordination.

"I'll have you…" Braddock shouted.

"Gentlemen, please, not in front of the men," Washington said calmly in another attempt to diffuse the escalating conversation.

The woodsmen whom the Major General had dismissed so easily earlier began laughing at his angry sputters, which intensified the older man's anger. Braddock continued his verbal assault on Jacob, saying, "I see you appear to prefer a French musket over our finely crafted weapons?"

"I 'acquired' this musket from a very co-operative French marine outside Fort Duquesne," Jacob said flippantly. "To be honest, I prefer my old Pennsylvania long rifle over the French or English musket; they both are horribly inaccurate and misfire more often than not."

As Washington geared up for another attempt at peacemaking, Braddock scoffed, "Bloody Americans, they don't have a clue about how to wage war. All they want to do is wobble behind trees and shoot from the bushes."

Jacob said nothing more. He understood that he had obviously not fallen into this powerful man's favor. All he wanted to do now was get into the camp.

Braddock pulled his horse and rode off, refusing to offer his goodbyes. His face was still red from their exchange.

Jacob stood by quietly, watching him ride away until Washington offered some advice, "Sims, you best watch yourself and keep your mouth shut. The Major General is a fine officer and holds little value for the likes of you."

"The feeling is mutual, I suspect," Jacob grumbled.

"As for the map, thank you. It is good to hear that Stobo is surviving well. As for you and your son, are you still going to enlist? I do not particularly appreciate your tongue, but we still need some good men. If you can shoot half as well as you talk, then you might prove to be of some use to me." Washington offered them both a smile.

"If I may, sir," Jacob began cautiously, not wanting to alienate Washington too, "my son and I would like to join up with one of the Ranging units. We both know these parts better than most, and our scouting skills would be more appreciated with said units."

"I wouldn't normally acquiesce to a request of such a brash and disrespectful fellow, at least not without putting you through your paces first, but I do see some value in you Sims. I will inform Captain Stevens' Provincial Rangers that you will be honoring them by joining their ranks. My only suggestion is to keep your nose clean and keep your opinions to yourself.

"As for you, son," he continued, looking at Joshua, "keep your father in line. You would be best not to follow in his footsteps; it would be far less troublesome." With that, Washington quickly departed to follow Braddock and his other advisors.

Jacob turned to Joshua, saying, "I fear I may have gotten us in some trouble already. Let's find these rangers and have some fun."

They shook the hands of the woodsmen who still lingered nearby, and wished them luck.

"I am still not convinced that getting involved in all of this is going to get us closer to Miss Maggie," Joshua said as they walked through the encampment to join up with the Virginia-based rangers. "It appears it will be more trouble for us and will just slow us down."

Jacob offered no answer and as they moved through the packed camp, he noticed an old man balancing on a well-worn stool, cleaning his aged squirrel rifle. "Excuse me, old-timer," he said brightly, "where can I find Captain Stevens and his rangers?"

Without bothering to look up, the man simply pointed towards the northern side of the woods and said, "Their tents are over that way, but they left about an hour ago. I guess they are out looking for some Frenchies or their savage friends."

Jacob thanked the man and asked, "How goes the hunting with that old stick of yours?"

The old man ignored his comment, offering only a low-pitched grunt and a spat of brown tobacco juice that landed just wide of Jacob's foot.

"Well, boy, let's get ourselves into the woods and track down these rangers," Jacob said as he rushed off to forest nearest the tents the old man had indicated.

"Good luck with that, boys, they have a good hour lead on you; you'll be lucky if you can find each other in those woods," The old man wisecracked, once again spitting stream of tobacco juice across the path.

Jacob lead the way as Joshua followed closely behind. They easily picked up the trail of the rangers, despite the darkness of the woods. By their tracks, Jacob was impressed that the unit of about twenty men appeared to be maintaining a single-file formation and were apparently spaced out in case of an ambush.

As he waited for Joshua to catch up, Jacob knelt down on one knee, checking out the prints left by the fast-moving men. "Take a look at this," he said when Joshua joined him. "These fellows are smart. Notice how they re-traced their footsteps to throw anyone tracking them off their movement. If I wasn't paying attention, there would be no way to notice their trick."

Joshua smiled and said, "That's an old Huron trick; they set many an ambush that way."

The two made good time, cutting a few miles off their trek by using an old Seneca path that Jacob had used many times in the past. They could now hear voices, most likely from the rear guard placed there to keep the main unit from being surprised from behind. By once again using the side path, they worked their way past the rear guard without being noticed. Jacob knew they were closing in on the heels of the main force.

"Those poor souls are damn lucky we are not a Huron or Shawnee hunting party looking for some trouble," Jacob whispered.

Not wanting to startle the men and cause an accidental shooting, Jacob and Joshua decide they should forewarn them of their arrival.

"Captain Stevens, may we approach?" Jacob called out. "We were sent by Lieutenant-Colonel Washington to join you."

He watched a group of about fifteen rangers quickly take up defensive positions behind some trees. A voice returned their call, "This is Captain Stevens, you may approach but first identify yourselves and keep your weapons above your heads."

"My name is Sims, John Sims, and I am with my boy, Joshua," Jacob replied, signaling Joshua to watch behind them in case the rear guard managed to move in to ambush them. "We were requested to join your ranger company and were told you were out in the woods."

They both stepped out slowly and waited for the hiding rangers to do the same. When they were fully out in the open and totally exposed, the rangers all stepped out with their rifles pointed directly at them.

Jacob remained calm and motioned to Joshua to stay where he was, then stepped towards a tall, slender man dressed in a green woolen vest and matching green breeches. He also wore a Scottish-style tam adorned with a bear claw and wild turkey feathers. His brain-tanned deer-skin leggings reached his upper thigh and he wore an old pair of moccasins. His uniform helped him blend into the surrounding wilderness and matched roughly what his men were wearing. Some of them had dark or light brown hunting shirts, instead of green, but no matter what they wore, it was all meant to keep them well hidden in the backdrop of the woods.

Jacob offered his hand to the man, who had also stepped forward, and said, "Captain Stevens? I am John Sims and this is Joshua; it's a pleasure to finally meet you."

Jacob remembered Stevens from the disaster at Fort Necessity and knew that he was a skilled and well-respected leader who was generally liked by his men. The one thing that had immediately struck Jacob was that Stevens not only dressed much like his men, but appeared to fight alongside them, which was something that was not usually done in the British army.

"Sims, where do you hang your hat?" Stevens politely asked.

"We are from the other side of the Susquehanna River area," was Jacob's guarded reply. "I'm a trapper and a farmer, when the land is workable."

He watched as Stevens quietly looked him over and by his hesitant reaction, Jacob was sure that Stevens recognized him as the Virginia volunteer who had stepped in to assist him after the surrender of the fort.

"Well you appear like you do know your way around these parts," Stevens said as he motioned his men to lower their muskets. "How long have you been tracking us?"

Jacob didn't want to come across too over-confident, so he was careful with what he said. "We left the camp about a half hour ago," he replied.

"Nice work, Sims; you might prove to be useful. Did you not run into our rear-guard somewhere along the trail?" As Stevens continued to press Jacob, Joshua just stood back and watched the exchange.

"We did, sir, maybe a half-mile back. We used an old Indian hunting path and worked our way around them."

Stevens continued to look him over, and to Jacob, it felt like Stevens was deliberately dragging out this interview to make certain this disheveled woodsman wasn't someone he knew.

After a few tense minutes, Stevens appeared to be satisfied that Jacob was who he said he was, and Jacob was able to relax.

"Well, Sims," Stevens said, shaking both his and Joshua's hands, "if you and your boy don't mind little pay, even fewer rations and basically being Braddock's substitute for his lack of Indian allies, you're welcome to join us. To be frank, Braddock sees no value in what a ranging company can provide him, and he is far too arrogant to even want to understand what we can do. Our boys are new to this as well, but most have been hunting for years and now they are here to hunt a different game—the French and Huron."

"Have you any fighting experience, Sims?" he asked after a brief pause.

"Nothing official, but I have fought off the odd Delaware and Shawnee from my trap lines," Jacob said with a smile.

Their conversation was interrupted by the return of the rear guard, which slowly walked into the small clearing.

"Good of you to find us, Taylor," Stevens barked at the surprised ranger.

Taylor glanced towards the two new recruits, and Jacob could see he was not happy that the two men had slipped past them.

Grumbling something under his breath, Taylor stood with four other men and said, "We saw and heard nothing, sir."

"So you are saying these men just appeared out of nowhere and never crossed your path?" Stevens mocked as the other rangers laughed.

Taylor remained beside his group and said nothing, but looked particularly furious at how these two made him look bad.

"We are heading out soon, so please move out to cover our advance and try not to get yourselves killed," Stevens ordered as some of the men heckled the obviously irate Taylor.

Taylor once again mumbled something incoherent under his breath before yelling at the rest of his men, "Get your sorry arses moving!"

As he watched Taylor depart, Stevens returned his attention to Jacob and Joshua, picking up the thread of conversation where it had left off. "My only battle experience was unfortunately at Fort Necessity. Not much to say, but I wouldn't have wished that terrible mistake on anyone—not even our Private Taylor. We did indeed lose more than a few good men at that meadow." Stevens lowered his head as he finished speaking.

"We did get word of the situation there, sir," Jacob responded as he thought of his brother Israel and how that battle changed his life forever.

"Well, enough about the past, we must head back before the British think we decided to go home. Why don't you and your boy join the advance guards and lead us home. If by chance you spot a buck or wild cat, take your shot, the boys could use a good meal tonight."

Jacob respectfully saluted and moved out with Joshua on his heels.

As they headed out, Stevens called after them, "Watch out for Taylor and his boys. They are good fighters, but they're all bastards, so take care."

Jacob and Joshua quickly switched to the same side trail they had used earlier, and it only took a few minutes to catch up to the slowly-moving guards. Taylor didn't even notice that Jacob and Joshua had joined them until he stopped to determine which way he and his guards should go.

Jacob could immediately smell the strong odor of rum on Taylor, who smirked when he saw that the two new recruits had joined their ranks. The man was heavyset and barely came up to Jacob's mid chest. He half-heartedly introduced his men to the new recruits, saying, "This lot is Kerr, Wallace and McDonald."

Jacob didn't bother to return the introduction and simply followed the others when they finally decided to keep moving towards the west. He and Joshua remained behind the others and could hear Taylor and his men talking amongst themselves and repeatedly casting glances back at them.

"We need to watch that rat," Jacob whispered to Joshua. "He's a drinker and reeks of rum, not something you want in a man leading the way home."

Jacob was far from a teetotaler, yet he had little respect for a man who drank too much. Rum surely gave a man a false sense of courage, especially when holding a loaded musket. Taylor struck him as a soldier that needed the boost to hide his fears, and a man like that leading the advanced guard was a disaster waiting to happen. Jacob had little time for men like him and decided that he and Joshua should stay behind and watch their backs.

"We'll see you back at the fort, gentlemen," Jacob said in an effort to distance himself as quickly as possible. "The Captain asked us to bring home some game for the boys tonight."

"Don't be a hero!" Taylor slurred loudly. "Leave us some of the savages to kill!"

Jacob and Joshua decided to turn south and get themselves on another side trail that would take them well past the four stragglers. They could still hear Taylor talking and Jacob said, "That Taylor is a no good drunkard and his men don't seem much better. My father always warned me about drunks, that you can't trust them and that rum makes a meek man a hero and a braggart even braver."

Joshua nodded and replied, "Rum was the plague of the Huron. The French traders would exchange it to them for valuable furs, knowing they had a weakness for it."

As they worked their way along the small trail, a noise just to their right made them both stop and take cover. Jacob glanced at Joshua, who was watching intently at some movement in the far tall bushes.

Jacob signaled to Joshua that he was going to move towards a better vantage point then got down on his stomach and crawled low to the ground under the thick brush. He reached an opening in the bushes that overlooked a small meadow. It was less than a half-acre, but it was the perfect place for deer to graze.

He could see that Joshua had worked his way just north of the clearing and it appeared that he had spotted what had made the noise. Moving himself to the other side of the opening, Jacob found a nice-sized chestnut tree that gave him enough cover to stand upright and get a much better view of the meadow.

From this vantage point, he could see that a mere twenty paces away grazed a herd of ten deer, unaware that they were being stalked by the two men. A large, multi-racked buck stood majestically above the brush, eating the small twigs and nervously moving his gaze over the surrounding woods.

This was their chance to be accepted into the ranger company; if they could take down at least one of the animals, it would feed the entire company. Jacob had his sights on the big buck. He was about to motion towards Joshua to take the smaller buck to his left, but he noticed that the boy already had his musket cocked and ready.

Jacob quickly took aim himself. He was still not entirely comfortable with the French musket he had acquired; he found it less comfortable than his prized long rifle. He concentrated to time his shot with Joshua's to keep either target from being scared off before the intended shot could reach it. He squeezed the trigger.

The small, secluded meadow echoed with the reverberation of the shot. As the heavy cloud of smoke cleared, Jacob briefly saw the back end of the deer herd scatter into the heavily-wooded area just to his far left.

He looked for Joshua through the haze and called out, "Did you get him?"

"Not entirely sure, but I think I hit something," the young man replied.

Jacob stepped out from behind the tree and before he got too far, a loud crack sounded and something hot passed right by his neck. Splinters from the chestnut tree splattered all around him, striking his face and arms. A large piece hit his forehead, drawing a small, steady trickle of blood that rolled down his nose and dripped onto his shoes.

He saw Joshua crumple to the ground and hoped he was just taking cover and was not hit. "Joshua, are you alright, lad?" he called.

He received no reply.

Fearing the worst, Jacob sprinted across the open expanse of the meadow with little thought for his own safety, and dove into the bushes where he had last spotted Joshua. He found the boy on his side, bleeding heavily.

As he carefully pulled him over to get a better look at him, Jacob whispered, "Joshua, can you speak, boy? For God's sake, speak."

He could see where all the blood was coming from; Joshua had a large, gaping wound in his shoulder. It was bleeding freely and Jacob's first reaction was to quickly remove his belt and tie it securely around Joshua's bicep to help ease the pain.

Jerking the belt hard, he barely heard Joshua whimper and was worried that he was losing consciousness. Satisfied the shoulder was bound enough to control the bleeding, he poured some water into Joshua's lips and removed his coat to prop up his head.

He felt slightly dazed and there was a severe pounding in his head from the impact of the large splinter. He heard voices all around him and could make out the familiar slurred growl of Taylor. Whether it was real or imagined, Jacob was now able to smell the awful reek of rum.

He became furious at the stupidity and carelessness of his fellow rangers. Guessing that in their drunken state, when they heard Jacob and Joshua shoot at the herd, they had blindly returned fire, inadvertently hitting Joshua.

As the men drew nearer, Jacob reloaded his musket and pulled out his tomahawk. Unable to control his rage, he let them come closer then let out a ferocious shriek and pounced on the first man. He drove the butt end of his musket into the unsuspecting man's temple. The force of the attack drove the man back into the others, knocking two of them to the ground.

He now stood face-to-face with the ranger called McDonald and before he could react, Jacob turned his hawk over and smashed it down against the man's collarbone. The impact shattered the man's right shoulder and he crumpled to the ground, screaming in pain.

Taylor and Kerr had managed to get to their feet just as Jacob turned his attention towards them. The rum had slowed their ability to react in time and Jacob threw himself headlong into them. He caught Kerr in the mid-section and slammed him hard against an old oak tree stump, knocking him out.

Taylor just stood frozen.

"What the hell…" was all Taylor had time to get out before Jacob drove his fist into the man's jaw.

Taylor went down and Jacob jumped on his limp body, throwing punches until the drunken man's face was a bloody mess.

Thankfully, before Jacob could do further damage, he heard a loud, forceful voice directly behind him shouting, "Stand down, Sims; one more punch and I'll shoot you dead myself.

Captain Stevens stood with his Queen Anne's pistol, cocked and pointing at the back of Jacob's skull.

Stopping immediately and falling off the unconscious, battered body of Taylor, Jacob broke down and cried.

Gathering his wits about him, Jacob muttered, "He shot Joshua; the damn drunken bastard shot Joshua."

Stevens ordered his men to search the bushes and, within minutes, they located the barely breathing Joshua, still bleeding from the wound, but not as bad as earlier. Jacob remained where he was until he regained his composure.

Surveying the carnage of his attack, Stevens kept his pistol aimed and asked, "Sims, what the hell happened here? We all heard the shouts and shots, and ran here as fast as we could. We assumed you were ambushed by some savages, but instead I find you practically killing one of my men and the rest of the lot beaten and bloodied. Now we find your son shot in the shoulder. To be honest, it certainly looks bad for you."

Stevens waited for an explanation and Jacob obliged by saying, "Sir, we moved ahead of Taylor and located a herd of deer we had tracked and before we knew it, Joshua was hit and I barely got out of the way of another one. After I helped Joshua, I saw Taylor and his drunkards and my temper got the best of me. All I wanted was to have that good-for-nothing drunk pay for his carelessness."

Jacob was now being held by two rangers and could only watch as Stevens checked on Joshua's condition. He heard him order four men to search the field for any signs of the deer herd and try to locate the musket ball that struck chestnut tree where Jacob had been standing.

A few of the others got Kerr, McDonald and Wallace to their feet and put them near their bloodied friend, Taylor, so Stevens could speak with them when he was ready.

Not soon after they went out into the field searching, Jacob saw the four rangers return. They had two bucks, one large adult and another smaller, younger male, which they dragged right to the feet of Taylor.

The two rangers who held his arms released Jacob. He understood that he was far from being cleared for his assault on his fellow rangers, no matter how much they were hated by the others, but the two bucks did ease some of the tension. When another ranger finally appeared with the stray musket ball he had dislodged from a tree, Stevens appeared to be far less upset with Jacob and now directed his fury towards Taylor's crew.

"This doesn't excuse you of your part in this, Sims," he said, "but now I know you didn't make this all up. Now I just want to know how one man could singlehandedly take out four, fully-armed rangers." Stevens gave a brief smile.

"Anger is a pretty strong emotion, sir," Jacob answered, then asked, "How does Joshua look? I know he lost a lot of blood."

"Private Murphy is a pretty good medical man," Stevens replied. "I'm not sure if he is a real doctor or not, but he can mend almost anyone. He did mention that your quick thinking to wrap your boy's shoulder might just have saved his life."

Taylor finally came to and was ranting to all his mates how Jacob had ambushed him and his men and they were forced to defend themselves.

Jacob heard his drunken accusations and walked over to face the still bloodied Taylor.

When Taylor saw him approach, he screamed, "That's the man! He's the one who shot at us then jumped us for no reason. Where is his boy? That coward didn't even show his face; he just shot at us from the trees."

Jacob just let him rant, knowing that the rum had clouded his memory. If he let Taylor keep talking, he would soon show himself to be a liar.

"Settle yourself, man, and tell me what happened, Taylor," Stevens said, standing over him, waiting to hear his version.

Jacob knew that sooner or later Taylor would show his true colors. The other rangers started to gather around the screaming man, wanting to hear what he had to say.

"As I said, Captain, that crazy woodsman attacked us for no good reason. They took two shots at us before we knew what hit us and all we were trying to do was get some cover." Taylor slurred most of his words as he struggled vainly to mask signs that he had been drinking.

Captain Stevens simply listened, nodding his head from time to time. Then he asked, "You say they both shot at you and your men?"

"Yes, sir, the bloody fools shot at us for no good reason."

"Were you and the men in the field or on the trail?" Stevens asked.

"Why, sir, we were obviously on the path moving north," Taylor replied, waiting for the other men to support his story.

Jacob looked at the other men, still nursing their wounds, and they offered nothing to substantiate Taylor's claims.

The stink of rum was all around the men and Jacob knew that Stevens could smell it to. The captain continued to press Taylor for more details, asking, "Tell me one thing, Taylor, how in God's name could Sims or his boy be shooting at you and all the while shooting down two deer in the back field?"

Taylor's demeanor began to change as he nervously looked around at the changing faces of his fellow rangers. "What deer?" he asked. "He and his good-for-nothing boy were shooting at us, isn't that right men?"

His men just kept their heads down, refusing to offer any support to assist him. Taylor knew that Stevens doubted his story and simply glared at Jacob, who returned his glare with a sly smile.

"This is what I make of the entire situation, Taylor," Stevens began, "You are a disgrace to our company and I have ignored the men's complaints of your drunken ways for far too long. To add to this, you are a liar and you have put us in harm's way. Do you know what the punishment is for being drunk on duty?" Stevens motioned two rangers to come to his side.

Taylor understood that his Captain was on to what really took place and with the others refusing to support him, he had no place to hide.

Bowing his head, Taylor replied, "Lashes, sir?"

"Correct, Taylor–lashes. Two hundred of them for lying to me and the men. After you have received your lashes, we will then deal with the fact you were drunk on duty today, and have been for months. That is a five hundred lash offense, but if you have ever seen the damage two hundred lashes does to a man, I fear another five hundred would surely kill you. You have made this very unpleasant for all of us, and as for Joshua, if that boy doesn't make it, you will be hanged." When Stevens finished speaking, he waited for Taylor to offer any form of an apology.

At Taylor's silence, Stevens continued, "I can see from the looks of your face that Sims has issued his own sentence for your carelessness. As for your lashes, I will leave it up to Sims and his son to decide your fate after you have received your initial punishment. I have not forgotten about the role your men played in this and they will be sentenced in due course."

When he had finished speaking to Taylor, Stevens shouted orders to the rest of the rangers, barking, "Now get this rabble out of here and get the injured men back to the fort!"

Jacob stood by quietly as the other rangers picked up the prisoners and pulled them ahead up the trail. He made no eye contact with Taylor or any of his men and waited to see what Stevens wanted from him.

Moments later, Stevens approached him and offered him his hand, "Let's move out, Sims, and get your boy back to the fort as soon as possible. Murphy and the fort's medical staff will be able to get Joshua back on his feet. As for Taylor, we will make sure he is dealt with severely and never allowed to be part of our company again."

Jacob accepted his captain's hand and said only, "Thanks."

"Now, move out and check on your boy; they rigged up a crude stretcher and I sent ahead for a wagon to get him back quicker." Stevens threw his rifle over his shoulder and ran to the head of the company.

Jacob tucked his tomahawk in his belt and shouldered his musket, then walked by Joshua side during the entire trip back to the camp.

Chapter | **Ten**

"**W**e must keep moving, Miss Maggie!" One-Ear urged Maggie as he moved up the trail ahead of her. "They could be right on our heels any minute."

She didn't need to be reminded of what they were running from. The shouts and war cries of the French and Huron reverberated through her mind as if the men were a few yards behind her. The fact that she and One-Ear had left them miles behind was of no comfort. She moved quicker every time she remembered Fredrick's bloodied body and the shots that had whizzed past her head. She was sore and tired, but One-Ear kept her moving and soon they ran through a natural break in the tree line just off the main trail.

Maggie watched One-Ear with admiration as he masterfully dodged, jumped and swerved, managing to avoid all the debris and rough thickets. She did her best to sidestep the numerous roots and skin-tearing thorn bushes that bordered the old trail, but she was still covered with scratches and stumbled periodically as she ran.

When she felt unable of taking another step, she halted and called out, "One-Ear, can we slow down and catch our breath? It looks like they have given up chasing us."

Slowing down slightly to look behind him, One-Ear replied, "We can't stop right here, we'll be safe just over this hill."

Maggie took a deep breath and reluctantly pressed on. She could see that One-Ear had already reached the top of the hill and had stopped on a small outcropping of rocks.

A few seconds later, she caught up to the young man and saw why he had paused. Their position presented them with a panoramic view of the entire valley below.

In addition to the grandeur of the view, they saw a large company of French regulars and their Huron, Delaware and Shawnee allies approaching from the north on the same trail. They had split into two smaller groups of about thirty men and were busy combing two lower trails that ran parallel to the lake.

"Did these soldiers come from the fort at Niagara?" Maggie asked.

"They must have; your Frenchman is obviously important to them," One-Ear replied.

"They are right in our path; what do you think we should do next?"

One-Ear was quiet for a few minutes before he answered, "We must wait them out and try to move past them during the night. You might want to pray to your God that they don't make it this far up the trail before nightfall.

"I thought your people didn't like to travel at night," Maggie said, "especially in the woods. What about the spirits who travel through the woods in the dark?"

"Our only hope is that the spirits who live amongst these woods will be kind enough to guide us past our enemies," One-Ear replied as he sat down and returned his concentration to the soldiers below.

"Why don't we head towards the east, work around them then cut back towards the lake?" Maggie suggested thoughtfully.

"Good thought, but I think we need to try to get past them and put some space between us and them. If we headed east, it would add at least a couple days to our trip and that might give the French enough time to organize and cover the entire lakeshore trail. If that happens, we will never be able to escape." He never took his eyes off the French below them.

Maggie sat beside him and watched as the men searched the vast wilderness for any sign of Fredrick. Finally, streaks of pink and red tinged the sky and the sun prepared to give itself over to the night. The separate French patrols met up with one another and began to set up their camp for the night. The Indians continued their search for a while longer before forming their own camp. They were far less formal than the French; most of the natives just found a tree to lean against, while others worked to get a fire started.

The two camps were no more than a hundred yards from each other, separated by a thick forested area and a small creek that meandered between them. The French had already sent out sentries to guard the north, west and eastern boundaries of the camp. The Huron sent out some of the Delaware and Shawnee scouts to guard the Indian camp and particularly the small creek that ran nearby.

The encampments sat directly in the path One-Ear and Maggie needed to use to make their escape. The camp fires were easily visible and the glow spread throughout the small valley. The night sky was also brightly illuminated by a full moon that looked massive, hanging in the cloudless sky above. Maggie could clearly see the expression on One-Ear's face as he pondered their next move.

"I still think heading east into the woods, and then cut back towards the lake makes the most sense," she offered again. "If you look we shouldn't have to travel too far east, just enough to skirt by their encampment."

"I just wished we knew if there are any more French soldiers around," One-Ear whispered, never taking his eyes from the fires. "I fear if we keep moving north, we will walk right into more French, but if we use the creek, they might continue moving south and we should be relatively free from their eyes. I was hoping they would not set up by the creek so we could just follow it out of the valley, but they are very smart."

"I agree that we should go deeper into the forest," Maggie replied.

"We will have to be careful of the sentries," One-Ear said, "but if we can clear them, we will have an opening to the eastern woods. In this darkness, the creek would assist us with our movement. It runs towards the east and as long as we can hear it, we might be fine." He didn't seem overly confident with his plan, but it was the only one he had.

"It will be much tougher to move through the forest than what we have faced so far," he cautioned Maggie, finally taking his eyes from the valley below and looking her square in the face. "My fear is that the wilderness will weaken you too much."

"If I am your only concern," Maggie responded, "please don't worry. I assure you I will keep up with you as long as you keep moving. If we get into a position of being captured, save yourself and let me accept my inevitable fate with the merchant."

One-Ear said nothing as they gathered up their gear and slowly worked their way down towards the valley floor. The challenge was to avoid all the same debris that made the trail difficult by day and deadly by night. The slightest trip or snapped twig could alert their enemies.

The campfires were like beacons, allowing them to judge their location and direction in relation to the camps. Maggie imagined that she could smell the musky odors of the men in the camps, mingled with the smoke and she was put off by the smell.

"Thank God for the moon tonight," she murmured, staying close to One-Ear's side.

He stopped and listened for any noise coming from the camps or the many sentries sent from each camp. "The moon is good for us, but it also presents the same light to the French and Huron," he countered.

Once they had worked their way to the valley, they could clearly make out the details of the two camps and were shocked to find that each still had several men sitting up around the fire pits. One-Ear grabbed Maggie's arm to make her stop and pointed ahead where French sentries were moving about, carrying torches to assist their movements. It appeared they were concentrating their efforts on the creek.

"They seem to be worried about the creek and the possibility of an attack," One-Ear explained. Again he pulled on Maggie's arm as they moved back towards the thicker forested trail they had just negotiated.

The voices of the sentries could be heard now, coming from either side of them. "The French care little if we hear them," One-Ear said softly, "but the Delaware and Shawnee know better than to warn their enemies of their approach. They could be anywhere in this darkness."

"What can we do now?" Maggie asked. One-Ear didn't respond immediately and Maggie sat by a tree as she waited for him to figure out their next move.

"I'm not sure what to do," One-Ear finally spoke, "they have us cornered. We might just want to walk back up where we were earlier." He continued to scan the area for an opportunity to move.

Maggie observed the two camps then looked towards One-Ear as he intently watched for any movement and listened for where the sentries were. She knew that their current location would leave them completely exposed with the impending sunrise, but she felt that moving back up the mountain would not be a good choice. They would likely be overtaken by the search parties before they reached the top.

The peace of the night was broken by the surprising arrival of a large contingent of French regulars, along with several Huron warriors, led by Fredrick. The results of One-Ear's attack were still very visible as Fredrick's head was wrapped with bandages and his face was covered with bruises. He was welcomed by the others and was noticeably angry, re-lighting several torches and ordering his men search around the camp.

The two observed Fredrick pacing around the perimeter of the camp, yelling at his men to keep searching the woods for any sign of his escaped prisoner.

"This can't be good for us," Maggie stated the obvious and ducked down into the thick brush, "How did they get past us?"

"Your Frenchman must be pretty upset to risk his men's lives travelling through the night to find you. They will not let us getaway easily; we must get moving now if we have any chance of escaping. They must have used the lake and canoed west of here."

The initial plan of using the creek was still a possibility, only now they would have to move farther west towards the lake. The more direct route had been taken away and their options were now perilously limited.

"We have to follow the creek west and then go the much longer way around by the lake," One-Ear continued. "It will be slow and add hours to our trip, but I see no other way. With all the additional soldiers, we have no chance to make it past them by the eastern route. He waited to see if Maggie had any ideas.

Maggie said nothing; she saw the logic in his plan. If they managed to work their way towards the lake, the possibility of finding the French landing site and canoes that Fredrick's group used would mean an easier escape.

While they continued to decide their next move, they heard Fredrick called back his men. It was futile to properly search the dark, thick woods and the other French officers appeared to have convinced that it would be far smarter to wait until the sun rises.

"Now we might have our opportunity, the creek should run into the lake and if we stay close to it we should find the lake at its end," One-Ear whispered as they quickly made it away from the French and were cleared of the camp in just a few minutes. They were still concerned that the French and Huron could be anywhere along the trail, but staying close to the creek meant they remained off the main trails and had a more direct way to the lake.

The sound and smell of the lake hit them as they continued walking by the soft mud of the creek bed. One-Ear had warned Maggie not to step too close to the mud, so they did not leave signs they had taken this route. He also did his best to sweep over their path with a pine branch on several occasions just to throw off any possible threat from anyone trying to track them.

They stopped about a mile before they reached the open lake, to collect themselves before facing the unknown. "They will have left behind a few Huron warriors to watch over the canoes," One-Ear said. "Unfortunately, we will not know how many until we get closer, but once we know better, we can decide what needs to be done."

They continued on at a much slower pace, watching and listening for any signs of the Huron guards. Once they reached the lake, they found themselves on a high sand ridge that presented them a good view of the canoes and the two Huron sitting by a fire on the small beach. One-Ear located a path down to the shore, but to reach the canoes they would have to make it across the guarded open beach. The only other possible way down was to climb a twenty foot cliff that dropped into the water.

"Are they the only guards or do you think they have a few hidden inland to warn the others?" Maggie asked, looking down towards the two Huron, who seemed oblivious to their presence.

"The Huron usually don't sacrifice themselves to draw an attacker in, but we cannot be sure," he replied. "Let me go down and take a better look and then decide what to do. Warn me if you see any other Huron."

Maggie sat and watched him work his way down the trail towards the beach. She watched intently to see if any other Huron were hidden in the rocks nearby. Her heart was beating uncontrollably, at once anticipating their escape and fearful of being recaptured.

One-Ear remained behind some large boulders, completely obscured from the view of the two Huron still sitting around the fire pit. When he made his way back up to Maggie, he said, "It will be difficult to make it across the open beach to get at the two Huron and I fear that one of us might die doing it. I got a good look at the cliff, though, and if we could climb down and use the water, we will have a better chance to surprise the Huron."

They moved closer to the cliff and Maggie saw that it was a sheer drop to the water. She could see very few places to hold onto and most of the rock face was wind-blown and sheered of any trees.

"What choice do we really have?" One-Ear said, noticing that Maggie appeared nervous.

"I don't know if I can do it, One-Ear," Maggie confided, "I am not ashamed to say it scares me that if either of us falls it will kill us." She stood over the cliff face, frozen and unable to move any further.

"Miss Maggie, you must trust me," One-Ear persuaded. "I would never let you die here; we have come too far and seen too much to give up this easily. As a boy I would climb up and down the lake cliffs much like this one and never fall. You just need to stay with me and follow my steps."

"As you can see, I am not a young boy," Maggie said with a smile as she strapped her musket tightly against her back and jammed her haversack under her shirt.

"Follow closely and try not to look down," One-Ear said as he started to slowly climb over the edge and onto the cliff face.

One of the reasons he had picked this particular spot was that he had noticed from below that it provided them a narrow but possible route right to the bottom. Maggie couldn't see this route from the top, but as they maneuvered their way down, she noticed that it was a much easier descent than she had expected.

The cliff face was pocked with large cracks that provided ample places to wedge a foot or hand. The cliff was also obscured by several overgrown shrubs that hid their climb from the unsuspecting Huron warriors, who still remained seated around the fire pit.

One-Ear worked his way almost to the bottom before he saw that the only way down to the water was to drop almost four feet directly into the cold water. The heavy waves over time had pounded most of the rocks into small stones, so they had little to be concerned about except the noise. Their splashes might alert the Huron who would great them with muskets aimed before they even got back to shore.

One-Ear stopped and softly called up to Maggie who had kept up with every one of his moves, "This is where we will get a little wet. Be mindful of your powder, we need it dry just in case we have to defend ourselves on the beach."

Maggie watched as One-Ear slowly guided himself down into the waist-deep frigid water. He made virtually no noise and stood right under Maggie and pulled her down beside him. Together they waded a few paces before climbing back onto some rocks that gave them a view of the several dozen canoes and French boats tied up on the shore. Maggie could also see the two Huron, still unaware that they were being watched.

"We do need to be careful that there are no other French or Huron around before we move to the canoes," One-Ear warned as he took a moment to check over his powder and musket. Maggie did the same, checking her powder horn and making sure no water had gotten into her musket.

They worked their way to the canoes and One-Ear took a moment to carefully cut several holes in the bottom of a few of them, just to slow down potential pursuers. One-Ear kept his eye on the nearby Huron and used his knife to slice through the bark, just below the water line. Maggie nervously watched, flinching at every slight noise that might alert the two Huron.

"Why don't we do this after we kill the guards?" Maggie softly asked.

"Once we attack these two, we will have no time," One-Ear replied, knowing that they would need to concentrate on reaching the canoes after the noise of their attack.

As they knelt together on the shore, he said, "We must strike fast and give them no opportunity to fight back. We each have only one shot and then we will have to use our muskets like clubs. We have only one chance at surprising them, so you aim for the warrior on the left."

They steadied their muskets and cocked back the hammers, pausing only a moment before One-Ear shouted, "Fire!" The Huron warriors jumped up when they heard his shout, but when the gun smoke cleared, Maggie could see the two Indians collapsed by the fire.

One-Ear immediately rushed onto the beach and charged towards the men. He didn't bother to re-load his musket, but had it ready to drive the butt into either of the Huron's heads.

Maggie reached the fire pit a few moments after and saw One-Ear turn one of the warriors over to check his condition. He did the same with the other and the shooters saw that each Huron had a large hole blown through his forehead.

"Good shot," One-Ear said quickly, "but we must get out of here. We still don't know if there are any others within earshot of us." One-Ear had already pulled a canoe out from the others and had it ready for Maggie. He steadied it as they both jumped in and paddled quickly to get away from the shore and any possible counter-attack from any other French or Huron in the area.

He called out to her, "I am shocked the French did not leave more men to guard their boats. They must have no reason to fear being attacked by the English this far north. They also did not think much of us and never expected us to be able to steal a canoe right from under their noses."

Maggie smiled, she was just happy they made it off the beach safely and without much of a fight. She had been moving so quickly to start paddling that she hadn't immediately noticed that the canoe One-Ear grabbed was full of supplies, tied down and secured to the bottom of the canoe's floor. She concentrated on her paddling, keeping pace with One-Ear to move them farther into the middle of the lake. The more distance they put between themselves and the French the better she felt.

Looking back towards the small beach and the cliff that she had just descended, Maggie wondered how they had made it with only a couple of minor scratches. The cliff, from the lake, appeared so much higher and, if she had seen it from here, she would have never even attempted to climb down it.

"Nice job with the remaining canoes; that should slow them down enough for us to get a few miles between them and us," Maggie called back to One-Ear.

"We still must keep our eyes out for any other French and Huron boats coming from Niagara," One-Ear responded.

With a steady pace they had moved far enough into open waters that they now would have no fear of being shot at from the shoreline. Thankfully, the lake was relatively calm and a light wind was to their backs. Maggie knew that if the wind was driving the waves towards them from the front, it would force them to use all their energy, making it much harder to guide the canoe away from the shore.

After a few moments, One-Ear gave Maggie some words of encouragement to keep up with his steady paddle strokes. She responded by saying, "I thought you said this lake was bad for storms and such, why would we chance being this far off shore if one hits us?"

Paddling harder to hold the canoe steady over a large wave that hit them, One-Ear replied, "Our choices are limited and we must push past any portage routes that the Huron frequent. The lake soon will narrow into a river that leads to the large falls, so if we move towards the other shore it will be much easier to negotiate. Also, the Huron always stick to the southern side of the lake and we are moving to the northern side."

"We are not heading towards Niagara, are we?" Maggie shot back.

"No, my thoughts are to head to the river my father's people live by. It drains into the lake and it can be used to work inland around the great falls."

They continued to paddle hard and keep their eyes on the distant shoreline to the north. Soon they were far enough away from the threat of any search parties or advancing troops moving from the French fort at Niagara that they were able to relax a bit.

Maggie could see how the lake started to narrow and the far shoreline become much more visible. The lake remained oddly calm and there was no sign of an impending storm, permitting them to head directly across the remaining open water to the mouth of the river, saving hours of time they would have otherwise spent following the much slower shoreline route.

With no sign of the French, One-Ear slowed his pace and called out to Maggie, "We can find a nice spot on the north shore and take some time to rest. This side of the lake is much more suitable to land a canoe since there are far fewer cliffs and many better beach areas. The water is also much better there and not as deep as the other side; we could normally wade out for several hundred feet and it never got higher than our hips."

Maggie simply nodded in agreement and continued to paddle. Once they got within a mile or so of the shore, the strong pull of the current guided them towards a nice, clear sandy area. They both pulled their paddles out of the water and let the waves drift them to shore. One-Ear jumped into the shallow water almost a hundred feet from the beach front and held onto the side of the canoe to keep it steady and watch for any underwater sand islands that might damage the bottom.

The current pulled them right to the shore and Maggie stepped out to assist One-Ear in pulling the canoe safely onto the beach. They both unloaded the supplies and laid them out on the sand.

"I will see what is around to eat," One-Ear said as he grabbed his musket and ran towards a nearby sand dune before Maggie could answer. She watched him struggle momentarily to climb the soft sandy incline, his every step burying his moccasins in the sand. He finally managed to get over the dune and was quickly out of sight. Maggie kept herself busy gathering up some dry wood and piling it up within a circle of rocks she had placed to make a fire pit.

Well before One-Ear returned, Maggie had a roaring fire going and she had even pulled over two large old logs to have a good place for them to sit. One-Ear proudly came back with a large sack full of wild berries and two good-sized rabbits that he had dangling from his musket barrel.

"Miss Maggie, you have been hard at work preparing the fire for these two fine rabbits," One-Ear said in appreciation when he saw her sitting, warming her wet clothes by the fire.

"I see you worked just as hard," she said with a smile. "Did you see anything out along the dunes?" She watched One-Ear skillfully cut and pull the skin off the meaty bodies of their dinner. Once they were cleaned he jammed the two skinned rabbits onto two long tree branches and placed them by the fire. He also stretched out the skins on a large, flat rock and held them in place with several smaller ones to dry out the pelts.

He finally sat on one of the logs and rotated the rabbits in the fire. The sizzle from the cooking meat sounded heavenly to Maggie who was starving and anxious to have a pleasant meal. She thought to herself that it was nice to finally have some food without the fear of being attacked or ambushed by a French patrol or a Huron war party.

Flipping the rabbits over one last time, One-Ear said, "At the top of the dunes you can see most of the surrounding countryside. This side has far fewer mountains and is flat, which makes it good for farming. I do know of several small villages that were around here when I was a young boy. This is the land of the Mohawk and Mississauga and they have always been friends to the English. They are mostly peaceful people who fish and plant large fields of maize and sometimes tobacco. The game is plentiful here and the turkey birds are especially good and their feathers are always good for trading with other tribes who pass through."

He carefully pulled one of the rabbits out of the fire and passed the branch over to Maggie for her to have the first try. Before she pulled off a piece she asked, "So if the Indians around here are friendly, we have little to worry about?"

"Unless you English did something to get them upset, they are very peaceful. They used to be enemies to the Huron, but I think that the Huron now stay farther north and many moved to the east to be closer to the French. My old home is only a few miles to the north of here, if we follow the long river that empties into the lake." One-Ear explained and grabbed the other rabbit and pulled a steamy piece of thigh off and tasted it.

Neither said anything else as they enjoyed their meals. Maggie loved the juicy, tender meat that was easy to pull off the bone and tasted wonderful. The wild berries certainly added to the pleasant meal, and she felt safe once again and just appreciated the quiet surroundings.

When most of the meat had been eaten and only a handful of the berries remained, Maggie reclined by the fire and rested her tired body for a few hours. She had her back to the lake, but when she saw One-Ear suddenly stand up and gaze intently out towards the water, she did the same.

The peace had been broken by the approach of two large canoes, each carrying well over a dozen Indians. They were now just beyond a small sand bank that jutted out into the lake. One-Ear didn't appear worried but did motion to Maggie to ready her musket just in case.

Maggie observed as One-Ear calmly waved towards the canoes and that was enough for them to decide to land on the beach. She was initially concerned because their sheer numbers were enough to overtake them both without much of a fight. Her concerns subsided once she saw that none of them raised a weapon or appeared threatening in any way.

She did keep her musket in arm's reach, but trusted One-Ear that there was no reason to panic.

He appeared as if he knew them and called out to one of the younger men as they pulled closer to the shoreline, "Wolf-Paw, it is me One-Ear."

Maggie could see the friendliness turn into pure elation as the young brave waved wildly and jumped from the first canoe.

The canoe hit the beach and One-Ear rushed towards the young man. All the other paddlers dropped their paddles and were out of the canoe cheering their old friend.

Left standing alone by the fire pit, Maggie watched the men continue their cheers and enthusiastically slap One-Ear on the back as he hugged the brave he called Wolf-Paw.

"Miss Maggie, please come here," One-Ear shouted back to her as he continued to be welcomed by the entire group that now included the men from the second canoe.

Maggie still remained cautious, but slowly made her way over to the large group of excited Indians.

"This is my brother Wolf-Paw and these are some men from my father's village," One-Ear proudly introduced his brother who was much older and taller than him.

"This is Miss Maggie Murray, my English friend," One-Ear then returned the introduction as Maggie politely smiled, not sure how they might accept her.

She was surprised by their kind greeting and how respectful they were towards her. They even presented her with two fine fox pelts and a beautiful wampum belt, hand-crafted with hundreds of small glass beads. They also handed her a new rifle that reminded her of the one she once used back in Pennsylvania.

Overwhelmed by their wonderful demeanor and kindness, Maggie was escorted back to the fire pit by several of the men and then watched as the rest brought three large hand-woven baskets full to the top with river trout, a recently cleaned deer and a bushel of freshly ground corn meal.

The men let Maggie relax while they prepared and cooked a feast. The aroma of the cooking food was carried by the cool lake breeze and engulfed the group around the fire pit as they told endless stories and rejoiced at their reunion.

It was fascinating to watch the men dance by the glowing fire pit as the celebration pressed into the early night. Maggie enjoyed the long shadows that mimicked every move they made.

Still full from the rabbit that they had eaten a few hours back, she was careful not to insult their generosity and tried a bit of everything. They had added some water to some of the corn meal and made large patties that they placed on the rocks around the fire. She particularly liked them. They offered her sweet honey to dip the patties into and she couldn't remember ever eating something so delicious. They even added some of the same berries that One-Ear had collected, which really added to the flavor.

Maggie enjoyed seeing One-Ear so happy and they occasionally smiled at each other as he went on sharing stories with his brother and the other men of the village. She caught One-Ear and his brother looking at her and smiling together as they talked.

Eventually the eating and dancing gave way to exhaustion and the sand flies that hovered over the fire all night. At this time of the early spring, the hordes of small flying insects swarmed a person, concentrating on the victim's head and neck. Some, such as mosquitoes, were relentless and left most of the men with itchy welts, while others just flew around their faces and were merely a nuisance. The strong fire did keep some of the flies away, but the sheer numbers made it unbearable at times.

Maggie wondered how she would get any sleep being exposed to the flies all night. They were not as relentless as the larger more aggressive woodland mosquitoes and biting gnats that she lived with in Pennsylvania, but it was necessary to rub the skin with sand to at least provide some protection and relief through the night.

Wolf-Paw had a couple of the men set up a nice spot for her right by the fire pit, using a large bear pelt to keep her off the sand and a small, tightly-woven reed hut that faced the warmth of the fire. Exhausted, she fell asleep being serenaded by the waves hitting the beach. She was surprised that throughout the night, the villagers maintained the fire to keep her comfortable.

Morning came way too soon and, much like the festivities of last night, Maggie was impressed by the men's energy level. Before she got up, they had already gathered some food and water for the morning meal, letting her once again relax. Several of the villagers had gone on the other side of the dunes to hunt and returned with a quick meal of a squirrel, muskrat and a couple large river otters that had a very musky smell to them.

Maggie just sat and watched all the men work and was given a nice hot cup of tea blended with berries and some herbs, to warm her while the fire was built up again.

One-Ear, clearly tired from all the celebration, sat down next to her and said, "Miss Maggie, how do you feel about going up the river a few miles to visit with some of my family? From there we can make our way around the fort at the falls and avoid the French. We will also be protected by staying on the land of the Mohawk and Mississauga; they are very friendly and we will not have to fear about being attacked or ambushed."

"I know, I feel much safer than I have for months, and the farther away we remain from the French, the better," she responded with a nervous smile as she sipped her tea.

"It will mean a greater distance to cover, but my brother offered to escort us as far as the other large lake that the French fort guards. He said that he will send word to the Mississauga to have a canoe and supplies ready for us to cross the lake, well past the fort's outer reaches. The land is far more welcoming to the English and my Mohawk people will certainly help us during our travels." One-Ear did his best to re-assure Maggie of their safety.

Once they had all eaten enough of the morning meal, the men started to load up the canoes with all the supplies and gear. Two of the villagers took the small canoe and let Maggie sit in the center of one of the large canoes. She offered to paddle, but the men refused, allowing her to enjoy the trip up the river.

The two men in the small canoe led the way and after a few minutes on the lake, they turned at the mouth of a large river that opened to a wide river that was bordered by tracts of farmland filled with endless rows of corn. Maggie saw two small villages situated across from each other and, as they passed, they were greeted with waves from the small children and calls from the adult villagers.

As they made their way farther up the wide river, the countryside opened up with small farms and large parcels of land rich with freshly-planted spring crops. The Indian population living here was made up of peaceful farmers and fisherman, but as they paddled, Maggie started to notice much larger villages. Some of them had massive longhouses and she noticed one in particular that even had a large palisade surrounding it.

One-Ear was in the same canoe as she was, but he was busy paddling and talking with his brother. He did tell her that there were many French traders in the area since his people preferred trading with the French. They felt that they treated them much better and the French copper pots were favored over the cheap English tin. He also mentioned that the English liked to trade rum for their pelts and corn, and many of the village elders refused to deal with them since they viewed English rum as evil.

Maggie enjoyed the trip, waving at the numerous children swimming in the clear water, watching the women cleaning their wares and the men out fishing the shoreline in their small, one-man boats in the tall reeds that populated the river's edge. Once, off in the distance, she saw a small cluster of wooden structures that had racks of unusually large brown leaves drying in the sun. Maggie pointed at them and asked One-Ear, "Is that tobacco?"

"Yes it is," he replied happily, "but we call it Indian tobacco as it far less bitter tasting than the Dutch or Virginia tobacco around your land."

She had never seen the young man as happy as he was now. Being amongst his people and experiencing their excitement when they saw him made her think of what it might be like if her family ever had the chance to be together again. The thought made her remember all the happier times they had spent together and how her children were coping with their new lives.

In spite of the clean, fresh river water splashing over the sides of the large cut-out canoe at regular intervals, Maggie remained fixated on the land that ran parallel with the snaking river as it meandered gracefully, wide in certain areas then narrowing substantially in others. It was fairly deep and, in spots, it was choked by the thick reeds, especially near the bend, where in places it was so narrow two canoes side-by-side barely fit.

Maggie loved the diverse landscapes that appeared to change at every turn. The open farm land moved into sections of dense, old-growth forests that reminded her of her homestead. The endless amounts of migrating birds, at times darkening the clear blue sky as they passed over their canoes, and the shore birds were just as spectacular and made her watch in awe. White Pelicans, egrets and herons nested and feasted on the abundant frogs and small fish that gave them a constant, easy food source.

She did notice some white people living in a few of the larger villages and she assumed they must be French or Canadian traders. They certainly did not exhibit the same enthusiastic welcoming as the Indians did. A few stopped to watch the canoes only after they noticed the strange white woman amidst the paddlers.

"I am surprised by the number of French traders living with your people, One-Ear," Maggie called out as they passed by one particular village that consisted of three small longhouses and a stout, heavily-bearded Frenchman who did not enjoy her stares.

"My brother told me that the French have tried to move into our territory and their numbers have been increasing every season, but the Mohawk have kept them under control. The Black Robes have always been in this area and try to push their religion on us. Most of them keep north, but they do sometimes venture into our villages. He also said our village has several French living there, especially over the winter season. Wolf-Paw warned me that a couple of them have the ears of the elder council and he senses some division within the village."

"Will we be as welcomed by them as your people have already greeted us?" Maggie asked nervously, her excitement noticeably diminished.

"We will be fine, the village had a hard winter and they should be happy the river is now cleared of all the ice and that the summer hunting grounds can be reached," One-Ear explained and then excitedly pointed towards the shore.

"That is my village!" he said as his smile overcame his entire face.

Seeing his happiness made Maggie happy, but she wasn't sure if this was the best place for her to be. Maggie could see the growing welcoming party as she sat up to get a better look at the village. From a distance, the village appeared much smaller, but as they paddled closer it reminded her of the village at Venango where One-Ear's uncle lived.

Some of the villagers were already in the river, swimming to the canoes and guiding them into the shore. Most of them stayed on the nice-sized landing area that led up to the main buildings. The village covered several acres and had high, spiked posts that surrounded the three sides of that did not face the river.

Maggie could smell the feast that was being prepared in their honor. As they came nearer, she saw five massive fire spits with roasting animals that she could not yet identify.

"Is this all for you One-Ear?" she asked.

"For us," he boasted with a smile, "they thought I had been killed by the Huron. They feel I must be blessed by the gods to have survived; they see me as special."

The canoes were now all being pulled by some of the villagers to avoid the rocks that dotted the shoreline. Before she could get herself up, Maggie was assisted by two villagers and helped over the rocks. They held her hands until they navigated over the slippery rocks and reached the sandy landing.

One-Ear was soon standing beside her, watching the villagers unload all the supplies from the canoes. Their own supplies were put in a hut across from the main long house. The other goods were presented to the gathering elders who stood by the entrance to the village.

Several of the men that had accompanied Maggie and One-Ear laid all the goods by the feet of elders and two of them stepped forward to receive the gifts. They appeared to be satisfied by what the men had brought back to the village and walked slowly back towards the village square. Maggie could see that there were many more French traders than she had expected, and they all stood comfortably amongst the elders. One Frenchman in particular stood whispering in their ears and pointed towards her; she avoided making eye contact and stayed close by One-Ear's side.

Maggie felt an odd sense of uneasiness that made her hesitant to enter the village. One-Ear noticed her uncertainty and whispered, "No reason to fear them, Miss Maggie, we are with friends now."

With a few claps and shouts, the once unorganized mob stepped into place and quickly formed two parallel lines.

Maggie had seen this before.

"Are they going to make us run through them?" Maggie gasped.

"This is just part of the ceremony of welcoming us to their village; I will be running it along with you," One-Ear responded calmly.

The scene, peaceful as it might be, brought back horrific memories to Maggie.

The once roaring and excited village was now silent, waiting. They stood with sticks, canes and anything else they could find to strike the runners.

The elders, along with the numerous Frenchmen, stood by a massive tree trunk that stood ominously in the center of the square.

The gauntlet was ready…

Two villagers approached Maggie and escorted her to the front of the lines. She looked back towards One-Ear and saw that his calm demeanor had changed to one of concern.

Maggie glanced towards the elders and saw the same Frenchman from earlier, again whispering in the ears of the two oldest leaders. When he finished, the two elders shouted at the villagers, who began to unleash a series of hideous cries. Maggie was pushed from behind and stumbled forward. She knew in an instant that this was not what One-Ear had thought would happen. She could hear his shouts, but he was held back by two more villagers.

She regained her balance and took a deep breath, knowing enough that she had to remain on her feet or be swarmed by the stick-wielding villagers. Sprinting as fast as she could, the first two strikes had little effect on her, but the sheer number of strikes soon overwhelmed her and less than half-way through, she fell. The villagers immediately began to swarm her and all she could do was cover her head and attempt to get back to her feet.

Unable to get back on her feet under the intensity of the swarm, Maggie found an outreached hand that she desperately grabbed onto. The hand pulled her up and the man it belonged to used his body to shield her face.

She could now see it was One-Ear and he was kicking and punching at anyone in his way. The line of villagers continued to strike at them and attempted to pull Maggie away from him. The constant strikes suddenly stopped and she finally had a moment to look up to see Wolf-Paw and several of the men forcefully breaking up the now disorganized gauntlet.

Maggie was in a daze but could hear the shouts and screams of the villagers as she maintained a firm hold on One-Ear's hand. One-Ear continued to battle the villagers as he pulled her towards the area where the elders were watching the proceedings carefully. After several long minutes, they stood, along with Wolf-Paw, directly in front of the five elders.

One-Ear stepped forward and showing his displeasure with the treatment they were given, screaming so all could hear, "Is this how we greet friends?"

Maggie just watched struggling to catch her breath as two of the elders stepped forward. The ever-present Frenchman remained beside them, obviously influencing their actions. They appeared undaunted by One-Ear's display of anger.

All Maggie could do was stand behind the two brothers as they stood up to the elders. Wolf-Paw stepped forward and demanded, "I thought we welcomed our people, but it appears we are now like French dogs and bite at all people, friend or foe?"

"Hold your tongue and stand back," one elder said angrily.

Maggie could clearly see the Frenchman smiling behind the elders, relishing in the influence he held over their heads. He appeared not much older than her Jacob, but was much shorter. From where she stood, he looked like he would not even reach her nose. His dirty reddish hair hung well below his deerskin shirt and he wore a breech cloth and leggings made in the style of his Indian friends. He had a light beard and pale skin that had yet to be browned by the hot summer sun. His skin was scarred from an obvious battle with small pox and his eyes appeared to be blue, but the effects of drinking rum with the elders made them look blood-shot and dark. As she looked him over, she felt no reason to fear him physically, but his strong influence over the elders created problems that even One-Ear could not fight.

"We meant no harm to this English woman," the same elder offered, "she is welcome in our village."

"Have the tribes in this land married with the French?" One-Ear remarked, finding it difficult to talk with the Frenchman present. "I understood the Mohawk, Cayuga and Mississauga people were friends with the English."

Before the others could reply, the Frenchman unceremoniously stepped forward saying, "I am Pierre DuPont and it was my fault that this happened. I merely explained to your elders that this is how the other tribes like the Huron and Delaware greet their visitors...especially the English ones. My apologies, madame." With that, he mockingly bowed his head toward Maggie.

She gave him no satisfaction of returning his gesture, instead locking her gaze past him at the elders.

"English prisoners are greeted that way, not visitors," One-Ear angrily replied. "Your English is too good for French trader."

"Well, young one, I spent a few years in an English prison; my English improved greatly under such circumstances," DuPont shot back.

"You didn't spend enough time," Wolf-Paw added.

"Why would a Frenchman be in an English prison when there has been no conflict between the English and French in these lands?" One-Ear pressed the Frenchman.

Before they could continue their argument, an elder spoke, "Enough, we have prepared a feast and will enjoy the company of our new visitors."

Seeing it was useless to speak any further, One-Ear and Maggie left with Wolf-Paw and some of his men.

The villagers, forced to wait during the uncomfortable exchange, moved from the beach towards the center of the village to begin the festivities.

"I am not hungry," Maggie said to One-Ear, while she straightened her clothes and checked herself for blood.

"I am sorry for all of this, Miss Maggie; I don't even know what to say, but it does show that this Frenchman holds too much power over this village." One-Ear was still visibly angry over the reception they had received.

Maggie, One-Ear and Wolf-Paw stood by and watched as the villagers gathered around the cooked animals and started to eat. In addition to slices of meat they cut from the smoking beasts, they indulged in the pots of vegetables and stacks of freshly baked corn bread.

"This was meant for you, brother," Wolf-Paw said sadly, "but these French dogs have moved in and taken great liberties with our elders. It appears they have poisoned many of the villages up and down our river."

"I don't want to insult the village, but I want to leave this place as soon as we can," Maggie said as she watched the Frenchman sitting amongst the elders. "That DuPont will only bring bad things to your village and I don't trust him."

"He married one of the granddaughters of an elder and that placed him in a position of influence. He has taken great advantage of it and has made it too easy for his fellow Frenchmen to come to our village and trade with us. They also make us pay high prices for their goods and give the elder's rum that clouds their minds."

Maggie had no interest in sharing food with these people and remained outside of the main square, observing the goings on. One-Ear remained by her side despite Wolf-Paw's urgings to at least join in some of the festivities. They waited until most of the villagers had slowed down from all the food and dancing, then headed for Wolf-Paw's small home near the far edge of the village. The sun had almost completely set and darkness was spreading into the village as the huge fires started to dissipate.

Maggie walked behind her escorts and in the dim light, she noticed several men standing directly in front of Wolf-Paw's home. The brothers noticed the same and slowed cautiously to see what the men might do.

One-Ear stopped completely and stood directly in front of Maggie to shield her from any possible attack. Wolf-Paw finally noticed that his brother had stopped and did the same. He stood several paces ahead of them.

Maggie could see that One-Ear was nervous and watched him check behind and strain to see the numerous laneways that separated the other houses. She knew they were in a terrible position if they were going to be attacked. Any attacker, with enough men, could easily encircle them using the cover provided from the many structures that led to One-Ear's brothers' home.

A heavily French-accented voice broke the dusky silence, "Do not be alarmed, we mean you no harm."

"I don't like this, Miss Maggie," One-Ear whispered, keeping his eyes focused on the men in front of him, "please stay behind me until I tell you to move. If they decide to fight, run as fast as you can towards the river and stop for nothing."

Maggie was prepared to do exactly what One-Ear said. She saw him ready his musket, which he thankfully had reclaimed from the hut where it had been deposited, despite his brother's insistence to let him take it back to his home. Maggie had followed suit, securing hers to her body after all the confusion of her failed gauntlet run. One-Ear made sure they both had their muskets, just in case such a situation occurred.

"Please, monsieur, we mean you no harm; we just need to speak with you," the same man called out once more.

One-Ear refused to move and kept Maggie behind him. They could see that the men decided to walk towards them. It was soon apparent that there were six Frenchmen, along with a handful of male villagers standing around the other homes.

"Can you see them?" Maggie whispered urgently. "They are all over us; they want to do more than just talk, One-Ear." She knew their options were limited, considering the superior numbers the French had on their side. "We can't fight them all," she added.

"Miss Maggie, please remain behind me," One-Ear said again. "We will see what they want before we make a bad decision. Again, if they attempt anything, just run towards the river and stop for no one. The darkness should cover your escape."

They watched as Wolf-Paw walked towards the Frenchmen and spoke with them. As hard as he tried, One-Ear could not hear any of their conversation. It appeared that the French showed no aggressive behavior towards his brother, but just continued to speak with him.

Deciding not to wait any longer, Maggie felt One-Ear push her back. She quietly stepped back a few paces but was blocked by a large body just as she was starting to turn. A set of hands locked her arms to her sides and covered her mouth. She could smell the odor of the roasted pig that this man had eaten earlier.

She had no time to warn One-Ear, who still stood watching his brother. She could only watch as One-Ear was swarmed by a number of men. He did his best to fight some of them, but their overwhelming strength knocked him down and, with one man on his back, his face was shoved into the ground.

Maggie could hear his shouts, but she was in no position to help him. After he was tied up, she was dragged towards the group standing in front of Wolf-Paw's house.

One-Ear was held down but managed to scream out, "What are you doing, my brothers, have you all gone mad?" A quick punch to the back of his head halted his questions. The blow forced his face back into the ground and bloodied his nose.

He could say nothing else to help Maggie.

The man who continued to grip her arms so tightly presented her to one of the French traders, saying, "Here she is, Mr. Dollard, as per our agreement." His voice was familiar; it was DuPont.

Just as she was taken into custody by several of Dollard's men, One-Ear's brother said to her, "I am sorry, madame, and my brother knew nothing of this, but the riches an Englishwoman could bring to our village in trade was too much to ignore. The French offered us a year's worth of food and supplies that would keep my people alive. We could not let our village suffer just because of my brother's friendship. I hope you understand."

Maggie said nothing and simply looked back at One-Ear's unconscious body that still had blood pooling around his face.

"We must move out; my friends are awaiting your arrival," Dollard said forcefully, then ordered Maggie's arms be bound with a tight leather rope line.

"If you choose to scream, we will be forced to cover up your mouth," he added as she was pulled towards a small back entrance in the village's make-shift palisade. "I will leave that up to you, madame."

She remained silent, fighting back her tears. She refused to give her captors any satisfaction.

Once they cleared the village's outer buildings, the men lit several torches. Maggie was forced to run through an open field, made difficult by the darkness and the rope that kept her secured. Thankfully, the field was relatively level except for a few small rocks.

With the additional light, she counted only four Frenchmen and no more than six Indians. The overshadowed moon and the speed of the men's movements still masked their faces, but she could hear them converse in French, deciding what route to take.

They kept up a hectic pace for several minutes until they reached a small creek. There stood several more Frenchmen waiting on the other side, securely holding four long flat bottom boats.

Without a word, she was pushed into one of the vessels and they were soon moving southward. All the men in her boat remained silent and the swishing of the paddles was the only thing that disturbed the silence of the night.

Slightly dazed and confused by the swiftness of what had just taken place, Maggie could only focus on the image of One-Ear lying still on the blood-stained ground. She prayed he was still alive, though she knew that if he was, he would be devastated by how his brother and the villagers had betrayed him.

Maggie knew they had negotiated a hefty deal for her that would secure the village's prosperity for the coming year, but One-Ear would still feel deceived. His heart would be broken, and the elation he had felt at reuniting with his brother would be crushed.

The boats that the French called bateaux were much more cumbersome than the birch bark canoes she had travelled in. They moved along the shallow creek, scraping the rocky bottom of the creek, which soon began to widen substantially. Maggie watched the boat ahead of her being steered by one of the Frenchmen, standing upright near the back and using an elongated paddle.

Another man used a torch to guide the bateaux around several large rocks and downed trees. She could also see that two of the boats were packed almost waist-high with traded goods. She was amazed at the skill shown by the men who safely steered the loaded boats without crashing them into the high banks.

They soon worked their way out of the shallow creek and veered into a much deeper, faster-moving river. All the bateaux's pulled over to the shore to ensure everything was secured down before they began their much faster-paced journey.

Maggie noticed that the paddlers appeared to be much more relaxed, probably because they had worked hard to distance themselves from any possible pursuers from the village. Once they had reached the more open river, they felt they could outrun any problems they might face.

"Madame, are you alright?" Dollard asked from just behind her.

Sitting there in the dark, wrapped up in her own thoughts, the sudden voice made her jump. "Considering my treatment, I am reasonable, sir," Maggie shot back, displaying her defiance and anger.

"Please," Dollard began by way of explanation, "you will be happy to know that what we traded for you will go a long way to make the village a much more livable place for the inhabitants." Caring little for anyone back at the village except One-Ear, Maggie replied, "And what value to you am I, monsieur?"

"Madame, we gave them 100 blankets, 50 brain-tanned deer skin leggings, 40 pounds of vermillion, two barrels of spices, 25,000 wampum glass beads, 20 barrels of salted pork and venison, 10 barrels of rum and several hundred pounds of powder and shot." She was shocked at what she had brought to the villagers, and had the incongruous thought that it was an excessive amount of payment for a single Englishwoman. Her resolve was diminished slightly, and she asked Dollard, "What are your plans for me now that you traded such a large portion of your supplies?"

"If we follow this river northeast, it will take us to the large lake near the fort at Niagara. My hope is we can parlay you into some Spanish gold. A proper French gentleman should pay a premium for such a beautiful prize." Dollard displayed no emotion while he spoke.

Feeling no better than a fur pelt or a piece of meat that could be traded to the highest bidder, Maggie said nothing. She just closed her eyes and listened to the water being effortlessly cut through by the paddles.

"Madame, I will cut the rope around your wrists to ease your comfort, if you assure me that you will not attempt to escape," Dollard said, trying to soften the situation.

"Sir, I will never give up and simply accept my situation, so therefore I cannot give you my word that I will not at least try to escape," Maggie coldly replied.

Dollard reached around her and sliced the rope close to her skin. The remnants of the rope fell to her feet and she rubbed her wrists and said nothing.

"No matter," Dollard said his frustration with her defiance evident, "any escape would leave you with hundreds of miles of uninhabitable forests to traverse, some never travelled by a white-skinned soul. You would most likely die a slow, horrible death and I would not lose any sleep if you chose that option." Maggie made no reply, but just closed her eyes and took a deep breath.

Chapter | **Eleven**

Jacob remained by Joshua's side the entire march back to the encampment. He held onto his cold hand and listened to his sickly moans that seemed to echo through the forest. He also kept his eyes on Taylor and his sorry lot, who were securely tied up and being escorted by a number of their fellow rangers.

He felt the glares from Taylor and his cronies, but relished the fact that he had given them such a good thrashing. Taylor's right eye was swollen shut and his coat was stained with blood that continued to leak from his broken nose. The others appeared no better and they marched with their heads down, never raising them throughout the trip.

Not concerned much with them, Jacob continuously checked on Joshua's bloodied shoulder, keeping the mass of flies off it and working to make sure no infection set in. He understood that the key was to keep the wound as clean as possible until they got to the fort's doctor, who could clean and dress it properly.

Thankfully, Captain Stevens sent two rangers ahead to inform the doctor of their arrival. The men had returned from their errand with a small munitions cart that cushioned its passenger from the bumpy, uneven trail, which was littered with rocks and roots. Joshua could now stretch out his legs and take some pressure off his shoulder and back.

He slipped in and out of consciousness, calling out, "Jacob, Jacob," several times. Jacob did his best to relieve his suffering, as did Captain Stevens. Stevens poured some rum from his silver flask into Joshua's mouth to help ease his pain.

"God, I hope he can make the rest of the trip," the captain remarked. "The boy has lost a lot of blood and most men would have been dead hours ago. If we can make it back soon, the doctor should fix him up proper."

Seeing him suffer so much, Jacob asked if they could stop the cart so he could take a better look at the wound. He removed the blood-soaked bandage that covered most of his shoulder. After asking a couple of men to help prop up the boy, he checked the shoulder on both sides and tried to move it to check if he had any mobility.

"Captain, I think we need to do something to stop the bleeding. It looks as if the ball went clean through and didn't hit any bone. The best thing would be to burn the wound on both sides to close it up."

"Can the poor boy take that kind of pain?" Stevens asked bluntly, looking directly at Jacob.

"His fever is not breaking and if we wait to get to the fort, I fear it will get infected. We both know he most likely would have no chance to survive after that," Jacob said, unable to make eye contact with his captain.

"You know your son, Sims, so what do you need from us?"

"First, give me your strongest man and some more of your rum. The rum will help clean the wound and numb it enough to limit his pain a touch. Also, the others don't need to watch this; they can get back to the fort and clean up the deer."

"Miller, I need you here to help Sims out," Stevens ordered his men. "Jenkins, take the rest of the men back to the fort, but leave four behind to watch our backs. Sims, I also wish to stay and help your boy if I could be of use." Stevens moved and stood on the other side of Joshua.

Jacob stood by and watched the rest of the men leave. Taylor and his men were escorted as well and as soon as they were all out of sight, the tricky operation commenced.

Picking up a small, thick branch off a nearby tree, Jacob quickly removed the bark and wrapped it in some cloth. He handed it to Captain Stevens and said, "Just before I light the wound, soak this with rum and place it between his teeth please."

Private Miller stood by and waited for Jacob to instruct him on what he wanted him to do.

"Have either of you seen this done before?" Jacob asked the two men, who shook their heads. "Once you get past the initial burn and horrid smell, it is not that bad…for us. Joshua might disagree, but he'll thank us some day." Jacob gave a weak smile in an attempt to lighten the tense situation.

"Well, I can't say I have seen this before, sir, and the way you describe it, I'm not sure I want to see it now," Miller replied, but stepped closer to the cart to await his orders.

Jacob nodded and said, "Mr. Miller, try to hold him down with all your weight. This is going to be painful and the less he moves the better."

"I have seen a man do it on his own leg once, but he…" Stevens said, but caught himself before he continued.

Jacob could see that Joshua was relatively calm and a fresh band of sweat lightly beaded on his forehead. He slowly started to remove the light bandage he had left on the wound and gently cut off the bloodied sleeve from around Joshua's arm.

"Mr. Miller, please get up on the cart and get behind Joshua. I need you to hold him up and give him the tightest bear hug you can. Keep your head on his other shoulder to protect yourself from any stray sparks."

Miller climbed up on the cart and pinned Joshua against his chest. Once he was comfortable he gave Jacob a nervous nod.

"Captain," Jacob said, turning to Stevens, "please soak the cloth and see if Joshua will take a good swallow of your rum. Will you also be kind enough to lend me your pistol and be ready to quickly take it from me and hand it back when I need it?"

With a weak whimper, Joshua took a bit of rum. He coughed most of it up, but Jacob hoped it was enough to deaden some of the pain. He would have liked to explain what he was going to do, but it honestly wouldn't matter much to Joshua now.

"This will have to be quick; expect him to scream, maybe even fight, but please do your best to hold him," Jacob warned the men while he checked over the entry and exit wound.

After splashing the entry wound with some rum, Jacob readied himself. He slowly dipped the spout of his powder horn into the wound and poured as much black powder in as he could manage. He then called out, "Your pistol, Captain, and please stand back."

"Here we go, Miller," Jacob said as he angled the flint onto the wound.

The pistol's hammer smashed down and a large spark hit the wound and ignited the powder. Smoke blinded the men and filled the forest with the salty smell of powder and the sick odor of Joshua's burning flesh.

Joshua jerked but made no sound. Miller hugged the boy closely while the powder seared his wound and turned the skin around it a deep black.

The odor of burnt flesh hit Jacob hard as it flooded him with memories of the stench of the burning at Fort Necessity. He turned his head and attempted to cover his nose.

Without hesitation, once the smoke cleared, Jacob asked Miller to turn Joshua's limp body around to expose the exit wound and asked Stevens to make sure the flint in his pistol was still in good condition. There was no time even to check the effectiveness of the first part of the operation.

"He's limp, sir," Private Miller said as he kept Joshua's body propped up to expose the exit wound, "I hope to God the poor lad makes it through all this pain."

"If we don't finish the job, he certainly will not," Jacob replied. "You are doing a fine job, Miller; just keep my boy steady once again."

Joshua was now sweating profusely and now Jacob could see that the exit wound appeared much larger than the front wound. He would have to use much more powder and that added to the risk. Jacob's only fear was that it might take several attempts to close the wound, causing too much trauma for the weakening boy.

Jacob held a full horn and began to pour in the powder, but stopped short of completely filling the wound. He worried that using too much powder might cause the blast to reopen the entry wound.

Stevens handed his pistol to Jacob and, much like before, the flint struck the hammer and the powder ignited. With the larger amount of powder, the smoke cloud was much thicker and Miller struggled not to cough and move the boy too much.

The smoke dispersed quickly and they were given a good view of the wound. Luckily, it appeared the powder had done its job and the hole was fully cauterized. For the moment, a second attempt appeared unnecessary.

Jacob poured his entire water canteen over the wounds to cool them. His skin made a sickly crackling sound and the men turned away quickly, their stomachs churning.

"Good lad," Miller said as he stroked Joshua's hair, still hugging him tightly.

"Hold him up the best you can, Mr. Miller, if you please," Jacob said. "We need to give his wounds one more check before we move him. You did a great job and I am in your debt." Miller smiled at the kind words.

Jacob and Stevens examined the wounds carefully. Both appeared to be closed and no blood was seeping through. It was now up to the doctor to dress the wounds and see if their efforts had worked.

Jacob knew that once the powder burns cooled and the blackened skin could be cleaned, Joshua would have a better chance to move on from all of this pain.

"You there," a grizzled old voice echoed behind them, "what are you doing to that poor lad, and what in God's name is that ghastly stench? It can be smelled all the way back to the camp!"

The men spun around to see who had spoken. It was the fort's doctor, who had trekked into the forest to find them when they hadn't returned immediately following their messenger. Jacob made no reply, but looked at the doctor expectantly.

"Back away now and let me see this poor lad," Dr. Wilson demanded gruffly. "I hope you didn't kill him with your wilderness sorcery."

Wilson was not as old as his voice suggested; he was actually only in his late thirties and a veteran of the wars in Europe. He was Major General Braddock's long-time personal physician and made no effort to hide his dislike of his newest posting here at Fort Cumberland. He was a rather short, thin man and Jacob's first thought was that he looked like he should be in the infirmary along with the other sick and wounded.

Jacob towered over the considerably smaller man and watched every move he made as he checked over Joshua's wound. Miller maintained his grip on Joshua and simply nodded a greeting towards the doctor.

"The poor lad," Wilson began quietly, "you men did a good job stopping the wound from bleeding him out. Certainly not my first choice of how to handle this type of wound, but very effective. How is the boy doing?"

Captain Stevens stepped forward and replied, "This is the lad's father, John Sims, and he was the one who did the fine work. The private and I just assisted."

"You most likely saved the lad," the doctor replied in a more positive tone, "although I will have to get him back to the fort to give him a closer check. He does have a slight fever, but we should be able to control that. Now let's get him back and clean him up."

Jacob was relieved by the doctor's hopeful words. He understood that infection was now the biggest enemy. Having once seeing a neighbor die from a small, insignificant cut on his finger, he knew they needed to get Joshua to the fort immediately. All that was left was to pray and remain by his side.

The two other men had also found hope and relief in the doctor's words. Stevens, Jacob and the doctor walked beside the cart as it was pushed back up the trail, and Miller remained holding Joshua against his chest, cushioning him from the bumps in the trail.

"Thank you gentlemen for all your kindness to my boy," Jacob said. "I will never forget it."

"No need for thanks," Miller replied and Miller nodded in agreement. "As rangers, we must always remain together and never leave one of our own behind."

The short trek back to the fort felt like it took hours. Jacob was the first to step from the thick forest wall and was astonished to see the swollen number of men within the encampment. There was certainly double the amount of men and artillery that had been there earlier in the day. Now they pressed the camp to the edge of the woods and pushed most of the companies closer together. Jacob saw a mosaic of colors as the call-to-arms had brought militia from as far south as the Carolinas. The green ranger uniforms were mixed with the red-coated Grenadiers, and both were interspersed with browns and blues of the other companies. The British regulars tried to keep themselves separated from the colonials, but the lack of room presented them with little choice but to pitch their white tents side by side.

Once the rest of the men with Jacob and Joshua had cleared the forest, Captain Stevens dismissed himself to tend to his duties. Private Miller carried Joshua from the cart to the doctor's cabin and Jacob followed right behind him. After the younger man placed Joshua on the only available cot in the congested room, the two rangers shook hands and Miller excused himself to get back with the others.

"Go to your mates," Dr. Wilson suggested without looking up as he started to clean the dressing on Joshua's wound. "The boy will be out for some time and if you want, you can come by later to check on him."

"Thank you for all your help; I will come back tonight," Jacob replied, leaving Joshua in the doctor's capable hands and heading back to the rangers' encampment.

Stevens' rangers had taken up a spot just to the left of the main gate, bordering the parade ground where the colonial militia and some newly recruited British regulars were constantly being drilled. With the number of soldiers increasing every day, the ranger camp had become far less sprawling and sat directly in front of a company of British regulars.

Jacob counted roughly thirty white canvas tents surrounding the much larger officers' tents that sat in the middle of the ranger camp. The largest tent, Jacob assumed, had to be Stevens'. It was guarded by a brown-shirted soldier who abruptly stopped Jacob before he approached any further.

"What do you want, you sorry lookin' mutt?" a thick Scottish accent barked as the guard held out a massive forearm to halt Jacob from getting any nearer.

"I am reporting to Captain Stevens," Jacob said, now standing face-to-face with the soldier and refusing to back down.

"Are you now?" the soldier replied, spitting a brown stream of tobacco juice just beyond Jacob's foot. "And who the bloody hell are you to be requesting a visit with the fine Captain?"

"I am certain I don't have to answer to you, or are you the captain's ears?" Jacob barked.

"Aye, we have a trouble maker amongst us now. I suppose you are the one who got my good friend Mr. Taylor in trouble and landed him in the captain's bad graces." The guard held his ground, still blocking the tent's entrance.

"I'm sure Taylor has never been in his good graces, and you should really think about getting some new friends."

Just then, the white flap of the tent flew open and the irritated voice of Captain Stevens shouted, "What is all this noise out here?"

"Beg your pardon, sir, but this woodsman wants to bother you and…"

"Stand down, Private McDonald," the captain interrupted, "I was expecting Mr. Sims, so let him pass before I have you join your friend Mr. Taylor."

"My apologies, sir," he said meekly.

As Jacob passed the red-faced private, he mockingly tipped his hat, saying, "Thank you, private."

McDonald sneered and spat another long stream of tobacco juice, this time towards a small dog quietly chewing on a leftover deer bone.

Jacob closed the flap and was directed to take a seat.

"Now, Sims, how is your boy holding up?" Stevens asked, lighting his pipe and offering some tobacco to his guest.

Declining the offer, Jacob said, "The doctor has him now and I expect he should be fine. Sore for a while, but fine all the same."

"That is good news, indeed. He seems like a very strong young man.

"Now, I know you are new within the ranks, but I saw and heard the men speak of your proficiency with your musket. The Major General wants to get the boys moving and we need to send out some advanced guards to be our eyes to protect the axe man from any savages milling about."

Jacob made no reply. He could never just leave Joshua behind.

Stevens noticed his hesitation and continued, "With all the issues with supplies and such, this army is a mess, but we still need to get moving. I really need a man like you to be my eyes. You know these parts and if you can somehow help this operation move forward steadily, we might just make bloody Fort Duquesne by summer's end."

"What about Joshua?" Jacob asked.

Stevens paused a moment before saying, "He is in good hands and there is nothing we can do for him now. I promise, once he is cleared by the doctor, I will send him forward to you."

Jacob truly did not like the idea of leaving Joshua behind, but leading a small scouting party would certainly go far towards possibly re-instating his standing in the army. He agreed that there was nothing he could do for Joshua at the moment and with Stevens' word that the boy would be sent forward once he recovered, he felt a little better.

"I'll scout for you, captain," he began, "but I honestly hate to leave my boy behind. When would you want me to leave?" Jacob said.

"You can rest tonight but I need you out before dawn. I have assigned four men to you and raised you to the rank of corporal, just to keep the others in line."

Jacob had hoped he would have had a few days to prepare and keep an eye on Joshua. Before he dismissed himself to ready his gear, he asked, "Can I make two requests, sir?"

Captain Stevens clearly wanted to finish this conversation and get back to other business, but he nodded, saying, "No promises, but speak your mind."

"Can I have Private Miller assigned to me, and can I get myself a proper long rifle? I hate this musket and am much more comfortable with a rifle."

"Private Miller has already been assigned to your group and you can certainly trade that musket for a rifle, if they have one," he said as he handed Jacob a small piece of parchment. "The English love their regulation musket and have little use for your long rifle, but take this signature to the quartermaster inside the fort and he will take care of you. Now if that is all, you need to get on your way."

Jacob offered a salute and stepped out of the tent into the light of the camp. McDonald greeted him with a smirk and spat some tobacco into the grass.

The sun was almost behind the ridges and that meant Jacob had only a few hours to gather some gear and get himself back out on the trail.

Ignoring the guard, Jacob immediately went off to find the quartermaster's post. The interior of the fort was just as active as the outer field. Red-coated soldiers, merchants and civilians were busily preparing for Braddock's long march to Fort Duquesne.

Jacob worked his way around the chaos and noticed a young girl washing some undershirts in a large soapy bucket. He paused before saying, "Excuse me Miss, could you direct me to the quartermaster's office?"

Without bothering to look up and still maintaining her brisk rhythm on the scrub board with one hand, she pointed to the far corner of the fort and said, "He should be there, sir."

"Thank you kindly, miss," Jacob replied and worked his way towards the office.

After knocking politely, Jacob stepped into a dark, musty space that most likely had been an old storage room before the need had arisen for a more formal quartermaster's office.

"Come in, lad; what do you want?" snapped a stern yet friendly voice from the shadows.

Jacob could barely make out a plump figure sitting in the dim light, working at a small desk piled with papers and books. "I was sent by Captain Stevens to retrieve some supplies for me and my men, sir," Jacob explained as he handed the man his captain's note.

"What is it you need? My supplies are limited and the English have tightened my inventory to only the bare necessities." He glanced briefly at the slip of paper and added it to the mountain on his desk.

"I need a rifle, preferably a long rifle, and whatever else the Captain had on that list," Jacob replied.

"A rifle? You know, those are difficult to find, and the English-made muskets I was sent are not worth the wood pile they were made from." The gentleman grimaced and put on a pair of wire glasses to take a better look at the note.

"I do happen to have a couple of locally-made rifles," he continued, "but most of these thugs don't appreciate real craftsmanship or accuracy. Most of the British prefer the damn Brown Bess musket; only God knows why. They might as well just shoot and pray the ball hits something instead of taking the trouble to aim." He chuckled lightly to himself.

Jacob was amused by the quartermaster. He was balding on the top of his head and the pair of round glasses he wore sat perched on the tip of his nose. His hair was neatly tied behind his head with a black silk bow. He carried himself as a man of some means and his nicely tailored pants and coat did give him an air of importance.

"Your rifles, are they made in Pennsylvania?" Jacob asked.

The man sneered, anticipating Jacob to make a disparaging remark about their quality, "Yes, lad, from right here in the Pennsylvania territory."

"I'll be happy to take them both, if I may," Jacob responded quickly. "Do you know exactly where they were made by chance?"

The man's demeanor changed as he saw that Jacob obviously appreciated the quality and craftsmanship of a Pennsylvania long rifle. "Sir, are you a Pennsylvania man?" he asked.

Jacob smiled and nodded.

The man held out his hand and said, "My name is Benjamin Franklin, Ben to my friends."

"My name is John Sims and I'm from the area around Butler Creek," Jacob said as he gripped Franklin's hand.

"Aye, I thought you had a slight Pennsylvanian accent. I have some family who lived around that area, but it is pretty much the edge of the frontier and I hear it's a tough place to live. You are welcome to the two rifles. I would rather give them to a fellow like you who values their accuracy and fine workmanship."

"Your name is familiar," Jacob said as he watched the quartermaster pull down the rifles from the top shelf behind his desk. "I thought you were the Post Master in these parts; how did you get yourself involved in all this mess?"

"I serve the King, and if he requests my services here, so be it. Braddock was having issues dealing with our fine Quaker neighbors and I was called in to broker some deals for horses and wagons. Take along these two full shot bags and two fine powder horns for your travels. I'll find you some ball molds and some other supplies to keep the rifles cleaned and ready."

"You are too kind, sir, and your help is much appreciated," Jacob smiled.

Franklin continued to check through several large crates and some smaller baskets that were spread around the floor. "The note also said you need a change of clothes and I do happen to have some breeches and shirts, but you are a big lad and I'm not sure I have anything that fits."

"It is no bother, sir; I will take whatever you have."

"We Pennsylvanians need to take care of each other because the bloody English think we are all Quakers and afraid to fight," the quartermaster said as he hurriedly filled a large canvas backpack with a variety of goods. "By the way, how did you find yourself with Stevens' Virginians?"

"Actually, it was all pretty easy," Jacob replied as he tried on a few green coats for sizing. "My son and I simply came to the fort and joined up."

"Your son? Where is he off to then?"

"He is under the care of the doctor after an unfortunate hunting accident," Jacob said quietly.

"Sorry to hear that. I hope he gets well soon. Here are your rifles and supplies, and it appears you found yourself a coat. Feel free to pick up a pair of boots on your way out."

"Thank you, sir, for everything; keep yourself well," Jacob said shaking Mr. Franklin's hand once more. As he grabbed a pair of boots and put them into his bulging sack, the quartermaster pulled down a ledger and entered this latest order into his records.

Jacob decided that the doctor had more than enough time to check Joshua over. It had been most of the day and he had only a few hours left before he needed to leave.

It was much darker around the camp with most of the small fires now just smoldering down to ashes, as Jacob managed to work his way into the fort, passed two sleeping guards and into the ever-expanding hospital.

"How are you feeling lad?" Jacob asked as Joshua sat himself up. "You look so much better than the last time I saw you!"

"Better, much better considering everything, and the doctor said I should be up on my feet in a week or so," Joshua said as he rubbed his shoulder and showed Jacob that he could lift his arm without too much pain.

It was clear to Jacob that he was attempting to put on a brave face but every small movement made him wince.

"I picked you up a nice rifle and some gear, so when you are ready to move out you can catch up with my unit."

"Catch up? You have yourself a unit already? That is good for you, what will become of me when you are gone?" Joshua seemed most concerned that he might miss out on a fight by being left behind.

"Captain Stevens asked me to head out at first light and do some advanced scouting for his company. He assured me that once you are healthy enough to move, you will be assigned to my unit. I am sorry to leave you, but he needs me to be the eyes for the army and guard the axe men who will be widening the trail for the wagons and supplies." Jacob felt tremendous guilt for leaving Joshua behind. The boy had always been right there for him when things got really rough. "I'll catch up to you in a week or so," Joshua said determinedly. "I have heard from a few of the sick regulars in here that Braddock wants to leave immediately. They have already been delayed by a month or so and he fears the men might become undisciplined and lazy. My only request is that you leave me a few Frenchmen to kill."

Joshua's smile alleviated some of Jacob's guilt. He could tell that it would not be too long before he was on his feet and scouting beside him once more.

"Is there anything you need from me before I leave?"

"I'm fine," Joshua said, smiling once more and shaking Jacob's outstretched hand, "just please don't get too far ahead of me."

The morning came fast and was greeted by a nearby pack of wolves howling at each other, along with a thick layer of dew that soaked anything left on the ground.

Jacob struggled to get himself up and rushed to the trailhead that would take him north towards Fort Duquesne. He could see Private Miller standing and waiting with three other men, who all appeared strong, healthy and eager to leave.

"I am Corporal John Sims," Jacob introduced himself confidently, offering Miller a friendly nod.

Miller stepped forward and saluted, "Sir, if I may, these are Privates Cullen, White and Sinclair and we are all ready to get moving."

"Thank you, Miller; Captain Stevens needs us to scout ahead to watch for any signs of savages or the French, and keep the trail clear of potential problems that might slow down the main army. We also have to provide some protection for the work details who will be widening the trail and have a terrible job ahead of them, cutting down trees and removing as many roots and rocks as they can. God knows, I am glad they are doing it and not me; it is certainly a thankless job."

Jacob was also eager to move out and was impressed by the looks of the men. Captain Stevens had certainly not unloaded the worst of the lot on him, and they appeared to be experienced in traversing these woods.

"My only requests are that you remain in single file just in case we are ambushed; a single shot could kill two of us if we are side-by-side. Also, we need to keep our voices down; our best weapon will be that the French and Huron never hear us coming or, better yet, have no clue that we are even out here. The Captain promised that we will have more men sent out to join us, but he had to wait to find out what Braddock's plans are for the march."

Satisfied he would not have to worry too much about these men, Jacob signaled them to head out and took up a position at the rear so he could get a better look at them in action. Private Cullen couldn't have been more than twenty, but he was tall and well-built. Jacob noticed that he had the hardened and calloused hands of a farmer and didn't appear to be afraid of hard work. White had a distinctive scar on the left side of his face that ran from his eyebrow to the corner of his mouth. He had the face of a fighter and that impressed Jacob. Sinclair had the thick, muscular forearms of a blacksmith and a smile that only the devil would appreciate. He was even younger than the others, but Jacob was glad they were on the same side of this fight.

The men were soon far from the coziness of the fort as they hiked steadily deeper into the wilderness. Once they were well down the main trail, Jacob took up his position in the lead of the small unit and had Private Miller take the rear.

Jacob signaled the men to stop for a moment and whispered, "I don't want to use the main trail. I know of a few old Delaware paths that will give us a decent view of the entire trail system."

After several hours of intense, non-stop trekking through tough terrain and throngs of the ever-present biting insects, they could hear the axes of the work crews just off to their right.

The scouting unit had seen nothing of interest during its trek and Jacob didn't want to get too far ahead of the engineering crews. He decided they should stop for the night and find a good spot to rest. He had no reason to inform the work crew that they were around and thought it would be a good way for his men to practice 'seeing but not being seen' by their enemies.

Jacob had sent Private White ahead to scout out some good terrain to set up a small camp. He soon returned to report back to Jacob. Keeping his voice down he said, "Sir, just up a ways is a small river; not sure where it goes, but it has some nice river trout in it. They are rather a fine fish to cook up on an open fire. The spot is flat and easy to defend if we had to."

"Sounds good; take Sinclair and ready the camp and we will be up shortly," Jacob ordered and watched the two men run up the trail.

"If you run into any trouble, get your tails back to us…understand?" he quietly called out and saw White wave back to acknowledge they heard the order.

Taking their time to reach the camp, the three rangers fanned out to check the area for any signs of the Delaware, Huron or possibly the French. Jacob had seen nothing to indicate that they had any reason to fear they might be attacked, yet he was worried that they had not seen any signs of the usual native population hunting or scouring around the woods.

The three met close to the place White had reported and they could smell the fire the men had set up, awaiting the arrival of the others. Jacob walked into the small clearing that sat right on the shore of a nice river and saw that the two had dragged a couple of fallen trees and placed them by the fire pit. He noticed that Sinclair was busy covering the second of two good-sized lean-tos with tree bark and White was already trying to catch some fish in the shallow river.

Already impressed by their skills, he was further thrilled when he saw White walk out of the water with five over-sized river trout dangling from a rope he had tied to a small branch.

"If we only had some pepper," Private White laughed and offered the others a sly grin.

"You boys did well; we will most likely be eating better than the others back at the fort tonight," Jacob said proudly. He encouraged the men to enjoy the feast, because there would probably not be many warm fires and good meals as they moved closer to Fort Duquesne.

He was adamant in his instructions to the men that one of them had to be on guard duty at all times. Each guard would have to stay alert and keep the fire going while the others tried to get a few hours of rest. There was still no reason to fear an attack, but Jacob knew that it was imperative that the men get themselves into a routine and used to being aware of their surroundings at all times.

The morning once again came too early and Jacob had taken the last watch to ensure that his men had gotten some good rest for the long trek ahead of them. He spent some of his time gathering up chestnuts and wild berries. He ground them between a couple of stones and had a nice pot of boiling water to make some tea for the men when they woke up.

The men were up as soon as the tea brew's aroma waffled around the small camp.

"My mother used to make a batch like this every so often, but we usually used it to seal holes in the outside walls of our cabin," Private Miller said as he stretched and cleared his eyes before he took a cup of the tea offered by Jacob.

"It makes a fine shoe polish as well," Jacob added with a smile as the others took their cups and slowly sipped the bitter brew.

He reached into his backpack and pulled out a small loaf of cornbread wrapped in a piece of cloth, a gift from the quartermaster. Jacob broke off a piece and tossed the remaining loaf to the still-laughing Miller, saying "This should hide some of the taste."

Jacob felt pretty good, much like he had during his earlier stint in Washington's militia. He loved the freedom of scouting and he understood the vital role it played in an army's advancement. He had heard from some of the men that Braddock did not see the importance of advanced scouts and had fought with his officers regarding the worth of sending out even a single unit to locate the enemy.

Standing by the river, watching it flow towards the south, brought back memories of the creek that ran by his homestead. His mind wandered, thinking about everything that he had lost and hoping Maggie and the kids were somehow still alive. It was the thought of once again being together that kept him going.

Returning to his current situation, he walked back to the men who were cleaning up the camp and getting their gear ready.

"Gentlemen," Jacob addressed his unit, "we should think about lightening our loads and carrying only what is essential. We have a lot of ground to cover and we don't want to be slowed down by heavy packs. Also, the trails ahead are narrower and we need to be careful not to have anything loose that can be snagged on a tree branch or the endless bushes that choke the woods." As he spoke, he emptied his pack and strapped on his powder horn and a small leather bag that held his pre-molded lead balls. He re-packed a few small pieces of cornbread, some dried pork and some extra flints in a smaller haversack that he flung over his other shoulder. A small sheathed knife was tied around his calf and he put another, larger one around his neck.

Before they headed out, he had the men clean and check over their weapons, not wanting any issues once they were out on the trail. As was typical of the colonial militia and ranging companies attached to the British army, these men had brought along their own rifles or muskets. The result was that each man was very proficient with his own gun, but each man was carrying a weapon of a different caliber or accuracy. Jacob noticed that Miller had a shorter musket that looked like he had cut some of the barrel down. White had an old squirrel gun with which, Jacob was told, he could hit anything within seventy paces. The others used guns that looked to be German-made and they appeared to be in good working order.

"Rub some mud on your barrels and any other metal on your weapons," Miller said as he picked up a handful of wet mud from the river's edge. "We don't need the savages to see us coming by the sun reflecting off the metal."

Jacob finally dressed in his green ranger coat and put on a matching green Scottish cap that was adorned with a nice piece of bear pelt sewn into the side. He was proud to wear such a nice uniform and liked how it merged so nicely with the surrounding, thick-forested wilderness. It was far better suited for this landscape than the bright red coats the British regulars wore, which could be seen for miles. Jacob kept his well-worn deerskin moccasins, but added a matching pair of green, thigh-high leggings that covered part of his new soft deerskin breeches. He felt oddly excited as he stood there in his completed ensemble, and even received a couple of mocking whistles from his men.

The others wore a more informal mix and matched uniform, but they were all dressed to blend onto the surroundings, far from the red preferred by the British regulars.

While they were preparing to head back out, Miller unexpectedly asked, "So, sir, where are we headed?"

Jacob had wrongly assumed Captain Stevens had informed the men of their scouting mission and was quick to answer Miller's question, "My apologies, lads, I thought the captain had mentioned to all of you where we were going. The plan is to scout the area as far as Fort Duquesne, then report back."

Once the men had safely stored away their unnecessary equipment and food high in the trees, far out of reach of any animals or the enemy, they headed back towards the work detail that had been making noise since they all got up. White was left to cover up any signs they had stayed the night, spreading sand and dirt over the fire and tossing the fallen tree trunks back into the forest.

"We'll double-back southward and catch up with the lads clearing the trail. From there, we'll split up; Miller and I will head north along the main trail to see if we can find any signs of savages milling about. The rest of you can make sure no one bothers the crew as they work." When Jacob finished speaking, he signaled the men to move out and they resumed their single-file line, spaced several paces apart.

They took their time to reach the work detail and were surprised by how little progress had actually been made on the trail since the men had begun. They were still only a mile or so from the fort and it had become evident that widening this old trail was backbreaking work, even for the seasoned Welsh axe men. They were forced to cut hundreds of trees and dig up the same amount of stumps that littered the path. It was time-consuming and tedious work that proved to be overwhelming for most of the detail.

Even a surprise visit the previous morning from Braddock himself hadn't spurred the men to move any more quickly. Jacob was told by the corporal in charge of the work detail that the Major General had appeared upset with the slow advancement. He even sent a whole company of colonial militia to assist with the work.

Despite the small amount of progress the men had accomplished, Jacob was impressed with the work they had done so far. This was once a narrow, albeit well-travelled pathway, and now it was three feet wider on each side. It could now accommodate eight men abreast or the hundreds of wagons that would be pulling supplies, cannon and the officers' personal items.

Jacob privately questioned Braddock's insistence of bringing along any form of artillery, be it cannon or mortars. Even with the trail cleared, the dense, suffocating forest would restrict any possible usefulness or advantage they might bring.

Learning very quickly that Braddock was not a man who took any suggestions well, the colonial and ranging troops had already begun rumbling about being led into another disaster. Jacob had heard some of these complaints from some of his own boys during dinner the previous night and tried to assure them that they would be the victors in any battle with the French. White was one of the loudest of the men to question some of the tactics being utilized by the British and knew that all the drilling and discipline would not prepare them for fighting in the wilderness.

Jacob had a hard time disputing some of their concerns, especially since he had firsthand experience with how British battle strategy failed in the forest.

After checking in with work crew's head officer and giving orders to his own men to keep a base camp nearby and report any findings to Captain Stevens, Jacob and Miller departed to scout towards the Forks.

They made excellent time and moved off the main trail to use the smaller, less-travelled side paths. When they had covered almost twenty miles and they were still a hundred plus miles from Fort Duquesne, Jacob realized that the mere distance they would have to cover would be close to impossible with such a large force.

They pressed on until they reached the outskirts of the destroyed Fort Necessity and, after covering the high ridges and swampy landscape that slowed them down repeatedly, Jacob suggested they find a place to spend the night and head back towards the work crew in the morning.

"We should rest. I know of a few safe places off trail in the rocky ridges that should give us some good cover. I thought we would cover more ground today, but the distance is far greater than I remembered. God knows how Braddock will get his entire army over the mountains and close enough to the French and still be in any shape to launch an attack."

He noticed the remnants of the place Washington had stopped and camped with his surviving troops after his surrender at the Great Meadows. They had certainly cared little about leaving behind several tents and endless supplies that had since been picked through, most likely by the Delaware and Seneca.

Jacob still could not get the image of an injured Israel, packed in with the hordes of the other injured men being burnt alive by drunken savages and their French allies. Their screams and desperate pleads haunted him to his day. He dearly missed his brother and longed for the days when they would hunt for hours or just trek through the backwoods without a care or concern.

Back to the task at hand, they soon found a good spot. It was nicely elevated above the main trail, and they both quickly cleared the area of loose branches and rocks. They piled leaves and moss for bedding and soon were lying across from each other eating some of the dried meat and corn bread that they both had packed.

Breaking the silence, Miller said, "Do you find it odd that we have seen neither hide nor hair of a single Delaware or Seneca since we left?"

"Funny, I was thinking the same," Jacob replied. "We have not even seen an old camp or markings on any trees."

Both men were extremely tired and they decided there was no need to have of one of them on watch through the night. Jacob had decided that they should not light a fire and both he and Miller set up several traps around the camp to at least warn them in case of an ambush.

Jacob had a reasonably good sleep considering the makeshift beds they each slept in were not overly comfortable. In the early morning, his sleep was interrupted by some noise from the main trail below.

He crawled to the edge of the ledge where they slept and squinted, attempting to get a better view of what was making the still muffled noise. He got a brief glimpse of four silhouetted figures that were still mostly concealed by the dawn mist. Their voices were now getting louder and Jacob could make out that there were at least two Frenchmen and possibly a couple of Indians.

After sliding slowly up next to Miller and nudging him awake, he signaled him to stay quiet. He pointed towards the lower trail and put four fingers up; Miller nodded and grabbed his musket. He moved closer to Jacob to see what was happening. "What did you see, sir?" Miller mouthed.

Jacob again pointed down and he saw that Miller could now see the four figures. Thankfully, the two men sat in a fairly good position, but they had no idea how many more could be lurking around them.

Keeping his eyes on the four men, Jacob sat and debated what move, if any, they should make. He wasn't one to wait too long and he would rather try to outrun the enemy than sit around waiting to be caught. If they were discovered, they could easily be pinned down and, if there were any other Frenchmen around, Jacob knew he and Miller would make easy targets.

Jacob whispered to Miller, "We need to get out of here; I think if we move slowly down the far ridge we might be able to work our way past them."

Miller agreed and they remained down and lowered themselves down the rocks that had provided them such good security through the night.

Their position was hidden from the view of the intruders and they were able to work their way down to the side trail fairly easily. They were careful not to make too much noise and soon, they could clearly hear the voices of the men.

Jacob could make out their conversation in French, and the men seemed to be arguing about what they should do next. Two of the men wanted to head back and were worried they had wandered too far away from their fort and likely run into the English. The two others, who Jacob guessed were Huron scouts, wanted to keep moving south and see for themselves the rumored massive English army.

The two Frenchmen were pretty adamant that they should head back and told the two scouts that they were welcome to continue on without them.

"Miller, you stay on this side; I'm going to work my way around closer to see exactly what we are dealing with." Jacob said quietly, not waiting for a response from Miller.

Jacob slowly stood up and stepped into the security of the trees. He had only moved a few paces before he got his first clear view of the still arguing men. There were definitely two French regulars along with two Huron scouts standing in a small clearing, apparently not concerned with being ambushed.

Jacob could also still see Miller, who remained down and watching what Jacob was doing. He signaled to him to stay hidden and wait until he came back.

He wished that Miller was by his side, but with the four men in clear view, any movement would be easily seen by them and Jacob would have no way to escape. Jacob's immediate concern was the very real possibility that there might be more than four of these men around the area.

After a few long minutes, Jacob could see that the Frenchmen finally decided to remain with the two Huron scouts and head southward, but that they let the Huron lead the way. As they began to move, Jacob saw one of the scouts point towards the trail where Miller was hiding.

Jacob held his breath as the two scouts walked towards Miller and luckily passed by him unaware that he sat almost a breath away from them. The Frenchmen followed up from behind and much like their Huron allies, walked past without noticing him.

They both waited several more minutes to make sure the men were not going to double-back and take them from behind.

"That was bloody close," Miller smiled, "I could smell the cheap rum on them."

"I think we should follow them, but from the far side trail. It will still give us a good view of them and we can see how far they intend to scout." Jacob said as they both moved forward and made the cut towards the much smaller trail to the east.

Observing every step, Jacob could see that the Frenchmen remained trying to convince the two scouts to turn back and head towards Fort Duquesne. The Huron still would have nothing to do with their suggestion and continued on. The Frenchmen knew not to fight with them and half-heartedly followed them.

Jacob assumed that the Huron were aware that they were being watched, especially since they reacted to every noise and the slightest movement of the branches caused from a squirrel or raccoon. He also knew they most likely were not as familiar with this area and that might have made them nervous and overly cautious. Either way, he knew enough about the Huron to fear and respect them at all times.

Worried that they might be getting too close to the advanced work crews who were in charge of moving ahead of the main crews to mark the trees that needed to be removed and survey the best route forward. Jacob and Miller decided to work their way around the scouting party and get between them and the crews. Jacob's hope was that, with the Frenchmen still complaining and the fact they had not seen any signs of the English, the Huron might give up and agree to return home.

It took about an hour for Jacob and Miller to get far enough ahead of the party that they felt there was enough room between them and the work crews. Jacob felt they now could talk and decide what they should do.

"I was thinking it might be a good idea for you to run back to the main work detail and get the other men to even up the numbers for us," Jacob suggested, as Miller took a much needed drink from a small stream that cut near where they were kneeling down.

"Beg your pardon, sir, but I think we would be better off if we stayed together. Two rangers against this scouting party seems like pretty even numbers to me." Miller smiled and looked up the trail for any signs of movement.

"The Huron are not as familiar with this territory," Jacob responded, "and it appears they are being extremely careful moving around the trail. Thankfully, they most likely have no idea about most of the side paths and, if we stick with them, we should be in a strong position to defend, if need be." Jacob replied and stopped as he heard voices to their left.

Soon they could again hear the two Frenchmen arguing with their Huron counterparts and becoming more insistent that they needed to head back. The Huron were pointing towards the trail and trying to convince the others that they must keep moving. Jacob could not hear the two Huron speaking and thought that with the scouting party's hesitation, it might be a good time to move.

With Miller still right by his side, Jacob whispered, "If you don't feel comfortable about leaving me, I think we should both run back to the work crews to get more men and come back to scare off these trouble-some scouts."

Miller agreed and waited for Jacob's signal to run.

Jacob could still hear the group discussing what they should do next, and he pointed to Miller to get up and slowly back away from their position. Jacob backed up as well then, on his command, they both turned and sprinted as fast as their legs could carry them towards the open side trail.

Running all out, Jacob finally slowed to catch his breath just as Miller fell awkwardly to the ground. Simply thinking he was exhausted, Jacob called out to him and offered him his hand. When he got no response, he pulled the younger man over onto his side and noticed a deep crimson pool of blood oozing from a gaping hole by his ribcage.

Miller was dead.

Turning just in time to see the two Huron scouts charging towards him at full speed with their war clubs raised, Jacob reacted quickly.

As he crouched low on the trail, he cocked back his loaded rifle, then hastily aimed and fired. A thick cloud of smoke engulfed and choked the small path. Jacob was temporarily blinded by the salty aftermath of his shot, but he heard one of the Huron scream.

He stood up quickly as the smoke cleared, and prayed that he had, at the very least, wounded one of savages. He knew he had no time to re-load, one of the disadvantages of preferring a rifle over a musket, and that this was not the best place to take a stand. He used the dissipating smoke as a cover and sprinted towards the main trail. Having many years of practice re-loading a rifle on the run, he soon had his weapon ready and ran behind a large hickory tree that gave him a chance to catch his breath.

Disoriented and not sure how many of the scouts were actually pursuing him, Jacob steadied his rifle up against the tree and aimed directly ahead of himself and waited. He could hear neither the rustling of branches nor the footsteps of the Huron scouts. Actually, the woods were deathly silent.

Still waiting and not sure if he should run or stay where he was or not, Jacob spotted something well up the trail. It appeared to be two figures side-by-side, walking close together and very slowly. The heavy brush still obscured any possible view of who was coming, but Jacob remained with his rifle aimed and steady.

The men were soon in full view and Jacob could see now that he had definitely hit one of the scouts right under his left rib cage. He was bleeding heavily and his partner was doing his best to keep him propped up and moving. Waiting for the right moment, Jacob let them get within a few paces and then stepped out from behind the tree. His rifle was raised and the Huron were only five or so paces directly in front of him.

Without bothering to give them a warning shout, Jacob fired toward the startled Huron. Then, before the smoke even began to clear, Jacob pulled the knife from his neck sheath and charged headlong toward them. His shot had knocked both savages down and he saw that the lead ball had hit the Huron who had been carrying his partner. It had struck him right above his left eye brow.

It was an instant kill.

Jacob now stood, peering down at the other severely injured Huron as the man struggled desperately to push his dead partner's body off of himself. His own deep wound was still bleeding heavily and Jacob was now close enough to hear the man's wheezy breaths barely exiting his throat.

Jacob kicked off the dead Huron and looked right into the scout's eyes. He could see that the man was suffering and there was nothing Jacob could do to ease his pain.

The wilderness was cruel at times and he knew what he had to do.

Jacob had been taught early on that if he ever found an animal slowly dying in one of his traps, the humane thing to do was to quickly put it out of its misery. A man was no different; even the hated Huron deserved a swift death without being left to fend off the many wild beasts that smell the blood and hang around for an easy meal.

He felt some remorse, but images of his defenseless brother's death put his mind back to what he had to do. Jacob was also aware of the fact that the French might still be nearby, so he fired off one last shot and watched the Huron take his final breath.

Jacob left the bodies where they lay. He knew that the animals would eventually feast on them, but that was just part of nature. He refused to scalp or mutilate their bodies in any way. He knew there was a large bounty on any Indian or French scalp, but if he scalped these men, he would be no better than the savages back at the Great Meadows. He certainly cared little for any trophies of the battle and any man who questioned his actions would be greeted by his fists.

With the threat of the Huron gone, and assuming that the French had no stomach to stand and fight, Jacob ran back to the smaller trail where Miller's body was. When he reached him Jacob found that Miller's body was already stiffening and that the Huron had not wasted an opportunity to scalp him, even in the middle of a skirmish. At that moment, Jacob wished he had not been so sympathetic towards either of the dead Huron.

He removed the brown sash that acted as his belt and opened it up. He placed it beside Miller's corpse and gently rolled the body onto the large sash that, when unraveled, was big enough to generously cover Miller's body. With both ends of the sash tied shut, the body was easier for Jacob to carry back to camp.

He was determined not to leave the young man behind and wanted to give him a proper burial. He pulled the heavy body up and over onto his shoulder and moved out. As he passed the two dead Huron, he decided to put down Miller's corpse and clean up the area. He picked up their discarded muskets and, having no way to carry them, he smashed the butts against a rock and bent the barrels over the same rock. He tossed their knives and one of their war clubs deep into the wilderness.

He decided to keep one of the clubs as a reminder of what happened here. The one that he kept had a carved rattle snake face that had a rounded ball cut into its mouth. It was adorned with several large turkey feathers and leather strips attached with deer sinew and maple sap. It was hand-carved and fairly rough to the touch, yet it was a beautiful piece that he knew would have been prized by the dead Huron scout. He also knew that one day, it could come in handy when his rifle couldn't be re-loaded quickly enough and his knife was not accessible. It might just save his life someday.

Arriving after dusk and greeted by several large camp fires that lit his final few miles on the trail, Jacob was tired and needed some water to drink. Private White was the first to notice him as he was taking the first shift on sentry duty.

Without bothering to call out a warning, White rushed over to Jacob and assisted him with the large sack he had on his back.

"Sir, I'm glad to see you made it back; we were all getting rather worried you might have met up with some savages. Where is Miller?" White asked as he put the sack on the ground.

"We did meet up with some Huron and a couple of French regulars," Jacob said as he sat down heavily. They killed Miller and I barely made it myself. I killed the savages and didn't want any other buggers to have Miller's body to feast on."

White could tell that his corporal was distraught and near tears, so he called for the other rangers, Cullen and Sinclair, to help. Soon, they had carried Miller's body to a more suitable location while it awaited burial.

They picked out a nice flat piece of land under an oak tree and began to dig a deep hole. Private White returned to Jacob and said, "By the way, sir, Captain Stevens arrived at the camp a few hours ago with the rest of the rangers and they set up a camp a half mile to the west of here. Would you like me to send for him?"

Jacob was physically and mentally drained and just sat on a fallen tree trunk and said nothing. He knew that White was dutifully waiting for his answer, so he replied, "Thank you, private, you should remain on watch and I'll go and report to the captain. I just want to check with the boys and see how they are managing."

He finally composed himself and walked towards the Virginia Rangers' encampment. Jacob heard the loud, boisterous laugh of Captain Stevens echo through the small clearing as he approached the two sentries guarding the eastern edge of the camp.

"Stop and identify yourself," one of the rangers called out.

"It is I, Corporal Sims reporting to Captain Stevens," Jacob replied.

"Pass, sir," the ranger said and the two men returned to their duties.

Jacob walked into the camp that had already been organized and had a nice copper pot boiling on the open fire.

"Sims, you are finally back!" Captain Stevens called out when he noticed Jacob enter the camp.

"Yes, sir," Jacob replied, approaching Stevens' tent that was set up in the middle of the camp, just by the fire. "I just returned and checked in with my men before I came here."

"I hope they are all well and have not run into any trouble with the French? We are all excited about the news that Braddock has issued orders for us to break camp and by dawn be ready to march towards Fort Duquesne."

"Regrettably sir, I have to report that Private Miller was killed fighting a French scouting party. He was brave and stayed by my side in a situation where most men would have turned and ran." Jacob could see that Stevens was visibly upset by the news.

"Damn good man he was and he will be missed by the men. Bloody horrible business this war stuff, Sims, bloody horrible. Did the French get his body?" "No sir, I carried him back and the boys are giving him a proper burial as we speak," Jacob replied.

"Good job, Sims, we can never leave a fellow ranger behind," Stevens said.

"So, the news is that the army is moving out, what are our orders?" Jacob asked, trying to change the subject.

"Well, we are to march ahead of the main column and keep the way clear. It took some convincing that we needed an advanced guard, since the Major General found no reason to do so, but our own Washington changed his mind and here we are."

"If I may, I could use some time to rest and be ready for the morning. I just carried his body almost thirty miles by myself and, to be honest, I am exhausted." Jacob noticed that while he made his request, Stevens was already signing a stack of orders and papers.

"This is no time to sleep, Sims; Braddock expects us to be well ahead of them and the axe men have made some progress with the help of additional militia units," Stevens said and returned to his work.

"What do you need me to do sir?" Jacob offered.

The aroma of cooked meat mingled with the anticipation of marching orders towards the French fort. The men's spirits were noticeably higher than in past days.

Stevens finished signing the last of the papers and got up before Jacob could say another word. "Sims, I am off to speak with Braddock and his aides. Come along if you want, and we can talk further on the way."

Jacob made his way through the camp right on Stevens heels. The Major General had moved his quarters to a large open area only a mile or so south of where the rangers were camped. The rest of the main army, except for the sick and wounded left behind at the fort, had set up just to the north and the two men could hear the singing and excitement that consumed the entire wilderness.

They reached the headquarters and were abruptly stopped by a red-coated grenadier, guarding the main entrance of the large white tent. "Halt sirs," he said brusquely, "no one is to trouble the Major General tonight on strict orders from Braddock himself."

"I am Captain Stevens of the Virginia Rangers and I have important information regarding the enemy," Stevens barked back, but his tone and rank had little effect on the stoic guard.

Jacob knew from his earlier experience as a colonial volunteer that the British regulars saw them as no better than the savages, so an officer in the colonial army carried no weight with even the lowliest regular.

"Nice to make your acquaintance, sir, but I still have my orders," the guard said without budging.

Stevens was clearly irritated and close to lashing out towards the insubordinate grenadier, but then a voice called out from behind the soldier, saying, "What do we have here?"

Jacob knew the voice all too well. It was his old commander, Washington.

The two rangers could clearly see that Washington was pale and sickly. Jacob guessed that if the army had not left, he would be under the care of the fort's medical staff.

"Stand down, men," he chided. "May I remind you that we are all fighting the French and Huron, not each other? Captain Stevens, how are you this exciting night?" Washington did his best to hide his ailment but he was not his usual confident, dominating self.

"Fine, sir, all things considered. This is Corporal Sims and he just returned from a scouting mission with some news and the body of one of my rangers." Stevens glared at the grenadier that still shielded the door to the tent.

"News? What news do you have that is more important than permitting this lad to fulfill his duties?" Washington asked arrogantly, noticing the angry looks being given the guard by both of the ranger officers.

"Well, sir…" Jacob started slowly, cautious that his former commander should not recognize him. "I, I mean we ran into a small scouting party of Huron and French regulars, maybe thirty miles northeast of this very spot."

When he had finished speaking, Jacob stood silently beside Stevens, watching Washington pace back and forth before them. He was mumbling under his breath and neither could make out what he was saying.

Thankfully, Stevens stepped forward and interrupted the sick officer before Jacob could do the same, grossly overstepping his own authority.

"Sir," Stevens said urgently, "we must speak with Major General Braddock before we depart in the morning, so he knows what we might be marching into."

Washington still appeared uncomfortable at the idea of disturbing Braddock, but he conceded to their suggestion, saying, "Certainly we should speak with the Major General regarding your first-hand news of the French. I know he was anticipating that the French would get word of our attack on the fort. Our intelligence told us they only have a small garrison manning it and are in no position to defend against a siege attack."

Jacob felt Washington's large hand on his shoulder as he was guided into the Braddock's headquarters. Stevens walked alongside and purposefully nudged the guard with his shoulder as he passed by. Jacob noticed it and smiled at Stevens' abrasive nature.

When they entered the front room of the canvassed quarters, Jacob was amazed at the beautifully handcrafted, solid oak officer's desk and matching chairs. This was no colonial volunteer's tent. Another piece in the room, a double-door dresser as tall as Jacob, took up nearly a whole wall and likely cost as much as he would make in wages during an entire year in the army.

Washington disappeared into another room of the tent as the two men stood uncomfortably waiting. Stevens let out a deep, frustrated puff of air and Jacob knew his captain was annoyed at how they were being treated.

They could clearly hear parts of the conversation between Washington and Braddock in the next room. The Major General sounded like he had little interest in speaking with the rangers, despite vigorous appeals from Washington. After a few long minutes, Braddock ordered Washington to bring in the two men, but just as a means of ending the discussion. When Washington open the private door and wave the two men in, Jacob hung back, waiting for Stevens to step forward first. They were ushered into a surprisingly small, plainly-decorated room that doubled as an office and sleeping quarters.

In addition to a small, nondescript bed that sat in one corner, there was a beautifully finished maple writing desk and chair and two decent arm-chairs. The desk was piled with an unorganized mess of papers and enveloped correspondence. Jacob noticed that Captain Stobo's map of Fort Duquesne was predominately displayed over a portion of the desk, obviously an important piece to Braddock's attack plan.

The Major General was still in his full uniform and was sitting with his back to them and his head down, signing papers and placing them on a larger pile to his right. Jacob was off to the side of the desk and could see that Braddock was pre-occupied with carefully placing his red wax seal on every piece he signed. He still wore his powdered white wig and, with his round-spectacled glasses perched on the edge of his nose, he reminded Jacob more of a grandfather figure than the leader of the British military contingent of North America.

Without offering them so much as a glance, Braddock growled, "You say one of you saw some Frenchmen with their heathen allies scouting in our territory?"

Stevens stepped forward and replied, "Yes, sir; Corporal Sims encountered some French regulars and at least two Huron scouts."

Jacob remained quietly off to the side, thinking it would be far better to let the officers talk amongst themselves than for him to be involved. He did not care for Braddock and knew that he in turn had no use for the colonial volunteers, and no respect for the Indians that inhabited the surrounding area. It was easy to see that he disliked the Indians, considering the fact there were no more than a handful attached to his army. Jacob felt that this was a mistake that might come back to haunt the older officer.

"Encountered?" Braddock barked.

Before Stevens could offer a reply, Jacob abandoned his plan and calmly responded to the disinterested commander, "Yes, sir, they attacked us and we had to defend ourselves. One of my men was killed during the attack by the Huron."

"Sims…Are you the same Sims I met earlier? You are now a Corporal are you? These bloody colonials certainly throw around titles like they are worthless." Braddock glanced at Washington with a sneer.

"I am the same, sir," Jacob said respectfully, ignoring the slight. "We ran into them about thirty miles up the trail from here."

"How did they react to your presence on our land?" Braddock removed his glasses and finally appeared somewhat interested.

"The French regulars were not much of a bother, but we had a good fight with the two Huron scouts."

"So typical of the damn French; as for those heathens, they are only good for stirring up the pot. They are brave when they are up against colonials, but I suspect they will turn and run when they face our seasoned, disciplined British regulars." Braddock was quick to dismiss the entire episode and returned to his papers.

Never one to be intimidated, Jacob pressed further, "You will find those Indians will be more trouble than just mere pot stirrers, sir. Ask your aide or Captain Stevens how well the Indians can fight."

Jacob knew he was pushing his luck and stepped back as Stevens pulled on his elbow. There was a moment of uncomfortable silence, broken only by the scraping of Braddock's pen on the papers in front of him.

Then, without acknowledging the presence of either ranger, Braddock said, "Mr. Washington, please advise Captain Stevens that we will indeed still be leaving at dawn, despite the presence of a handful of French and their savages. Please tell Colonel Dunbar that the captain will be leaving before the main column and his ranging company will clear the trails of any savages or roaming Frenchmen in our way.

"We shall all sleep better knowing they have our backs," he added mockingly added as he returned once more to his work.

Jacob stood silently, watching Stevens and Washington offer up respectful salutes, and thinking to himself that this foolish officer would do his best to get all of them killed. Without receiving a return salute or any other gesture, the three men quickly exited Braddock's office.

Waiting for one of the two officers to comment about what had just happened, Jacob instead heard Washington repeating the same orders to Stevens and dismissing himself to speak with Dunbar.

Standing there in bewilderment, unsure of what had just happened, Jacob decided he had enough and was about to vent his frustrations until Stevens stepped in and offered an explanation.

"The Major General has decided to divide the army into two brigades led by the two Scots, Colonels Halket and Dunbar. Our men, as you heard, are attached to Dunbar's 48th foot. We are also with several units of Provincials and a South Carolina Independent Company. Between the two brigades, we have near 1600 men, not including a number of wagoners and camp followers."

"That is more than a few men and wagons to get through the mountains and the swamps," Jacob commented. "Not to mention all the artillery pieces our commander feels are so critical to drag all the way to Fort Duquesne." He thought to himself that this could either be an amazing victory or a defeat even worse than what happened at Fort Necessity. He truly felt that the latter scenario was the more likely, especially after speaking to the arrogant and dismissive Braddock.

"The fact that he has also dismissed any help from the Indians in this area will prove to be a mistake that might cost us all our lives," Jacob added boldly, not caring that he had just overstepped himself. "Have you heard if we have any Indians on our side? If not, does the man realize we are travelling through Delaware and Shawnee territory? Any stragglers will make easy targets for them and only end up adorning their scalping poles."

"I have seen a few Mingo warriors hanging around, but they are little concern to us," Stevens said absently. "You heard the Colonel; we leave before dawn, so ready the men and I'll be by shortly to speak with them." Without another word, Stevens left to find Dunbar and reconfirm his orders.

Chapter | **Twelve**

When Maggie finally opened her eyes, the sky had lightened a bit in the east. As she looked through the predawn dimness, there was not a hint of any villages or farms like those that had dotted the creek she had travelled with One-Ear.

This river was a stark contrast, miles of untamed, dense wilderness. The surrounding forest was so thick that parts of its canopy hung well into the river and took the efforts of a man in each boat to stand and push the branches out of their path.

Maggie rubbed at her tired eyes then continued to take stock of her situation. She was in one of four heavily-laden boats with Mr. Dollard manning the front of the one she was being held in. The boat crews were masterful, quickly maneuvering the low-riding boats around the endless branches and rocks that lined the river. They never missed a beat, even as they were forced to kneel down at times to avoid the obstacles and pulled around rocks that jutted out from below the surface.

"Madame, we will be stopping soon," Dollard said, jarring her back to the reality of her situation. "There is a fine area to land the boats only a few miles ahead where we can rest and have some food."

The rest was not meant for her; the men had pushed themselves to the brink of exhaustion. They had travelled most of the night, guided by small torches that only gave them a few feet of visibility. She could tell, though, that they had travelled these waters many times before, and probably didn't even need the lights to guide them. The four boats slid gracefully across the water, snagged only a few times by sunken logs or rocks.

Maggie may not have been physically exhausted, but she was emotionally spent. She was stiff, tired, hungry and severely disappointed. She had been so looking forward to feeling safe in the hospitality of One-Ear's village, but it was not to be. She certainly had not expected that she would once again be heading towards Fort at Niagara, a place fraught with new dangers. She expected she would see Fredrick there, not to mention the French merchant who had initially purchased her.

Worse than all her disappointment was the last image she had of One-Ear, lying motionless on the ground. It still haunted her and she prayed he was still alive. She knew two things for certain. If he had survived, he would be completely devastated by the deception his fellow villagers had committed, and if he was healthy enough, he would be out searching for her.

She didn't have high hopes that he would find her though. They had made very good time in their swift boats, and the distance between them was most likely too great to make up before she reached the Fort at Niagara. However, if she had learned one lesson over the past months, it was to always maintain some hope.

Maggie prayed that if she ended up making it to the fort, the merchant would turn out to be a good man and would treat her well, possibly even selling her to a nice family in Quebec. The image of living the rest of her days as nothing better than a slave, while never seeing her family again made her weep inside, but she would never give such satisfaction to her captors. Externally she remained strong and defiant and never yielded to her tears.

Less than an hour later, the sun had made its appearance over the eastern horizon and the men pulled the boats towards the left bank of the river. There was a clearing on the shore and several of the men jumped out of the boats to secure them with ropes to two large shade trees. The men ignored Maggie and she remained in the boat as they hauled some of the goods off and set up a small camp.

Maggie curiously scanned the area and noticed it was a rather beautiful spot, considering her circumstance. A few of the men were building and preparing a large fire pit while others pulled several fallen tree trunks nearby and began to meticulously hack off most of the smaller branches and trim a few notches in them. When they had finished, they placed the cleaned logs in a comfortable semi-circle around the fire. Meanwhile, another group of the men finally asked her to get out of the boat. They were polite and indicated that they wanted to remove the rest of the gear. When the boats were empty, the men turned them over to carefully check the hulls for any damage or leaks.

She was left standing by the bank just watching all the work being done. Dollard had already taken two men with him down an old pathway, presumably to hunt some game. Just a few minutes after they had disappeared into the woods, Maggie heard the echoes of musket fire. It wasn't long before they returned, triumphantly carrying two large deer and what looked like a small wild pig.

As a makeshift spit was added to the fire pit, one of the men drove a sharpened wooden branch through the pig's body and placed it over the fire. The fire roared uncontrollably as the pig's cooking flesh spewed juice as it roasted, and the men all cheered.

Maggie was directed to sit by the fire; she had a great view of the cooking beast and enjoyed the wonderful smell that surrounded the small landing. She watched as two of the hunters quickly skinned the two deer with skill and precision and neatly carved one of them into several pieces. Once a second fire pit was completed, they tossed the meat into a large pot placed right in the fire, covered it with some water, herb roots and berries they had gathered up from the immediate area.

Maggie enjoyed the hectic action, yet felt guilty that she just sat and watched. Once everything appeared to be in order, Dollard came over and took a seat beside her.

"Is this feast to your satisfaction, madame?" he asked.

"I assume this is not just for me, but it is impressive all the same," Maggie replied politely, not interested in indulging in a lengthy conversation with him. "Your men are well suited for this life."

Dollard made no reply, but watched the men as they worked feverishly. Finally, he said, "These men have been hardened by this fine country, and become well-adapted to this unforgiving land."

An hour later, Maggie was given a plate filled with seasoned venison stew and a nice piece of flavorful roasted pork. She also ate several slices of hard tack cornbread. She watched as the men drank a few bottles of wine they had warmed over the fire. Maggie sampled some but found it bitter tasting, reminding her of the root wine favored by the Dutch settlers near her old homestead.

After indulging in the feast, most of the men laid down in the soft grassy meadow to rest. The remaining men repacked the boats and cleaned up the mess from the feast. They discarded the remains of the roasted pig in the nearby wooded area and hung the carcass of the second deer from a high branch to keep wild cats and bears away from the camp until they were ready to leave.

Finally tired from sitting on the hard log, Maggie stood up and walked back towards the river. Dollard was busy ensuring that all the supplies were properly packed and the boats were still in good shape.

When he saw Maggie, he said, "Madame, please feel free to wander up the path a bit and stretch your legs. I trust you will not be foolish enough to escape, since we both know these woods are no place for a woman venturing all alone." The other men around the boats began to laugh.

Needing to get away from all of this and realizing this would probably be the last time she would enjoy such freedom, Maggie politely waved at Dollard and walked towards the narrow path the hunters had used. The path was well-travelled and was surrounded by waist-high grasses and various wild flowering plants. With the mid-morning sun heating up, combined with the buzzing noise of the throngs of insects all around her, she took a deep breath and walked. She followed the path through a small meadow until it emptied into the darkness of the massive wilderness.

She was out of sight of the beach area and was lost in the enjoyment of gathering up a handful of colorful flowers. There was a brief thought of running but she knew that would be a death sentence and a far worse fate than what awaited her at the Fort at Niagara.

Lost in the peacefulness of the moment, she was startled by a flock of wild turkeys that suddenly flew up right in front of her.

She stopped in her tracks.

Maggie could hear nothing, but she knew that birds rarely flew away in such manner unless they were frightened by something. She knew she couldn't have scared them, because they were too far in front of her.

She stood frozen in the meadow, scanning the forested area for anything that might have caused the turkeys to scatter. Maggie could see the flock had all landed far off to her right and settled back down, but she was still cautious.

In the midst of the silent stillness, a familiar voiced called out to her from the woods, "Miss Maggie, don't be afraid it is me One-Ear."

Excited, but wary that this could be someone's idea of a cruel joke, Maggie waited before she called back, focusing her eyes on the path that blended into the wooded area ahead of her.

Finally ducking down to get some cover, Maggie called back softly, "The One-Ear I know was left for dead; how could he be speaking to me now?"

She also knew not to call out too loudly, just in case it truly was One-Ear and she alarmed her French captors.

"My head aches, but I am well enough to find you and take you back from the Frenchmen who took you from me. My brother realized his mistake and he brought some of the villagers to come and take you back." One-Ear slowly stepped out from the darkness and revealed himself to Maggie, who remained hiding within the tall grass.

She could hardly contain her excitement when she got a good look at him standing in the sunny light.

He was almost unrecognizable. His face was painted with the rubbings of black ashes and vermillion. His bare chest was completely blackened and his arms were adorned with tattoos of a snake and a howling wolf. His hair was impressively decorated with a number of wild turkey feathers with red and blue beads. Maggie had never seen him look so striking and at the same time so ferocious.

"One-Ear, I am glad you are safe, but what are you going to do against all these Frenchmen?" She again called out softly as she started to work her way closer to where he stood.

One-Ear remained where he was and signaled Maggie to move quickly towards him. She reached him and then saw over fifty, well-armed warriors and his brother, Wolf-Paw, standing within the tree line.

The villagers were in a semi-circle around the small meadow and anyone coming through on the trail would be funneled into a killing zone, leaving the narrow pathway back to the river as their only escape route.

One-Ear was greeted by a big hug and he reluctantly returned it, careful not to show too much emotion and appear weak to his fellow warriors. Maggie wiped the tears from her eyes and watched him motion to the villagers to remain concealed in the tree-line.

He stood proudly beside Maggie, seemingly expecting the French to come charging into the meadow at any moment. "I will stay by your side no matter what," he said, and Maggie could see the seriousness in his eyes. "If the French want you bad enough, they will have to kill us all to get you."

Maggie could say nothing, but she was impressed by how quickly he had matured into a strong leader, displaying no outward fear.

"If they come," he continued, "I have several more warriors hidden from them by their camp. They have no means of escape, and if they run for their boats I have given the others strict orders to kill them all."

Not sure what she should do, Maggie asked, "What happened to that DuPont beast and his control over the elders?"

One-Ear maintained his watch over the trail and simply pointed to a bloody scrap of hair that dangled proudly from his belt. Maggie was speechless once more, realizing how seriously he was guarding her life.

Offering no explanation, One-Ear suddenly started to move towards the narrow path that had led Maggie to him, and she remained by his side. Soon, she heard the voices of several Frenchmen call out to her, "Madame, Mr. Dollard needs you back at the boats."

One-Ear whispered to her not to reply, "Let them come out into the open; if they are foolish enough to fight then I need you to run for cover in the woods."

The group of Frenchmen innocently walked into the open meadow before they got a clear view of the two lone figures standing in the waist-deep meadow grass.

They appeared puzzled by the appearance of this lone Indian and Maggie standing waiting for them, and they called out once more to her, "Madame, please come to us."

Maggie stood by One-Ear and watched as one of the Frenchmen in the party turned and ran back towards the camp. One-Ear did nothing to prevent him from informing the others and remained defiantly standing in the meadow. Maggie knew the remaining Frenchmen would do nothing until the others returned and it felt like hardly any time had lapsed before all the French boatmen arrived with Dollard in the lead.

He was visibly upset and clearly intended to approach her before thinking better of it. Instead, he shouted forcefully, "Madame, you must come with us immediately!"

One-Ear stepped in front of her, clearly displaying to Dollard he had no intentions of letting Maggie go with them.

"You are that boy from the village! You know we had a deal with your elders and Mr. DuPont for this Englishwoman. She belongs to us, and you must give her to me now." Dollard was now clearly incensed that this savage would think to double-cross him. He turned to his men and ordered them to ready their muskets.

"I don't want any more bloodshed on my behalf, please be careful," Maggie pleaded with One-Ear, but she could see he was not going to back down without a fight.

As the pair watched the French disperse along the path and form a line, Maggie noticed One-Ear reach down and pull the bloody scalp from his belt.

Holding it high into the air to make sure all the men could see it, he unleashed a hideous scream that vibrated around the small meadow. He stopped and then called out to the Frenchman, "This is what is left of your friend DuPont; you and your men will face the same fate if you do not leave this land now.

Maggie could see the fear in some of the men's eyes as they intently looked at the fresh scalp that dripped blood down One-Ear's outstretched forearm.

As menacing as the scene looked, Dollard defiantly lashed out, "If that is Mr. DuPont's scalp, then I truly fear for your village's safety. The Governor in Montreal will not stand for such actions against his subjects.

One-Ear said nothing and just signaled with his other hand.

Maggie stepped back as the warriors, still concealed by the woods started to screech out a cry similar to that which One-Ear had unleashed earlier. The meadow thundered with the cries of the fifty or so warriors, and the Frenchmen were visibly shaken. Even Dollard briefly stepped back, but caught himself and remained where he was.

The warriors stepped out in unison and readied their weapons. Maggie thought it was a wondrous sight to behold as One-Ear said to her, "Miss Maggie, stay here. The Frenchmen will do nothing since they have no place to run."

As he explained the situation to her, they heard Dollard scream towards them, "We are not afraid. Do you forget that we are allies with the great Mississauga people? They will not look kindly on your treatment of us on their land."

Once again Maggie witnessed One-Ear calmly wave his hand.

With that, twenty warriors from the nearby Mississauga village moved in on the startled Frenchmen, taking up a position that blocked any possible escape back towards the landing area.

"They were easily convinced to take up arms against you French," One-Ear shouted back. "If you still have thoughts of fighting your way through us, just know that I have more warriors at this very moment destroying your boats. The contents of your boats are now property of the Mississauga and they are taking it all back to their village." One-Ear smiled at Maggie, satisfied he had covered all his options.

The tension was high as Maggie had her eyes fixed on Dollard, praying he would back down and save his men's lives.

Everything went crazy all of a sudden as Dollard called out to his men and ordered them to run for a small patch of trees that could possibly provide some of the men some cover.

Maggie just stood by and waited for One-Ear to react, but he refused to, still remaining calmly beside her. He showed no fear and he slowly passed a musket to Maggie, saying, "Use this, if necessary. We will need all the help we can get since the foolish Frenchman is determined to get himself and all his men killed."

She momentarily hesitated, but her choices were limited and she wanted no part of remaining as a captive of the French. Maggie also knew that Dollard was a smart man and he was only trying to give himself more time to decide what he needed to do to get his men out of this bad situation.

Both adversaries were stubborn, but both knew that Dollard's position was hopeless and One-Ear was presenting him an opportunity to reconsider his actions. Maggie feared that either One-Ear or his fellow warriors would lose patience and open fire on the trapped Frenchmen. She decided to plead to One-Ear to avoid any more killing, "We should at least speak with Dollard and see if he would just let us go."

"The French would only return to our village with more men and kill us all. We have to end this now and send a message all the way to Quebec that we will not be taken advantage of…we must fight them now." He spoke without emotion.

Maggie said nothing more and watched as the French desperately piled rotted logs, fallen trees and branches to give them some fortification against the expected attack. She was confused as to why One-Ear just stood back and let them give themselves cover while his warriors just howled and screamed sporadically to try to unnerve the boatmen.

Remaining in the open field and unafraid of the French, One-Ear waved his hand once again and that sent some of his warriors through the concealed woods and within clear firing range of the enemy. As of now, over half of his warriors could fire endlessly into the French makeshift fortification without fear of return fire. He also waved to the Mississauga to remain where they were and guard the only escape route. Maggie understood that One-Ear did not want the Mississauga to get directly involved in this dispute, unless it became necessary.

Before One-Ear could issue any further instructions, Dollard screamed, "Fire!"

The small meadow was immediately filled with smoke and the deafening echoes trembled through the woods. The mass of lead balls could be heard striking branches and tree trunks, but they initially did little damage. The Frenchmen shouted as they quickly re-loaded their muskets and readied themselves to fire again.

One-Ear coolly ducked down and waited.

Only a few seconds later another round was fired off by the French but One-Ear felt nothing whiz by him. This time the French had directed this volley towards the unsuspecting Mississauga warriors.

Maggie lifted her loaded musket to her shoulder but could only watch helplessly as several warriors collapsed in pain. The swiftness and confusion resulted in the surviving Mississauga warriors running in disorder towards the river bank.

Dollard's plan was obvious now—to clear a path to the river and try to escape from there.

Maggie shouted above the hideous noise, "You need to do something before the French escape."

All she heard was a shrieking, blood-curdling cry emanating from One-Ear as he fired off a quick round then threw down his musket and pulled out his war club from his belt. Maggie stood rooted to the spot and watched as he ran directly towards the Frenchmen. He was immediately joined by the entire group of warriors who saw him charge.

The woods and the small meadow exploded with rage as she tried her best to give some cover fire, some of the other villagers joined in with her and fired but most wildly ran full speed into the French. One-Ear had made it all the way within a few paces as Maggie directed her small group to move up closer and continue to fire.

The French were overwhelmed by the onslaught as One-Ear and more than thirty warriors swung and kicked their way into the small fortification. The Frenchmen used the butt ends of their muskets to attempt to stop the savage attack.

In a matter of minutes, the gun fire on both sides had ceased and the warriors had switched primarily to their war clubs. Maggie remained behind as the others in her line ran to get their spoils of battle.

She could hear the horrible cries from the dying men, many of whom pleaded for their lives. As the frenzied warriors took scalps and proudly paraded them around like some kind of grotesque trophy, Maggie saw One-Ear walk away from all the killing to speak with the remaining Mississauga allies.

The war cries had lessened in frequency, but not in volume. Their scalping tasks finished, the villagers began to strip off the dead anything they thought was valuable enough to take back to the village.

One-Ear left his allies, who seemed to be satisfied with the rewards for their support, and slowly walked back towards Maggie. She could see he was still breathing and sweating heavily. He had smattering of blood on his chest and arms that she knew was not his. She was glad to see that he carried no scalps or souvenirs from his heroic charge, and that he was not as excited about the victory as his fellow warriors.

He walked to her side, sat down on the ground by her feet and cried.

Maggie knew he did not want the others to see his emotions, so she stood in front of him to block him from the view of the villagers.

"Thank you for rescuing me…again," Maggie offered. "I am so sorry you had to do all of this and risk the lives of your villagers."

He remained silent.

It was then that Maggie noticed several of the villagers were gathering up the dead and wounded warriors. She saw that Wolf-Paw's bloodied body had been placed among the dead.

Understanding his loss, she knelt beside him and pulled him close. She let him cry on her shoulder and her kindness helped him regain his composure so he could continue to lead his warriors.

"Thank you, Miss Maggie," One-Ear said, rubbing his eyes clear of the tears that soaked his face. "We have both lost too much, and I fear there will be more losses to come."

"What do we do next?" she asked. "We can't return to your village; the French will certainly search for me there first. I cannot let them be punished because of me."

"I must ensure that my brother's body will be safely taken back to his village. I have spoken with the Mississauga people and they have been kind enough to provide us with a canoe and an escort as far as the wild river that flows from the great falls. We can only hope that the French will not find this place for several weeks, yet I fear word will soon reach them back at the Fort at Niagara." One-Ear looked towards the small clump of woods that now housed the dead and mutilated bodies of several Frenchmen.

Maggie said nothing and avoided looking at the death scene left behind by the victorious warriors. It took little time for the vultures to appear above the dead bodies and she heard several of the villagers firing at a number of coyotes gathering to scavenge on the corpses.

"The beasts can already smell the scent of the dead and that will certainly make it easy for anyone out searching for the missing Frenchmen to locate them. We must leave now before the French are alerted; one of the villagers said he thought he saw one of the men being sent ahead to tell the fort to expect their arrival."

As One-Ear and Maggie moved towards the path that led to the river, several Mississauga warriors approached him and spoke for a few minutes.

Maggie watched as they disappeared up the path to the beach then looked at One-Ear.

"We should leave immediately; the Mississauga said they are fearful that the French will return with more soldiers and punish anyone they think was involved in this slaughter. I just hope we don't run into them on the river or before we make it past the fort."

Maggie followed him towards the row of dead warriors. The stench of death washed over her again and she stood a little apart as she patiently waited for One-Ear to pay his respects to his brother. He knelt down and spoke a few words before sprinkling some tobacco over the body. He then rubbed something onto Wolf-Paw's face and upper chest and then covered his body.

As he continued to kneel by the body, Maggie moved up the path to the beach to give him some privacy. When she reached the landing area, she was struck by the memory of how peaceful it had been only a few hours earlier as the French prepared their feast. Their boats were now ransacked and battered so badly they could likely never be used again.

A number of Mississauga warriors were already bobbing on the water in their canoes, waiting for One-Ear to arrive so they could depart. They made no eye contact with Maggie and she made no effort to offer a greeting to them.

She stood by the large fire pit that still had a few charred remains of the roasted pig clinging to the spit. The distinct smell of pork perversely mingled with the stench of the rotting corpses and she had to cover her nose to lessen the smell.

A few minutes later, One-Ear ran down the pathway and, without saying a word, went directly to the canoe that still rested on the beach. Maggie immediately followed and helped One-Ear and a Mississauga paddler push it into the shallow part of the river. They jumped in and soon were following the other Mississauga paddlers down the narrow river towards the land of the thunderous falls.

She sat in the middle of the canoe with One-Ear in the front and the Mississauga warrior taking up the rear.

"I am so sorry for your brother's death," Maggie said, attempting to break the uncomfortable silence.

One-Ear said nothing and was clearly not in the mood to talk, so Maggie was left to watch the other canoes slide swiftly across the surface of the river. She was impressed by the rhythmic stroke of the paddlers. They were so synchronized, they made it appear effortless.

The paddlers barely looked up, concentrating on their stroke and listening to the cadenced grunts of the lead man in each canoe, who kept the paddlers on pace. She watched the men in the back seats pull and move the face of their paddles through the water to steer around the rocks and logs with ease. The rear paddlers were the eyes of the canoes and they gently guided them without losing pace.

So focused was Maggie on watching the men, that she was startled when One-Ear broke their silence, saying, "Thank you, Miss Maggie, but I do blame my brother for all of this. My heart is still heavy with sadness that he had to die to make everything right, but I did pray for him to be forgiven by the Spirits so he can once more live in peace."

"I will hope for that as well. If it makes you feel better, I have already forgiven him for everything. He was only trying to do what was best for his people and we can't fault him for that." She continued to watch their progress and asked, "How much farther is it to the place where the Mississauga will leave us?"

"We are nearly there, as the river we are on will turn towards the south and take us away from the fort. Once we stop, we will have to decide if we want to carry the canoe overland or leave it behind and travel the rest of the way by foot. We will be deep in French territory once more, and will have to be very cautious. The French fort is several miles north of us and the river that empties into the lake is far too fast and dangerous for us to travel on."

Maggie could see that the mist from the falls was getting heavier and she could hear the thunderous roar emanating from the mass of water that pounded over the high, watery cliffs.

"Now you know why we call this place 'Thunder Water'," One-Ear said with a smile.

"I can't believe the noise; it's almost deafening!" Maggie cried.

While they talked, the Mississauga pulled canoes to the left and floated close to the shore line looking for a good place to land.

Slowing his own pace, One-Ear continued, "I have seen small children cry when they are near its shore."

The constant pounding was hard on her ears and she did her best to soften the noise by keeping her ears covered with her hands. One-Ear just laughed at the sight of her and softly landed the canoe on a small, cleared area.

Once all the formalities of thanks and exchange of some supplies were completed, the Mississauga warriors quickly left.

One-Ear, Maggie and one tiny canoe, resting peacefully on the river's edge, were left deep in French territory alone. Without a word, they each grabbed a musket left for them by the Mississauga and took a look around the area. One-Ear asked Maggie to stay near the canoe and to fire off a warning shot if she ran into trouble. He would follow a trail of crushed cattails that headed north.

He returned after a few long minutes and said, "We need to decide what to do next. The Mississauga said we must carry the canoe overland to the north. We will be on the opposite shore, across from the trail that leads to the fort. They brought us here so we can bypass the fort and reach the lake and from there we could paddle past the fort and reach the Mohawk valley in a week or so. It's a much rougher and longer route, but they told me fewer French and Huron live in this area and it is much safer. We will be moving away from the falls, so the noise will be at our backs and soon only be a slight whisper."

Maggie listened to both options, but wanted no part of the French or their fort. Without hesitating, she said, "If we load our backs with our supplies, the canoe is light and the land towards the lake appears much flatter than we have travelled on to this point. I would rather keep away from the French and get to the lake."

One-Ear was in agreement and they pulled the canoe further onto shore so they could organize the supplies.

"The Mississauga also mentioned that the last time they visited the supply post at the fort, the French regulars and their Huron allies appeared to be getting ready to leave for the south. They heard that they were going to Fort Duquesne to re-enforce the soldiers there. There had been some scouts who had told them that the English had brought many men and were marching through the forest to attack the fort as we speak." One-Ear tossed a loaded haversack over his shoulder and helped Maggie do the same.

Maggie made no reply; she was busy checking her powder horn and wrapping a small deerskin sack of lead balls around her belt. Before they departed, the Mississauga had presented her with a beautiful, maple war club with a face of a wolverine carved at the ball end. One-Ear told her they were impressed with her bravery during the battle and wanted her to have this piece as a sign of their respect. She proudly displayed it, placing it in her sash. The people of One-Ear's village had also given her a newly-made pair of buffalo skin leggings and a skirt that she wore over her breeches. One-Ear had given her a hand-made knife that hung around her neck in a porcupine quilled sheath and a black and white wampum belt that she proudly wrapped around her waist.

She looked at One-Ear for approval and he offered a smile. He had also traded for some knives and a tomahawk that would surely come in handy on their travels.

"We should leave now to use all the light we can before darkness sets in. The Mississauga mentioned there were a few old winter camps along this route that might be a good place to spend the night. They also knew of an old winter village of their northern brothers that sits this side of the river from the fort, where we could possibly stay there a night or two." With that, One-Ear dragged the canoe closer to them and, with one big pull, he had it up on his shoulders, waiting for Maggie to work her way underneath it to do the same.

She was happy to find the canoe was rather light and easy to maneuver. The only drawback was that she could not see where she was going, but she simply watched her own feet and followed One-Ear's lead.

The land was far more level than they had traversed earlier in their journey. Even with its thick forests and trails that had not been travelled very often, they found it much easier to trek across this terrain. High ridges nearby even tended to protect this land and it almost seemed to alter the weather to a much calmer, warmer climate. It was less swampy than the land to the south and, besides the long river that linked the falls to the lake, there weren't as many rivers and creeks as Maggie was used to in and around her Pennsylvania homestead.

After a day and a half of trekking along the relatively cleared trail and thankfully seeing no visible signs of the enemy, One-Ear continued to lead the way and they were soon on a small trail situated directly across from the French fort. They were separated by a deep ravine that contained the fast-moving river, which had been churned up by the massive volume of water that flowed over the falls nearly twenty miles to the southwest. The area, although level, was heavily dotted with large boulders and rocky fields that required more attention to their footing.

Just as they got their first clear view of the French Castle, Maggie asked, "Can we stop for a moment so I can rest my shoulders?"

"This seems like a good place," One-Ear replied, "and we can see what the French are up to." He pulled the canoe up and over his head, taking most of the weight off of Maggie's shoulders before swinging it down to the ground.

As Maggie stretched out her arms and back and walked a few paces towards the edge of the ravine, One-Ear made sure the canoe was still in good condition and tipped it upside-down to keep the bottom from being accidently damaged.

"Be careful, Miss Maggie," he called out, "the drop-off is deadly, not to mention we don't want to be spotted by French patrol from across the river."

"I can't believe the power of the river down there. I have never seen so many whirlpools and rapids in my life!" she said in awe as she peered over the edge.

She returned to One-Ear, who was resting against a large boulder with his eyes closed.

Not wanting to disturb his rest, Maggie quietly sat by the canoe and looked for some food in her haversack. She opened up a cloth that had some corn bread and some hard bread. Another cloth held a nice piece of cheese and Maggie used her neck knife to cut a thin slice off for her bread.

It might have been the smell of the cheese, or that he only needed a moment to rest, but One-Ear opened his eyes and looked towards Maggie. She greeted him with a smile and tossed him a piece of bread and the bundle of cheese. They remained quiet and focused on feeding their tired bodies.

They both enjoyed the snack and One-Ear was soon back on his feet, looking at the French fort.

"You know, the French built this castle and tried to explain to the Mohawk that it was only there to be used as a trading post. Over the years, they built up the castle and added several other buildings and an outer earth wall that made it far less of a simple trading post and more of a fort. I see with the threat from the English, they have used the excuse now to build a tall wooden palisade around the land-facing side. They have also added a few more cannon then the last time I visited." One-Ear shook his head nervously.

"Do you want to keep moving and use what is left of the light before we stop?" Maggie asked.

"We should think about stopping soon since I am not sure what lies ahead of us. I have never travelled on this side of the river before, and I would rather find a good place to sleep and get a fresh start in the morning."

Maggie agreed and they quickly swung the canoe up again, working their way along the trail. This time, after the short rest, Maggie found the canoe far easier to carry, even though her shoulders still ached.

They maintained a steady pace until One-Ear stopped without warning. Luckily, Maggie was paying attention and caught herself before she knocked him over.

"What did you hear?" Maggie asked as they quickly dropped and placed the canoe on the side of the trail.

One-Ear moved a few feet ahead and waited. Maggie stayed by the canoe and waited for him to signal what to do. He remained motionless for what felt like minutes, but he soon walked back to Maggie and said, "Sorry, but I am sure I heard Huron voices. Not sure if it carried from across the river, but I am sure it was Huron. We should stop here for the night; the boulders will give us good cover and a place to hide the canoe."

Maggie read the wary look on his face and followed his lead. They pulled the canoe up the side of a small slope beside the trail and covered it with some fallen branches. Once he was satisfied no one was around, One-Ear pointed to a group of huge boulders that provided a nicely sheltered spot to sleep without being seen from the trail.

The added height gave them an even better view of the fort and once they had both scrambled up onto one of the boulders, they both could see the winding trail that they needed to traverse in the morning. The lake could be seen clearly from their vantage point as well, and it gave Maggie some hope that they would soon be away from the French and the threat of the Huron.

One-Ear pointed to a similar trail that followed the other side of the river. They could see a number of Canadian Militia and several Indians running south along the ridge.

"I am glad we are on this side," One-Ear said quietly. "The woods to the east would have been filled with the French and their Indian allies. We would have no chance of making it through all of them."

Maggie nodded her agreement; she was just happy they were far enough away from an imminent threat for the moment. Tired from carrying the canoe and from all the emotions of the last several days, Maggie instinctively started to gather up some small pieces of branches and dried moss that were all around their small camp.

"Miss Maggie, we cannot have a fire tonight. We are far too close to the French and we are not sure how far their influences reach in these parts. Our Mississauga brothers can easily turn on us if they are offered enough from either the French or Huron, so we need to be very careful. I think we both have had our fill of them and I want no part of being a prisoner in their fort."

Maggie stopped and smiled, "I am so lucky you are here with me One-Ear. I would never have thought of that and would have just started a fire for my own comfort."

One-Ear opened his pack and pulled out several pieces of corn bread and various dried meats. He laid them out and sliced off a chunk of bread with his knife and handed it to Maggie. "It's not much," he said as he cut a slice for himself, "but it will fill our stomachs enough to give us energy to make the next leg of our trip."

They sat quietly, enjoying the peacefulness of their surroundings, and shared several pieces of salty, dried meat.

Maggie took in all the sounds that surrounded her, the tranquil chirping of birds and rustle of small creatures in the woods, the rushing river below and the far off sounds of men working at the fort. Amazingly, in addition to all these sounds, she could still hear the dull roar of the falls some twenty or so miles off to the south. She felt, for one night at least, that her fear and all the killing were well behind her. When she was full, she cleaned up and packed the food back into One-Ear's haversack while he was collected large pieces of spongy moss and what leaves he could find to make a comfortable place for them to sleep.

Maggie saw that One-Ear was exhausted and, once he was satisfied that she was happy with her bed, he dropped off immediately. She couldn't remember the last time he had fallen asleep before she did; he normally saw it as his duty to remain awake long after she was sleeping to guard their various encampments.

She intently watched the rhythmic movement of his chest, and when his breathing had deepened, she turned her thoughts to her family. It had been a long time since she had had a moment to herself to just think, and she wondered what her family was doing right then. Had Jacob survived and tracked down the merchant? Was he rotting in some French prison or, worse, was he dead at the hands of the Huron?

And what had become of her children? It felt like a lifetime had passed since she had held them or kissed them goodnight. Maggie hoped they were still alive and somewhat happy with their new families. She prayed they remembered her and still hoped to be reunited someday. James and Becky would be fine, strong enough to survive, but she feared for little Henry and Mary the most. They were young and could easily forget about their past English family.

That life seemed so far away, so distant in her past that she honestly did not know who she was now. A fire would have been nice at the moment, not to warm her feet but to dry the tears that dripped down her face and landed just by her moccasins. She was glad that One-Ear was in a deep sleep, so he would not see her so upset. Maggie could no longer fight the tears and fought hard not to sob loud enough to wake him. She was overwhelmed, not by fear or pain, but by the deep sense of loss and gut-wrenching grief that she had managed to keep hidden from all her captives and friends.

This was one of the first moments she truly felt alone, despite One-Ear sleeping just a few feet away. Maggie finally came to the realization that she might never see her family again. The sheer distances that separated them all was a factor, but it had to do more with all the individual experiences they were being forced to deal with. The scars that would be left from their ordeals would make a reunion difficult, and would certainly prevent them from ever returning to the same kind of life they had enjoyed before.

Maggie understood that her old life, her first life was over now and she had to fight to survive in this new life. That was all that really mattered now.

She cried well into the night, trying to muffle any sounds that might disturb One-Ear's much-needed sleep. Although she only managed to get a few hours of sleep, she felt very well-rested. She had relieved herself of the burden she had allowed to sit and fester within her for so long.

Her tears had turned into determination—the determination to live.

Chapter | **Thirteen**

Jacob returned to the camp, frustrated with the utter stupidity of the senior officers. He realized that they had learned nothing from the mistakes made at the Great Meadows and if they continued on with their plans for this upcoming battle, they would certainly meet with the same results.

He now needed to find a way to survive this mess and get himself north to track down Maggie.

Walking through a number of the encampments, he could hear the various units readying themselves for the march ahead. Some were singing and playing songs on their fiddles or flutes, the more seasoned veterans of the many European wars were meticulously cleaning and shining their muskets.

"Don't shine up that steel too much or the savages will see you from miles away once the sun hits it," Jacob suggested to a couple of nearby Scotsmen, but his idea was met with a sneer and a gob of tobacco juice spat towards him.

Working his way to the first tents in his own camp, Jacob finally realized that Joshua was nowhere to be seen. He was surprised by his absence, especially since the doctor appeared to pretty confident he would up on his feet within the week. Anxiety washed over him, but he was unable at the moment to make the short walk back to the fort.

He moved towards a large open fire that provided enough light for the entire unit and saw only a handful of men sitting around without employment. None of them bothered to acknowledge his arrival or even glance his way.

Jacob whistled as loudly as he could to get all the men's attention. Most came directly, but there were always a few in any unit who took their time to join the others. Not bothering to wait for those uninterested men, Jacob began, "Gentlemen, we have orders to leave before first light and be the advanced scouts to clear the way for the main army. Captain Stevens will be by shortly to advise us of our marching orders, so I would suggest that you ready yourselves for our trip and pack lightly."

The men were excited and gave up a unanimous cheer, which set off a number of distant cheers from other units around the large encampment. The entire army was happy to finally depart and get away from all the endless drills and marching about for nothing.

Jacob continued, despite the dull roar that was taking over the camp, "Keep your packs light, men. We are far better off keeping only the essentials…a horn, powder, a good supply of lead, a good knife and a hatchet. Anything else will tend to get caught in the trees and brush and only slow us down."

"What about the wounded, like the boy?" an all too familiar voice cracked out. "Are they going to be left behind?"

Unable to locate the owner of the voice, but well aware of whose it was, Jacob called back, "Private, you concern yourself with your own duties and leave those decisions to the Captain."

"Yes, sir, just concerned, sir. These woods are full of all sorts of dangers and I wouldn't want anything to happen to the boy." Private Taylor finally stepped out into the open with a smirk on his face. His friends laughed and waited for the corporal's reaction.

Jacob had only just gotten himself calmed down after his conversations with the fools at Braddock's headquarters, and now he was face-to-face with the man who had recklessly shot Joshua. It took all of his self-control to speak in an even tone. "Private, I have experienced your lack of discipline in these woods once already, and you should be more concerned about your own greasy scalp. By the way, how is your back from the lashes?"

Most of the men laughed, which only made Taylor fume more. By this time privates White and Sinclair had moved in beside Jacob to even up the numbers a bit.

Taylor, unwilling to let the conversation go, added, "My back is fine, the captain decided to rescind my sentence on account of the lack of evidence."

Jacob watched as the others started to disperse and go about their duties, then stepped towards Taylor and said, "I will speak with the captain about his sudden change in your punishment, but know this, these woods can engulf a man pretty easily and his body would never been seen again…"

Taylor got the warning and only responded with his familiar smirk, deciding to head back towards his tent to ready himself for the march. His fellow low-lives submissively followed him like obedient, trained dogs.

"We will have to keep our eyes on that lot," Jacob said to the two privates as they all walked back to their tents.

"The best thing is to cut the snake's head off," Private White suggested.

"True, but we need to catch the bloody snake first," Jacob half-jokingly replied.

Jacob walked away, and forced himself to calm down after his encounter with Private Taylor.

Deciding to walk off his anger, he briskly walked back to Fort Cumberland.

The hospital had outgrown its rooms within the fort and was now located just outside the walls, in two large officer's tents. One housed the less injured or sick and the other held the men sick with severe fevers, contagious stomach ailments and others who were too fatigued to do much. Most of the men would miss the upcoming battle and would be forced to listen to the expected returning men's stories of their great victory.

Jacob was greeted by two grenadiers sitting on a couple of gun powder barrels, keeping themselves busy by wiping down their muskets.

"What is your business?" one of them barked, not even bothering to look up.

"A little respect, privates," Jacob replied. He hadn't expected anything from these British privates; he had experienced the condescension of

British regulars time and time again, but he was still not in the mood for more disrespect after his run in with Taylor.

The pair of guards glanced up briefly and the same soldier scoffed, "Again, what is your business…sir?"

Before the discussion could escalate, a white-coated doctor pulled back the flap of the main door and hissed, "Please keep it down, gentlemen; these poor souls need their peace and quiet."

Stepping forward and ignoring the two grenadiers, Jacob spoke up, "I am Corporal Sims, doctor; could you please update me on my son who has been in your care for the better part of the week."

The doctor stood rubbing his arms with a well-used cloth, and finally said, "Aye, you talking of the young lad, Joshua? He is fine and recovering well. The boy is strong and fought off most of the damn fever that has swept through both tents."

Overjoyed at this news, Jacob asked, "When will he be well enough to travel? Can I speak with him?"

The doctor tossed the cloth onto the ground, just short of a small pile of similar towels and said, "He won't be going anywhere for about a week and no one, not even Braddock himself, is permitted inside the tents. We have all the sick patients we can handle without exposing healthy men to the illnesses. You will just have to wait."

Knowing he had to get back to his camp, and that trying to convince this doctor to let him in would be futile, Jacob asked, "Could you please pass on the message that his father came by and I will see him on the trail in a week or so?"

The doctor pulled back the large canvas flap and replied, "No promises, I have a lot more important issues to deal with, like your Washington's illness and getting him back to active duty. He is certainly my worst patient. He's only just arrived and I already pray for the day he is out of my hair."

As Jacob watched the doctor disappear behind the flap, he looked at the two insolent grenadiers who laughed at how the doctor treated him. Having no patience with these two, Jacob walked away but heard one of them say something indistinguishable under his breath.

He decided to put these two arrogant British regulars in their place. After walking back and pulling a barrel up in front of them, Jacob took a seat and said, "Listen, lads, there will be a moment in these woods when the Huron are all around you yet completely out of sight. When they start screaming their horrific war cries, the wilderness will be echoing with their yells and you will have no place to run. You go ahead and line up in your formations, firing blindly into the woods at your unseen enemy and see how many of your friends fall around you. Your nice red coats and fancy caps will make nice targets for the French and their savages to aim at. You will be bloody grateful then, when the 'colonials' charge into the woods and clear out them and save your lives."

He stood up and left before the men could offer a reply, and he smiled all the way back to his camp. Jacob hoped to rush back before anyone noticed he was absent. The darkness was an issue yet he had travelled this trail so many times over the past year that he was sure he could navigate it blindfolded.

The first thing he noticed when he got there was that the large fire was still roaring. On the other side of the fire pit, he could see Captain Stevens, standing alone, staring into the mass of burning logs and branches, deep in thought.

"Good evening, sir," Jacob said quietly, trying not to startle him. "The men have been told to ready themselves and we should be ready to go well before dawn."

Jacob stepped up close beside him as his captain answered softly, being careful not to let the men overhear, "It is interesting how much this army needs us, but still has such little use for us."

Stevens sat down and grabbed a stick to poke the fire. Embers shot into the air and lit up the blackened sky. Jacob took a seat beside him and said, "What are your thoughts of this Braddock fellow? He seems to care nothing for the Indians or their way of fighting and is determined to fight like we are all back in Europe."

Stevens let out an uncharacteristic sigh and confided in Jacob, "We both have seen how a European-trained army fairs against experienced frontier fighters. The poor British regulars will be shot to pieces where they stand. Braddock is your typical British officer and I fear his overconfidence will get us all killed. I must say that Halket and Dunbar appear to be stand-up fellows, but as for our man, Washington, he is far more interested in getting himself a commission than ensuring that the colonial units are used properly."

"It's unfortunate, sir, that the entire army sees us as either scouts or heathens, but never sound strategists or fighters." Jacob replied.

"Well, regrettably, Braddock's regard for us isn't even *that* high," Stevens said drily. "He views us as an undisciplined, crude horde that is an embarrassment and a hindrance to him. He is of the opinion that there is no need for a large advanced scouting party and that the ranging companies are no better than baggage carriers and wagoners. His order for us to help guard the axe men and carpenters by clearing the forward trails is just busy work to keep us out of the way. I don't think he sees a real threat in the French or Huron. I have had my fill of the British and there will be a day when we will not need their muskets or forts."

Waiting a moment while Stevens stood up and tossed a few more small branches on the fire, Jacob said, "Sir, I know we have far more important things to concern ourselves with, but I would like to speak to you about Private Taylor."

Before he could continue, Stevens interrupted, "I know, Sims, I have not forgotten about his punishment, but the doctor gave us all strict orders not to flog or beat any of the men until he has dealt with all the sick. He said he had no more space for the injured and any men condemned to receive lashes would have to wait. I will deal with Taylor and his lot after we take Fort Duquesne."

Jacob could tell by his captain's tone that any more discussion on that topic would only upset him further, so he decided not to push his own concerns, "Very well, sir."

"We should both get some rest; we will need to leave in only a few short hours. The sun will be rising soon enough and then the entire army will be on the move. Good night, Sims." Stevens nodded and excused himself.

"'Night, captain," Jacob replied and kept his seat by the fire.

After spending some time alone thinking about Maggie and his kids, Jacob tried to get a few hours of sleep in his small, uncomfortable tent. The thing was so short that it barely covered his tall frame, but it felt strangely roomy in Joshua's absence.

As Captain Stevens had predicted, the early morning came quickly and Jacob had only managed to grab a couple hours of good rest. The predawn also brought with it a strange air of excitement and anticipation that rippled through the ranger camp.

The men started up groggily, but soon snapped into shape once Captain Stevens readied himself to address them. Jacob stood by his side, and as he looked about, he was impressed at how good most of the men looked. He knew they were eager to get moving and would be far more comfortable in the wilderness than they had been, sitting around the camp being ordered around by the British regulars.

Jacob called the men to attention as Stevens adjusted his powder horn and haversack.

All eyes were on the captain as he began to speak, "At least the weather is clear and once the sun rises above the ridge, we will be well on our way towards the French at Fort Duquesne. I have received our orders and we are part of the informal forward guard in charge of keeping the main trail clear of any trouble, and to provide protection for the work crews. I am sending ahead twenty men, to be picked and commanded by Corporal Sims, to scout the area for any signs of savages or any Frenchmen foolish enough to get in our way." The men interrupted Stevens with a loud cheer.

Gesturing with his hands for the men to quiet down, Stevens continued, "Your enthusiasm is well noted and expected. As for the rest of us, we will stay with the work crews and assist them as needed. It is imperative that we clear the way for the main force and keep any 'problems' to a minimum. Are there any questions?"

The orders were straightforward and Stevens expected no one to ask a question until Private Taylor, his mouth packed with tobacco, piped up, "Can I volunteer to join Corporal Sims and be part of the forward scouting party? I do know these parts better than most, though I'm not bragging, sir."

Stevens ignored the request and Jacob stepped up to answer instead, "As Captain Stevens clearly stated, I will be hand-picking the scouting party, and all volunteers will be considered."

Jacob made no eye contact with the smiling Taylor and dismissed the men at Stevens' nod.

The captain departed to check in with his own commander as Jacob readied his pack and gave his rifle one last check over. It appeared that most of the men wanted to go out with him, but he had already decided on who would be in his detail.

All the men had already grabbed their gear and were waiting in an uneven line for their assignments. Stevens came back into camp just as Jacob began to call out the names he had chosen for his party.

"When you hear your name called, please form up behind me," Jacob barked. "We will be leaving immediately, so have your packs ready for inspection."

"White, Sinclair…" Jacob went through the list, "Kerr, Wallace, McDonald…" He continued until he had named nineteen of his twenty men.

"Private Taylor, please form up."

Taylor strolled past Jacob and offered a confident grin.

"Eyes forward, Taylor and present your pack," Jacob ordered and the private flinched.

"Privates White and Sinclair, would you be kind enough to inspect the men's packs. Remember, only the necessities may come along; I can't have men bogged down with extra weight or getting caught on every low tree branch along the way."

"Yes, sir, only the necessities," the two men replied.

Taylor lost his smile.

White began to pull out most of the contents of Taylor's haversack, and then dumped the rest onto the ground. Jacob walked by and kicked at the various pieces thrown about the dew-soaked dirt.

"You were told to bring only the essentials, private, not your entire bloody tent," Jacob shouted, causing the rest of the men to gather around.

"I need all of this to fight the savages," Taylor said, squirming uncomfortably.

"Four knives, a blanket roll, two bayonets, two hatchets, extra pants, three shirts, a pipe, tobacco and enough food to feed a dozen men? I will do you a favor and repack your haversack for you, Taylor."

Jacob quickly kicked some of the items to one side, and then picked up the pipe and tobacco, throwing them into the woods. Taylor fumed and called out for Stevens to stop Jacob from ruining his personal goods, "Captain, please do something about this! That was a piece of good Virginia tobacco!"

Stevens ignored his pleas and stood by to watch the proceedings.

Jacob jammed a shirt into the pack, followed by a rolled-up a pair of pants. He then split the food into four piles and scooped some dried meat, a piece of corn bread and a piece of cheese onto an old neck cloth. After adding the food packet to the haversack, he tied it off and left one knife and hatchet for Taylor to pick up. He threw the pack at Taylor and said, "Now get yourself in line and let's move out."

Taylor said nothing and picked up the knife and hatchet.

Jacob smiled to himself. It had felt good putting Taylor in his place, but now could expect some form of retaliation.

He decided to split the group into five smaller units. Jacob went ahead of the main unit with the Nettle brothers, Jack and Jeremy, Charlie Walker and a man they all called Spencer. Private White took four men and covered the left flank, while Private Sinclair left with another group to watch the far right flank.

Private Taylor and his crew were left to guard the immediate front of the work crews, while Jacob assigned the rear guard to a fellow Scotsman, named McCrea and four experienced woodsmen.

Jacob ordered them all to stay together in their groups and, if they were in trouble, to send a runner back to the main force to alert the men of the potential danger.

The trudging was slow and tedious. Jacob was careful not to get too far ahead of his men and kept in constant contact with White and Sinclair. The area had been hit with some heavy spring rains that softened the trails to the point where places that were once dry meadowland were now marshy bogs, infested with swarms of biting bugs and venomous snakes.

He was surprised by how slowly the work crews were progressing; it would certainly be a concern for Braddock's advancing army. There was word that more men were being added to the crews, but it would matter little the number as their speed was hindered more by the mountainous terrain and thick, overgrown forests than by a lack of manpower.

A few days into their trek, Jacob was called back to speak with Captain Stevens. He left his small group of rangers early in the morning with orders to continue searching the immediate area, but not to go further than the ruins of Fort Necessity at the Great Meadows.

Jacob reached Stevens' company near an encampment set up for the growing work crews. The confusion on the trail was noticeable right away, and the tension was multiplied by the news that Braddock himself was arriving shortly for a firsthand look at the lack of progress being made.

Jacob saw some of Braddock's aides arrive, but saw no sign of Washington, who must have still been ill and under the doctor's care. Once Braddock arrived, there were numerous heated conversations going on at once, especially between Braddock and his engineers.

Standing near an old oak tree, Jacob watched as the hard working crews continued to cut down trees that were larger in girth than ten men holding hands around its trunk. The Welshmen's skills were amazing as was their sheer determination in removing as many of the old growth trees as they could. The follow-up crew was no less impressive as they endeavored to pull up the massive stumps and the heavy, far-reaching roots.

"It's absolutely back-breaking work, lad; I know I would be bedridden for a month after just one day of hacking at these trees," Captain Stevens said as he moved up beside the startled Jacob.

"I agree, sir; they are an impressive lot. So how are things, sir?"

"I'd be a liar if I said that all is well. The Major General is upset with the lack of progress by the axe men and how little they have advanced. I honestly feel he is underestimating the vastness of this wilderness and his English arrogance must have felt that it would just yield to his superiority. For now, his true enemies are these mountains and the swamps that stop him at every turn." Stevens kept his voice low, remembering that camps were often infested with listening ears.

"What did he really expect?" Jacob commented, never taking his eyes from the men who still had nearly a hundred miles of forest to chop through. "This ground was never meant for the transport of cannon and heavy artillery wagons."

"How are your men holding up?" Stevens asked as he guided Jacob to a small tent near Braddock's temporary headquarters. "Your reports are very detailed and I do appreciate you keeping me abreast of what is going on beyond the main work crews."

"The lads are doing well, but I think they will be much happier once we find some Frenchmen and a chance for some action."

Stepping into the modest tent, Stevens offered Jacob the lone chair while he sat on the small cot he used for his bed. Stevens made sure the tent's flap was tied down to give them more privacy, and then poured two small cups of rum.

After handing one of the cups to Jacob, the captain removed his hat and ran a weathered hand through his uncombed hair. Jacob could see that Stevens was concerned by what was happening.

When he had tipped the entire contents of the small cup into his mouth in one gulp, Stevens put the empty vessel back on the small table and asked, "How is that boy of yours?"

"I tried to look in on him before we headed out, but I was not permitted to see him. The doctor said he was much better and he hoped that Joshua would be back on the trail with in the week, as long as he doesn't catch the fever that has a good share of the men ill." Jacob politely drank down the rum and put the cup back on the table. He was not much of a drinker; he didn't particularly enjoy the taste or the way it gave men more courage than they showed when they were sober.

His father had always warned him of the evils of rum and the root beers that many of the frontier men tended to enjoy. He was told that such drinks dulled a man's senses and that made him weak. Jacob had also seen the effect that rum had had on the savages back at Fort Necessity. He preferred to keep his wits about him and not give his enemy any advantage.

"Well, you must be wondering why I called you back here. I wanted to get your opinion on something that some of the officers have been bantering back and forth about. I think it was our Washington who first suggested that we might want to consider splitting up our force into two smaller forces and send one ahead, unencumbered by wagons or the heavy guns. That group could traverse through the wilderness much faster and set up an attack. It is very apparent that Braddock is upset with slow movement of the main troops and wants to expedite the advancement. What do you think of that?"

Jacob was careful not to overstep his authority by answering too hastily, and decided he should clarify the situation first. "Who is for the idea of splitting the forces, and what would the army do once it reached Fort Duquesne? An army without the support of artillery would be foolish to attack a manned fort, and I know how foolish the English can be."

"As I said, Colonel Washington is steadfastly in favor of such an idea. Meanwhile, Braddock has been busy ordering all unnecessary baggage, wagons and civilians back to Fort Cumberland. I heard rumors that Washington was down to a single piece of luggage. Halket and Dunbar appear to be leaning towards sending some troops ahead but their numbers appear to rather different."

"It does make some sense to move a strong contingent forward, and the lads have been as far as the Great Meadows now, without seeing a single sign of the French or their Indian allies. I feel we should, at least, send a few companies forward to keep the trail clear, since past the Meadows it is in far better shape than what we are dealing with now. Do we have any other information about the French or the garrison strength at Fort Duquesne?"

"I also agree with sending some troops ahead, but it is just a matter of how many to commit. Braddock had a report from some Delaware around the area that the fort was severally undermanned and was down to less than a hundred regulars." Stevens poured another shot of rum in his cup and offered the same to Jacob, who respectfully declined.

"So now Braddock is listening to the Delaware?" Jacob said in disbelief. "Does he realize that they are loyal to the French and there is a good possibility that they want to coax us into an ambush? I would feel much more comfortable if you let me take a couple of men to scout ahead for ourselves and get an accurate picture of what we are getting ourselves into." He made his offer humbly, careful not to insult his commander.

Stevens stood up and opened the flaps on his tent, tying them both back to let in some much needed fresh air. Jacob remained seated and watched him stand in the middle of the opening, watching the activity around the wilderness camp.

Jacob waited a moment before picking up his hat and rifle and standing behind Stevens' left shoulder with his head pressed uncomfortably against the roof of the tent. He wanted nothing more than to get back to his men.

"Sir?" he said. "Should I be getting back now?"

Stevens still blocked the opening, but nodded and said, "You should, and I want you take a look around, like you suggested, and try to confirm what we are heading into. If the Delaware are correct, then we must press ahead. If you can return with anything that might help us, do it sooner rather than later. Our leader has proven he is certainly not a patient man."

Jacob dismissed himself and immediately returned to the trail that would take him back to his men.

He located White and Sinclair just before nightfall and they both appeared to be in good spirits. They reported that there was no sign of the enemy, but wanted to press on further up the trail to hopefully run into a French trader or, better yet, a small French scouting party.

All three men felt concerned by the lack of signs of any Delaware or Seneca around the area. Jacob knew this was one of their favorite places to hunt and if they were not here, then it was possible that they might be with the French closer to Fort Duquesne. If the French had convinced most of the Eastern Woodland people to help them fight the British, Braddock would be in for more of a fight then he had ever dreamed.

Jacob knew that with the rate of the army's current pace, they would soon be stretched out enough along the trail that they would become easy targets for the hit-and-run tactics of the Indians. Added to their troubles were the massive cannon that would be next to impossible to budge over the mountains or through the endless swamps that would soon smother the advancing army. Jacob's hand-picked men were well-seasoned, but even they had difficulties traversing the constant bogs and rivers that were around every corner of this trail. Even they were physically taxed by the terrain of the mountains. Jacob couldn't imagine how the artillery would be carried over the relentless, impassible ground, let alone the heavy wagons and munitions supplies that were probably far more important than any cannon or mortar.

Desperate to find out the strength and health of the enemy, Jacob decided to leave Private White back to command the party of rangers that would be remaining behind. They were to keep scouting the upper trails and keep protecting the hardworking axe men who were fighting to clear the main trail as fast as humanly possible.

The entire scouting party had managed to advance to within sixty or so miles of the ridge that overlooked Fort Duquesne, so Jacob sent most of the others back with White and took Private Sinclair and the two Nettle brothers ahead towards the fort.

Captain Stevens had also asked Jacob to keep his eye out for a possible better pass through the mountains. Braddock and his aides seemed most concerned about that part of the trail, considering the struggle the work crews had already faced clearing the first part of the trail.

Jacob had become aware of more rumors as he moved through the work crews to get back to his men. In addition to report that the Delaware had reported a small garrison at the fort, it was also rumored that the French garrison at the fort was not only small, but decimated by sickness as well. It was also reported that a couple of loyal Iroquois scouts had reported that some of the Delaware, Seneca and Shawnee delegations were reconsidering their alliance since the French were so undermanned and the British army was purported to be so large.

Jacob could only hope that the Indians would remain neutral and let the two European armies fight each other, waiting to get involved until there was a true victor. As soon as he arrived on the frontier, Jacob learned quickly how unpredictable the Indians could be when dealing with their white allies.

Hoping to cover the last sixty miles to the fort as rapidly as possible, Jacob picked not only the fastest of his men, but the three he felt knew the terrain the best.

"Gentlemen, we need to get a decent look at the fort and send back a rough count of the garrison's size to Major General Braddock. We must assume that the savages who have been so conspicuous by their absence must be congregating by the Forks, adding to strength of the French contingency. I need you to move as fast as possible and keep up, so that we might cover the distance quickly and get word of our findings back to the army."

The four rangers made it to the ridge after pushing themselves hard for a good day and a half. Free of the issues that slowed down the main force, the men were now standing on the top ridge that gave them a panoramic view of the entire fort that sat at the confluences of three rivers, the Ohio, the Allegheny and the Monongahela. The scene brought back some chilling memories to Jacob who had last scene the area when he and Joshua escaped from the stockade and faced down certain death at the hands of the French merchant.

Jacob honestly could never tire of the beauty that engulfed the area below. Viewing the thick wilderness of the valley and the prime location of the fort, he understood fully just how critical the impending battle was in the British bid to control the Ohio Valley. He could imagine that if the artillery made it this far and was placed in just the right spots, the constant barrage of cannon and mortar fire could rain down on the fort and deci-mate it with horrific results.

"Damn fine spot for a fort, sir," Private Sinclair said, interrupting Jacob's thoughts.

"Aye, it certainly makes an interesting place for a siege," he answered, still thinking of what might happen.

Deciding to stay on the ridge with the youngest Nettle brother, Jack, Jacob asked Sinclair and Jeremy Nettle to work their way down the steep mountain trail and get as close as they could to the river.

"Keep your heads down and do not take any unnecessary risks," Jacob ordered. "I don't want the bloody French army on our tails, even if they are sick and under-manned."

Turning to Jack Nettle, he asked, "What can you see of the French?"

"The garrison appears to be in order, not that I would know otherwise. Their numbers look strong, possibly three hundred or so regulars. If you look beyond the fort's eastern walls, you can see there is an encampment of Canadian militia, but I can't get a good enough look to estimate how many there are. You can't really see much of any of the savages but you can see a handful of canoes beached on the river side of the fort."

Impressed by the young Nettle's attention to detail, Jacob peered around several of the trees and confirmed the young ranger's findings. "It certainly appears that the French are in much better shape than we were led to believe. I think we will give the other two a few more minutes to report back then send one of you back to inform Captain Stevens."

When Jacob finished speaking, he and Jack waited in a tense silence for about three minutes, until Sinclair and Jeremy reappeared just from beyond the trail head. Sinclair ran directly over to Jacob and reported what they had seen, "Sir, we managed to get as far as the lower shoreline. We had to stop and take cover after we noticed a large Indian encampment on the far west side of the river. Only God knows for sure, but there had to be several hundred Huron, Delaware, Shawnee and Seneca warriors milling about."

"Thank you, private; we had no way of seeing their camp from where we stood. You lads did a good job and I am glad you made it back safely." Jacob offered his hand to both of the men.

He took a moment to scratch down a few notes on a plain piece of parchment that Stevens had given to him:

'Garrison is welled manned with regular troops and Canadian militia. No sign of illness, as reported. A large number of savages camped near fort. In all they appear to be well prepared for us.

Your servant, Corporal Sims'

Rolling it up and securing it with a small piece of cloth, Jacob asked if any of the men would prefer to volunteer or if he should just pick one to make the hazardous trek back to Captain Stevens.

Young Nettle stepped forward and offered to take it back, saying, "Sir, we all know I am by far the fastest, so if you are agreeable, I would like to take the note back."

Jacob hesitated, looking first towards Jack's older brother for his approval. With a quick nod, Jeremy agreed adding, "Just keep moving, boy, and don't stop for anyone –friend or enemy."

With that, Jacob gave young Jack his own, full canteen of water and a few extra pieces of corn bread for his travels. Jeremy stepped up and hugged his brother and gave him a beautiful silver pocket watch that had once belonged to their father. It was distinctly engraved with the Jeremy's name and had their family coat-of-arms stamped on the facing.

"For luck, Jack," he said hugging him once more, "but I expect it back when we meet up again."

"Private," Jacob said when the brothers had finished their goodbyes, "take the main trail until you hit the old Gist plantation, then head south-west along the side trail and keep to that until you reach the work crews. Godspeed to you lad."

The young Nettle nervously saluted and tucked the paper roll into his inner coat pocket. With a quick wave and a smile, Jack was off quickly down the trail.

"He is a brave lad and it wouldn't hurt to say a little prayer for his safe travels," Jacob said as the three remaining rangers stared down the trail towards home.

The young private made it in relatively good time back to the encampment where he had slept just a night earlier with his brother and the others. He stopped briefly for some water and a piece of salted pork, and then took off again towards the axe crews.

Jack knew he was close to the work crew from the echoes of trees falling and the voices that could be heard for miles. Slowing slightly to catch his breath, he was brought to a stop by several of his ranging mates.

He was relieved to see familiar faces, and then a voice called out from behind the two large rangers that were blocking his way.

"Hello boy, where are you off to?" Private Taylor asked as he brushed past his two friends Wallace and Kerr and stepped right up in front of the young man.

"Speak up, boy," he said louder; "I have orders to stop anyone coming through my territory." Taylor spat at the feet of the visibly frightened young Nettle.

"I–have a report–from Corporal Sims for Captain Stevens," Nettle stuttered nervously, but stood his ground against Private Taylor, who had stepped closer to him.

The stink of rum waffled off of Taylor's breath and clothing. Jack had been warned by his brother not to cross Taylor and his gang since they tended to fight for themselves and not for the British. Careful not to upset Taylor, Jack attempted to step back, but Kerr had worked his way behind him and blocked his retreat.

"No need to run, boy; we are all friends here," Taylor smiled as the others laughed. "Sims, you said? Well, give me the note and I will have one of my lads take it to our fine captain. You have done a great duty to all of us and you deserve to rest and have a bite to eat."

"Can't do that, sir; I have my orders…" Jack replied but was interrupted by Taylor before he could continue.

"That's a shame, boy; I was hoping you would be kinder to your old Private Taylor but…"

Before Taylor finished, Private Kerr came up from behind and drove a small hatchet into the back of Jack's neck.

He started to fall immediately and was dead before he slumped to the ground. His blood seeped into the spongy moss below him.

"Search his pockets!" Taylor screamed at Kerr and Wallace.

Kerr pulled back Jack's outer jacket and grabbed at the top pocket of the blood-soaked inner coat. He pulled out a rolled-up piece of paper and handed it to Taylor.

"Good job, lads; now scalp the poor bugger and cut him up some to make it look like some damn savage attacked him," Taylor ordered coldly.

Before the two did their dirty work, Taylor's eye caught upon a shiny object in the boy's jacket pocket.

"Wait a moment, lads," Taylor barked. "Pull that item from his jacket and hand it over."

Wallace quickly pulled out a silver watch with a long silver chain wrapped around it. As he handed it to Taylor, he let the chain unravel so they could all get a good look at it.

"Nice, I think I will keep this for my troubles," Taylor smirked, wiping off the cover and putting it into his pocket. "It is for the best anyway, we need it to look like a savage killed him, and they would certainly not leave such a nice piece behind."

Taylor took the note over to a small tree stump, motioned the two men to continue on with their duties and sat down. He opened the note and after reading it, he tore it into small pieces and buried it within the roots of the stump.

Once the others returned from dumping the mutilated young Nettle's body, Taylor handed Kerr a piece of paper and a small lead pencil to take a note.

"Take this down, Kerr, word-for-word:

'Captain Stevens, I report that the fort appears to be poorly garrisoned and noticeably undermanned. There is also no sign of any savages, thinking they might all be at the Fort at Niagara. It seems we will have no issues in taking the fort from the French.

Your Servant, Corporal Sims.'"

Figuring the captain had never corresponded with Sims before and had never seen his handwriting before, Taylor rolled up the fake note and tied it with the same piece of cloth that was used on the original.

"Kerr, be a good lad and run this back to Stevens and make sure he reads it. Report back to me with his reaction to the note."

He stood proudly as he watched Kerr run down the narrow trail towards the temporary British camp.

Jacob, along with Jeremy and Sinclair, made it back to the camp that they had used only a few nights earlier, not far from where the other rangers should be. All appeared peaceful and they decided to stretch out their tired legs before they made the last part of their return journey.

"Should we be worried about Jack?" his brother asked, giving voice to Jacob's own thoughts. "I'm a little surprised he hasn't returned to us yet."

"Most likely he is resting with the other boys and will be meeting up with us shortly," Jacob said, trying not to show that he was actually worried about the young boy.

The three men set off again, and within a few short miles they were amongst the other rangers that they had left behind. Jacob immediately requested that someone retrieve Private White and have him report to him directly. There appeared to be some extra patrols out in the woods and after a short wait, Private White caught up with Jacob and the two others.

"Sorry I didn't get here sooner, sir, but there is some trouble at camp and I was trying to get as much information for you as possible."

"What kind of trouble?" Jacob asked.

"I would rather speak alone, sir, if that is alright," White he said to Jacob, while looking directly at Nettle.

"Lads, why don't you find some food and I'll speak with you later," Jacob said before returning his attention back to White. "So, what is the problem?"

White hesitated, making sure no one was around to listen in on their private conversation. "Well, sir, it seems a patrol found one of our men butchered and left for dead in the woods."

"Do you know who it might be?" Jacob asked immediately.

"The body was severely mutilated, sir; it looks like the work of savages. They did such a job on the body, though that it is hard to identify him. I was hoping you might be able to." As he explained the situation, White noticed the color draining from Jacob's face.

"So no one has touched the body?" Jacob asked as he followed the private. "Do you at least know how long it has been there?"

"As far as I know, no one has touched the body, and it looks like it has been there only a day or two. It is pretty fresh since the animals have not had a chance to feed on it. I must warn you, sir, it is rather gruesome."

They reached a small clearing, not far off the main trail, and at first glance, the body was nearly impossible to recognize. Kneeling down beside the bloated corpse, Jacob confided to White who had remained back because of the strong smell, "I've seen much worse, to tell you the God's honest truth, but you are right, it looks like the body has been here no more than a day. The bloody maggots have just got to him and there is no sign of marks from a coyote or wild cat."

The scalped, brutalized corpse was badly disfigured yet Jacob knew who it was.

His worst fears had been realized as he recognized the size of the body and the hints of blonde hair left on the sides of his head. Jacob said, "Damn it. This was the young boy I sent ahead of us to deliver a message to Captain Stevens. It's Jack Nettle, I'm sure of it. Did anyone check the body for a note?"

"No, sir, we left him as he was found. Honestly, no one dared to touch him, let alone search through his pockets."

"Bloody hell," Jacob said as he slowly pulled back on the boy's coat and hesitantly reached into the inner pocket. "This is a terrible work, Private White."

"Yes, sir," White managed to say as he watched his Corporal rummage around in the pockets of the dead ranger.

Jacob could find nothing. He checked and re-checked each pocket and found them all empty.

"Did you get any reports of savages in the area?" Jacob demanded, now visibly upset. "We travelled up and down this trail and saw nothing."

"No, sir, we have not seen a single sign of either the French or savages since I have been on ranger detail here."

"We'll have to speak with Jeremy before he finds out from one of the men," Jacob said sadly. It was a hard conversation to have with anyone, but he knew it would be harder for Jeremy since he and his brother were close, and it was his self-imposed responsibility to keep his younger brother safe.

Most of the rangers had started to gather around the small clearing and Jacob called out to one of the men, "Get all the men together; I need to get some more answers."

Jacob only had to wait a couple minutes and all the men were present. He asked White to double-check who was missing from their ranks, and while the private did that, Jacob asked to speak privately with Jeremy.

The young man knew from Jacob's face that the news was not good. "Sir," he asked, "what is wrong? I have not seen Jack since we returned and I'm getting worried; this is not like him at all."

Jacob was not prepared to tell one brother that his younger brother had been brutally murdered, especially since he knew how heart-wrenching it was to lose a brother. He knew that he would never wish that kind of pain on anyone, not even his worst enemy…not even Private Taylor.

He thought back to that dark day in his own life, when he was forced to leave behind his injured brother to be killed at the hands of the Huron and Canadian militia, and he tried to imagine how he would have wanted to be told if he wasn't already aware of the situation.

"Jeremy," he began quietly, "I have some tough news for you and the only way to tell you is just say it. Jack has been found dead and we are not sure exactly what happened to him. At first glance, it does seem like an ambush by some of the savages, but…"

"What savages, sir?" Jeremy jumped in before Jacob could finish. "There have been no reports or sightings of savages in this area since Private Miller was killed. For God's sake, we travelled all the way up to the fort and back and saw nothing the entire length of the trail."

Tears welled up in the young man's eyes as he tried to continue, "Sir, how could this have happened?"

"I can promise you that I will find out what exactly happened and how Jack died. Now, return to your tent and take as much time as you need. I'm just going to inform the others of the news and I don't think you need to hear it again." Jacob wasn't really sure what more he could do for Jeremy at the moment.

White did a roll call and the only two men who were not accounted for were Jack Nettle and Private Kerr. "All present except for young Nettle and Private Kerr, and Kerr might have deserted," White reported when Jacob returned.

Jacob immediately sought out Private Taylor and found him smiling by an old oak tree surrounded by his gang, except for the missing Kerr. He was finding it very difficult to control his temper as he said, "Taylor, I suppose you know nothing of the whereabouts of your friend, Private Kerr? And wipe that bloody smirk off your face, you piece of scum."

Taylor initially kept quiet, but then decided to defend himself against Jacob's personal attack, saying, "This country is not for the weak or stupid. Any man can die unexpectedly or be overwhelmed by all of this."

Jacob waited a moment so he could catch his growing rage.

Re-focusing his attention towards Private Taylor, who still stood by the tree confidently smiling, Jacob snapped, "Taylor, what do you have to smile about? We lost one of our own and the other appears to be a deserter."

He said nothing and just looked directly at Jacob, silently urging him to do something.

Ignoring him, Jacob asked of the men, "Did anyone see either Jack Nettle or Private Kerr last night or early this morning?"

No one stepped forward to say anything, either because they feared Taylor or because they did not want to get involved in the feud between the two men.

"Just 'cause we haven't seen any savages, doesn't mean they are not around," Taylor blurted out. "They could be watching us now as we speak." Taylor gave Jacob an even bigger smile, pushing Jacob to do something he might regret.

The men had no idea what to do, so they all stood around with their heads down, sensing the mutual hatred that flowed between the pair. No one wanted to get in the way and just hoped the corporal and private would get their personal issues resolved so they could all get back to the work at hand.

Jacob had had enough.

"Gentlemen, arrest Private Taylor and tie him up. Make sure you bind his legs, and when Private Kerr decides to return, arrest him as well." Jacob motioned to White and Sinclair to follow his orders.

A low murmur rocked the camp as the two men reluctantly walked towards Taylor.

Before they reached him, Taylor stood up and yelled defiantly, "On what charges am I being arrested?"

Jacob stared directly at him, almost looking right through him and snapped back at him, "This is the British army, Taylor, and you are currently being held for insubordination and disrespecting an officer. I will also be personally investigating your involvement in Private Nettle's murder."

Taylor had no time to reply as White and Sinclair bound his hands and legs with rope. He winced with the pressure applied by the men, but said nothing.

"If either privates McDonald or Wallace decide they want the same treatment, please oblige them," Jacob added as he watched them pull Taylor across the ground and secure him to a large hemlock tree.

Most of the others just stood in silence, waiting for all this to play out.

"You men are dismissed to return to your previous assignments. Private White, would you please gather a small crew and give Private Nettle a proper burial."

Jacob was still upset and knew that he had probably over-stepped his authority, but if he wanted to check around the area for some clues surrounding what really happened to Jack, he needed Taylor out of the way.

Private Sinclair walked directly over to Jacob after he had tied Taylor to the tree, and asked, "Sir, what are your plans? If I may, we both know that you can only hold Taylor for a few hours before some officer sets him free."

"Aye, I know, Sinclair," Jacob confided, "but I need some time to find out what really happened to the Nettle boy. I really need to find Private Kerr, since it appears he might hold the key to what happened." Jacob confided.

Thinking it would be best to speak with Captain Stevens, Jacob decided he should send one of the men to inform him of what had happened. He also sent out two patrols to search around a ten mile perimeter around the camp to see if they could find any signs of savages. Jacob also sent a larger crew out to guard the work crews, who were being pushed even harder since Braddock's visit.

Jacob returned to the spot where Jack Nettle was found and searched the area. Instead of waiting for Stevens to return, Jacob called on Private White to find ten men and get them ready to depart immediately, "I want to follow the trail that Jack took to see if there are any clues that might help me solve his murder."

White left as ordered and a few seconds later, Private Sinclair came running towards Jacob, shouting, "We found Kerr, sir!"

Chapter | **Fourteen**

Maggie slept for a few hours and rose to get her gear together before One-Ear awoke. It was still dark, but the night sky's full moon provided more than enough light to gather what she needed. She was happy to leave this area and get past the French. One-Ear had told her about the land they were heading for and that the tribes were much closer with the English.

It was the land of the Six Nations People.

Maggie had heard about the powerful tribes that lived in New York, especially around Albany and the Lake George region. Besides getting away from the constant threat of being re-captured by the French or their Indian allies, One-Ear told her that her two boys were most likely living with the Mohawk or Cayuga, since they preferred 'young white male children' to re-populate their numbers. They often traded with the Wyandot and Abenaki people, who often purchased white captives from the Huron on their way back to Canada.

When One-Ear got up, he immediately began prepping the canoe for the short portage to the large lake on which the fort was positioned.

"We must get moving and pass by the fort well before first light," he said as he pulled the canoe up and rested it on his shoulders. "The lake is nearby and if we walk fast enough, we should be past the French before the sun rises, and then we will have an easy paddle to the land of my Mohawk brothers."

"Let me help you carry that," Maggie said as she picked up her pack. "You will be exhausted by the time we get to the lake."

"No need, if you carry my pack then I should be able to move much faster if you walk ahead and guide," One-Ear said and she knew him well enough to know that he would not change his mind.

Maggie was both surprised and happy that they were in sight of the lake after only a short walk up the trail. The rising sun was still struggling to reach above the eastern skyline and its bright red hue reflected nicely on the calm waters of the large lake.

One-Ear stopped just short of a small cliff that would take them down to the sandy shore. He placed the canoe down and walked a few feet ahead, checking the area.

"Is there a problem?" Maggie asked innocently, not sure what he was looking for.

"No, I was just always taught to check around before you place your canoe in the water. The cliff gives a Frenchman or some resting Huron some good cover and they would easily hear us before we knew they were around."

Maggie took some time to look around as well and could see the beautiful silhouette of the large stone structure that sat across the river. One-Ear had told her that the Indians called it 'The Castle' and it was originally meant as a place of peace built by the French for all the tribes in the area. As usual, though, the French continued to build up the fortification from the lake inward, despite their assurances that it was only a meeting place for trading and gatherings. It was now an important fortification for the French and was essential in supplying the forts to the south with food and powder.

She was also mesmerized by the size of the lake. It was noticeably calmer than the volatile lake they had travelled on earlier. By now, One-Ear had returned from his search and noticed her staring out into the mass of water.

"I have been told that some people have called this an ocean, but I have no idea if that is true," One-Ear said.

"I have seen an ocean and this is just as impressive," Maggie replied, still looking beyond the French fort.

"We need to keep moving," One-Ear urged as he once again rested the canoe on his shoulders. "The French will be guarding the lake soon and they might even send out some patrol boats to watch the shoreline."

Once the canoe was in the water and their gear was secured, they paddled straight north and then slowly turned back towards the shore once they were several miles past the last French outpost. It was far easier to paddle on this calm lake compared to the stormy, treacherous lake they barely survived on several months back.

The sun was well over the eastern sky by the time they reached a small rocky area that One-Ear pointed at before they turned towards it.

"This place is good to stop and decide where we should go. I have used this place before and it is safe and also has a good trail that takes us to a large village that sits just up the river from here."

Maggie nodded her approval as they pulled hard towards the shore and paddled directly into the sandy cove. One-Ear jumped into the shallow water and pulled the canoe onto the shore.

When Maggie stepped out of the canoe, she helped One-Ear carry it fully up on to the sand, where they were able to unload their supplies, dump the water out of the bottom of the canoe and set it upright to dry in the sun.

As One-Ear busily collected dry wood from around the beach, Maggie cleared a place for a fire pit and placed some rocks in a circle. She also piled some small twigs and branches in the pit and waited for One-Ear to return with some larger logs.

After just a few minutes, One-Ear had a good fire going and they dragged a large log over to the fire where they both took a well-deserved seat. Maggie had missed having a fire and it was refreshing to enjoy the warmth despite the lack of wind coming off the lake.

"Where are we going from here?" Maggie asked as she opened up her haversack and pulled out some bread.

"We are where we need to be now. This is the land of the Iroquoian People and they are the most powerful tribes in all the lands. The French still use the lake to get back to Quebec, but that is because the Mohawk elders permit them to. The English call the group of tribes the Iroquois Confederacy but we call ourselves Haudenosaunee, or the People of the Longhouse. The Mohawk, Cayuga, Onondagas, Oneidas, the Eastern

Seneca and Tuscarora people make up the tribes whose powers reach as far as all the great lakes and the distant ocean." As he explained, One-Ear appeared happy to be back where he had once lived.

"It is good to see you smile," Maggie said as she enjoyed a peaceful slice of bread with some salted pork.

The fire helped warm them up and dry their clothes after the trip on the water. The small cove was secluded enough that it protected them from the winds that suddenly began to whip up and created large waves that smashed onto the shore.

"Looks like we just made it to shore in time before the winds picked up," Maggie said as they both watched the white-capped waves reach almost to where they had safely beached their canoe.

"The weather has appeared to have made our decision much easier. From the waves, I fear we would be foolish to use the lake much more and should stay on land until we reach the village of the Onondagas. It should take us most of the daylight to reach it, but they will be a gracious host towards a Cayuga warrior and an English white women…once we explain our journey to the elders." One-Ear dragged the canoe into a small clump of wind-swept trees that leaned down towards the sand instead of upright towards the sky.

Satisfied that no one would spot the canoe from the lake, unless they landed on the beach, One-Ear poured some water over the fire and Maggie piled scoops of sand over the remaining embers. They took a moment to scatter the circle of rocks to ensure no one from the water would notice anyone had landed there.

One-Ear lead the way and once they used a well-traversed trail that brought them up to a small, grassy field, the two turned east and moved along a relatively flat dirt trail.

After a life time of travelling through mountains, bug-infested swampy bogs and paths that, most of the time could barely fit only one person, Maggie liked the easier terrain of this land. While the thickly-forested wilderness still stretched as far as they eye could see in most directions, the much better-organized trails that they had used so far were better suited for quick movement and provided a much more efficient way to travel from village to village.

One-Ear maintained a quick pace and they finally saw a group of Indians advancing towards them from a northern path that intersected the trail they had been using.

One of the men called out to One-Ear as he slowed to greet them. Maggie could hear them talk and look towards her but she had no idea what they were talking about. They did appear to be friendly and they were laughing and sharing smiles when One-Ear called Maggie to come over and join them.

Translating as they spoke, One-Ear offered a greeting from the men who One-Ear said were from a Seneca village in the mountains of eastern Pennsylvania near the New York border.

"They told me that there is a large meeting of all the most powerful chiefs and elders from as far away as the land of the Ottawa at the village we were heading to. The Englishman William Johnson is there offering peace wampum belts to all the tribes. They said it would be safe to go there and we would be well taken care of." One-Ear laughed and continued to listen intently as the men continued to speak.

Maggie stayed beside One-Ear, waiting for him to tell her what they were saying.

"They also spoke about a large British army marching towards the Forks, but the French recruited hundreds of Huron, Delaware, Shawnee and even some Mississauga warriors to help them fight the English. They laughed at the English General because he felt he didn't need any help from the Indians, although they did get the word that the Six Nations people would stay neutral during the battle."

As fast the men had appeared, they departed. One-Ear exchanged hand-shakes and they all politely nodded towards Maggie. She smiled and was relieved when they all left and let them continue on towards the village.

"Do you think it is safe for us to go to the village with all the Indians there?" Maggie innocently asked.

"We are not all bad, despite what you have experienced." One-Ear said bluntly.

Grabbing him by the arm and stopping him from going further, Maggie replied, "You know that is not what I meant, but you must admit, the Indians I have run into so far have not been overly friendly towards white people."

"We will be safe…I promise."

Nothing else was said until they reached the outskirts of the first notice-able signs of a village. They had to stop when they were blocked by acres of corn that appeared to go on forever. Not wanting to walk through the field and risk damaging some of the crop, One-Ear pointed to a path that ran down alongside the far field.

"I have never seen so much corn in my life." Maggie said, awed by the sight of the perfect rows of corn stocks bending in the wind.

"Wait until you see the village. The previous places we have been in would fit into this a hundred times over."

The smell of fire and celebration was everywhere in the air. Large clouds of smoke blended into the sky and were pushed by the winds that once again were picking up.

Several women were out checking the stocks and pulling out dead or dying plants that might infect the main crop. They carried their young ones on their backs, but to Maggie they still appeared graceful. Some older children ran freely through the maze of stocks, laughing and playing before they noticed two strangers coming up the path. They briefly stopped to look at them, but soon returned to their games and thought nothing of the visitors.

Before they reached the main entrance of the village, One-Ear stopped to speak with Maggie. She had already slowed down to take an admiring look at the fortified village that had walls made out of tree-trunk-sized posts driven into the ground. Maggie guessed they had to be twenty feet high and could not imagine how deeply they would have been placed in the ground to remain upright.

"These are good people and we need to treat them with respect. I will bring you to the Englishman they call Johnson as soon as I can and maybe he can help you. Also, stay close to me until I have a chance to explain our story to the chief of the village." One-Ear finished his instructions just before several warriors came outside the village's formidable walls and stopped them.

Speaking in broken English, they cautiously asked One-Ear who he was and why he was with this white woman.

"We have escaped from the French and have travelled over two great lakes to find our freedom. We just want to speak with the leader of this village and ask if we may stay until we decide where we might travel next."

Maggie remained beside One-Ear, as he had directed her, and just smiled as cordially as was possible. She only hoped the nervousness she felt in her stomach did not show on her face.

The guards appeared to be satisfied with One-Ear's explanation and escorted the two of them inside the first set of walls. Maggie was surprised to see that the outer wall was actually just the first in a set of walls that weaved along like a maze. She assumed it was to stop an attack if they had breached the first wall.

They were left for a moment by their escorts and soon met up with more warriors. One-Ear once again explained why they had come and, much like before, they walked with them until they were in the main area that was as large as any city Maggie had seen in Europe. The distinguishing feature of the village was the long houses that were each more than hundred paces long and were staggered in all direction throughout. The largest sat near the middle of the village and Maggie thought it might be the elders home or the meeting house.

Smoke flowed from each house, some having six or seven plumes of smoke billowing from its roof. There were thousands of natives walking about and it appeared like they were a mixture of many tribes.

"Where do we go now?" was all Maggie could think to say.

"We just wait until another greeting party comes to us and then follow them," One-Ear said, clearly not sure what to expect next.

As had happened earlier, another group approached them but this one was much friendlier than the previous two. Several women came over and touched Maggie's hair and rubbed her skin. They were also friendly, smiling at her and offering her berries.

Maggie graciously accepted the gift and smiled back at them. "Thank you," she said, but they did not respond.

An elder soon came over and again greeted them, inviting One-Ear to join him. He agreed and when Maggie followed, she was immediately stopped. One-Ear appealed to the elder, but he said that she was to go with some of the village women to get cleaned up.

One-Ear had no choice, unless he risked insulting the elder. "Maggie, they wish to clean you and have you ready for a great feast they have planned for nightfall. These women will help you, so please go and I will call for you as soon as possible."

Left behind, Maggie walked with two women, who looked almost her age, to a much smaller house that had many more women sitting outside. Some were busy weaving baskets out of reeds, others working on some furs and a couple doing some delicate quill work that caught Maggie's eye.

Noticing her fascination with their work, the one quilter patted the blanket where she was sitting with all her quills and dyes, asking Maggie to sit with her. She was much older than the others and when Maggie sat beside her she took her hand in hers and touched the still hard porcupine quills.

Maggie smiled and said, "Beautiful, I have never seen such wonderful work in my life."

The woman laughed and began to show how she softened up the quills in her mouth then dipped them in some dye. She then began to weave them together, using some deer-skin as a backing. Maggie was amazed at her patience and skill, as she meticulously weaved then asked Maggie to hand her quills of different colors. It wasn't long until Maggie could see the piece take shape, it was a small, colorful pouch and the intricate design appeared to be that of a turtle.

Before the woman was done, two more women opened a small skin flap over the door and motioned for Maggie to enter. The elderly quilter simply smiled and nodded to her, letting her know that it was alright to go in. Stepping from the sunny outside into the large, dark house, Maggie took a moment to get her eyes to adjust. The room was smoky and smelled of dried herbs and fruit, an odd mixture but pleasant all the same.

There was a good-sized wooden trough that resembled a canoe with its ends cut down. It was full of steamy water and one of the two women was busy dropping flower petals into the water as the other, without warning, started to take Maggie's old clothes off. It had been awhile since she had taken off her outer clothing and she knew the smell must have been rather strong. At first she resisted but after a friendly smile and a point towards the water trough, she understood they wanted to give her a bath.

Stepping up into the hot bathwater and not used to having an audience, Maggie quickly dunked under the water, despite how hot it felt. Maggie was much taller than any of the villagers she had seen and the wooden tub was so short that she had to press her knees close to her chest but all the same it was still better than a cold river or choppy lake. The women laughed at the face Maggie made as she finally relaxed and splashed some water over her face. The woman who had been cutting up the flower petals handed Maggie a large wooden cup to pour the water over her head.

She hadn't realized how much she missed having a moment to take a real bath, she had been in several of the rivers along the way to have a quick clean, but nothing this nice. The other woman put some finely ground up stone-like material in her hands and asked Maggie to sit up. Again she hesitated but the woman softly rubbed the gritty mixture over her back and gave it a good scrub. Expecting it to hurt, Maggie flinched but soon relaxed again, enjoying the rubbing that really invigorated her skin.

Maggie was then handed a sweet smelling liquid that the woman pointed to her head, understanding she wanted her to rub it into her hair, Maggie obliged. Her once brown hair had been blackened with the fifth of the last several months and her once pale European skin was nicely tanned from all her time out in the sun.

After taking a few minutes to soak in the wooden tub, she was embarrassed at the dirt scum that rose to the top of the water. The women left for a moment then returned with a large blanket that they wrapped around Maggie once she stepped out of the water. They sat her down by a small fire pit and began to comb out her hair with a piece of carved deer bone. As the one woman combed out the knots, the other braided the completed side.

Never in her life had she been so well taken care of and once they were done, they gave her an ankle length, brain-tanned dress that was colorfully decorated with quills and ribbons. She felt wonderful in her new attire and laughed to herself about what Jacob might think of her if he saw her now.

Maggie also thought back when her Huron captors took her two girls and put similar outfits on them, then paraded them in front of their white mothers before they were taken away. She wondered why she was being cleaned up. Was it to be paraded in front of the visiting chiefs and elders? Was she going to be some savage's prize or, worse, slave?

She tried not to think about it and only wished that One-Ear would return soon to be by her side.

Before she stepped back into the sunlight, the elderly quilter came in and presented her with a beautiful neck bag that she hung around her neck. Maggie graciously accepted the thoughtful gift and gave the woman a hug that she happily returned. The woman then stepped back to take a better look at Maggie's new dress and said, "You are as beautiful as the morning sky and I will call you, 'Morning Fire'. She looked at the others and repeated the name and they repeated it back.

The elderly woman grabbed Maggie's hand and proudly took her outside to present her to the growing throngs of village women and children. She lightly pushed Maggie in front of her and then spoke to the crowd, "May I present, Morning Fire; she is now a friend to all the Six Nations people."

Maggie uncomfortably stood in front the hundreds of eager onlookers as they stared and pointed at the white woman who looked more Indian now, than Scottish. Her skin had been tanned a brownish red hue and she thought she could pass for a native.

Some of the women and several of the smaller children approached her to get a better look; they were fascinated by this once white woman who towered over them, as tall as the tallest male warrior in the village, and now looked like them. Smiles and some clapping greeted her and then the crowd soon dispersed. Maggie was happy once the last of the villagers returned to their regular daily chores.

Shortly after the crowd left, One-Ear came by and was initially shocked by Maggie's new look.

"Miss Maggie, you look wonderful," He blurted out, blushing at this 'new' woman he saw standing in front of him.

Maggie said nothing. She had sat back down with the elderly woman who was still working with the endless supply of quills.

"Who gave you the neck bag?" One-Ear asked as he noticed her new necklace.

"This fine woman made it for me," Maggie replied and handed a quill dyed in vermillion to the woman. "She has been wonderfully gracious and kind to me since we came here."

"You have no idea who this woman is and what she gave you, do you?" One-Ear grinned.

"I assumed she is an elder," Maggie replied innocently.

"She is much more; you have made a friend with the village matriarch. She is the grandmother of the most powerful Ottawa chief, the one they call Pontiac. He is here for this meeting and has come all the way from the western region, where the last of the great lakes reach. She is the most senior elder, the one that the other male elders come to ask council with. Her husband was once a leader of the Ottawa but moved to New York when he fell in love with her. She is a Mohawk and you are lucky that she has taken you under her wing. As for the bag, it is a wish bag and the wearer has the protection of the strongest of our Gods, the one who guards over this world and keeps us safe…it is a true honor that she presented it to you and it gives you special privileges throughout the village."

"Can you please thank her for me?" Maggie asked as she smiled at the elder.

"Her English is good and she can understand everything you have said since you arrived," One-Ear laughed as the woman smirked while she concentrated on her quill work.

"Does she have a name, so I can at least address her properly?" Maggie continued.

"Well she is much like your English Queen, but without a King. I have not seen her for years, but when I lived near this village we called her 'Morning Sun'.

"She told me that my name now was Morning Fire."

"You are truly lucky Miss Maggie and you should consider yourself privileged to be under her wing," One-Ear said as he looked behind him, "One last thing. I must leave again for the grand meeting. The village is having a huge celebration tonight to celebrate their alliance with the English and we have been asked to attend. I will come back later and we can go together."

"Remember, you mentioned the Englishman Johnson is here and I would enjoy meeting with him. Can I come with you now and watch the grand meeting?"

Morning Sun looked up at him and nodded her approval. "Women are not usually invited, but it appears you can," he said as he looked at the elder.

The older woman stood up and said, "She is strong and brave. I want her to go with you and then I shall speak with her about thoughts of the meeting." Looking at Maggie, she continued, "Go and listen. When you return, we can speak and you can tell me your story."

Maggie politely hugged her and left with One-Ear.

While they walked, he continued in wonder at Maggie's new-found standing, "I still cannot believe you have been taken in by such an important elder. She has the ear of all the chiefs from here to the ocean and back towards the lake people. Her words are like they were spoken directly from the Gods, and the men do as she says."

"You must point out her grandson to me," Maggie said as they stepped into a large covered area that held more than a hundred men, plus the dozens of chiefs that sat at the front and their numerous aides.

Maggie was noticed right away, yet no one said anything about why she was there. She sat beside One-Ear and could see that she was the center of attention, something that was also noted by the first speaker.

One-Ear pointed out William Johnson, who was seated among the chiefs and reminded Maggie of a wealthy landowner back in Scotland. The elder's grandson, Pontiac, sat to the left of Johnson.

As Johnson rose to speak first, as the honored guest, he was interrupted by Pontiac, who jumped up and began his own speech first. His opening words were directed at Maggie, "I am honored to see my grandmother's friend has sat among us. She is more beautiful than what has been spoken by others, and I hope she will be kind enough to sit by my side at our great celebration tonight?"

Maggie was unsure what to do, so she offered Pontiac a gracious bow, thus accepting his invitation.

One-Ear then whispered to her while the Ottawa chief continued to address the others, "You have certainly caught the eye of all the important people in the village today. Chief Pontiac is one of the most powerful men here, outside of the Six Nations, and his request should be taken as a great honor. I only hope there is enough room for me at your table!"

"Stop it!" she nearly giggled. "He is merely a man, and I want to bring you to his table as my guest."

Maggie returned her attention to the regal-looking Ottawa chief as he finished his opening remarks and began his speech. She had no idea what the Ottawa chief was saying, and even One-Ear only understood a few words, as Pontiac spoke in a form of Algonquin. He mixed in several phrases from the Ottawa dialect that made it difficult to translate enough so it would make sense to her. His passion and unbridled fury did hold Maggie strangely captivated, no matter what tongue he spoke in.

"The Ottawa are not friends with the English, so I am surprised he has decided to speak among the Iroquois, who have such a strong alliance with the English," One-Ear whispered to Maggie at one point.

Maggie looked at William Johnson to see his reaction to be usurped by Chief Pontiac. He did not seem offended, but did appear concerned by some of the chief's words. Maggie found him to be as impressive a figure as the Ottawa chief, and she really hoped she would have a moment to speak privately with him concerning her own family's circumstance.

Pontiac continued to speak for over an hour, pointing several times at Johnson and his English delegation. When he had finished, the representative members of the Confederacy politely cheered, but they were very careful not to insult their English allies.

One-Ear and Maggie sat through the entire day of speeches. Each remaining speaker was very cordial and confirmed the Confederacy's agreement to remain neutral in the war between the French and British, and committed to keep trading with the English.

Maggie watched Pontiac's reaction to the many speeches, pledging solidarity with the English. She noticed him shake his head on several occasions and One-Ear explained that it was when each of the Six Nations chiefs accepted the word of the English that they would remain off of the lands of the Iroquois, allowing the native people to keep the land to live on.

When the last speaker had finished, William Johnson stood up and briefly spoke his thanks as he personally gave each chief a peace wampum belt and a medal as a gift from the King, "Thank you for hosting this gathering. Please accept these gifts as a gesture of peace from your King, who watches over you from across the great waters."

Pontiac was the last chief approached by Johnson, who offered the gifts politely, but the Ottawa chief refused to touch them. Instead, he let one of his men accept the items, which were quickly placed inside a bag.

One-Ear saw this exchange and whispered to Maggie, "The Ottawa need to be careful that they do not insult the English, but at the same time, they cannot threaten their relationship with the French. Pontiac is smart enough to know that the French have probably already heard that he is here, and that they must be uneasy at the thought that one of their strongest allies is sitting among the English."

"The politics and allegiances within the tribes are interesting," Maggie replied. "I never realized the division was based on their relationship with the French or English."

"Many of us like how the French treat us with respect, but the truth is that it is all about land," One-Ear said bluntly. "The French and English will both lie to protect their own interests." He stood up once the other delegates appeared to be finally ready to enjoy the feast being prepared by the villagers.

Before they left to eat, Maggie reminded One-Ear that she wanted to speak with William Johnson. They weaved their way through the many groups of Indians busy discussing the meeting, and finally stood directly by the English delegates.

Maggie noticed Johnson speaking with one of his aides, and she pulled on One-Ear's hand and confidently walked over to him to introduce herself. "Excuse me, sir, would you be kind enough to give me some of your time?" she asked politely.

Johnson dismissed his aide and turned his attention towards this curious woman, who appeared more white than native, but sat with them and was accompanied by a young Cayuga warrior. He bowed his head and said, "Madame, my name is William Johnson, and I am the King's Indian Agent to the Six Nations people."

"It is a pleasure to meet you, sir, my name is Maggie Murray of Pennsylvania and this is my friend One-Ear."

Johnson bowed his head again and said with a smile, "Please take a seat so we can speak. I must say you are a long way from home and I am curious how you came to be in this fine land."

They sat across from Johnson, and once she had made herself comfortable, Maggie replied to his question, "It has been a long journey, and by God's hand One-Ear has kept me safe through many dangerous situations. My husband volunteered to fight with the Virginia militia and soon after he left, my four children and I were captured by a French-backed, Huron raiding party. They burned our home and took my children and I have no idea where they might be now."

"I am certainly sorry for your loss," Johnson said sympathetically, "but I am not sure how I can help you."

"Well, sir, their children's names are James, Becky, Henry and Mary Murray. I'm aware of your close relationship with the Indians, and I was hoping you could possibly help me find them. One-Ear himself is a Cayuga warrior who was captured by the Huron and adopted into their tribe. He feels my children might have been moved into this area and adopted into one of the Six Nations tribes. I only ask you to speak with the chiefs and inquire if they have seen or adopted any white children into their villages over the past year."

Maggie could see that Johnson was genuinely concerned and she watched as he rubbed his chin, contemplating how he might help. "As your Cayuga friend knows," he began slowly, "sadly, the Indians buy and trade in white children pretty regularly, despite my constant objections of such practices. I can make you no promises that my position holds much merit concerning this kind of situation, but I will speak to the chiefs and hopefully, we can get you some answers. I am sorry to have to tell you, but your children could be anywhere from the Pennsylvania territory to Quebec and any lands in between."

Maggie understood his position and was pleased that at the very least he would speak with the chiefs. Her expectations were low that anything would come of it, but she had to pursue every avenue.

When Maggie had nodded her thanks, Johnson said, "Pardon my rush, but I must head to the celebration and speak with some of the villagers. Would you be kind enough to accompany me to the feast?"

"You have been more than kind, sir, and I mustn't keep you from your business. As for your invitation, I sadly must decline. The Ottawa chief asked me to sit with him and I already accepted; it would be rude to not go now."

"Aye, that Pontiac is not a man to cross; maybe you can use your charm to convince him to join our side instead of remaining blindly loyal to the French." Johnson smiled and excused himself.

Maggie and One-Ear were left standing alone in front of the English delegate area and One-Ear said, "Well, we should work our way back towards the celebration house and find the Ottawa."

"Yes, we should," Maggie agreed and walked with One-Ear through the nearly deserted meeting house. "What did you think of this William Johnson?"

"He appeared to be an honorable man, but one can never tell." One-Ear said ominously.

"I like him; he came across so caring and legitimately concerned," Maggie replied.

They walked slowly through the village, alive with activity. One-Ear stopped right outside the feast hall and they could see the chiefs and villagers beginning to take their places. "Before we sit with the Ottawa," One-Ear said urgently, "I must tell you that they have a deep hatred for the English. The French have used this for their own good, and that is why the Ottawa always lead the Indian allies into battle. They often live separately from the other tribes before a fight, seeking little contact with them. They are ferocious in battle and usually fight for their own causes."

Maggie looked at One-Ear after spotting Pontiac standing with his fellow Ottawa warriors, and asked, "Why would he want to share dinner with me, a white English woman?"

"His intentions are unknown to me; I only said something to warn you that the Ottawa are short-tempered and aggressive. Pontiac is a person to be careful with. He is afraid of no man, white or Indian. If he wants something he will kill for it, or just simply take it."

Once they reached the Ottawa, Maggie was happy to see the elder that had been so kind to her, Morning Sun. Maggie gave a polite nod and smile to Pontiac, who, despite his stern exterior, returned her smile. Maggie then greeted Morning Sun, saying, "I am so happy you are here, I must thank you for all your kindness towards me."

"Morning Fire, you remind me so much of me when I was a young lady. We have a connection that only the Gods understand, but I feel we have been together at one time and our bond has finally brought us together again." With that, Morning Sun moved over so Maggie and One-Ear could sit beside her. When they got themselves comfortable, Pontiac took a seat on the other side of his Grandmother and remarked on how happy he was that Maggie had accepted his invitation to sit with the Ottawa.

"My grandson appears like a wolf on the outside, but has the heart of a loving mother bear," Morning Sun laughed, careful not to let Pontiac hear her remarks. "His smile is something he needs to use more, but he feels it is a sign of weakness. He prefers to frighten his enemies from the outset, instead of drawing them in with kindness before striking."

Maggie shared in the older woman's laughter and said, "I have a son like that who is kindness itself, but guards it like a weakness."

"Tell me about your family."

"My husband is fighting with the English, although I have not seen him in over a year, and my four children were taken from me by the Huron," Maggie confided.

"You are travelling alone in this wilderness?" Morning Sun looked surprised.

"No, my friend One-Ear has been with me since my children were taken. He has kept me safe and well-fed…I am very lucky to have him with me."

Morning Sun reached over Maggie and grasped One-Ear's hand, "You are Cayuga?"

"Yes," One-Ear respectfully answered.

"You make all the Cayuga people proud," she said and squeezed his hand. "Where are your parents, young Cayuga?"

"They are dead; I was taken by the Huron and adopted into their tribe, but I ran from them. I am all alone except for Miss Maggie…I mean Morning Fire."

Morning Sun smiled and then turned to Pontiac to speak with him. As the feast began, each group was presented with a large wild pig, skewered and placed on a bed of leaves. The women of the village brought around wicker pots full of corn, beans and cooked potatoes. They also had herbs and berries to enjoy and several cut spring squash and loaves of corn bread.

There were wooden kegs of rum, barrels of bitter, root beer, and cool fresh water to drink and enjoy. The beer and rum were abruptly refused by Pontiac and his warriors, as they preferred the fresh water to keep their senses.

Maggie could see that Pontiac was amused by what Morning Sun had told him and she caught him glancing at her on several occasions.

The entire village was busy enjoying this amazing feast and Maggie and One-Ear were lost in the festivities. Once Maggie had finished her meal,

Pontiac had one of his men deliver a plate of berries and bread to her. She accepted his gesture and ate the entire plate of food.

Morning Sun broke the silence that had descended while they ate, "Morning Fire, it appears my grandson is very fond of you. I have never seen him look so peaceful and he rarely lets himself have so much enjoyment."

When Maggie had finished the fruit plate, she could not eat another bite, despite the fact she had eaten so little over the last few months. One-Ear had finished as well and had stretched his legs out and was soon fast asleep.

Most of the Ottawa did the same, except for Pontiac and his grandmother. The three sat quietly amongst the sleeping men.

The Ottawa chief finally broke the silence, "Did you eat enough? Most white people would be too frightened to share our food."

Maggie noticed his smile and cordially replied, "You are a great host and it was an honor to eat amongst your people."

Morning Sun whispered something in Pontiac's ear, as they both shared a smile.

She then turned to Maggie, "Morning Fire, you have found a piece of Pontiac that I have never seen before. You have been good for him and I wish you to remain friends for many years. You will always be welcome in the land of the Ottawa."

Maggie thought nothing of this statement and replied, "He is a good and strong man and I would count myself lucky to be called his friend."

Pontiac continued the conversation, "If all the English were like you, I would never wish to fight with them."

Maggie did not know what to say and simply smiled at his eerie compliment and said nothing.

The night sky had blanketed the village despite the large fires that had been lit, and the celebration started to break up as more of the warriors fell asleep. Even Pontiac was asleep, and Morning Sun finally got up.

"You might want to come with me," she told Maggie. "With all these men around and the amount of rum they consumed, a young woman might not be safe despite her strength."

"I would feel much better with you, thank you. I must ask about the rum and why your grandson refused the offer of drink?"

"He has never tasted the white man's drink. He feels it is their way to control the Indians and he does not like how it affects the men's minds. It is poison to him and his people and any member of his tribe who takes up the drink is no longer welcomed."

The two ladies entered the same house where Maggie had bathed hours earlier. They slept on two warm bear skins and enjoyed a peaceful night.

Morning came too early for Maggie's liking, but she rose and helped Morning Sun gather some berries and draw water from a nearby stream.

As the two women walked up the path towards Morning Sun's house, they saw Pontiac and several of his warriors waiting outside the entrance.

"Wonder what is happening?" Maggie said.

"Maybe he is leaving to return to his home and he wants to say goodbye," Morning Sun suggested.

Just as she finished her thought, several of the warriors approached Maggie and grabbed her by the arms. Her first reaction was to pull away, but they had a strong grip on her so she screamed.

The noise drew the attention of several of the village men who rushed over to see what was happening. Pontiac stepped up and slapped Maggie across the face, not hard but enough to silence her. She was shocked by his actions as he just looked at her defiantly.

"What is the meaning of this, Grandson?" Morning Sun asked.

"I am leaving to fight with the French and I want this woman to come to my home," Pontiac said simply, dismissing any objection.

The noise had attracted almost the entire village, and Pontiac stood before them holding a trump line that had been secured by his warriors around Maggie's hands.

Once he was aware of what was happening One-Ear ran over to where Maggie was being held. William Johnson ran over as well and demanded, "What is the meaning of this?"

"This does not concern you, Englishman. I have taken this woman as my wife and she must return with me to the village of my people." Pontiac spoke calmly and his warriors raised their muskets in defense of their chief.

The villagers and the chiefs had no recourse but to accept Pontiac's claim. They did not want to cause troubles with the Ottawa over some white woman, so they backed down.

Johnson was also powerless to do anything.

One-Ear was not just going to stand by and watch Maggie be taken away, no matter if it was the Ottawa chief. Without thinking, he foolishly charged towards Pontiac armed only with a small neck knife. One of Pontiac's warriors appeared to be anticipating the attack and leveled his musket.

A lone shot echoed through the village and when the white smoke lifted, the warrior stood with his musket still resting against his shoulder. His well-aimed shot struck One-Ear in full stride and Maggie screamed as she watched her friend's limp body roll twice along the ground, finally coming to rest just by the warrior's feet.

Maggie's last desperate glance towards One-Ear left her with an image of his lifeless body in a grotesque pose and his brave attempt to rescue her once again.

Pontiac pulled on Maggie's trump line and led his men towards the opening in the village wall. No one in the village dared to move until the Ottawa warriors had disappeared into the maze of the outer wall.

Once again Maggie was a prisoner.

Chapter | **Fifteen**

Jacob waited for Private White to reach him before he asked, "Where is the bloody deserter?"

"Sir, please come with me and I will explain along the way." White immediately turned and ran back towards the camp while Jacob did his best to keep up.

"Private, slow down for a moment," Jacob called out, but White continued running until he reached a large oak tree that had several other rangers waiting by it.

Jacob ran up beside White and after struggling to get air into his lungs for a few seconds, he was struck by a sight that would have made most men lose the contents of their stomach.

It was Private Kerr.

His bloodied body was tied around the tree, naked and scalped. If it wasn't for the bushy beard that always distinguished him from the other rangers, he would have been next to impossible to identify.

"Cut him down," Jacob ordered.

No one was willing to touch the body after it crumpled to the ground after White cut the rope that bound him.

"Please do something with the body," Jacob said. "I am going to take a look around and see what is going on. Either we are all so blind that we can't see there are savages all around us, or one of our own is a murderer."

Jacob needed to speak with Captain Stevens immediately. The ranger he had sent out to inform the captain of the situation had not reported back and Jacob was nervous that he might have met the same fate as Jack and Kerr.

He asked White to accompany him and they were just about to head out when Stevens rode up the trail and blocked their way. "Sims, what is going on? It appears that all hell has broken loose."

Stevens handed the reins to a nearby ranger and dismounted. He walked up to Jacob and launched right into his tirade, "I hear nothing from you for days, then yesterday I get a note delivered by Private Kerr, who didn't even go with you, saying that the French situation is exactly what we had heard. Now this morning, I get word that one of my men is dead and another is being held prisoner. I demand an explanation! What do you have to say, Sims?"

Jacob tried to remain calm and began speaking without trying to come across as too defensive, "Sir, I did send a message to you that the French and Indians amassed at the fort were far more numerous than we were led to believe, but young Jack Nettle was carrying it before he was killed, not Private Kerr. I have no idea who gave such note to Kerr to deliver, but you need to come over here and see what is left of our Private Kerr now."

Once Stevens saw the mangled body, his tone was much less accusatory. "Have you seen any signs of Indians?" he asked, watching his men wrap Kerr's body with a large cloth blanket, then tying up both ends.

"Not on any of the trails that we followed, sir. The only savages we saw were at Fort Duquesne and there were well over five hundred. I fear all the Indians around these parts have joined up with the French."

"This changes everything. I relayed a message to Braddock that the fort was undermanned and we needed to strike before they are re-enforced. He was planning to send out a company of our best men under Colonel St. Clair to reach the fort ahead of the artillery and remaining companies." Stevens fell silent, momentarily lost in his thoughts.

Jacob and White stood by patiently as their captain contemplated what should be done next.

Understanding that the movement of twelve hundred troops along the narrow, twisted, rugged hills and numerous creeks would not likely be much faster than waiting for the axe men to finish their work, Jacob spoke up before Stevens could.

"Sir, we need to get out ahead of them to discourage any potential problems. Most of these men and officers have never experienced a march through this terrifying wilderness. The narrowness of the trail will most likely present them with no opportunity to use a flank guard and that will make them easy targets and expose them to hit-and-run attacks. They're going to be stretched out for miles too; some of the parts are so narrow, they'd be lucky to stand three men abreast."

Stevens remained silent a moment longer before speaking, "We do need to get our company out there to assist the first unit. We can figure out what happened here later; our priority must be getting to St. Clair's army and providing them protection and advanced scouting. I do know that a small group of savages under Chief Monocatuca was attached to their unit, but after what you told me about the loyalty of the savages, we can't be sure he will be of any help."

It took Jacob only a few minutes to gather all the men together. There was a small contingent that was still out scouting the area, but word had been sent out to recall them.

Stevens returned after speaking with a couple of Braddock's aides about his plan. "Sims, are all the men ready to move out? I left a very small number of the men, including Taylor and his cronies, behind to help guard the axe men. They are still attempting to clear the road for the artillery and wagons."

Jacob said nothing of Taylor, deciding that would be a much better discussion after they had defeated the French, "The men are all here except for about ten men who are out scouting. They have been informed of our plan and will be meeting up with us along the trail."

"Good work, Sims. Form the men up and let's get out of here."

Jacob addressed the men briefly to explain what they needed to do, "We will be getting back out on the trail to once again scout for any problems we might run into. Braddock has decided to send out an advanced column to reach Fort Duquesne within a week or two. We all know that the trails or not meant for such a large amount of men to travel on, so we must be their eyes. Private White and his men will protect the column's immediate flanks; I will take an advanced guard farther up the trail to keep our eyes out for the enemy; and the remaining men will extend farther from the sides of the column to clear the woods of any possible ambush."

The men were visibly excited about the prospects of the upcoming battle and that worried Jacob, so he added, "Make for damn sure you keep your eyes open lads. We are all happy this day has finally come but please be wary. The enemy will soon know we are approaching, if they don't know already. Keep your wits about you and be careful."

With that, they men organized themselves and moved out.

Jacob got word from Captain Stevens that the column was on the move, and his group of twenty-five rangers double-timed it up a side trail to keep a good distance between them and the British regulars. Jacob had informed Stevens of a good side path that would cut miles off their journey, and likely pull them well ahead of the main company. From their higher trail, they could see the stretched-out line of men from the trail.

As the rangers trekked ahead then worked their way back alongside the column, they remained hidden enough that even the most experienced grenadiers had no idea they were being watched. Jacob imagined how easy it would be to start an attack on this unit, starting with the stragglers and smaller groups at the rear. Without the ranger units Braddock found so unimportant, these men would be completely exposed to their enemies.

Word was sent out to Jacob to wait for St. Clair and the main body of regulars to reach an old encampment, situated a few miles south of Fort Necessity. Jacob knew it well since it was used a year earlier by Washington's men as they retreated from their defeat at the Great Meadows.

St. Clair arrived in due time and gave the order to set up camp. He had set a frenzied pace that day, and while they still had a great distance to cover,

Jacob was impressed with how far the column had progressed. The men had been greatly taxed by the rough terrain and were beyond exhausted.

When their encampment, set up in a circular arrangement with wagons and officers' cents in the center, was finished, St. Clair sent out several guard units to relieve the rangers and keep an eye out for the French or savages. He also sent out Chief Monocatuca and his warriors to scout further ahead.

Captain Stevens arrived amidst these preparations and Jacob asked, "How was it on your end, sir?"

"Oddly impressive; that St. Clair will drive this column to the gates of the fort before we know it. I just hope the rest of the army can keep up and not miss out on the fight." Stevens smiled as he continued to watch the British camp take shape.

"Seen many stragglers, sir?" Jacob continued.

"A few were picked up by White's men. I can see it being a problem once the column starts to cover the more challenging parts of the journey."

Stevens then gave the order for the rangers to set up camp a few yards north of the British and left to meet with Colonel St. Clair to exchange updates.

The ranger camp was far less formal than the main camp, although they were just as cautious. Jacob oversaw the men and sent pairs of men twenty paces from each of the four corners of the camp to stand guard. They would be relieved every four hours around the clock.

The captain soon returned from his meeting with St. Clair and found Jacob to update him. "That St. Clair is certainly a straightforward gentleman," he began, "he suggested we join up with Lieutenant Colonel Gage's vanguard in the morning.

"He also mentioned that Colonel Dunbar will be setting up a supply camp back at the Little Meadows once we move the column past it. In addition to two of the cannon, they left several of the heavy wagons and some of the wagoners and colonial troops from Virginia to watch over the camp. St. Clair really wanted to move forward with more speed and felt his pace was hindered by the unnecessary artillery and wagons."

Jacob listened silently, but was impressed that one of the British officers had finally realized that this terrain was not meant to support the heavy cannon and wagons that Braddock thought were so critical to their attack.

"St. Clair also told me that he is concerned for the men, especially the European-trained troops. They are visibly disturbed by the vast, silent wilderness and he is considering flying the colors with full pipe and drum corps to motivate the men and ease their fears."

"I'm not sure that is the smartest plan, Jacob said. "The savages and the French will hear us coming for miles and there will go our element of surprise."

"I fear the element of surprise is long gone, Sims. The French, especially their savages, know we are out here by now, and I think we should be prepared for some attacks to slow us down sooner rather than later."

Jacob had suggested that his men get some good rest because there might not be another opportunity to get much over the next few days. Most of the men were like him, though, and only needed a few hours of rest to revitalize them before they were anxious to get back out on the trail.

Once the camp was set up, there were still a couple of hours of daylight left. Feeling antsy, Jacob decided to take a small group of ten men out and search up the trail a bit to see what the next day would bring.

There were still no visible signs of Indians, but Jacob kept his men in single file and had them on full attention. Suddenly, he noticed something amiss up ahead and stopped moving. He motioned for two of the men to move forward with him, and signaled the others to fan out into the cover of the woods, in a defensive position. Fully exposed, but moving slowly, Jacob's senses were on high alert. He heard muted groans coming from somewhere out of his sight. He signaled his rangers to stop and then motioned for them to listen ahead.

The noise came again.

They all heard it that time.

Jacob continued to lead the way and they walked forward with their rifles cocked and at the ready. It was only a few moments before they found the body one of their Indian scouts.

The body had been scalped, mutilated and propped up against a large boulder for all who were passing to see.

It was the first warning sign that the French knew the British were on the move.

Jacob got two of the rangers to drag the body off the trail and placed into the woods. There was no reason to frighten the British regulars this early into the campaign, they would soon see far worse than any man should be forced to experience.

As the men moved cautiously ahead towards a small elevated area that exposed them to a blind spot, the groans they heard earlier grew louder. Not wanting to send any of the men into a potential ambush, Jacob decided to call out over the rise to see if anyone would answer.

"Identify yourself, man," he called out.

The still unseen man called out in a tongue that Jacob did not recognize. He was not comfortable with the situation and refused to send his men into harm's way. Jacob motioned to the others to stay where they were and lowered himself to the ground. He advanced up the rise on his stomach and, taking a deep breath, slowly poked his head up over the hill until he could see the groaning man. It was Chief Monocatuca, bound to a tree but still alive.

Scanning the surrounding grounds, Jacob noticed a handful of additional dead scouts, laid out right in front of the chief's feet. Not sure why they didn't kill the chief, Jacob guessed that it was out of respect or they didn't want the chief dead…yet.

Scrambling quickly over the small hill, Jacob untied the chief and assisted him back over the small rise. He ordered one of the men to take him back to St. Clair's camp. The chief was in reasonably good condition but the trauma of seeing his warriors killed in front of him had clearly shaken him.

"We need to search ahead, men," Jacob said, "but I fear we might be walking into a possible ambush. If any of you want to return to camp, please do it now and I will not think any less of you."

No man took the option and they all moved forward. After checking the trail for a few miles, Jacob decided it would be best to return to their camp. They had seen no further signs of any savages and did not want to get too far north and be forced to set up a small overnight camp.

At nearly the same moment they decided to turn back, shots rang out and the men instinctively took cover. Having no idea where the attackers were, Jacob ordered a slow retreat. He and three other rangers set up a rear guard to hold off any further attack.

All of the men remained disciplined and moved back quickly, but always aware that they might be ambushed at any moment. A few more intermittent shots rang out, but Jacob saw no need to waste their own ammunition.

The men managed to get back safely to the camp. Having now confirmed that there were indeed Indians out in the woods, Jacob knew that the attacks would become more frequent as the army moved forward.

It was clear that this was the second warning sign to the British that the French and their allies were now in the woods.

Captain Stevens was waiting by Jacob's tent and spoke as soon as Jacob returned, "Sims, I heard what happened to you and the lads; this situation is getting interesting. One of your men returned with the chief and he looked pretty shaken."

"Aye, sir, a little too interesting, but at least we know for certain that the French and the savages know we are coming."

After few days of re-organizing the men and scouting the area to ensure it was safe to move out, the officers were assured it was safe to move forward. Jacob and his ranging company encountered no further attacks or signs that the French remained in the immediate area.

The British once again advanced, only this time much slower. The terrain was certainly a factor but the men were being far more cautious.

The noise from the sheer number of men, horses and wagons that clamored across the trail must have been easily heard all the way to Fort Duquesne by the French. Jacob had heard that most of the senior British officers prayed that the French would either just simply abandon the fort all together or stay and fight from behind the walls of the fort. They were still holding out hope that this would be like the civilized fights of Europe.

Jacob had set up a forward guard in a valley just beyond the second river crossing, as well as a large contingent of men guarding the main water crossing while main column finished its fording. He trekked back to the crossing site to report to Stevens, who had ridden through the shallow water with Captain Stewart's Virginia light horsemen.

After waiting for the captains to find a suitable area for their horses to feed, Jacob approached them, saying, "All of our men forded successfully and are set up as an advanced guard to watch over the main crossing."

"Good job, Sims. Do you know Captain Stewart from Virginia?"

He remembered Stewart from Fort Necessity. He was part of Washington's staff and although his light horsemen did not directly participate in the disaster, he did provide the retreating army with some much-needed cover.

Jacob held out his hand to the captain, who shook it and asked, "What do you think, corporal; isn't it rather an impressive sight?"

"Very impressive indeed, sir; the French must be shaking in their boots."

"Just wait until you hear the pipes and drums playing and see the colors flying in the wind, it would be hard not to be impressed. The woods have been echoing with their tunes all morning and my men and I got a nice view of them from the far ridge." Stewart added before excusing himself to check on his men.

"Stay safe, Stewart, and I'll save you a pint of ale once we take the fort." Stevens confidently shouted.

Stewart waved and offered a salute as he rode away.

Jacob and his captain gazed back across the river as the army organized itself to cross the last ford. "Back to business, Sims," Steven said, shaking himself out of his reverie. "What can you tell me about the terrain around these parts?"

"To be frank, sir, the next few miles are going to be treacherous and would be a perfect place for the French to set up an ambush. We have to inform Lieutenant Colonel Gage and the other commanders that we must be extremely cautious in our advancement."

Before Stevens could respond, the first company of grenadiers began its impressive march through the shallow water of the second ford. Jacob saw what Stewart was talking about when the drummers started to beat their rhythmic tune and the pipers played a haunting melody that made the wilderness come alive. It was difficult not to show excitement and Jacob was exhilarated by the entire show. He could see that all the colonial troops were fixated by the wondrous display of British power and glory.

"Bloody hell, Sims, how can the French stop this?" Stevens said in awe, but Jacob made no answer and just enjoyed the display.

The fording took most of the day, but went relatively smoothly. As the rangers prepared for the next leg of the trek, many took time to lighten their packs even more. Most only carried a weapon, an extra shot bag and a full powder horn.

Captain Stevens had been met by one of Lieutenant Colonel Gage's aides and Jacob expected that they would be moving out very shortly. Stevens pulled his horse up alongside Jacob and said, "Several hours ago, one of Braddock's engineering companies was sent ahead with the remaining Indian scouts and a small group of militia to get an idea of the terrain and obstacles ahead. It is time to get the army moving, so I'd like you to take thirty men ahead with a few of Captain Stewart's light horsemen and move forward to offer them some protection and scout out any other dangers along the trail. Lieutenant Colonel Gage's vanguard will focus on providing protection for the front of the army, allowing you to be the forward scouts. Stewart's men will move into the east side of the woods to do some further scouting."

With a quick salute to his captain, Jacob rounded up thirty of the best rangers and gave them their assignment. Just as he was about to move out behind them, Stevens added, "Sorry, Sims, I forgot one last thing. Could you please take this boy along with you? I heard he is pretty adept with a rifle."

Jacob looked puzzled for a moment until he saw Joshua step around Stevens' horse.

"I hope you were not planning to leave without me and keep all the fun for yourself?" Joshua said and laughed at Jacob's surprised face.

"Get yourself up here with me, boy, and let's find us some Frenchmen to kill!" Jacob called out and greeted the young man with a hearty handshake.

Between the earlier scene with the drums and pipes, and this reunion with Joshua, Jacob felt invincible as he ordered the men forward. His resolve did waver slightly, though, as they entered the dark, silent wilderness and the landscape brought on flashbacks of the disaster at Fort Necessity. The sloped high ground that ran parallel to this trail would be a great place for a handful of well-armed men to set up an ambush. The massive trees would give them an excellent cover and they could shoot all day at the enemy below and never be seen.

He had heard that Gage's vanguard called the dark valley trail the Shades of Death. Apparently, despite being highly-disciplined soldiers, the men had moved into the sea of trees only after they had been convinced by threats of flogging, or worse, from their commanding officer.

Jacob himself had never entered this shallow valley, always preferring to trek on the trail that ran above. He was hesitant as he led the men slowly along the trail. It narrowed tightly in some places and opened quite nicely in others. His only thought was if they could safely get past this valley, the remaining leg of the trail to the fort would be easier to defend.

As they moved forward cautiously, Jacob spoke softly to Joshua, "I am glad that you made it, but are you sure you are healthy enough to fight?"

Without taking his eyes off the trail in front of him, Joshua responded quietly, "The shoulder is still sore, but I tested it by shooting of a few rounds back at Fort Cumberland and it felt alright. Honestly, my choices were limited. The doctor said I have restricted mobility in my shoulder and could either be sent to Philadelphia for surgery or live with the pain. I insisted that I wanted to get back to my unit, and he respected that. I can still shoot and that's all that really matters."

Jacob looked around at his men and saw that Gage's men were only a hundred yards behind them, exercising the same slow and cautious advance.

Pointing at a spot just ahead of their current position, Jacob suggested, "Do you see that slope right ahead of us?" When Joshua nodded, Jacob continued, "If we run into trouble, we must get the men up there. It will give us a place to offer some cover fire as the main column passes by."

Suddenly, the unnatural hush that had descended upon the valley was shattered by two of the King's engineers as they ran back towards Jacob's men at full speed, screaming, "Indians! Indians!"

Before Jacob had a chance to ask any questions or issue any orders, the crack of musket fire echoed through the woods ahead of them. He knew that the only men ahead were a few remaining engineers with some of their allied Indian scouts and militia.

On Jacob's command, the thirty rangers ran up the slope to see what exactly was happening.

A mere fifty paces away, French and Huron, led by a strange white man in Indian clothing, were exchanging fire with the handful of Brits and allied Indians. As Jacob surveyed the scene before him, he could hear Gage screaming at his men to move quickly and set up in formation.

It was difficult to know the size of the enemy. The French and their Indian allies remained at the trail head, just as it curved around a bend. Jacob thought that if it wasn't the entire French force, it could just be a scouting party that had accidentally run into the engineers. Once those same British engineers had made it back to the relative safety of the rangers, Jacob gave the order for his men to fire at will in an attempt to push the French back.

He raised his own rifle and took aim at the oddly-dressed Frenchman, howling like his savage allies. A quick shot rang out and Jacob could see that he had hit his mark. The Frenchman fell directly back onto the grassy floor and appeared to be dead. The shot made the increasing numbers of French and Indians stop, even amid continued firing from the rangers.

Their enemy's confusion gave the two companies of grenadiers that followed Gage's vanguard the opportunity to pull up to the small ridge ahead of the ranger's location. Several independent militia units came running down the trail to reinforce the regulars.

Two six pound cannon were quickly pulled into position by horses. The gunners unhitched the team and immediately fired off a few rounds just to add to the confusion.

Covered by the slope at their forward position, Jacob and half dozen rangers maintained rhythmic volleys of fire straight towards the middle of the French forces. Jacob watched as most of the Indians and the Canadians began to run, but were rallied by some of the French officers. They then began to split their forces and spread out across the high ground.

By now, the disciplined British grenadiers had opened up a continuous volley fire into the woods, and Jacob found himself mesmerized as he watched them through the thickening white smoke. One rank knelt while the other stood behind it, and they would alternate their shots so that while one rank shot, the other was reloading. While they looked impressive with their military precision, their shots were not effective, as the French and Indians simply remained behind the mass of trees, firing back whenever there was a pause between volleys.

Jacob and his fellow rangers concentrated their fire on the front ranks of the regulars and Canadian militia, forcing them back and seeing most of the militia run screaming, "Sauve qui peut…sauve qui peut."

The rangers fired at will and tried to aim their shots, unlike the disciplined grenadiers, who seemed to shoot blindly, in their hope to drive back the French. The experienced French regulars had learned from the Indians that if they stayed behind the trees and shot after the volley, the British made far easier targets.

Jacob decided not to advance his men towards the retreating militia, since the French regulars maintained their position and did their best to return fire. The grenadiers, on the other hand, greeted this small retreat with loud cheers, which were short lived.

A different French officer had stepped forward and once again rallied the men, ordering them to disperse further into the wooded area surrounding the enemy. They quickly followed orders and unleashed a deadly volley into the ranks of the cheering grenadiers.

Confusion quickly changed sides as the French regained their composure and poured more fire directly into the British advanced company. The grenadiers had not been prepared for this, and were completely exposed to an enemy that was able to blend with the trees.

White smoke hung low in the air like a thick morning mist, and through it, Jacob could barely make out what was happening, despite the fact he was only a short distance from the grenadiers. Their sickening screams told him they were in trouble and he needed to do something to relieve them.

"Wilson," Jacob screamed to the man next to him, barely audible over the thunderous musket fire, "move towards the grenadiers and see what the hell is happening. Find Gage and tell him the French have fanned out along the high ground and we are all taking heavy fire."

He knew they were in trouble; it was Fort Necessity all over again. The British were unable to see their enemy, but were taking merciless fire that was decimating their ranks.

By now, the flank guards were surrounded and overwhelmed. Jacob and his small group of rangers were in danger of being cut off from the main army. All he could hear was the war cries from the savages and the now muffled yells from the devastated British soldiers.

The woods were now full of white smoke that added to the confusion. Jacob's men were now between the grenadiers and the remaining companies of the advanced column. Their advance only added to the slaughter, presenting the enemy with additional, easy targets.

Jacob knew he needed to act and motioned Joshua to run towards the spot he had pointed out earlier. It was on a good slope and laced with some boulders that would help provide some relief. Unfortunately, it also meant that they would have to run across a patch of ground that would leave them completely exposed to their concealed enemy. It would position them near the trail head and between the two enemy armies who by now had spread themselves on both sides of the valley.

Joshua stood up to run, but was instantly frozen by the image that met his eye. Jacob moved up behind him and understood what had affected him so. He immediately ordered the men to retreat back towards their previous position.

The once disciplined, impressive line of grenadiers was now a red mass of dead and injured men. The few that were not injured still continued to fire off shots even though they couldn't see the enemy. Some of the men even stood in for the dead gunners, but only wasted the cannon balls as they never came in contact with the enemy. All it did was add more blinding white smoke to the already congested valley.

They were highly-disciplined and highly-trained, but not for this kind of fight. The French position had changed to allow them to fire into the grenadiers from both sides, leaving Jacob and his fellow rangers helpless to relieve their suffering.

The battle had raged for over an hour and had broken down the organized units of British soldiers into small pockets of desperate men struggling to survive. Jacob knew by this point that the battle was lost and it was now his duty to save as many of the men as possible. His only priority now was to get as many rangers as he could out of the congested 'death valley' and back towards the river. If they could make it across the second ford and re-organize what was left of the devastated army, the French and the allies might think to chase them down. That would force them to cross the same river and bring them out in the open.

He knew it would be hell getting past the incessant French firing, not to mention the hordes of confused and packed-in British regulars blocking the trail.

"Boys," he screamed as he motioned towards a group of man-sized boulders on a patch of sloped ground just to the south of them, "you can see it is bloody murder all around us, but we can't just sit back and do nothing. We must get into the woods."

Shouting frantically, Jacob boldly stood up and ran as fast as he could directly to the first set of boulders, only a few paces in front of the woods where the French sat firing at will. He could feel Joshua right on his heels and they were able to make it without mishap, as the French still concentrated most of their efforts on the grenadiers and the rest of Braddock's army that was still struggling to advance.

When they reached the cluster of boulders, fallen trees and scattered rocks, Jacob, Joshua and a handful of other rangers began to fire into the exposed flank of a large company of militia and Huron warriors. Initially, the French had no idea where the fire was coming from, but when they noticed the small unit of rangers, they reorganized their attentions towards the bold rangers.

The small piece of ground where the rangers stood to fight elevated them enough to provide a slight panoramic view of the entire battlefield. Even through the dense smoke, Jacob was shocked at the scene of disaster. The French and their allies had taken up a position that was within close range of the British guns and artillery, but they still were well-covered by a line of massive trees. He could see that the British troops had been reduced to a confused, crushed and frightened mass, blindly firing at anything… even their own men.

Jacob also spotted Braddock, foolishly still mounted on his horse and sitting high above his frightened men. He was still screaming orders in a valiant attempt to direct them. Washington was also in the middle of a pack of men, still trying to rally the troops amidst chaos. He too was on the back of a horse, providing an excellent target for the French.

Jacob was shocked that neither officer had been injured, considering the carnage that lay below them.

The small but effective group of rangers bravely kept up a steady fire, despite witnessing how the enemy had fanned out further along both sides of the entire ridge and had the entire British line covered now. Even with their unfailing fighting spirit, the rangers could do little to halt any progress the enemy was having on the decimated British below their position.

They watched the French regulars, along with their savages and undisciplined militia purposely targeted the officers. Jacob had already seen many dead officers carried off the field during this brief battle, and knew how it affected the discipline and efficiency of the regulars to lose their commanders. The enemy strategically remained hidden behind trees or kept on their stomachs, firing freely into the mass of red-coated targets who had no place to hide.

Jacob's band of rangers kept up their fire into the French lines until they realized that they were taking fire from their own troops below. The small unit was being forced from the security of the boulders, not from the enemy but from the panicking grenadiers who were shooting blindly at anything that moved. Jacob called out to his men, "Sorry, lads, but we have to get out of here. Our own side is shooting at us and we need to get back down into the valley before they kill us all…now follow me."

Once again, Jacob bravely led his men through the heat of the battle. Miraculously, they found Captain Stevens and the rest of their company immediately.

"Damn fool Braddock has gotten us all killed," Stevens shouted when he saw Jacob and his men come to join what was left of the rangers. Many had died or were injured and unable to return fire, but the rest had kept their fire and fight alive and were ready to keep going.

"Sir, if we all get into the woods, we can fight them like we have been trained," Jacob screamed at the Stevens, whose face was blackened by the dense powder that continued to send pungent clouds of white smoke that burned the men's eyes and throats.

Stevens made no answer.

As they attempted to survive the endless, deadly fire, Jacob heard the desperate shouts from Braddock. He was still making an easy target of himself, riding around his dying men attempting to rally them. He yelled for the men to stay in formation and keep returning fire.

Frustrated at the foolishness and unwavering arrogance of the entire army, especially Braddock, Jacob saw Colonel Washington slowly ride past, shouting at anyone who could hear him. Jacob rushed towards him and pleaded, "Colonel, we have to get into the woods, it's our only chance."

Washington peered down at Jacob, who saw that the colonel's coat showed the holes of several lead balls that had passed through it without striking his body. After a brief moment of thought, he ordered, "Men, move towards the woods and take the fight to them."

Jacob relayed the order to the rest of the men, many of whom rushed into the woods without a minute's delay. Jacob and Joshua were just about to move out after them when Braddock pulled his horse alongside Washington's and screamed almost incoherently, "What in God's name are you cowards doing? Stay in your line and fight; we are not savages!"

Washington said nothing, but could not halt the first group of men who had already charged up the slight slope.

Joshua could not hear Braddock over the noise and confusion, and before Jacob could call him back himself, he saw Braddock, consumed with rage at the sight of some of the men moving into the woods, lunge forward to stop the erratic charge.

With his sword overturned, the Major General swiped at several of the men and then, with a wild backswing, he smashed it hard against Joshua's skull. Joshua never saw Braddock or heard his rants as he slumped to the ground.

His fellow rangers stopped running and shooting, even some of the disciplined grenadiers could not believe the sight of one of their own officers attacking a young soldier who was just following orders. They stared desperately at their fallen mate, who appeared dead. They were shaken back into reality by a volley blast that smashed all around them.

Captain Stevens, having seen the entire incident, rushed heedlessly to Joshua's side ignoring the intensity of the enemy fire. Braddock said nothing more, pulling on his reins and jerking his horse back towards another small group of grenadiers fighting near a particularly narrow point on the trail. Washington remained mounted, looked towards Jacob and then obediently followed his commander.

Jacob could not believe his eyes.

Stevens pulled up Joshua's limp body and called out that he was not dead, just dazed. By now, several of the rangers had formed up in front of Stevens to provide him with some cover.

Jacob did not hear him. He was deafened and blinded by a rage he had only ever felt when he was forced to leave his twin brother behind at Fort Necessity to die.

He checked his rifle and, without a thought except for indignation at the insane actions of a stubborn, arrogant British Major General, he aimed his rifle at the head of the unsuspecting Braddock.

He squeezed the trigger and a cloud of white smoke momentarily blinded his view.

Seconds later, he ran forward to see if he had indeed hit his intended target. He saw Braddock slumped on his horse as two grenadiers and one of his aides struggled to keep him from tumbling to the ground.

Jacob was unsure if he was dead, but he knew the lead ball had hit him either in the chest or shoulder. Despite the fact that he had aimed for his head, Jacob was satisfied with the amount of blood that was quickly staining the commander's outer coat.

He had expected to be arrested on sight, but the grenadiers and all the officers that were in the area were far too busy removing Braddock from his horse and moving him from the battlefield. The only prayer Jacob uttered as he ran coolly back to where the rangers were fighting was that they would assume it was a Frenchman who fired the shot.

Returning quickly, he noticed that Joshua had been moved behind a tree and that one of the men had wrapped his head in a make-shift bandage. Stevens stayed by the boy's side, while still attempting to keep his surviving rangers in good order.

"Are you alright, lad?" Jacob asked as he knelt down by the glassy-eyed Joshua.

"A small headache, but fine considering the circumstances," he replied, rubbing his head.

Captain Stevens left them, but returned quickly with a sick look on his face. "All is lost, Sims; we must get the lads back towards the river before the bloody French lose control over the savages or their militia. Braddock's been hit and the situation ahead is one of utter panic. I saw Washington trying in vain to get the men to retreat in some kind of order, but they are just running."

"My fear is the same as yours," Jacob relied, "if we don't move soon, the bloody savages will be all over us."

The men had been informed of the situation and were already pulling the wounded out of the piles of the dead and near-dead. Jacob left Joshua to be escorted by two rangers and moved ahead to see what was happening. When he was just out of sight of his unit, he was intercepted by Private Taylor who greeted him with his all too familiar smirk.

"Nice shot, Sims," Taylor said as he blocked Jacob's way.

Jacob said nothing and attempted to push Taylor aside.

The private stood his ground and latched onto Jacob's arm, "What do you think your Captain Stevens will say when I tell him what I just witnessed?"

Jacob jerked his arm free and pushed his face closer to Taylor, "What did you see, you drunken, no-good fool? All the lads know you are just an old, rum-loving liar."

Taylor remained face-to-face with Jacob, now clearly irritated by his tone, "Listen, boy, murder is a serious offense and I will make sure you are left hanging on some bloody tree along this trail, if I have to do it with my own hands."

Jacob had little to fear from Taylor, but he did inwardly shudder at the possibility that others might have seen his shot. Growing tired of this conversation, he drove his fist into Taylor's stomach and then smashed the butt of his rifle into his temple.

He stood over Taylor's body and watched him struggle to catch his breath. Thankfully, the shroud of white smoke that had hovered around them all day had not yet lifted, and Jacob viciously brought his foot down hard onto Taylor's exposed jaw.

Jacob felt Taylor's jaw displace and break just before the beaten drunk spat up a mouthful of blood and blacked out. Jacob coldly walked away, leaving the man bloodied and unconscious. He hoped that if the private's jaw was indeed shattered, it would keep him quiet for the time being and give Jacob some time to figure out what he would have to do next.

Gathering his wits and controlling his temper, Jacob could see that the one-sided battle was now turning into a complete route. Most of the rangers were in full retreat mode, picking up the injured as they went. Jacob pointed out Taylor's body and had two rangers pick him up and drag him along.

A little ahead of the small group of remaining rangers, Jacob could still see Washington riding his horse around, doing his best to keep the men orderly as most of them ran back towards the river. A good number of them just threw down their muskets and packs and ran as fast as they could towards the river, where only a few hours earlier, they had crossed feeling invincible.

Stevens reached Jacob, who was keeping the men moving. The captain was still visibly shaken, and said, "The savages are moving out of the woods and brutalizing the dead and wounded. I saw a small pocket of New York militia and some grenadiers caught between us and the marauding Huron."

"Let me move back and speak with Washington to have some men attempt to relieve the troops at the rear of this retreat," Jacob suggested.

"Do what you think is best, but I must get these men out of here," Stevens said, squaring himself for the task ahead.

Jacob turned and ran to where he had last seen Washington. He saw him now in the distance with the remaining officers, who were placing Braddock's body into the back of one of the last remaining wagons.

Washington was still trying valiantly to get some of the regulars to organize a rear-guard to cover the retreat, but his efforts were still greeted with deaf ears. Jacob was disgusted by the actions of the British regulars. They had been so disciplined but were now no better than an uncontrolled mob. They made easy targets for the avenging savages and the Canadian militia, who were bent on getting their hands on trophies of the battle. Some were run down and butchered outright, while even more were taken prisoner to face fates that would prolong their worst fears.

Jacob looked at most of the colonial troops, who did remain disciplined and tried their best to fight as they retreated. He decided that they would be more likely to step up and aid him.

Just as he was hoping to rally a few of the colonial troops, Jacob heard a voice call to him from his right, "Sims, come to me."

He looked up and saw Washington desperately calling to him, "Sims, get some of your Virginians and set up a rear guard. We must hold them back so this doesn't become a complete catastrophe. I must attend to the Major

General and have the doctors assist him. For the love of God, just get us some time to cross the river."

Jacob could tell that the usually calm Washington was leaning toward desperation as he did his best to lead the remaining troops and keep his commander alive in the face of a disaster. Having no other option but to follow the order, Jacob obediently called back, "I will sir, and the rangers will hold the line for you."

It only took a few minutes to amass men from his company along with an odd mixture of green, brown and red coated survivors. All told, he had over one hundred men to serve as the rear guard. They got in formation and answered the continuous volleys sent by the advancing French and Huron.

Thankfully, most of the enemy, especially the Huron and Ottawa, were more content with pillaging the dead for their trinkets and war prizes than fighting the survivors as they retreated. The scene of Huron warriors prancing around with the mitre caps and coats of the numerous dead grenadiers made the men of the rear guard fight with a renewed vigor.

The field in front of them was now filled with uncontrolled French-allied Indians and the equally savage Canadian militia. Jacob's guard kept up their fire on the French regular troops who moved in to advance onto the retreating British.

Captain Stevens had passed through the rear guard with the injured and dying, as Jacob motioned to him to keep moving out, "I will stay as long as possible, sir, take the boys to the river and join up with Washington. We will be there shortly."

"Good luck, Sims, and stay alive," Stevens called out and gave a haphazard salute.

Jacob saw Private Taylor, still unconscious and being carried by two rangers. Joshua joined up with the guard, ensuring Jacob that he was fine and fit to fight. Happy to see him looking much better, Jacob waited until he was by his side before speaking, "Good to see you, lad. I wouldn't think any less of you if you stayed with Stevens and the other injured."

"You want me to miss all this fun?" Joshua replied sarcastically as he nervously peered ahead at the horrible scene of looting and some of his fellow mates being taken prisoner.

The men also saw some of the Indians get their hands on liquor that they pillaged from a number of the wagons abandoned by the fleeing

British. The next few hours would be a scene that most of the men brave enough to remain behind would soon wish to forget.

The hysterical screams from the unlucky men, who were unable to escape the clutches of the marauding victors, hit the rear guard especially hard. Many hung their heads or shot off volleys just to obscure the heart-wrenching noise. Jacob felt the worst for the severely injured that could not be moved by the retreating rangers and were brutally murdered by the ravaging savages.

Scanning the rest of the field, Jacob saw British artillery pieces and wagons of powder, supplies and officers' personal possessions dragged off the field by the enemy. Everything had been hastily abandoned by the gun crews and wagoners as they retreated amongst the throngs of their fellow soldiers.

He could see some of the French regular troops slowly advancing towards their position only to be pushed back by a massive volley from Jacob's guard. He guessed the French had no idea if the British were going to re-organize and strike at them again. Hoping they would be satisfied with their victory and 'spoils of war', he ordered another massive volley to discourage them from advancing much further.

Nightfall was also fast approaching, and the French themselves would soon have to organize their return to Fort Duquesne. Jacob could see that they now only half-heartedly returned the odd volley and appeared to be more concerned with controlling their Indian allies and own militia.

It did seem that the threat of being overrun by the advancing French was all but over, so Jacob ordered the men to retreat back towards the river. He gave authority to Private White to get the men across both fords and then set up a camp, with full sentries and patrols.

"Joshua and I will remain here until we are sure the French are only interested in returning to Fort Duquesne. If we run into trouble, I will send Joshua to the camp to have you form up and come to my aid. Any questions, private?"

"No, sir, I will get the men to the other side of the river to camp and await your further orders," White said and moved out with the men.

Joshua sat beside Jacob as the others left and asked, "What is the plan, sir? Not much only two men can do if the French decide to come after us."

"I just want to see what they are thinking. Honestly, they appear not overly interested in fighting much more. I don't plan on staying here much longer; I just wanted a private moment to confess something I did."

Jacob could see that Joshua was not giving him his full attention, as he kept watching the grim scene before him.

"I shot Braddock."

Joshua looked at Jacob with disbelief, "When?"

"After he hit you, I lost my head and I thought no one was watching," Jacob confided.

"Why did you do it? Don't you know that you could be hanged?"

"I thought he had killed you and I wanted him dead," Jacob explained, ashamed of his actions.

"Thank you, sir, for watching my back. I can't say I would do the same for you, but I would certainly think about it," Joshua replied, then remembered something Jacob said earlier. "You said you thought no one was watching?"

"Yes, it does not end there. Private Taylor said he saw the entire thing and threatened he would tell Captain Stevens."

"Taylor is a drunk and no one would listen to him," Joshua reassured Jacob.

"Time will tell, lad…only time will tell. Now let's get out of here and find the boys." As Jacob spoke, the sun quickly set and left the field a dark and painful reminder of the disaster that was in full bloom only a few long hours earlier.

It was easy to locate the camp that sat only a few paces from the second ford. White had done a fine job setting up sentries and keeping several fires ablaze throughout the hundred or so men.

Jacob went directly to White and said, "Thank you for your help, private; the camp appears to be in order."

"Thank you, sir; I have several fires lit to make it look like there are more of us than there actually are…just in case the French had thoughts of following us. I also sent a few of the regulars ahead to inform the officers that we pulled out and have the rear secured."

Tired from the intensity of the battle and the events that followed, Jacob thanked White and asked him to remain in charge as he wanted to check in with Washington and check the status of Braddock.

Having little to fear from being attacked by any savages, Jacob and Joshua took the trail south to find Washington's encampment.

The trail was littered with debris left behind by the desperate retreating army. Jacob lost count of the men far too injured to continue on, abandoned by the side of the trail to cry out alone through the night. Understanding that there was little they could do to comfort them, Jacob pushed forward with Joshua right behind him.

"A bloody awful way to die, lad, alone and waiting to be eaten by a wild cat or attacked by some savage," Jacob said. "I feel for these men, but we can do little to comfort them, so keep your head down and keep moving. Managing to avoid the many canteens, bayonets, cartridge boxes and enough muskets to supply a company for a year in the pitch darkness, the two men remained focused on the trail. After an hour or so of ignoring the pleas and listening to the young soldiers begging for their mothers, the two made it to a small clearing that was now a crude encampment, packed with men from all different companies, huddled together in a mass of tears and failure.

Washington and his surviving officers didn't even bother to set out sentries or set up a perimeter guard. Added to their troubles, they had no tents and were forced to sleep amongst the hordes of mosquitoes and flies that ate at them without mercy. A few of the rangers, adept to such harsh conditions, had some fires going and Jacob could smell the familiar aroma of cooking deer meat.

Before he found Washington, Jacob was met by a sullen Captain Stevens. Joshua was sent over with the other ranging companies to have a quick bite to eat and get comfortable for the night.

"Damn shame, Sims; we went from an impressive, invincible army to a sad, broken company of men, bent only on making it back alive to Fort Cumberland. What the hell happened?" Stevens shook his head in total disbelief.

"To be frank, sir," Jacob replied, "the first problem was the arrogance of the British in thinking that they are so far superior to all the Indians, colonists and their French counterparts. The second problem was in having a commander who just set foot on this land lead us into a battle that he could never win."

"Keep your voice down, lad. The officers are already having a hard time keeping the men from deserting. Mistakes were made and lives have been lost, and those are two things we can never change. Now the poor men don't even have any rum to drown their sorrows. It's a bloody shame." Stevens was more distraught then Jacob had ever seen him.

Leaving Stevens to his thoughts, Jacob departed to locate Washington. Finding him alone, leaned up against a tree, Jacob cleared his throat before he spoke.

"Sims, you made it," Washington whispered, not wanting to draw the attention of the other officers. "I suspect that the French were satisfied by their route and decided not to chase us all down?"

"Correct sir, they were far too busy attempting to control their savages and Canadians. We remained back a bit and the men are camped just on this side of the river."

"Good work, Corporal; I will be sure to mention your fine work in my report," Washington whispered again, never lifting his head.

Jacob could see that the colonel was tired and desperate to get the men safely back to Fort Cumberland.

"How is the Major General?" Jacob asked innocently.

"Not well, I fear this wilderness is no place for such a severe injury to occur, not to mention the painful wagon ride over these horrendous roads. I have my fears he will expire before we reach the fort."

Jacob excused himself and went to locate Joshua. He was happy to find that the older Nettle brother and Private Sinclair had made it through the battle with only some minor cuts and bruises. They shared smiles, but it was short lived as they were lost in the thoughts of the day's battle.

White and the remaining company of the rear guard arrived at the camp early the next morning, just as the main body of men struggled to get itself organized. The long, drawn-out line of survivors stretched for miles as the men did their best to keep moving.

Joshua remained with the other rangers while Jacob moved up by the wagon that carried the dying Braddock. He could see the large, bloody wound that by now soaked the entire front of the Major General's coat. By his looks and the ungodly noises he made every time they went over a rock or root, Jacob could see that Washington was most likely correct that Braddock would never make it back to the fort.

Sadly relieved, but at the same moment frightened that somebody other than Taylor had witnessed the shooting, Jacob kept by the wagon's side to keep a close eye on Braddock's condition during the last two days of the pathetic march home.

At the last temporary encampment, Jacob took some time to look in on Private Taylor. He was satisfied to find that the distasteful man would not be able to speak for quite some time yet.

Noticing that the trail was taking them close to Fort Necessity, Jacob remained close to Washington. As they passed over a small creek, the now covered wagon suddenly stopped as the wagoner called out to Washington, "Sir, the Major General has not moved for the past few miles and I fear the worst."

Washington rushed over to Braddock's side and confirmed the wagoners fears.

Braddock was dead.

Not wanting to alarm the troops, Washington sent an officer back towards the main body of men and ordered them to halt and take some time to rest. Jacob stepped up and helped several of the officers to pull Braddock's limp body out of the covered wagon and lay him on the ground.

Washington and the others just stared at their once proud commander, now resting peacefully on the ground he could not defend.

"Sir," Jacob addressed Washington directly, "we must bury the Major General before we attract the wolves or coyotes. May I be bold and suggest we place him where he lies? If we do so, the grave site will be more than obscured by the hundreds of men that will follow us on the trail."

"We cannot permit it, sir!"

"He deserves a better fate than that."

"I must protest, sir!"

The officers gathered around Braddock vehemently shouted their opposition to such a degrading idea, but Washington was the most senior officer, and they would respectfully abide by his decision.

"Regrettably, the corporal is correct with his assessment," Washington began elegantly. "We can't transport the Major General's body over this terrain and keep it safe. What of the mountains or the many swamps we have not yet traversed? If we place him here, the men will cover up any signs of his grave and therefore he will not be an easy target for the returning savages who would love to desecrate his remains. Has he not suffered enough without having to face such indignities?"

While still objecting to the thought of entombing such a man in the heart of this ungodly wilderness, the officers relented and carefully wrapped the Major General in his scarlet sash and lowered him into a deep hole that was quickly dug by several of the grenadiers.

Washington said a few words before Braddock was somberly covered up with dirt, which was then packed down. The wagon made several passes over the grave to conceal its whereabouts.

The officers could barely hide their emotions. Many of them walked away and kept to themselves for the next few miles.

With Braddock's burial, Jacob avoided the chance that some doctor might pull out the lead ball from Braddock's wound and discover that it came from a British weapon, more specifically a rifle. He could not take such a chance.

The only remaining link was Private Taylor and Jacob could not wait for him to recover and tell whoever would listen that Jacob shot Braddock. He had to deal with Taylor before they reached Fort Cumberland, or any thoughts of finding Maggie would be lost.

Jacob left Washington and his officers to deal with their own pains and doubled back to look for Joshua. After travelling only a mile or so, he found Taylor amid the growing number of men who needed assistance to continue on. Taylor was on a native-style stretcher, made from some coats and two large branches that provided little comfort but could be hauled over the trail by a horse.

Jacob was relieved to find him still unconscious, though he was muttering something under his breath. Trying to decide what he should do, Jacob ordered the horseman to halt so Taylor could be examined by him.

"How has he been?" Jacob asked the horseman who had grabbed a handful of grass to feed to his hungry animal.

"Pretty quiet most of the time; he calls out some incoherent name every-so-often, but I just ignore him." The horseman was clearly much more concerned with his horse than talking with Jacob.

Trying to look busy, Jacob pulled opened Taylor's vest pocket and felt something inside. Curious but careful not to draw the attention of the horseman, Jacob put his hand inside and pulled out a pocket watch. It was the same watch that the young Nettle boy was given by his brother before he left to take the message to Stevens.

The tides had just turned. Although the watch certainly did not convict Taylor of young Jack's murder, it did tie him to it somehow. After placing the watch in his own pocket for safe keeping, Jacob told the horseman to continue on. He stood back and watched as Taylor's stretcher bumped down the rocky trail.

Jacob took a deep breath, stared back at the pathetic sprawling line of the remains of a once mighty army and knew what he needed to do next…

Timeline of **Important Events**

1755 January	Major General Edward Braddock departs from Cork, Ireland with two regiments. They land in Virginia in March.
1755 May	Braddock's army leaves from Fort Cumberland, marching towards Fort Duquesne.
1755 June 18	The heavy wagons are left behind with Colonel Dunbar, as the decision to split the troops into two units is made. An advanced army of approximately twelve hundred men is sent ahead.
1755 June 24	As the large advanced army moves within forty miles of Fort Duquesne, French and Indian raids increase.
1755 July 7	The British are now within nine miles of the heights surrounding Fort Duquesne, when the French, with their allies, send a strong war party out to ambush them.
1755 July 9	The Battle of Monongahela begins as the two forces collide in a small valley. Braddock's army is routed by a smaller French force, a short distance from the shores of the Monongahela River. Braddock is wounded and leaves Washington in charge of the retreat.
1755 July 13	Braddock dies, ironically only a short distance from Fort Necessity. He is buried on the trail.
1755 July 17	The shattered remains of the army arrives at Fort Cumberland.

Author's **Historical Note**

Shades of Death covers Braddock's fateful expedition into the heart of the Pennsylvanian territory in the spring of 1755 and although it is fiction, I did attempt to remain true to my interpretations of what documentation there was available.

As we know it ended in a complete route but logistically it was a rather impressive feat by Braddock and his army to traverse such diverse wilderness. They clear cut and hacked their way along mountains, swamps and endless forest that concealed their ever-present enemy. Most of the British forces had never been in North America and the frontier must have been both frightening and breathtaking.

Militarily Braddock made a number of critical errors, both personally and strategically, not the least was his failure to value the native population in his battle plan. Despite the pleas from frontiersmen like Jacob, he ignored any attempt to even keep the surrounding tribes neutral.

In the summer, I was fortunate to have the opportunity to visit the great site at Fort Necessity and walk the actual trail that Braddock used to march towards Fort Duquesne. The noise of the heavy wagons, the sheer number of men marching along the trail, the heat and the mass of bugs must have been staggering to witness.

The Scottish and Irish companies coined the phrase 'Shades of Death' on their way towards the Forks, when they were faced with the ocean of pine trees once they made it over the mountains. Just stop and think what you might have thought seeing such a sight for the first time!

Added to this, they had never seen many of the wild creatures that populated the endless forests. Noises and calls that were so unfamiliar to them must have been both terrifying and fascinating at the same moment. Imagine the stories and rumors that must have spread around the camp fires each night.

About the actual battle, I tried to show it through one man's eyes. That was a particular challenge considering the British were spread over a mile along the trail. I do want to mention one point regarding the actions of the British regulars during the battle. There have always been rumors that some of the colonial militia, including Washington, accused the British regulars of cowardly actions during the battle.

My only point on this is how could anyone stand in formation and shoot at an unseen enemy be called a coward? The confusion, the panic, the sight of seeing their dead mates falling everywhere around them and the clouds of smoke that would have suffocated the elongated battle scene, would have made any soldier question his courage. It would have been pure hell and anyone who stood there in the heat of the battle and took the heavy volume of fire, has my respect.

As for Braddock's death, we will never know if he was shot by one of his own men or the French. He certainly made an easy target, foolishly sitting on his horse throughout the battle. With all the confusion during the heat of the battle one could easily image that he could have been mistakenly shot by one of his own men. Medical reports from the field doctors had stated that some of the returning injured soldiers had been shot by their own mates.

On the historical ramifications, if Braddock would have garnered some assurances from the natives to assist in his efforts, the outcome could have been different. If he would have let the men fight a more 'wilderness style', especially after the tide of the battle turned, the day might have been won. History is full of 'what if's' and that is what makes this story most intriguing.

The disaster left the known frontier defenseless. The British immediately abandoned the many settlers and retreated back to Maryland. It also cost millions monetarily, in today's terms, in lost artillery equipment, wagons and horses, as well as, shot, powder and men. The loss and value of supplies affected the British influence in the area over the next several years. The remainder of 1755 and 1756 left the Ohio Valley undefended to be ravaged by the French-backed Delaware and Seneca, resulting in hundreds of innocent settler families being murdered or taken captive.

That is something for another story and I am sure Jacob and Maggie will have something to say about the events that will follow.

Acknowledgments

I must again express my gratitude to all the living historians, artisans, authors, artists and re-enactors who share my passion and love for this mostly forgotten time.

Robert Griffing, John Buxton, David Wright, Doug Hall, the cover artist, Todd Price plus several other amazing artists that have continued to inspire me. I have had the pleasure meeting many of them and their kindness and friendship made me appreciate their hard work and dedication even more.

The great people at Lord Nelson's Gallery in Gettysburg, PA gave an unknown writer a chance and decided to carry my first novel. They also invited me to History Meets the Arts in June and that was a highlight both personally and professionally. Thanks to George, Philippe and Marsha who welcomed me and my family into theirs!

Again, I must thank Frank and Lally House for extending an invitation to the CLA Show in Lexington, KY. The kindness of the folks at Lord Nelson's gave me an opportunity to sign books and meet many great people who encouraged me and offered kind words about my writing. Donna and Jack Vargo of Beaver River Trading Company, who invited me to an event at Ogdensburg, NY and made me and my family feel extremely welcome.

Roger Moore, Ghost in the Head, Mad Anne Bailey, Tim L. Jarvis and many more people who took time to talk with me over a number of summer events inspiring me to continue on with my journey...Thanks!

Once more, I want to clarify that any depictions of First Nations People in this novel are strictly fictional. It was simply a snapshot in time. They truly were the empire that lost the most and have been unfairly treated, both then and today.

Jacob and Maggie will also be enduring through their own journey in the wilds of the frontier and please continue to follow them as they fight to reunite and find their family. Cheers and good tidings to all!

References and
Recommendations

I would remiss if I forgot to direct interested readers to further materials on the French and Indian War. These are a few of my favorite books and other great resources to consider.

Books:

- Ian McCulloch and Timothy Todish. *Through So Many Dangers.* New York. Purple Mountain Press Ltd., 2004. This book introduced me to the Scottish influence during the war and more importantly to the breathtaking artwork of Robert Griffing.

- Fred Anderson. *Crucible of War.* New York. Vintage Books, 2001. The best and most extensive account of the war. Simply a must read for anyone interested in this time period.

- Osprey Publishing. There numerous works on the war and look particularly for anything written by Rene Chartrand.

- *The Art of Robert Griffing*, by George Irwin. New York. East/West Visions. 2000. The follow up, *The Narrative Art of Robert Griffing*, by Tim Todish. Gibsonia, Pennsylvania. Paramount Press Inc. 2007. Once again for their amazing artwork and for putting faces and emotions to a war long forgotten.

- Robert Lickie, *A Few Acres of Snow.* Toronto. John Wiley & Sons Inc., 1999. Another outstanding piece of work on the war.

Other **Sources:**

- *Muzzleloader* magazine, by Scurlock Publishing Company. An amazing bi-monthly publication that keeps this period alive.

- Lord Nelson's Gallery, est. 1990 in Gettysburg, PA. A great place to view and purchase artwork depicting this war.

- DVDs on the war include the Paladin Communications great series, *Young George Washington, The Complete Saga, The War That Made America*. PBS Home Video, 2005. Narrated and hosted by Graham Greene.

- Douglas "Muggs" Jones has produced a great series of DVD's from the School of the Longhunter Series. Entertaining, informative and well worth purchasing. For more information check- www.douglaswjonesjr.com.

Look for Author and Historian Brady J. Crytzer's newest book, *Guyasuta and the Fall of Indian America* (Scheduled for release in April 2013)

Also by Mr. Crytzer, *Major Washington's Pittsburgh and the Mission to Fort Le Boeuf* (2011) and *Fort Pitt: A Frontier History* (2012)

Another author I would like to mention is Tim L. Jarvis and his new book, *Shadow In The Forest, Woodland Warriors of the Mississippi Valley*. Please look for it at your local book store or at www.warriorstrail.com.

Websites:

www.nightowlstudio.net	www.doughallart.com
www.lordnelsons.com	www.onthetrail.com
www.keithrocco.com	www.smoke-fire.com
www.paramountpress.com	www.andrewknezjr.com

I am also a proud member of the CLA (www.longrifles.com) and the NMLRA (www.nmlra.org).

Historical Sites and Events:

History Meets the Arts, Gettysburg, PA in June. Great artwork, Great atmosphere and Great people. Please check www.lordnelsons.com for details.

It's a good idea plan a visit when they have a reenactment scheduled. Try Fort Fredrick, MD in late April, Fort Niagara in July and Fort Necessity anytime in the summer for their great atmosphere and historical accuracy. Fort Ligonier is another special place and the staff is second to none!

In Canada, make sure you visit the Fortress at Louisbourg and Quebec City. Visiting either place is like going back in time.

Visit a First Nations event in your area. It is one of the best cultural events to attend and they deserve our support. If you visit a historical site during a re-enactment you will see firsthand how critical the natives were to both sides and how much they truly lost during and after the French and Indian War.

Another reason to attend an event is Suzanne Larner. Suzanne does an amazing first person characterization of the true story of 'Mad Anne Bailey'. Captivating, informative and touching, it is a presentation that is a must see and gives you a real picture of the struggles a frontier family faced in the 18th century. Much like what Maggie Murray and her family experienced in the first two novels. Please check Suzanne's blog at http://madannebailey.blogspot.com/ for schedule of events and more information.

Special Note: 2013 is the 250th Anniversary Commemoration of Bushy Run Battlefield in August. Please check their website: www.bushyrunbattlefield.com for the schedule of events. DO NOT miss this! I have visited the battlefield and it is simply breathtaking and highly recommended.

This is only a snapshot of what is available to the reader interested in expanding his or her knowledge of this great period. Please support our historical sites and buy a membership or plan a visit. Make your own list and remember to read, visit, watch, and enjoy. You will be amazed at what you will learn and what they didn't teach you in school.

If you see me at an event doing a book signing or just enjoying the sites, take a moment to introduce yourself and say hello.

Author | **S. Thomas Bailey**

About the Author

S. Thomas Bailey is an award winning author and independent researcher of early North American life. A raw historian at heart, and a writer by choice.

Bailey's own sense of history is enriched by a Mi'kmaq grandfather and a family tree that can be traced back to the young surveyor, James Cook, who began his career mapping out the St. Lawrence River system during the French and Indian War.

He resides in a quiet hamlet north of Toronto, Ontario, with his wonderfully supportive wife and two amazing children. His family spends their spring and summers visiting French and Indian War sites, attending re-enactments and living history events and spreading the word about this wonderful period in North American history.

Bailey looks forward to continuing Jacob and Maggie's story. Watch for additional novels in The Gauntlet Runner Series, coming soon.

Follow, contact or connect with S. Thomas Bailey for updates and events :

www.thegauntletrunner1754.com

thegauntletrunner1754@yahoo.com

or on www.facebook/TheGauntletRunner

CPSIA information can be obtained
at www.ICGtesting.com
Printed in the USA
LVHW041023211218
601184LV00001B/59